THE MASTER OF BALLANTRAE

and

WEIR OF HERMISTON

and other Fragments

ROBERT LOUIS STEVENSON
1850-1894

THE MASTER OF BALLANTRAE

and

WEIR OF HERMISTON

and other Fragments

R. L. STEVENSON

With Introductions by

NEIL MUNRO

and

LOUIS J. McQUILLAND

COLLINS

LONDON AND GLASGOW

GENERAL EDITOR: G. F. MAINE

First published in this edition, 1953
Latest reprint, 1974

PRINTED IN GREAT BRITAIN
COLLINS CLEAR-TYPE PRESS

ROBERT LOUIS STEVENSON

ROBERT LOUIS STEVENSON was born on November 12th 1850 in Edinburgh. He was the only child of Thomas Stevenson, a distinguished civil engineer and of his wife Margaret Isabella, daughter of the Reverend Lewis Balfour, minister of Colinton.

Stevenson's whole life was dominated by a pulmonary affliction, periods of comparative good health alternating with prolonged spells of acute illness and invalidism. As a young child, owing to a religious upbringing in which the main emphasis was laid on sin and its dire consequences in after-life, he lived in terror of death and damnation, indulged in disturbing guilt phantasies and suffered from constant nightmares. Of all games he liked hide-and-seek best for it lent itself to any kind of make-believe. For the same reason he liked the 'Penny plain and Twopence Coloured' toy theatres to which he had been initiated at the age of six.

He went successively to a number of schools, mainly at Edinburgh, but his schooling was neither exacting nor very strenuous. In 1863 he accompanied his parents on a long tour through southern France and Italy; other holidays were spent at Scottish holiday resorts and later at Swanston, near Edinburgh. In 1867 he entered Edinburgh University to study for a science degree, but he was bent on becoming a writer, not a civil engineer.

Stevenson loved his native city—its architectural beauties, its history and associations—but he hated its climate which was bad for him and was deeply disturbed by an element of deceitfulness and duplicity which seemed to him characteristic of town and inhabitants alike. There was the polite, highly respectable façade, and behind it a life of squalor, vice and misery. His own life as a young man brought him into close contact with the less polite, less respectable side of Edinburgh, and his views on matters of religion, morals and sex led to many conflicts with his father. In 1871 he abandoned his engineering studies and started reading law, his intention, however, of taking up a literary career remaining unchanged. (In 1874 he was called to the Scottish Bar but never practised in earnest.)

In 1873 he made the acquaintance of Mrs. Sitwell and Sidney Colvin, then Professor of Fine Art at Cambridge, and from this meeting sprang a lifelong friendship which was of the greatest importance to Stevenson's development and literary career.

5

Sidney Colvin later became editor of his works and correspondence. During the winter of 1873-74 spent in the south of France, he began to write stories and essays, many of which appeared in the *Cornhill* magazine, and were collected later in the volume *Virginibus Puerisque* (1881). The next three years (1875-78) were spent in congenial company mostly in France, especially at Fontainebleau and Barbizon. There he met his future wife Mrs. Osbourne an American lady who, estranged from her husband, had come to spend some time in Europe, accompanied by her son Lloyd and her daughter Isobel.

By now his writings were beginning to attract the public's attention. His first two books: *An Inland Voyage* and *Travels with a Donkey in the Cévennes* appeared in 1878 and 1879 repectively.

In the summer of 1878 he left England for San Francisco where two years later he married Mrs. Osbourne, by then divorced. Later in 1880 the couple returned to Europe. Their movements during the next seven years were dictated by the grim realities of Stevenson's health. Davos (1880-82), the French Riviera (1882-84), Bournemouth (1884-86) were their successive places of residence, with occasional visits to Scotland and London. During these years Stevenson wrote and published some of his most famous works: *Treasure Island*, first serialised in the periodical *Young Folks*, appeared in 1883; *Prince Otto* in 1885; *The Strange Case of Dr. Jekyll and Mr. Hyde* in 1886; *Kidnapped* in the same year; *The Black Arrow* in 1887. In between appeared books on travels, short stories and volumes of poetry. In 1885 in Bournemouth, Stevenson made the acquaintance of Henry James, with whom he established an intimate and lasting friendship.

In August 1887, accompanied by his wife, his stepson and his mother—his father having died that year—Stevenson left Europe for America, never to return. He remained in America just under a year, mostly at a health resort at Saranac Lake, during which time he contributed a series of articles for *Scribner's Magazine*, wrote the novel *The Wrong Box* (in collaboration with Lloyd Osbourne) and began *The Master of Ballantrae.*

In June 1888, he set out with his family on a cruise to the South Pacific, which took him to the Marquesas, Tahiti and Honolulu (where he spent six months and visited the leper settlement of Molokai) and then from Honolulu (in June 1889) to the Gilbert Islands, arriving in Samoa at Christmas 1889. After a short visit to Sydney, and further cruises, Stevenson decided to live permanently in Samoa. In November 1890 he settled at Vailima where he built a house and gradually established himself as a sort of Island Chieftain, surrounded by his family and faithful retainers. He took an active part in the island's internal political affairs, recording his experiences and observations in *A Footnote to History* (1892). Other works written during that time include: *The Wrecker* (in collaboration with Lloyd Osbourne), *The Ebb-Tide, Catriona,* and finally *Weir of Hermiston,* left unfinished at his death.

Stevenson's last years at Samoa were happy, and his health much better than it had been during most of his life. He died suddenly on December 3rd 1894, and was buried with all the honours and ceremonial due to a chieftain, on top of Mount Vaea 1300 feet above the Pacific. He was mourned not only by his family and his islanders but by the whole civilized world.

H. d. R.

THE MASTER OF BALLANTRAE

TO

SIR PERCY FLORENCE AND
LADY SHELLEY

HERE is a tale which extends over many years and travels into many countries. By a peculiar fitness of circumstance the writer began, continued it, and concluded it among distant and diverse scenes. Above all, he was much upon the sea. The character and fortune of the fraternal enemies, the hall and shrubbery of Durrisdeer, the problem of Mackellar's homespun and how to shape it for superior flights; these were his company on deck in many star-reflecting harbours, ran often in his mind at sea to the tune of slatting canvas, and were dismissed (something of the suddenest) on the approach of squalls. It is my hope that these surroundings of its manufacture may to some degree find favour for my story with seafarers and sea-lovers like yourselves.

And at least here is a dedication from a great way off; written by the loud shores of a subtropical island near upon ten thousand miles from Boscombe Chine and manor: scenes which rise before me as I write, along with the faces and voices of my friends.

Well, I am for the sea once more; no doubt Sir Percy also. Let us make the signal B. R. D.!

R. L. S.

Waikiki,
  May, 17, 1889.

CONTENTS

CONTENTS

INTRODUCTION

THAT generation of contemporary readers who followed the early career of Stevenson as a romancer, from *Treasure Island* through *The Black Arrow*, *Prince Otto*, *Dr. Jekyll and Mr. Hyde*, and *Kidnapped*, could not complain of any monotony in the author's choice of themes, characters, treatment, or locality. He never repeated himself. The success of *Treasure Island* might have tempted an impecunious writer to follow up that paying lode with successive stories of the same facile character till the vein ' petered out.' Indeed he entertained that idea, himself, for a little. Gratified by the ease with which *Treasure Island* had come to him, as compared with previous literary efforts in which style had been his aim rather than more popular entertainment, and by the modest pecuniary reward thus secured, he wrote to W. E. Henley, ' I'll make this boys' book business pay. I love writing boys' books. I'll be the Harrison Ainsworth of the future.'

In that transient mood he was already thinking of a ' pendant,' as the artists used to say, to the first story—a picture to balance it on the other side of the mantelpiece. It must, nevertheless, to be amusing for himself, be totally different from *Treasure Island*, however melodramatic. *Treasure Island* was merely a gay experiment on the part of one who held the sensible conviction that a literary artist should be able to make a good job in any genre; having proved to himself, to his father, and his stepson Lloyd Osbourne, that he could handle buccaneers with more sensational effect than could the serial writers for boys' journals whose peculiar craft it was to do so, piracy and foreign parts were finished for him. His next adventure must be nearer home, on land, with highwaymen in jolly old England.

It was to be *Jerry Abershaw; a Tale of Putney Heath;* but *Jerry* was never written. Instead, the readers of *Young Folks* had the adventures of *The Black Arrow*, in whose carpentry Stevenson discovered that writing determinedly for boys is really not much fun at the age of thirty-two. *The Black Arrow* pleased the boys more than *Treasure Island* did, but its potboiler quality was so manifest to the author or the publishers that it was four or five years before it reappeared in volume form.

To classify Stevenson's works at this period in strict chronological order is not easy, for they were, in some cases, tentatively started years before their appearance as books, but they may, for convenience sake, be all attributed to the first eight or nine years of his married life. *Prince Otto* was, in a sense, conceived before *Treasure Island*; it existed before 1880 as a play entitled *Semiramis: a Tragedy*. Into its reincarnation as a novel he put, between 1883 and 1885, a vast amount of fastidious though intermittent labour, all the craft and all the style at his command. It had distinction and charm, but added little or nothing to the author's vogue in the bookshops.

Followed, *The Strange Case of Dr. Jekill and Mr. Hyde*, in 1886, 'conceived, written, re-written twice and printed inside ten weeks,' to placate that exigent gentleman, ' Byles the Butcher '—a moralistic shilling shocker which might well have created apprehension among the author's more intimate and expectant friends. It sold like *The Mystery of a Hansom Cab*, found an enormous public which had hardly heard of Stevenson before, and by its success commercially and as *réclame*, gave the author his first chance to indulge himself in some more deliberate fiction wherein his long-pondered principles of romance could be put in practice.

Fortunately, for the reassurance of his friends, there appeared a few months later *Kidnapped*. It had succeeded *The Black Arrow* as a serial story in the same boys paper, and appeared simultaneously in *The Century Magazine* of America. In its writing Stevenson made a discovery—that dealing with a land and race he knew and a manner of life less remote than that of the Spanish Main, Old England, Ruritanian realms, and the days of Robin Hood, could engage his serious artistic interest and skill without alienating juvenile readers. In starting *Kidnapped* he had still his eye on youth, but the book's best qualities emerged later when that particular audience was forgotten, and the only boy to be pleased was one who had not forgotten his romantic dreams of the eighteenth century Highlands.

For adult readers, here was a new Stevenson, the first glimpse of a story-teller in the lineage of Walter Scott and one whose future work would be worth watching. He realised, himself, that *Kidnapped* had a quality of permanence in it, and put his own name to the story instead of the nom-de-guerre he had used for its predecessors.

Throughout those eight years during which the urgency of making a living for himself and his household forbade too much indulgence in the luxury of self-expression, there was in suspense in the author's mind a novel of a more ambitious kind, some idea of which had come to him in August, 1881, in the course of a journey from Pitlochry to Braemar, 'conceived in Highland rain and the blend of the smell of heather and bog-plants,' and

by a mind at the moment occupied by stories of Jacobite intrigues.

In 1887, living in the hamlet of Saranac, New York State, he
had read for the third or fourth time Marryatt's *Phantom Ship*,
and one frosty night, walking on the veranda of his house, was
moved, as he says, by the spirit of emulation. ' Let us make
a tale,' he said to himself; ' a story of many years and countries,
of the sea, and the land, savagery and civilisation; a story that
shall have the same large features and may be treated in the
same summary elliptic method as the book you have been reading
and admiring.'

Realising that Marryat, no less than Homer, Milton, and
Virgil, profited by the choice of a familiar and legendary subject,
he sought for one, and remembered an old story often related
to him by an uncle, of an Indian fakir buried in a trance and
resuscitated afterwards. ' The next moment,' he says, ' and I
had seen the circumstances transplanted from India and the
tropics to the Adirondacks wilderness and the stringent cold of
the Canadian border. Here, then, almost before I had begun
my story, I had two countries, two of the ends of the earth
involved, it fitted at once with my design of a tale of many
lands.'

The Scottish phase of the story and the Scottish characters
were, it seems, the last to suggest themselves to Stevenson; they
were, as he tells us, the subconscious elements stored up in his
mind in the journey between Pitlochry and Braemar.

This genesis of *The Master of Ballantrae* is narrated at length
in the volume of Stevenson's called *The Art of Writing*. There
could be no more striking evidence that at the time he was still,
so far as fiction was concerned, in some vital respects the amateur,
and failed to recognise that his uncle's story—like most stories
uncles and other amiable persons tell to novelists—could not
plausibly be expanded into a tale of ' many years and countries,'
nor possibly make anything but an inharmonious patch on any
kind of Scots novel—a Jacobite romance in particular.

Aristotle's laws of unity in time, action, and place have been
generally regarded as for the dramatist only, but they are of
equal importance to the novelist, and though we need not accept
them too literally, we should be aware that any violent departure
from them enormously adds to the labour of the story-teller and
tends to mar the perfect ensemble. Had we not the author's
word for it, there would be something incredible in this account
of the genesis of *The Master of Ballantrae*, and most people who
read the story without having seen the author's account of its

origin, not unreasonably conclude that the exhumation incident was the expedient of a tired man who, having got so far with his novel and reached a point where his fancy flagged, seized upon the first lurid incident that came to his mind to carry the tale a stage further. It reads like an interpolation, wholly out of key with everything that precedes it, though really that particular incident was obviously being prepared for from our first introduction in Chapter Seven to the incongruous person of Secundra Dass.

No book of Stevenson's—not even *Weir of Hermiston*—opens more delightfully, with the atmosphere of a land and period familiar through Scott, but seen from a new angle. We have come again, in Stevenson's work, into a country he knew and loved, whose landscape and the emotions it aroused and the characters it evoked were simultaneously conceived and in the happiest accord. It was really not the uncle's Indian incident that pitched the key and dictated the story to start with, but the recalled emotion of the Perthshire moors and a certain ' winter walk,' perhaps, on the coast of Ayrshire.

There are twelve chapters in the novel; the first ten of them must have been a delight to all readers who had been following Stevenson through his divagations into foreign fantasies and been eagerly expectant to see him in his work come home again to the land of his heredity wherein any author will always find emotions and effects that have the stamp of authenticity. Here, as in *Kidnapped*, were convincing portraits, a background of veritable history, real native airs. Mackellar, the faithful land steward, was an amalgam of all the more lovable qualities of Scott's domestic retainers, lifted to a higher social plane to justify intellectual flights to which a more homespun character could not have risen; the family of Durrisdeer which he served with feudal loyalty had every quality of vraisemblance, even in its blackguard member, the Master himself, and his earlier adventures.

Though the Aristotelian unities might be disregarded in *The Master of Ballantrae*, a single purpose, a unifying central idea was not lacking—it was that favourite philosophical theory of Stevenson's that in a bad man may be all the machinery to be a good one, made useless by ' the malady of not wanting.' The brilliant Mephistophelian brother James and Mackellar, his philosophic contrast, carry the whole machine on their backs, when they are off the stage it takes all his time for the Chevalier Burke and the supernumeravies to keep our interest from temporarily flagging.

Yet, in spite of that egregious final chapter, ('Steep, steep, sir!' confessed Stevenson to Henry James), and our bewilderment at finding ourselves unnecessarily in a Wilderness so ill-suited to bring out the character and genius of either Mackellar or the Master, we feel constrained to go back again and again to those charmed earlier scenes where climate and character are conceived as one; to listen to the crafty Master's singing in the hall of Durrisdeer; to see the flaming candle in the frosty midnight air of the vacant duel ground; to recapture the emotion of that wild winter morning when through a landscape drenched in a not unpleasing melancholy, two of the most memorable characters in English fiction set out from that tragic dwelling whence

> ... the folks are all departed,
> The kind hearts, the true hearts, that loved the
>   place of old.

NEIL MUNRO

Summary of events during the Master's wanderings

THE full truth of this odd matter is what the world has long been looking for, and public curiosity is sure to welcome. It so befell that I was intimately mingled with the last years and history of the house; and there does not live one man so able as myself to make these matters plain, or so desirous to narrate them faithfully. I knew the Master; on many secret steps of his career I have an authentic memoir in my hand; I sailed with him on his last voyage almost alone; I made one upon that winter's journey of which so many tales have gone abroad; and I was there at the man's death. As for my late Lord Durrisdeer, I served him and loved him near twenty years; and thought more of him the more I knew of him. Altogether, I think it not fit that so much evidence should perish; the truth is a debt I owe my lord's memory; and I think my old years will flow more smoothly, and my white hair lie quieter on the pillow, when the debt is paid.

The Duries of Durrisdeer and Ballantrae were a strong family in the south-west from the days of David First. A rhyme still current in the countryside—

> Little folk are the Durrisdeers,
> They ride wi' ower mony spears—

bears the mark of its antiquity; and the name appears in another which common report attributes to Thomas of Ercildoune himself—I cannot say how truly, and which some have applied—I dare not say with how much justice—to the events of this narration:

> Twa Duries in Durrisdeer,
>   Ane to tie and ane to ride.
> An ill day for the groom
>   And a waur day for the bride.

Authentic history besides is filled with their exploits, which (to our modern eyes) seem not very commendable: and the family suffers its full share of those ups and downs to which the great houses of Scotland have been ever liable. But all these I pass over, to come to that memorable year 1745, when the foundations of this tragedy were laid.

At that time there dwelt a family of four persons in the house of Durrisdeer, near St. Bride's, on the Solway shore; a chief hold of their race since the Reformation. My old lord, eighth of the name, was not old in years, but he suffered prematurely from the disabilities of age; his place was at the chimney side; there he sat reading, in a lined gown, with few words for any man, and wry words for none: the model of an old retired house-keeper; and yet his mind very well nourished with study, and reputed in the country to be more cunning than he seemed. The master of Ballantrae, James in baptism, took from his father the love of serious reading; some of his tact perhaps as well, but that which was only policy in the father became black dissimulation in the son. The face of his behaviour was merely popular and wild: he sat late at wine, later at the cards; had the name in the country of 'an unco man for the lasses;' and was ever in the front of broils. But for all he was the first to go in, yet it was observed he was invariably the best to come off; and his partners in mischief were usually alone to pay the piper. This luck or dexterity got him several ill-wishers, but with the rest of the country, enhanced his reputation; so that great things were looked for in his future, when he should have gained more gravity. One very black mark he had to his name; but the matter was hushed up at the time, and so defaced by legends before I came into those parts, that I scruple to set it down. If it was true, it was a horrid fact in one so young; and if false, it was a horrid calumny. I think it notable that he had always vaunted himself quite implacable, and was taken at his word; so that he had the addition among his neighbours of 'an ill man to cross.' Here was altogether a young nobleman (not yet twenty-four in the year '45) who had made a figure in the country beyond his time of life. The less marvel if there were little heard of the second son, Mr. Henry (my late Lord Durrisdeer), who was neither very bad nor yet very able, but an honest, solid sort of lad like many of his neighbours. Little heard, I say; but indeed it was a case of little spoken. He was known among the salmon fishers in the firth, for that was a sport that he assiduously followed; he was an excellent good horse-doctor besides; and took a chief hand, almost from a boy, in the management of the estates. How hard a part that was, in the situation of that family, none knows better than myself; nor yet with how little colour of justice a man may there acquire the reputation of a tyrant and a miser. The fourth person in the house was Miss Alison Graeme, a near kinswoman, an orphan, and the heir to a considerable fortune which her father had acquired in trade.

This money was loudly called for by my lord's necessities; indeed the land was deeply mortgaged; and Miss Alison was designed accordingly to be the Master's wife, gladly enough on her side; with how much good-will on his, is another matter. She was a comely girl, and in those days very spirited and self-willed; for the old lord having no daughter of his own, and my lady being long dead, she had grown up as best she might.

To these four came the news of Prince Charlie's landing, and set them presently by the ears. My lord, like the chimney-keeper that he was, was all for temporising. Miss Alison held the other side, because it appeared romantical; and the Master (though I have heard they did not agree often) was for this once of her opinion. The adventure tempted him, as I conceive; he was tempted by the opportunity to raise the fortunes of the house, and not less by the hope of paying off his private liabilities, which were heavy beyond all opinion. As for Mr. Henry, it appears he said little enough at first; his part came later on. It took the three a whole day's disputation, before they agreed to steer a middle course, one son going forth to strike a blow for King James, my lord and the other staying at home to keep in favour with King George. Doubtless this was my lord's decision; and as is well known, it was the part played by many considerable families. But the one dispute settled, another opened. For my lord, Miss Alison, and Mr. Henry all held the one view: that it was the cadet's part to go out; and the Master, what with restlessness and vanity, would at no rate consent to stay at home. My lord pleaded, Miss Alison wept, Mr. Henry was very plain spoken: all was of no avail.

'It is the direct heir of Durrisdeer that should ride by his King's bridle,' says the Master.

'If we were playing a manly part,' says Mr. Henry, 'there might be sense in such talk. But what are we doing? Cheating at cards!'

'We are saving the house of Durrisdeer, Henry,' his father said.

'And see, James,' said Mr. Henry, 'if I go, and the Prince has the upper hand, it will be easy to make your peace with King James. But if you go, and the expedition fails, we divide the right and the title. And what shall I be then?'

'You will be Lord Durrisdeer,' said the Master. 'I put all I have upon the table.'

'I play at no such game,' cries Mr. Henry. 'I shall be left in such a situation as no man of sense and honour could endure. I shall be neither fish nor flesh!' he cried. And a little after he had another expression, plainer perhaps than he intended. ' It is your duty to be here with my father,' said he. ' You know well enough you are the favourite.'

' Ay? ' said the Master. ' And there spoke Envy! Would you trip up my heels—Jacob? ' said he, and dwelled upon the name maliciously.

Mr. Henry went and walked at the low end of the hall without reply; for he had an excellent gift of silence. Presently he came back.

' I am the cadet and I *should* go,' said he. ' And my lord here is the master, and he says I *shall* go. What say ye to that, my brother? '

' I say this, Harry,' returned the Master, ' that when very obstinate folk are met, there are only two ways out: Blows—and I think none of us could care to go so far; or the arbitrament of chance—and here is a guinea piece. Will you stand by the toss of the coin? '

' I will stand and fall by it,' said Mr. Henry. ' Heads, I go; shield, I stay.'

The coin was spun, and it fell shield. ' So there is a lesson for Jacob,' says the Master.

' We shall live to repent of this,' says Mr. Henry, and flung out of the hall.

As for Miss Alison, she caught up that piece of gold which had just sent her lover to the wars, and flung it clean through the family shield in the great painted window.

' If you loved me as well as I love you, you would have stayed,' cried she.

' I could not love you, dear, so well, loved I not honour more,' sang the Master.

' Oh! ' she cried, ' you have no heart—I hope you may be killed! ' and she ran from the room, and in tears, to her own chamber.

It seems the Master turned to my lord with his most comical manner, and says he, ' This looks like a devil of a wife.'

' I think you are a devil of a son to me,' cried his father, ' you that have always been the favourite, to my shame be it spoken. Never a good hour have I gotten of you, since you were born; no, never one good hour,' and repeated it again the third time. Whether it was the Master's levity, or his insubordination, or Mr. Henry's word about the favourite son, that had so much disturbed my lord, I do not know; but I incline to think it was the last, for I have it by all accounts that Mr. Henry was more made up to from that hour.

Altogether it was in pretty ill blood with his family that the Master rode to the North; which was the more sorrowful for others to remember when it seemed too late. By fear and favour he had scraped together near upon a dozen men, principally tenants' sons; they were all pretty full when they set forth, and rode up the hill by the old abbey, roaring and singing, the white cockade in every hat. It was a desperate venture for so small a company to cross the most of Scotland unsupported; and (what made folk think so the more) even as that poor dozen was clattering up the hill, a great ship of the king's navy, that could have brought them under with a single boat, lay with her broad ensign streaming in the bay. The next afternoon, having given the Master a fair start, it was Mr. Henry's turn; and he rode off, all by himself, to offer his sword and carry letters from his father to King George's Government. Miss Alison was shut in her room, and did little but weep, till both were gone; only she stitched the cockade upon the Master's hat, and (as John Paul told me) it was wetted with tears when he carried it down to him.

In all that followed, Mr. Henry and my lord were true to their bargain. That ever they accomplished anything is more than I could learn; and that they were anyway strong on the king's side, more than I believe. But they kept the letter of loyalty, corresponded with my Lord President, sat still at home, and had little or no commerce with the Master while that business lasted. Nor was he, on his side, more communicative. Miss Alison, indeed, was always sending him expresses, but I do not know if she had many answers. Macconochie rode for her once, and found the Highlanders before Carlisle, and the Master riding by the Prince's side in high favour; he took the letter (so Macconochie tells), opened it, glanced it through with a mouth like a man whistling, and stuck it in his belt, whence, on his horse passageing, it fell unregarded to the ground. It was Macconochie who picked it up; and he still kept it, and indeed I have seen it in his hands. News came to Durrisdeer of course, by the common report, as it goes travelling through a country, a thing always wonderful to me. By that means the family learned more of the Master's favour with the Prince, and the ground it was said to stand on: for by a strange condescension in a man so proud—only that he was a man still more ambitious— he was said to have crept into notability by truckling to the Irish. Sir Thomas Sullivan, Colonel Burke, and the rest, were his daily comrades, by which course he withdrew himself from his own country-folk. All the small intrigues he had a hand in fomenting; thwarted my Lord George upon a thousand points; was always for the advice that seemed palatable to the Prince, no matter if it was good or bad; and seems upon the whole (like the gambler he was all through life) to have had less regard to the chances of the campaign than to the greatness of favour he might aspire to, if, by any luck, it should succeed. For the rest, he did very well in the field; no one questioned that; for he was no coward.

The next was the news of Culloden, which was brought to Durrisdeer by one of the tenants' sons—the only survivor, he declared, of all those that had gone singing up the hill. By an unfortunate chance John Paul and Macconochie had that very morning found the guinea piece—which was the root of all the evil—sticking in a holly bush; they had been 'up the gait,' as the servants say at Durrisdeer, to the changehouse; and if they had little left of the guinea, they had less of their wits. What must John Paul do but burst into the hall where the family sat at dinner, and cry the news to them that 'Tam Macmorland was but new lichtit at the door, and—wirra, wirra—there were nane to come behind him?'

They took the word in silence like folk condemned; only Mr. Henry carrying his palm to his face, and Miss Alison laying her head outright upon her hands. As for my lord, he was like ashes.

'I have still one son,' says he. 'And, Henry, I will do you this justice—it is the kinder that is left.'

It was a strange thing to say in such a moment; but my lord had never forgotten Mr. Henry's speech, and he had years of injustice on his conscience. Still it was a strange thing, and more than Miss Alison could let pass. She broke out and blamed my lord for his unnatural words, and Mr. Henry because he was sitting there in safety when his brother lay dead, and herself because she had given her sweetheart ill words at his departure, calling him the flower of the flock, wringing her hands, protesting her love, and crying on him by his name—so that the servants stood astonished.

Mr. Henry got to his feet, and stood holding his chair. It was he that was like ashes now.

'Oh!' he burst out suddenly, 'I know you loved him.'

'The world knows that, glory be to God!' cries she; and then to Mr. Henry: 'There is none but me to know one thing—that you were a traitor to him in your heart.'

'God knows,' groans he, 'it was lost love on both sides.'

Time went by in the house after that without much change;

only they were now three instead of four, which was a perpetual reminder of their loss. Miss Alison's money, you are to bear in mind, was highly needful for the estates; and the one brother being dead, my lord soon set his heart upon her marrying the other. Day in, day out, he would work upon her, sitting by the chimney-side with his finger in his Latin book, and his eyes set upon her face with a kind of pleasant intentness that became the old gentleman very well. If she wept, he would condole with her like an ancient man that has seen worse times and begins to think lightly even of sorrow; if she raged, he would fall to reading again in his Latin book but always with some civil excuse; if she offered, as she often did, to let them have her money in a gift, he would show her how little it consisted with her honour, and remind her, even if he should consent, that Mr. Henry would certainly refuse. *Non vi sed saepe cadendo* was a favourite word of his; and no doubt this quiet persecution wore away much of her resolve; no doubt, besides, he had a great influence on the girl, having stood in the place of both her parents; and, for that matter, she was herself filled with the spirit of the Duries, and would have gone a great way for the glory of Durrisdeer; but not so far, I think, as to marry my poor patron, had it not been—strangely enough—for the circumstance of his extreme unpopularity.

This was the work of Tam Macmorland. There was not much harm in Tam; but he had that grievous weakness, a long tongue; and as the only man in that country who had been out—or, rather, who had come in again—he was sure of listeners. Those that have the underhand in any fighting, I have observed, are ever anxious to persuade themselves they were betrayed. By Tam's account of it, the rebels had been betrayed at every turn and by every officer they had; they had been betrayed at Derby and betrayed at Falkirk; the night march was a step of treachery of my Lord George's; and Culloden was lost by the treachery of the Macdonalds. This habit of imputing treason grew upon the fool, till at last he must have in Mr. Henry also. Mr. Henry (by his account) had betrayed the lads of Durrisdeer; he had promised to follow with more men, and instead of that he had ridden to King George. 'Ay, and the next day!' Tam would cry. 'The puir bonnie Master, and the puir, kind lads that rade wi' him, were hardly ower the scaur, or he was aff—the Judis!—Ay, weel—he has his way 'ot: he's to be my lord, nae less, and there's mony a cold corp amang the Hieland heather!' And at this, if Tam had been drinking, he would begin to weep.

Let anyone speak long enough, he will get believers. This

27

view of Mr. Henry's behaviour crept about the country by little and little; it was talked upon by folk that knew the contrary, but were short of topics; and it was heard and believed and given out for gospel by the ignorant and the ill-willing. Mr. Henry began to be shunned; yet awhile, and the commons began to murmur as he went by, and the women (who are always the most bold because they are the most safe) to cry out their reproaches to his face. The Master was cried up for a saint. It was remembered how he had never any hand in pressing the tenants; as, indeed, no more he had, except to spend the money. He was a little wild perhaps, the folk said; but how much better was a natural wild lad that would soon have settled down, than a skinflint and a sneckdraw, sitting, with his nose in an account book, to persecute poor tenants! One trollop, who had had a child to the Master, and by all accounts been very badly used, yet made herself a kind of champion of his memory. She flung a stone one day at Mr. Henry.

' Whaur's the bonnie lad that trustit ye? ' she cried.

Mr. Henry reined in his horse and looked upon her, the blood flowing from his lip. ' Ay, Jess? ' says he. ' You, too? And yet ye should ken me better.' For it was he who had helped her with money.

The woman had another stone ready, which she made as if she would cast; and he, to ward himself, threw up the hand that held his riding-rod.

' What, would ye beat a lassie, ye ugly——? ' cries she, and ran away screaming as though he had struck her.

Next day word went about the country like wildfire that Mr. Henry had beaten Jessie Broun within an inch of her life. I give it as one instance of how this snowball grew, and one calumny brought another; until my poor patron was so perished in reputation that he began to keep the house like my lord. All this while, you may be very sure, he uttered no complaints at home; the very ground of the scandal was too sore a matter to be handled; and Mr. Henry was very proud and strangely obstinate in silence. My old lord must have heard of it, by John Paul, if by no one else; and he must at least have remarked the altered habits of his son. Yet even he, it is probable, knew not how high the feeling ran; and as for Miss Alison, she was ever the last person to hear news, and the least interested when she heard them.

In the height of the ill-feeling (for it died away as it came, no man could say why) there was an election forward in the town of St. Bride's, which is the next to Durrisdeer, standing on the

Water of Swift; some grievance was fermenting, I forget what, if ever I heard; and it was currently said there would be broken heads ere night, and that the sheriff had sent as far as Dumfries for soldiers. My lord moved that Mr. Henry should be present, assuring him it was necessary to appear, for the credit of the house. 'It will soon be reported,' said he, 'that we do not take the lead in our own country.'

'It is a strange lead that I can take,' said Mr. Henry; and when they had pushed him further, 'I tell you the plain truth,' he said, 'I dare not show my face.'

'You are the first of the house that ever said so,' cried Miss Alison.

'We will go all three,' said my lord; and sure enough he got into his boots (the first time in four years—a sore business John Paul had to get them on), and Miss Alison into her riding-coat, and all three rode together to St. Bride's.

The streets were full of the riff-raff of all the countryside, who had no sooner clapped eyes on Mr. Henry than the hissing began, and the hooting, and the cries of 'Judas!' and 'Where was the Master?' and 'Where were the poor lads that rode with him?' Even a stone was cast; but the more part cried shame at that, for my old lord's sake, and Miss Alison's. It took not ten minutes to persuade my lord that Mr. Henry had been right. He said never a word, but turned his horse about, and home again, with his chin upon his bosom. Never a word said Miss Alison; no doubt she thought the more; no doubt her pride was stung, for she was a bonebred Durie; and no doubt her heart was touched to see her cousin so unjustly used. That night she was never in bed; I have often blamed my lady—when I call to mind that night, I readily forgive her all; and the first thing in the morning she came to the old lord in his usual seat.

'If Henry still wants me,' said she, 'he can have me now.' To himself she had a different speech: 'I bring you no love, Henry; but God knows, all the pity in the world.'

June the 1st, 1748, was the day of their marriage. It was December of the same year that first saw me alighting at the doors of the great house; and from there I take up the history of events as they befell under my own observation, like a witness in a court.

2

Summary of events (continued)

I MADE the last of my journey in the cold end of December, in a mighty dry day of frost, and who should be my guide but Patey Macmorland, brother of Tam! For a tow-headed, barelegged brat of ten, he had more ill tales upon his tongue than ever I heard the match of; having drunken betimes in his brother's cup. I was still not so old myself; pride had not yet the upper hand of curiosity; and indeed it would have taken any man, that cold morning, to hear all the old clashes of the country, and be shown all the places by the way where strange things had fallen out. I had tales of Claverhouse as we came through the bogs, and tales of the devil as we came over the top of the scaur. As we came in by the abbey I heard somewhat of the old monks, and more of the freetraders, who use its ruins for a magazine, landing for that cause within a cannon-shot of Durrisdeer; and along all the road the Duries and poor Mr. Henry were in the first rank of slander. My mind was thus highly prejudiced against the family I was about to serve, so that I was surprised when I beheld Durrisdeer itself, lying in a pretty, sheltered bay, under the Abbey Hill; the house most commodiously built in the French fashion, or perhaps Italianate, for I have no skill in these arts; and the place the most beautified with gardens, lawns, shrubberies, and trees I have ever seen. The money sunk here unproductively would have quite restored the family; but as it was, it cost a revenue to keep it up.

Mr. Henry came himself to the door to welcome me; a tall dark young gentleman (the Duries are all black men) of a plain and not cheerful face, very strong in body, but not so strong in health: taking me by the hand without any pride, and putting me at home with plain kind speeches. He led me into the hall, booted as I was, to present me to my lord. It was still daylight; and the first thing I observed was a lozenge of clear glass in the midst of the shield in the painted window, which I remember thinking a blemish on a room otherwise so handsome, with its family portraits, and the pargeted ceiling with pendants, and the carved chimney, in one corner of which my old lord sat reading in his Livy. He was like Mr. Henry, with much the same plain countenance, only more subtle and pleasant, and his talk a thousand times more entertaining. He had many questions to ask me, I remember, of Edinburgh College, where I had just received my mastership of arts, and of the various professors, with whom and their proficiency he seemed well acquainted; and thus, talking of things that I knew, I soon got liberty of speech in my new home.

In the midst of this came Mrs. Henry into the room; she was very far gone, Miss Katharine being due in about six weeks, which made me think less of her beauty at the first sight; and she used me with more of condescension than the rest; so that, upon all accounts, I kept her in the third place of my esteem.

It did not take long before all Patey Macmorland's tales were blotted out of my belief, and I was become, what I have ever since remained, a loving servant of the house of Durrisdeer. Mr. Henry had the chief part of my affection. It was with him I worked; and I found him an exacting master, keeping all his kindness for those hours in which we were unemployed, and in the steward's office not only loading me with work, but viewing me with a shrewd supervision. At length one day he looked up from his paper with a kind of timidness, and says he, 'Mr. Mackellar, I think I ought to tell you that you do very well.' That was my first word of commendation; and from that day his jealousy of my performance was relaxed; soon it was 'Mr. Mackellar' here, and 'Mr. Mackellar' there, with the whole family; and for much of my service at Durrisdeer, I have transacted everything at my own time, and to my own fancy, and never a farthing challenged. Even while he was driving me, I had begun to find my heart go out to Mr. Henry; no doubt, partly in pity, he was a man so palpably unhappy. He would fall into a deep muse over our accounts, staring at the page or out of the window; and at those times the look of his face, and the sigh that would break from him, awoke in me strong feelings of curiosity and commiseration. One day, I remember, we were late upon some business in the steward's room. This room is in the top of the house, and has a view upon the bay, and over a little wooded cape, on the long sands; and there, right over against the sun, which was then dipping, we saw the freetraders, with a great force of men and horses, scouring on the beach. Mr. Henry had been staring straight west, so that I marvelled he was not blinded by the sun; suddenly he frowns, rubs his hand upon his brow, and turns to me with a smile.

'You would not guess what I was thinking,' says he. 'I was thinking I would be a happier man if I could ride and run the danger of my life, with these lawless companions.'

I told him I had observed he did not enjoy good spirits; and that it was a common fancy to envy others and think we should be the better of some change; quoting Horace to the point, like a young man fresh from college.

'Why, just so,' said he. 'And with that we may get back to our accounts.'

It was not long before I began to get wind of the causes that so much depressed him. Indeed a blind man must have soon discovered there was a shadow on that house, the shadow of the Master of Ballantrae. Dead or alive (and he was then supposed to be dead) that man was his brother's rival: his rival abroad, where there was never a good word for Mr. Henry, and nothing but regret and praise for the Master; and his rival at home, not only with his father and his wife, but with the very servants.

They were two old serving-men that were the leaders. John Paul, a little, bald, solemn, stomachy man, a great professor of piety and (take him for all in all) a pretty faithful servant, was the chief of the Master's faction. None durst go so far as John. He took a pleasure in disregarding Mr. Henry publicly, often with a slighting comparison. My lord and Mrs. Henry took him up, to be sure, but never so resolutely as they should; and he had only to pull his weeping face and begin his lamentations for the Master—'his laddie,' as he called him—to have the whole condoned. As for Henry, he let these things pass in silence, sometimes with a sad and sometimes with a black look. There was no rivalling the dead, he knew that; and how to censure an old serving-man for a fault of loyalty, was more than he could see. His was not the tongue to do it.

Macconochie was chief upon the other side; an old, ill-spoken, swearing, ranting, drunken dog; and I have often thought it an odd circumstance in human nature that these two serving-men should each have been the champion of his contrary, and blackened their own faults and made light of their own virtues when they beheld them in a master. Macconochie had soon smelled out my secret inclination, took me much into his confidence, and would rant against the Master by the hour, so that even my work suffered. 'They're a' daft here,' he would cry, 'and be damned to them! The Master—the deil's in their thrapples that should call him sae! it's Mr. Henry should be master now! They were nane sae fond o' the Master when they had him, I'll can tell ye that. Sorrow on his name! Never a guid word did I hear on his lips, nor naebody else, but just fleering and flyting and profane cursing—deil hae him! There's nane kent his wickedness: him a gentleman! Did ever ye hear tell, Mr. Mackellar, o' Wully White the wabster?

No? Aweel, Wully was an unco praying kind o' man; a dreigh body, nane o' my kind, I never could abide the sight o' him; ony-way he was a great hand by his way of it, and he up and rebukit the Master for some of his on-goings. It was a grand thing for the Master o' Ball'ntrae to tak up a feud wi' a' wabster, was-nae't?' Macconochie would sneer; indeed, he never took the full name upon his lips but with a sort of a whine of hatred. 'But he did! A fine employ it was; chapping at the man's door, and crying "boo" in his lum, and puttin' poother in his fire, and pee-oys[1] in his window; till the man thocht it was auld Hornie was come seekin' him. Weel, to mak a lang story short, Wully gaed gyte. At the hinder end, they couldnae get him frae his knees, but he just roared and prayed and grat straucht on, till he got his release. It was fair murder, a'body said that. Ask John Paul—he was brawly ashamed o' that game, him that's sic a Christian man! Grand doin's for the Master o' Ball'ntrae!' I asked him what the Master had thought of it himself. 'How would I ken?' says he. 'He never said naething.' And on again in his usual manner of banning and swearing, with every now and again a 'Master of Ballantrae' sneered through his nose. It was in one of these confidences that he showed me the Carlisle letter, the print of the horse-shoe still stamped in the paper. Indeed, that was our last confidence; for he then ex-pressed himself so ill-naturedly of Mrs. Henry that I had to reprimand him sharply, and must thenceforth hold him at a distance.

My old lord was uniformly kind to Mr. Henry; he had even pretty ways of gratitude, and would sometimes clap him on the shoulder and say, as if to the world at large: 'This is a very good son to me.' And grateful he was, no doubt, being a man of sense and justice. But I think that was all, and I am sure Mr. Henry thought so. The love was all for the dead son. Not that this was often given breath to; indeed, with me but once. My lord had asked me one day how I got on with Mr. Henry, and I had told him the truth.

'Ay,' said he, looking sideways on the burning fire. 'Henry is a good lad, a very good lad,' said he. 'You have heard, Mr. Mackellar, that I had another son? I am afraid he was not so virtuous a lad as Mr. Henry; but dear me, he's dead, Mr. Mackellar! and while he lived we were all very proud of him, all very proud. If he was not all he should have been in some ways, well, perhaps we loved him better!' This last he said looking musingly in the fire; and then to me, with a great deal

[1] A kind of firework made with damp powder.

of briskness, ' But I am rejoiced you do so well with Mr. Henry. You will find him a good master.' And with that he opened his book, which was the customary signal of dismission. But it would be little that he read, and less that he understood; Culloden field and the Master, these would be the burthen of his thought; and the burthen of mine was an unnatural jealousy of the dead man for Mr. Henry's sake, that had even then begun to grow on me.

I am keeping Mrs. Henry for the last, so that this expression of my sentiment may seem unwarrantably strong: the reader shall judge for himself when I have done. But I must first tell of another matter, which was the means of bringing me more intimate. I had not yet been six months at Durrisdeer when it chanced that John Paul fell sick and must keep his bed; drink was the root of his malady, in my poor thought; but he was tended, and indeed carried himself, like an afflicted saint; and the very minister, who came to visit him, professed himself edified when he went away. The third morning of his sickness, Mr. Henry comes to me with something of a hang-dog look.

' Mackellar,' says he, ' I wish I could trouble you upon a little service. There is a pension we pay; it is John's part to carry it, and now that he is sick I know not to whom I should look unless it was yourself. The matter is very delicate; I could not carry it with my own hand for a sufficient reason; I dare not send Macconochie, who is a talker, and I am—I have— I am desirous this should not come to Mrs. Henry's ears,' says he, and flushed to his neck as he said it.

To say truth, when I found I was to carry money to one Jessie Broun, who was no better than she should be, I supposed it was some trip of his own that Mr. Henry was dissembling. I was the more impressed when the truth came out.

It was up a wynd off a side street in St. Bride's that Jessie had her lodging. The place was very ill inhabited, mostly by the freetrading sort. There was a man with a broken head at the entry; half-way up, in a tavern, fellows were roaring and singing though it was not yet nine in the day. Altogether, I had never seen a worse neighbourhood, even in the great city of Edinburgh, and I was in two minds to go back. Jessie's room was of a piece with her surroundings, and herself no better. She would not give me the receipt (which Mr. Henry told me to demand, for he was very methodical) until she had sent out for spirits, and I had pledged her in a glass; and all the time she carried on in a light-headed, reckless way—now aping the manners of a lady, now breaking into unseemly mirth, now making coquettish advances that oppressed me to the ground. Of the money she spoke more tragically.

'It's blood money!' said she; 'I take it for that; blood money for the betrayed! See what I'm brought down to! Ah, if the bonnie lad were back again, it would be changed days. But he's deid—he's lyin' deid amang the Hieland hills—the bonnie lad, the bonnie lad!'

She had a rapt manner of crying on the bonnie lad, clasping her hands and casting up her eyes, that I think she must have learned of strolling players; and I thought her sorrow very much of an affectation, and that she dwelled upon the business because her shame was now all she had to be proud of. I will not say I did not pity her, but it was a loathing pity at the best; and her last change of manner wiped it out. This was when she had had enough of me for an audience, and had set her name at last to the receipt. 'There!' says she, and taking the most unwomanly oaths upon her tongue, bade me begone and carry it to the Judas who had sent me. It was the first time I had heard the name applied to Mr. Henry; I was staggered besides at her sudden vehemence of word and manner, and got forth from the room, under this shower of curses, like a beaten dog. But even then I was not quit, for the vixen threw up her window, and, leaning forth, continued to revile me as I went up the wynd; the freetraders, coming to the tavern door, joined in the mockery, and one had even the inhumanity to set upon me a very savage small dog, which bit me in the ankle. This was a strong lesson, had I required one, to avoid ill company; and I rode home in much pain from the bite and considerable indignation of mind.

Mr. Henry was in the steward's room, affecting employment, but I could see he was only impatient to hear of my errand.

'Well?' says he, as soon as I came in; and when I had told him something of what passed, and that Jessie seemed an undeserving woman and far from grateful: 'She is no friend to me,' said he; 'but indeed, Mackellar, I have few friends to boast of, and Jessie has some cause to be unjust. I need not dissemble what all the country knows: she was not very well used by one of our family.' This was the first time I had heard him refer to the Master even distantly; and I think he found his tongue rebellious even for that much, but presently he resumed—'This is why I would have nothing said. It would give pain to Mrs. Henry . . . and to my father,' he added with another flush.

'Mr. Henry,' said I, 'if you will take a freedom at my hands, I would tell you to let that woman be. What service is your money to the like of her? She has no sobriety and no economy

—as for gratitude, you will as soon get milk from a whin-stone; and if you will pretermit your bounty, it will make no change at all but just to save the ankles of your messengers.'

Mr. Henry smiled. 'But I am grieved about your ankle,' said he, the next moment, with a proper gravity.

'And observe,' I continued, 'I give you this advice upon consideration; and yet my heart was touched for the woman in the beginning.'

'Why, there it is, you see!' said Mr. Henry. 'And you are to remember that I knew her once a very decent lass. Besides which, although I speak little of my family, I think much of its repute.'

And with that he broke up the talk, which was the first we had together in such confidence. But the same afternoon I had the proof that his father was perfectly acquainted with the business, and that it was only from his wife that Mr. Henry kept it secret.

'I fear you had a painful errand to-day,' says my lord to me, 'for which as it enters in no way among your duties, I wish to thank you, and to remind you at the same time (in case Mr. Henry should have neglected) how very desirable it is that no word of it should reach my daughter. Reflections on the dead, Mr. Mackellar, are doubly painful.'

Anger glowed in my heart; and I could have told my lord to his face how little he had to do, bolstering up the image of the dead in Mrs. Henry's heart, and how much better he were employed to shatter that false idol; for by this time I saw very well how the land lay between my patron and his wife.

My pen is clear enough to tell a plain tale; but to render the effect of an infinity of small things, not one great enough in itself to be narrated; and to translate the story of looks, and the message of voices when they are saying no great matter; and to put in half a page the essence of near eighteen months—this is what I despair to accomplish. The fault to be very blunt, lay all in Mrs. Henry. She felt it a merit to have consented to the marriage, and she took it like a martyrdom; in which my old lord whether he knew it or not, fomented her. She made a merit besides, of her constancy to the dead, though its name, to a nicer conscience, should have seemed rather disloyalty to the living; and here also my lord gave her his countenance. I suppose he was glad to talk of his loss, and ashamed to dwell on it with Mr. Henry. Certainly, at least, he made a little coterie apart in that family of three, and it was the husband who was shut out. It seems it was an old custom when the family were alone in Durrisdeer, that my lord should take his wine to the chimney-side, and Miss Alison, instead of withdrawing, should bring a stool to his knee, and chatter to him privately; and after she had become my patron's wife the same manner of doing was continued. It should have been pleasant to behold this ancient gentleman so loving with his daughter, but I was too much a partisan of Mr. Henry's to be anything but wroth at his exclusion. Many's the time I have seen him make an obvious resolve, quit the table, and go and join himself to his wife and my Lord Durrisdeer; and on their part, they were never backward to make him welcome, turned to him smilingly as to an intruding child, and took him into their talk with an effort so ill-concealed that he was soon back again beside me at the table, whence (so great is the hall of Durrisdeer) we could but hear the murmur of voices at the chimney. There he would sit and watch, and I along with him; and sometimes by my lord's head sorrowfully shaken or his hand laid on Mrs. Henry's head, or hers upon his knee as if in consolation, or sometimes by an exchange of tearful looks, we would draw our conclusion that the talk had gone to the old subject and the shadow of the dead was in the hall.

I have hours when I blame Mr. Henry for taking all too patiently; yet we are to remember he was married in pity, and accepted his wife upon that term. Once, I remember, he announced he had found a man to replace the pane of the stained window, which as it was he that managed all the business, was a thing clearly within his attributions. But to the Master's fancies, that pane was like a relic; and on the first word of any change, the blood flew to Mrs. Henry's face.

' I wonder at you! ' she cried.

' I wonder at myself,' says Mr. Henry, with more of bitterness than I had ever heard him to express.

Thereupon my old lord stepped in with his smooth talk, so that before the meal was at an end all seemed forgotten; only that, after dinner, when the pair had withdrawn as usual to the chimney-side, we could see her weeping with her head upon his knee. Mr. Henry kept up the talk with me upon some topic of the estates—he could speak of little else but business, and was never the best of company; but he kept it up that day with more continuity, his eye straying ever and again to the chimney, and his voice changing to another key, but without check of delivery. The pane, however, was not replaced; and I believe he counted it a great defeat.

Whether he was stout enough or no, God knows he was kind enough. Mrs. Henry had a manner of condescension with him, such as (in a wife) would have pricked my vanity into an ulcer; he took it like a favour. She held him at the staff's end; forgot and then remembered and unbent to him, as we do to children; burthened him with cold kindness; reproved him with a change of colour and a bitten lip, like one shamed by his disgrace; ordered him with a look of the eye, when she was off her guard; when she was on the watch, pleaded with him for the most natural attentions, as though they were unheard-of favours. And to all this he replied with the most unwearied service; loving, as folks say, the very ground she trod on, and carrying that love in his eyes as bright as a lamp. When Miss Katharine was to be born, nothing would serve but he must stay in the room behind the head of the bed. There he sat, as white (they tell me) as a sheet and the sweat dropping from his brow; and the hand-kerchief he had in his hand was crushed into a little ball no bigger than a musket-bullet. Nor could he bear the sight of Miss Katharine for many a day; indeed, I doubt if he was ever what he should have been to my young lady; for the which want of natural feeling he was loudly blamed.

Such was the state of this family down to the 7th April, 1749, when there befell the first of that series of events which were to break so many hearts and lose so many lives.

On that day I was sitting in my room a little before supper when John Paul burst open the door with no civility of knocking, and told me there was one below that wished to speak with the steward; sneering at the name of my office.

I asked what manner of man, and what his name was; and this disclosed the excuse of John's ill-humour, for it appeared the visitor refused to name himself except to me, a sore affront to the major-domo's consequence.

' Well,' said I, smiling a little, ' I will see what he wants.'

I found in the entrance hall a big man, very plainly habited, and wrapped in a sea-cloak, like one new landed, as indeed he was. Not far off Macconochie was standing, with his tongue out of his mouth and his hand upon his chin, like a dull fellow thinking hard; and the stranger, who had brought his cloak about his face, appeared uneasy. He had no sooner seen me coming than he went to meet me with an effusive manner.

' My dear man,' said he, ' a thousand apologies for disturbing you, but I'm in the most awkward position. And there's a son of a ramrod there that I should know the looks of, and more betoken I believe that he knows mine. Being in this family, sir, and in a place of some responsibility (which was the cause I took the liberty to send for you), you are doubtless of the honest party?'

'You may be sure at least,' says I, 'that all of that party are quite safe in Durrisdeer.'

'My dear man, it is my very thought,' says he. 'You see, I have just been set on shore here by a very honest man, whose name I cannot remember, and who is to stand off and on for me till morning, at some danger to himself; and, to be clear with you, I am a little concerned lest it should be at some to me. I have saved my life so often Mr.——, I forget your name, which is a very good one—that faith, I would be very loath to lose it after all. And the son of a ramrod, whom I believe I saw before Carlisle. . . .'

'Oh, sir,' said I, 'you can trust Macconochie until to-morrow.'

'Well, and it's a delight to hear you say so,' says the stranger. 'The truth is that my name is not a very suitable one in this country of Scotland. With a gentleman like you, my dear man, I would have no concealments, of course; and by your leave I'll just breathe it in your ear. They call me Francis Burke—Colonel Francis Burke; and I am here, at a most damnable risk to myself, to see your masters—if you'll excuse me, my good man, for giving them the name, for I'm sure it's a circumstance I would never have guessed from your appearance. And if you would just be so very obliging as to take my name to them, you might say that I come bearing letters which I am sure they will be very rejoiced to have the reading of.'

Colonel Francis Burke was one of the Prince's Irishmen, that did his cause such an infinity of hurt, and were so much distasted of the Scots at the time of the rebellion; and it came at once into my mind, how the Master of Ballantrae had astonished all men by going with that party. In the same moment a strong foreboding of the truth possessed my soul.

'If you will step in here,' said I, opening a chamber door, 'I will let my lord know.'

'And I am sure it's very good of you, Mr. What-is-your-name?' says the Colonel.

Up to the hall I went, slow footed. There they were, all three—my old lord in his place, Mrs. Henry at work by the window, Mr. Henry (as was much his custom) pacing the low end. In the midst was the table laid for supper. I told them briefly what I had to say. My old lord lay back in his seat. Mrs. Henry sprang up standing with a mechanical motion, and she and her husband stared at each other's eyes across the room: it was the strangest challenging look these two exchanged, and as they looked, the colour faded in their faces. Then Mr. Henry turned to me; not to speak, only to sign with his finger; but that was enough, and I went down again for the Colonel.

When we returned these three were in much the same position I had left them in; I believe no word had passed.

'My Lord Durrisdeer, no doubt?' says the Colonel, bowing, and my lord bowed in answer. 'And this,' continues the Colonel, 'should be the Master of Ballantrae?'

'I have never taken that name,' said Mr. Henry; 'but I am Henry Durie, at your service.'

Then the Colonel turns to Mrs. Henry, bowing with his hat upon his heart and the most killing airs of gallantry. 'There can be no mistake about so fine a figure of a lady,' says he. 'I address the seductive Miss Alison, of whom I have so often heard?'

Once more husband and wife exchanged a look.

'I am Mrs. Henry Durie,' she said; 'but before my marriage my name was Alison Graeme.'

Then my lord spoke up. 'I am an old man, Colonel Burke,' said he, 'and a frail one. It will be mercy on your part to be expeditious. Do you bring me news of—— ' he hesitated, and then the words broke from him with a singular change of voice— 'my son?'

'My dear lord, I will be round with you like a soldier,' said the Colonel. 'I do.'

My lord held out a wavering hand; he seemed to wave a signal, but whether it was to give him time or to speak on, was more than we could guess. At length he got out the one word, 'Good?'

'Why, the very best in the creation!' cries the Colonel. 'For my good friend and admired comrade is at this hour in the fine city of Paris, and as like as not, if I know anything of his habits, he will be drawing in his chair to a piece of dinner.—Bedad, I believe the lady's fainting.'

Mrs. Henry was indeed the colour of death, and drooped against the window-frame. But when Mr. Henry made a movement as if to run to her, she straightened with a sort of shiver. 'I am well,' she said, with her white lips.

Mr. Henry stopped, and his face had a strong twitch of anger. The next moment he had turned to the Colonel. 'You must not blame yourself,' says he, 'for this effect on Mrs. Durie. It is only natural; we were all brought up like brother and sister.'

Mrs. Henry looked at her husband with something like relief

or even gratitude. In my way of thinking, that speech was the first step he made in her good graces.

' You must try to forgive me, Mrs. Durie, for indeed and I am just an Irish savage,' said the Colonel; ' and I deserve to be shot for not breaking the matter more artistically to a lady. But here are the Master's own letters; one for each of the three of you; and to be sure (if I know anything of my friend's genius) he will tell his own story with a better grace.'

He brought the three letters forth as he spoke, arranged them by their superscriptions, presented the first to my lord, who took it greedily, and advanced towards Mrs. Henry holding out the second.

But the lady waved it back. ' To my husband,' says she, with a choked voice.

The Colonel was a quick man, but at this he was somewhat nonplussed. ' To be sure! ' says he; ' how very dull of me! To be sure! ' But he still held the letter.

At last Mr. Henry reached forth his hand, and there was nothing to be done but give it up. Mr. Henry took the letters (both hers and his own), and looked upon their outside, with his brows knit hard, as if he were thinking. He had surprised me all through by his excellent behaviour; but he was to excel himself now.

' Let me give you a hand to your room,' said he to his wife. ' This has come something of the suddenest; and, at any rate, you will wish to read your letter by yourself.'

Again she looked upon him with the same thought of wonder; but he gave her no time, coming straight to where she stood. ' It will be better so, believe me,' said he; ' and Colonel Burke is too considerate not to excuse you.' And with that he took her hand by the fingers, and led her from the hall.

Mrs. Henry returned no more that night; and when Mr. Henry went to visit her next morning, as I heard long afterwards, she gave him the letter again, still unopened.

' Oh, read it and be done! ' he had cried.

' Spare me that,' said she.

And by these two speeches, to my way of thinking, each undid a great part of what they had previously done well. But the letter, sure enough, came into my hands, and by me was burned, unopened.

To be very exact as to the adventures of the Master after Culloden, I wrote not long ago to Colonel Burke, now a Cheva-lier of the Order of St. Louis, begging him for some notes in writing, since I could scarce depend upon my memory at so great an interval. To confess the truth, I have been somewhat embarrassed by his response; for he sent me the complete memoirs of his life, touching only in places on the Master; running to a much greater length than my whole story, and not everywhere (as it seems to me) designed for edification. He begged in his letter, dated from Ettenheim, that I would find a publisher for the whole, after I had made what use of it I required; and I think I shall answer my own purpose and fulfil his wishes by printing certain parts of it in full. In this way my readers will have a detailed, and, I believe, a very genuine account of some essential matters; and if any publisher should take a fancy to the Chevalier's manner of narration, he knows where to apply for the rest, of which there is plenty at his service. I put in my first extract here, so that it may stand in the place of what the Chevalier told us over our wine in the hall of Durrisdeer; but you are to suppose it was not the brutal fact, but a very varnished version that he offered to my lord.

3

The Master's wanderings:
From the Memoirs of the Chevalier de Burke

. . . I LEFT Ruthven (it's hardly necessary to remark) with much greater satisfaction than I had come to it; but whether I missed my way in the deserts, or whether my companions failed me, I soon found myself alone. This was a predicament very disagreeable; for I never understood this horrid country or savage people, and the last stroke of the Prince's withdrawal had made us of the Irish more unpopular than ever. I was reflecting on my poor chances, when I saw another horseman on the hill, whom I supposed at first to have been a phantom, the news of his death in the very front at Culloden being current in the army generally. This was the Master of Ballantrae, my Lord Durrisdeer's son, a young nobleman of the rarest gallantry and parts, and equally designed by nature to adorn a Court and to reap laurels in the field. Our meeting was the more welcome to both, as he was one of the few Scots who had used the Irish with consideration, and as he might now be of very high utility in aiding my escape. Yet what founded our particular friendship was a circumstance, by itself as romantic as any fable of King Arthur.

This was on the second day of our flight, after we had slept one night in the rain upon the inclination of a mountain. There was an Appin man, Alan Black Stewart (or some such name,[1] but I have seen him since in France), who chanced to be passing the same way, and had a jealousy of my companion. Very uncivil expressions were exchanged; and Stewart calls upon the Master to alight and have it out.

'Why, Mr. Stewart,' says the Master, 'I think at the present time I would prefer to run a race with you.' And with the word claps spurs to his horse.

Stewart ran after us, a childish thing to do, for more than a mile; and I could not help laughing, as I looked back at last and saw him on a hill, holding his hand to his side, and nearly burst with running.

'But, all the same,' I could not help saying to my companion, 'I would let no man run after me for any such proper purpose, and not give him his desire. It was a good jest, but it smells a trifle cowardly.'

He bent his brows at me. 'I do pretty well,' says he, 'when I saddle myself with the most unpopular man in Scotland, and let that suffice for courage.'

'O, bedad,' says I, 'I could show you a more unpopular with the naked eye. And if you like not my company, you can " saddle " yourself on some one else.'

'Colonel Burke,' says he, 'do not let us quarrel; and, to that effect, let me assure you I am the least patient man in the world.'

'I am as little patient as yourself,' said I. 'I care not who knows that.'

'At this rate,' says he, reining in, 'we shall not go very far. And I propose we do one of two things upon the instant: either quarrel and be done; or make a sure bargain to bear everything at each other's hands.'

'Like a pair of brothers?' said I.

'I said no such foolishness,' he replied. 'I have a brother of my own, and I think no more of him than of a colewort. But if we are to have our noses rubbed together in this course of flight, let us each dare to be ourselves like savages, and each swear that he will neither resent nor deprecate the other. I am a pretty bad fellow at bottom, and I find the pretence of virtues very irksome.'

'O, I am as bad as yourself,' said I. 'There is no skim milk in Francis Burke. But which is it to be? Fight or make friends?'

[1] *Note by Mr. Mackellar.* Should not this be Alan *Breck* Stewart, afterwards notorious as the Appin murderer? The Chevalier is sometimes very weak on names.

'Why,' says he, 'I think it will be the best manner to spin a coin for it.'

This proposition was too highly chivalrous not to take my fancy; and, strange as it may seem of two well-born gentlemen of to-day, we span a half-crown (like a pair of ancient paladins) whether we were to cut each other's throats or be sworn friends. A more romantic circumstance can rarely have occurred; and it is one of those points in my memoirs, by which we may see the old tales of Homer and the poets are equally true to-day—at least, of the noble and genteel. The coin fell for peace, and we shook hands upon our bargain. And then it was that my companion explained to me his thought in running away from Mr. Stewart, which was certainly worthy of his political intellect. The report of his death, he said, was a great guard to him; Mr. Stewart having recognised him had become a danger: and he had taken the briefest road to that gentleman's silence. 'For,' says he, 'Alan Black is too vain a man to narrate any such story of himself.'

Towards afternoon we came down to the shores of that loch for which we were heading; and there was the ship, but newly come to anchor. She was the *Sainte-Marie-des-Anges*, out of the port of Havre-de-Grace. The Master, after we had signalled for a boat, asked me if I knew the captain. I told him he was a countryman of mine, of the most unblemished integrity, but, I was afraid, a rather timorous man.

'No matter,' says he. 'For all that, he should certainly hear the truth.'

I asked him if he meant about the battle? for if the captain once knew the standard was down, he would certainly put to sea again at once.

'And even then!' said he; 'the arms are now of no sort of utility.'

'My dear man,' said I, 'who thinks of the arms? But, to be sure, we must remember our friends. They will be close upon our heels, perhaps the Prince himself, and if the ship be gone, a great number of valuable lives may be imperilled.'

'The captain and the crew have lives also, if you come to that,' says Ballantrae.

This I declared was but a quibble, and that I would not hear of the captain being told; and then it was that Ballantrae made me a witty answer, for the sake of which (and also because I have been blamed myself in this business of the *Sainte-Marie-des-Anges*) I have related the whole conversation as it passed.

'Frank,' says he, 'remember our bargain. I must not object

to your holding your tongue, which I hereby even encourage you to do; but, by the same terms, you are not to resent my telling.'

I could not help laughing at this; though I still forewarned him what would come of it.

' The devil may come of it for what I care,' says the reckless fellow. ' I have always done exactly as I felt inclined.'

As is well known, my prediction came true. The captain had no sooner heard the news than he cut his cable and to sea again; and before morning broke, we were in the Great Minch.

The ship was very old; and the skipper, although the most honest of men (and Irish too), was one of the least capable. The wind blew very boisterous, and the sea raged extremely. All that day we had little heart whether to eat or drink; went early to rest in some concern of mind; and (as if to give us a lesson) in the night the wind chopped suddenly into the north-east, and blew a hurricane. We were awaked by the dreadful thunder of the tempest and the stamping of the mariners on deck; so that I supposed our last hour was certainly come; and the terror of my mind was increased out of all measure by Ballantrae, who mocked at my devotions. It is in hours like these that a man of any piety appears in his true light, and we find (what we are taught as babes) the small trust that can be set in worldly friends: I would be unworthy of my religion if I let this pass without particular remark. For three days we lay in the dark in the cabin, and had but a biscuit to nibble. On the fourth day the wind fell, leaving the ship dismasted and heaving on vast billows. The captain had not a guess of whither we were blown; he was stark ignorant of his trade, and could do naught but bless the Holy Virgin; a very good thing, too, but scarce the whole of seamanship. It seemed, our one hope was to be picked up by another vessel; and if that should prove to be an English ship, it might be no great blessing to the Master and myself.

The fifth and sixth days we tossed there helpless. The seventh some sail was got on her, but she was an unwieldly vessel at the best, and we made little but leeway. All the time, indeed, we had been drifting to the south and west, and during the tempest must have driven in that direction with unheard-of violence. The ninth dawn was cold and black, with a great sea running, and every mark of foul weather. In this situation we were over-joyed to sight a small ship on the horizon, and to perceive her go about and head for the *Sainte-Marie*. But our gratification did not very long endure; for when she had laid to and lowered a boat, it was immediately filled with disorderly fellows, who sang and shouted as they pulled across to us, and swarmed in on our deck with bare cutlasses, cursing loudly. Their leader was a horrible villain, with his face blacked and his whiskers curled in ringlets; Teach, his name; a most notorious pirate. He stamped about the deck, raving and crying out that his name was Satan, and his ship was called Hell. There was something about him like a wicked child or a half-witted person, that daunted me beyond expression. I whispered in the ear of Ballantrae that I would not be the last to volunteer, and only prayed God they might be short of hands; he approved my purpose with a nod.

'Bedad,' said I to Master Teach, 'if you are Satan, here is a devil for ye.'

The word pleased him; and (not to dwell upon these shocking incidents) Ballantrae and I and two others were taken for recruits, while the skipper and all the rest were cast into the sea by the method of walking the plank. It was the first time I had seen this done; my heart died within me at the spectacle; and Master Teach or one of his acolytes (for my head was too much lost to be precise) remarked upon my pale face in a very alarming manner. I had the strength to cut a step or two of a jig, and cry out some ribaldry, which saved me for that time; but my legs were like water when I must get down into the skiff among these miscreants; and what with my horror of my company and fear of the monstrous billows, it was all I could do to keep an Irish tongue and break a jest or two as we were pulled aboard. By the blessing of God, there was a fiddle in the pirate ship, which I had no sooner seen than I fell upon; and in my quality of crowder I had the heavenly good luck to get favour in their eyes. *Crowding Pat* was the name they dubbed me with; and it was little I cared for a name so long as my skin was whole.

What kind of a pandemonium that vessel was, I cannot describe, but she was commanded by a lunatic, and might be called a floating Bedlam. Drinking, roaring, singing, quarrelling, dancing, they were never all sober at one time; and there were days together when, if a squall had supervened, it must have sent us to the bottom; or if a king's ship had come along, it would have found us quite helpless for defence. Once or twice we sighted a sail, and, if we were sober enough, overhauled her, God forgive us! and if we were all too drunk, she got away, and I would bless the saints under my breath. Teach ruled, if you can call that rule which brought no order, by the terror he created; and I observed the man was very vain of his position. I have known marshals of France—ay, and even Highland chieftains—that were less openly puffed up; which throws a singular light on the pursuit of honour and glory. Indeed, the longer we live, the more we perceive the sagacity of Aristotle and the other old philosophers; and though I have all my life been eager for legitimate distinctions, I can lay my hand upon my heart, at the end of my career, and declare there is not one—no, nor yet life itself—which is worth acquiring or preserving at the slightest cost of dignity.

It was long before I got private speech of Ballantrae; but at length one night we crept out upon the bowsprit, when the rest were better employed, and commiserated our position.

'None can deliver us but the saints,' said I.

'My mind is very different,' said Ballantrae; 'for I am going to deliver myself. This Teach is the poorest creature possible; we make no profit of him, and lie continually open to capture; and,' says he, ' I am not going to be a tarry pirate for nothing, nor yet to hang in chains if I can help it.' And he told me what was in his mind to better the state of the ship in the way of discipline, which would give us safety for the present, and a sooner hope of deliverance when they should have gained enough and should break up their company.

I confessed to him ingenuously that my nerve was quite shook amid these horrible surroundings, and I durst scarce tell him to count upon me.

' I am not very easily frightened,' said he, ' nor very easily beat.'

A few days after, there befell an accident which had nearly hanged us all; and offers the most extraordinary picture of the folly that ruled in our concerns. We were all pretty drunk: and some bedlamite spying a sail, Teach put the ship about in chase without a glance, and we began to bustle up the arms and boast of the horrors that should follow. I observed Ballantrae stood quiet in the bows, looking under the shade of his hand; but for my part, true to my policy among these savages, I was at work with the busiest and passing Irish jests for their diversion.

' Run up the colour,' cries Teach. ' Show the——s the Jolly Roger! '

It was the merest drunken braggadocio at such a stage, and might have lost us a valuable prize; but I thought it no part of mine to reason, and I ran up the black flag with my own hand.

Ballantrae steps presently aft with a smile upon his face.

' You may perhaps like to know, you drunken dog,' says he, ' that you are chasing a king's ship.'

Teach roared him the lie; but he ran at the same time to the bulwarks, and so did they all. I have never seen so many drunken men struck suddenly sober. The cruiser had gone about, upon our impudent display of colours; she was just then filling on the new tack; her ensign blew out quite plain to see; and even as we stared, there came a puff of smoke, and then a report, and a shot plunged in the waves a good way short of us. Some ran to the ropes, and got the *Sarah* round with an incredible swiftness. One fellow fell on the rum barrel, which stood broached upon the deck, and rolled it promptly overboard. On my part, I made for the Jolly Roger, struck it, tossed it in the sea; and could have flung myself after, so vexed was I with our mismanagement. As for Teach, he grew as pale as death, and incontinently went down to his cabin. Only twice he came on deck that afternoon; went to the taffrail; took a long look at the king's ship, which was still on the horizon heading after us; and then, without speech, back to his cabin. You may say he deserted us; and if it had not been for one very capable sailor we had on board, and for the lightness of the airs that blew all day we must certainly have gone to the yard-arm.

It is to be supposed Teach was humiliated, and perhaps alarmed for his position with the crew; and the way in which he set about regaining what he had lost was highly characteristic of the man. Early next day we smelled him burning sulphur in his cabin and crying out of ' Hell, hell!' which was well understood among the crew, and filled their minds with apprehension. Presently he comes on deck, a perfect figure of fun, his face blacked, his hair and whiskers curled, his belt stuck full of pistols; chewing bits of glass so that the blood ran down his chin, and brandishing a dirk. I do not know if he had taken these manners from the Indians of America, where he was a native; but such was his way, and he would always thus announce that he was wound up to horrid deeds. The first that came near him was the fellow who had sent the rum overboard the day before; him he stabbed to the heart, damning him for a mutineer; and then capered about the body, raving and swearing and daring us to come on. It was the silliest exhibition; and yet dangerous too, for the cowardly fellow was plainly working himself up to another murder.

All of a sudden Ballantrae stepped forth. ' Have done with this play-acting,' says he. ' Do you think to frighten us with making faces? We saw nothing of you yesterday, when you were wanted; and we did well without you, let me tell you that.'

There was a murmur and a movement in the crew, of pleasure and alarm, I thought, in nearly equal parts. As for Teach, he gave a barbarous howl, and swung his dirk to fling it, an art in which (like many seamen) he was very expert.

'Knock that out of his hand!' says Ballantrae, so sudden and sharp that my arm obeyed him before my mind had understood.

Teach stood like one stupid, never thinking on his pistols.

'Go down to your cabin,' cries Ballantrae, 'and come on deck again when you are sober. Do you think we are going to hang for you, you black-faced, half-witted, drunken brute and butcher? Go down!' And he stamped his foot at him with such a sudden smartness that Teach fairly ran for it to the companion.

'And now, mates,' says Ballantrae, 'a word with you. I don't know if you are gentlemen of fortune for the fun of the thing, but I am not. I want to make money, and get ashore again, and spend it like a man. And on one thing my mind is made up: I will not hang if I can help it. Come: give me a hint; I'm only a beginner! Is there no way to get a little discipline and common sense about this business?'

One of the men spoke up: he said by rights they should have a quartermaster; and no sooner was the word out of his mouth than they were all of that opinion. The thing went by acclamation, Ballantrae was made quartermaster, the rum was put in his charge, laws were passed in imitation of those of a pirate by the name of Roberts, and the last proposal was to make an end of Teach. But Ballantrae was afraid of a more efficient captain, who might be a counterweight to himself, and he opposed this stoutly. Teach, he said, was good enough to board ships and to frighten fools with his blacked face and swearing; we could scarce get a better man than Teach for that; and besides, as the man was now disconsidered and as good as deposed, we might reduce his proportion of the plunder. This carried it; Teach's share was cut down to a mere derision, being actually less than mine; and there remained only two points: whether he would consent, and who was to announce to him this resolution.

'Do not let that stick you,' says Ballantrae, 'I will do that.'

And he stepped to the companion and down alone into the cabin to face the drunken savage.

'This is the man for us,' cries one of the hands. 'Three cheers for that quartermaster!' which were given with a will, my own

voice among the loudest, and I dare say these plaudits had their
effect on Master Teach in the cabin, as we have seen of late
days how shouting in the streets may trouble even the minds
of legislators.

What passed precisely was never known, though some of the
heads of it came to the surface later on; and we were all amazed,
as well as gratified, when Ballantrae came on deck with Teach
upon his arm, and announced that all had been consented.

I pass swiftly over those twelve or fifteen months in which
we continued to keep the sea in the North Atlantic, getting our
food and water from the ships we overhauled, and doing on
the whole a pretty fortunate business. Sure, no one could wish
to read anything so ungenteel as the memoirs of a pirate, even
an unwilling one like me! Things went extremely better with
our designs, and Ballantrae kept his lead, to my admiration,
from that day forth. I would be tempted to suppose that a
gentleman must everywhere be first, even aboard a rover: but
my birth is every whit as good as any Scottish lord's, and I am
not ashamed to confess that I stayed Crowding Pat until the
end, and was not much better than the crew's buffoon. Indeed,
it was no scene to bring out my merits. My health suffered
from a variety of reasons; I was more at home to the last on
a horse's back than a ship's deck; and, to be ingenuous, the
fear of the sea was constantly in my mind, battling with the fear
of my companions. I need not cry myself up for courage; I
have done well on many fields under the eyes of famous generals,
and earned my late advancement by an act of the most distinguished valour before many witnesses. But when we must proceed
on one of our abordages, the heart of Francis Burke was in his
boots; the little egg-shell skiff in which we must set forth, the
horrible heaving of the vast billows, the height of the ship that
we must scale, the thought of how many there might be there
in garrison upon their legitimate defence, the scowling heavens
which (in that climate) so often looked darkly down upon our
exploits, and the mere crying of the wind in my ears, were all
considerations most unpalatable to my valour. Besides which,
as I was always a creature of the nicest sensibility, the scenes
that must follow on our success tempted me as little as the chances
of defeat. Twice we found women on board; and though I
have seen towns sacked, and of late days in France some very
horrid public tumults, there was something in the smallness of
the numbers engaged, and the bleak, dangerous sea-surround-
ings, that made these acts of piracy far the most revolting. I
confess ingenuously I could never proceed unless I was three

parts drunk; it was the same even with the crew; Teach himself was fit for no enterprise till he was full of rum; and it was one of the most difficult parts of Ballantrae's performance to serve us with liquor in the proper quantities. Even this he did to admiration; being upon the whole the most capable man I ever met with, and the one of the most natural genius. He did not even scrape favour with the crew, as I did, by continual buffoonery made upon a very anxious heart; but preserved on most occasions a great deal of gravity and distance: so that he was like a parent among a family of young children, or a schoolmaster with his boys. What made his part the harder to perform, the men were inveterate grumblers; Ballantrae's discipline, little as it was, was yet irksome to their love of licence; and what was worse, being kept sober they had time to think. Some of them accordingly would fall to repenting their abominable crimes; one in particular, who was a good Catholic, and with whom I would sometimes steal apart for prayer; above all in bad weather, fogs, lashing rain and the like, when we would be the less observed; and I am sure no two criminals in the cart have ever performed their devotions with more anxious sincerity. But the rest, having no such grounds of hope, fell to another pastime, that of computation. All day long they would be telling up their shares or glooming over the result. I have said we were pretty fortunate. But an observation falls to be made: that in this world, in no business that I have tried, do the profits rise to a man's expectations. We found many ships and took many; yet few of them contained much money, their goods were usually nothing to our purpose—what did we want with a cargo of ploughs, or even of tobacco?—and it is quite a painful reflection how many whole crews we have made to walk the plank for no more than a stock of biscuits or an anker or two of spirits.

In the meanwhile our ship was growing very foul, and it was high time we should make for our *port de carénage*, which was in the estuary of a river among swamps. It was openly understood that we should then break up and go and squander our proportions of the spoil; and this made every man greedy of a little more, so that our decision was delayed from day to day. What finally decided matters, was a trifling accident, such as an ignorant person might suppose incidental to our way of life. But here I must explain: on only one of all the ships we boarded, the first on which we found women, did we meet with any genuine resistance. On that occasion we had two men killed and several injured, and if it had not been for the gallantry of Ballantrae we had surely been beat back at last. Everywhere else the defence (where there was any at all) was what the worst troops in Europe would have laughed at; so that the most dangerous part of our employment was to clamber up the side of the ship; and I have even known the poor souls on board to cast us a line, so eager were they to volunteer instead of walking the plank. This constant immunity had made our fellows very soft, so that I understood how Teach had made so deep a mark upon their minds; for indeed the company of that lunatic was the chief danger in our way of life. The accident to which I have referred was this:—We had sighted a little full-rigged ship very close under our board in a haze; she sailed near as well as we did—I should be nearer truth if I said, near as ill; and we cleared the bow-chaser to see if we could bring a spar or two about their ears. The swell was exceeding great; the motion of the ship beyond description; it was little wonder if our gunners should fire thrice and be still quite broad of what they aimed at. But in the meanwhile the chase had cleared a stern gun, the thickness of the air concealing them; and being better marksmen, their first shot struck us in the bows, knocked our two gunners into mincemeat, so that we were all sprinkled with the blood, and plunged through the deck into the forecastle where we slept. Ballantrae would have held on; indeed, there was nothing in this *contretemps* to affect the mind of any soldier; but he had a quick perception of the men's wishes, and it was plain this lucky shot had given them a sickener of their trade. In a moment they were all of one mind: the chase was drawing away from us, it was needless to hold on, the *Sarah* was too foul to overhaul a bottle, it was mere foolery to keep the sea with her; and on these pretended grounds her head was incontinently put about and the course laid for the river. It was strange to see what merriment fell on that ship's company, and how they stamped about the deck jesting, and each computing what increase had come to his share by the death of the two gunners.

We were nine days making our port, so light were the airs we had to sail on, so foul was the ship's bottom; but early on the tenth, before dawn, and in a light lifting haze, we passed the head. A little after, the haze lifted, and fell again, showing us a cruiser very close. This was a sore blow, happening so near our refuge. There was a great debate of whether she had seen us, and if so whether it was likely they had recognised the *Sarah*. We were very careful, by destroying every member of those crews we overhauled, to leave no evidence as to our own persons; but the appearance of the *Sarah* herself we could not keep so private; and above all of late, since she had been foul, and we had pursued many ships without success, it was plain that her description had been often published. I supposed this alert would have made us separate upon the instant. But here again that original genius of Ballantrae's had a surprise in store for me. He and Teach (and it was the most remarkable step of his success) had gone hand in hand since the first day of his appointment. I often questioned him upon the fact, and never got an answer but once, when he told me he and Teach had an understanding 'which would very much surprise the crew if they should hear of it, and would surprise himself a good deal if it was carried out.' Well, here again he and Teach were of a mind; and by their joint procurement the anchor was no sooner down than the whole crew went off upon a scene of drunkenness indescribable. By afternoon we were a mere shipful of lunatical persons, throwing of things overboard, howling of different songs at the same time, quarrelling and falling together, and then forgetting our quarrels to embrace. Ballantrae had bid me drink nothing, and feign drunkenness, as I valued my life; and I have never passed a day so wearisomely, lying the best part of the time upon the forecastle and watching the swamps and thickets by which our little basin was entirely surrounded for the eye. A little after dusk Ballantrae stumbled up to my side, feigned to fall, with a drunken laugh, and before he got his feet again, whispered me to 'reel down into the cabin and seem to fall asleep upon a locker, for there would be need of me soon.' I did as I was told, and coming into the cabin, where it was quite dark, let myself fall on the first locker. There was a man there already; by the way he stirred and threw me off, I could not think he was much in liquor; and yet when I had found another place, he seemed to continue to sleep on. My heart now beat very hard, for I saw some desperate matter was in act. Presently down came Ballantrae, lit the lamp, looked about the cabin, nodded as if pleased, and on deck again without a word. I peered out from between my fingers, and saw there were three of us slumbering, or feigning to slumber, on the lockers: myself, one Dutton and one Grady, both resolute men. On deck the rest were got to a pitch of revelry quite beyond the bounds of what is human; so that no reasonable name can describe the sounds they were now making. I have heard many a drunken bout in my time, many on board that very *Sarah*, but never anything the least like this, which made me early suppose the liquor had been tampered with. It was a long while before these yells and howls died out into a sort of miserable moaning, and then to silence; and it seemed a long while after that before Ballantrae came down again, this time with Teach upon his heels. The latter cursed at the sight of us three upon the lockers.

' Tut,' says Ballantrae, ' you might fire a pistol at their ears. You know what stuff they have been swallowing.'

There was a hatch in the cabin floor, and under that the richest part of the booty was stored against the day of division. It fastened with a ring and three padlocks, the keys (for greater security) being divided; one to Teach, one to Ballantrae, and one to the mate, a man called Hammond. Yet I was amazed to see they were now all in the one hand; and yet more amazed (still looking through my fingers) to observe Ballantrae and Teach bring up several packets, four of them in all, very carefully made up and with a loop for carriage.

' And now,' says Teach, ' let us be going.'

' One word,' says Ballantrae. ' I have discovered there is another man besides yourself who knows a private path across the swamp; and it seems it is shorter than yours.'

Teach cried out, in that case, they were undone.

' I do not know for that,' says Ballantrae. ' For there are several other circumstances with which I must acquaint you. First of all, there is no bullet in your pistols, which (if you remember) I was kind enough to load for both of us this morning. Secondly, as there is some one else who knows a passage, you must think it highly improbable I should saddle myself with a lunatic like you. Thirdly, these gentlemen (who need no longer pretend to be asleep) are those of my party, and will now proceed to gag and bind you to the mast; and when your men awaken (if they ever do awake after the drugs we have mingled in their liquor), I am sure they will be so obliging as to deliver you, and you will have no difficulty, I daresay, to explain the business of the keys.'

Not a word said Teach, but looked at us like a frightened baby as we gagged and bound him.

' Now you see, you moon-calf,' says Ballantrae, ' why we make four packets. Heretofore you have been called Captain Teach, but I think you are now rather Captain Learn.'

That was our last word on board the *Sarah*. We four, with our four packets, lowered ourselves softly into a skiff, and left that ship behind us as silent as the grave, only for the moaning of some of the drunkards. There was a fog about breast-high upon the waters; so that Dutton, who knew the passage, must stand on his feet to direct our rowing; and this, as it forced us to row gently, was the means of our deliverance. We were yet but a little way from the ship, when it began to come grey, and the birds to fly abroad upon the water. All of a sudden Dutton clapped down upon his hams, and whispered us to be silent for our lives, and hearken. Sure enough, we heard a little faint creak of oars upon one hand, and then again, and further off, a creak of oars upon the other. It was clear we had been sighted yesterday in the morning; here were the cruiser's boats to cut us out; here were we defenceless in their very midst. Sure, never were poor souls more perilously placed; and as we lay there on our oars, praying God the mist might hold, the sweat poured from my brow. Presently we heard one of the boats where we might have thrown a biscuit in her. ' Softly, men,' we heard an officer whisper; and I marvelled they could not hear the drumming of my heart.

' Never mind the path,' says Ballantrae; ' we must get shelter anyhow; let us pull straight ahead for the sides of the basin.'

This we did with the most anxious precaution, rowing, as best we could, upon our hands, and steering at a venture in the fog, which was (for all that) our only safety. But Heaven guided us; we touched ground at a thicket; scrambled ashore with our treasure; and having no other way of concealment, and the mist beginning already to lighten, hove down the skiff and let her sink. We were still but new under cover when the sun rose; and at the same time, from the midst of the basin, a great shouting of seamen sprang up, and we knew the *Sarah* was being boarded. I heard afterwards the officer that took her got great honour; and it's true the approach was creditably managed, but I think he had an easy capture when he came to board.[1]

I was still blessing the saints for my escape, when I became aware we were in trouble of another kind. We were here landed at random in a vast and dangerous swamp; and how to come at the path was a concern of doubt, fatigue, and peril. Dutton, indeed, was of opinion we should wait until the ship was gone, and fish up the skiff; for any delay would be more wise than to go blindly ahead in that morass. One went back accordingly to the basin-side and (peering through the thicket) saw the fog already quite drunk up, and English colours flying on the *Sarah*, but no movement made to get her under way. Our situation was now very doubtful. The swamp was an unhealthful place to linger in; we had been so greedy to bring treasures that we

---

1 *Note by Mr. Mackellar.* This Teach of the *Sarah* must not be confused with the celebrated *Blackbeard.* The dates and facts by no means tally. It is possible the second Teach may have at once borrowed the name and imitated the more excessive part of his manners from the first. Even the Master of Ballantrae could make admirers.

had brought but little food; it was highly desirable, besides, that we should get clear of the neighbourhood and into the settlements before the news of the capture went abroad; and against all these considerations, there was only the peril of the passage on the other side. I think it not wonderful we decided on the active part.

It was already blistering hot when we set forth to pass the marsh, or rather to strike the path, by compass. Dutton took the compass and one or other of us three carried his proportion of the treasure. I promise you he kept a sharp eye to his rear, for it was like the man's soul that he must trust us with. The thicket was as close as a bush; the ground very treacherous, so that we often sank in the most terrifying manner, and must go round about; the heat, besides, was stifling, the air singularly heavy, and the stinging insects abounded in such myriads that each of us walked under his own cloud. It has often been commented on, how much better gentlemen of birth endure fatigue than persons of the rabble; so that walking officers who must tramp in the dirt beside their men, shame them by their constancy. This was well to be observed in the present instance; for here were Ballantrae and I, two gentlemen of the highest breeding, on the one hand; and on the other Grady, a common mariner, and a man nearly a giant in physical strength. The case of Dutton is not in point, for I confess he did as well as any of us.[1] But as for Grady, he began early to lament his case, tailed in the rear, refused to carry Dutton's packet when it came his turn, clamoured continually for rum (of which we had too little), and at last even threatened us from behind with a cocked pistol, unless we should allow him rest. Ballantrae would have fought it out, I believe; but I prevailed with him the other way; and we made a stop and ate a meal. It seemed to benefit Grady little; he was in the rear again at once, growling and bemoaning his lot; and at last, by some carelessness, not having followed properly in our tracks, stumbled into a deep part of the slough where it was mostly water, gave some very dreadful screams, and before we could come to his aid had sunk along with his booty. His fate, and above all these screams of his, appalled us to the soul; yet it was, on the whole, a fortunate circumstance and the means of our deliverance, for it moved Dutton to mount into a tree, whence he was able to perceive and to show me, who had climbed after him, a high piece of wood, which was a landmark for the path. He went forward

[1] *Note by Mr. Mackellar.* And is not this the whole explanation? since this Dutton, exactly like the officers, enjoyed the stimulus of some responsibility.

the more carelessly, I must suppose; for presently we saw him sink a little down, draw up his feet and sink again, and so twice. Then he turned his face to us, pretty white.

'Lend a hand,' said he, 'I am in a bad place.'

'I don't know about that,' says Ballantrae, standing still.

Dutton broke out into the most violent oaths, sinking a little lower as he did, so that the mud was nearly to his waist, and plucking a pistol from his belt, 'Help me,' he cries, 'or die and be damned to you!'

'Nay,' says Ballantrae, 'I did but jest. I am coming.' And he set down his own packet and Dutton's, which he was then carrying. 'Do not venture near till we see if you are needed,' said he to me, and went forward alone to where the man was bogged. He was quiet now, though he still held the pistol; and the marks of terror in his countenance were very moving to behold.

'For the Lord's sake,' says he, 'look sharp.'

Ballantrae was now got close up. 'Keep still,' says he, and seemed to consider; and then, 'Reach out both your hands!'

Dutton laid down his pistol, and so watery was the top surface that it went clear out of sight; with an oath he stooped to snatch it; and as he did so, Ballantrae leaned forth and stabbed him between the shoulders. Up went his hands over his head—I know not whether with the pain or to ward himself; and the next moment he doubled forward in the mud.

Ballantrae was already over the ankles; but he plucked himself out, and came back to me, where I stood with my knees smiting one another. 'The devil take you, Francis!' says he. 'I believe you are a half-hearted fellow, after all. I have only done justice on a pirate. And here we are quite clear of the *Sarah*! Who shall now say that we have dipped our hands in any irregularities?'

I assured him he did me injustice; but my sense of humanity was so much affected by the horridness of the fact that I could scarce find breath to answer with.

'Come,' said he, 'you must be more resolved. The need for this fellow ceased when he had shown you where the path ran; and you cannot deny I would have been daft to let slip so fair an opportunity.'

I could not deny but he was right in principle; nor yet could I refrain from shedding tears, of which I think no man of valour need have been ashamed; and it was not until I had a share of the rum that I was able to proceed. I repeat, I am far from ashamed of my generous emotion; mercy is honourable in the warrior; and yet I cannot altogether censure Ballantrae, whose step was really fortunate, as we struck the path without further misadventure, and the same night, about sundown, came to the edge of the morass.

We were too weary to seek far; on some dry sands, still warm with the day's sun, and close under a wood of pines, we lay down and were instantly plunged in sleep.

We awaked the next morning very early, and began with a sullen spirit a conversation that came near to end in blows. We were now cast on shore in the southern provinces, thousands of miles from any French settlement; a dreadful journey and a thousand perils lay in front of us; and sure, if there was ever need for amity, it was in such an hour. I must suppose that Ballantrae had suffered in his sense of what is truly polite; indeed, and there is nothing strange in the idea, after the sea-wolves we had consorted with so long; and as for myself, he fubbed me off unhandsomely, and any gentleman would have resented his behaviour.

I told him in what light I saw his conduct; he walked a little off, I following to upbraid him; and at last he stopped me with his hand.

'Frank,' says he, 'you know what we swore; and yet there is no oath invented would induce me to swallow such expressions, if I did not regard you with sincere affection. It is impossible you should doubt me there: I have given proofs. Dutton I had to take, because he knew the pass, and Grady because Dutton would not move without him; but what call was there to carry you along? You are a perpetual danger to me with your cursed Irish tongue. By rights you should now be in irons in the cruiser. And you quarrel with me like a baby for some trinkets!'

I consider this one of the most unhandsome speeches ever made; and indeed to this day I can scarce reconcile it to my notion of a gentleman that was my friend. I retorted upon him with his Scotch accent, of which he had not so much as some, but enough to be very barbarous and disgusting, as I told him plainly; and the affair would have gone to a great length, but for an alarming intervention.

We had got some way off upon the sand. The place where we had slept, with the packets lying undone and the money scattered openly, was now between us and the pines; and it was out of these the stranger must have come. There he was at least, a great hulking fellow of the country, with a broad axe on his shoulder, looking open-mouthed, now at the treasure, which was just at his feet, and now at our disputation, in which we had gone far enough to have weapons in our hands. We had no sooner observed him than he found his legs and made off again among the pines.

This was no scene to put our minds at rest; a couple of armed men in sea-clothes found quarrelling over a treasure, not many miles from where a pirate had been captured—here was enough to bring the whole country about our ears. The quarrel was not even made up; it was blotted from our minds; and we got our packets together in the twinkling of an eye, and made off, running with the best will in the world. But the trouble was, we did not know in what direction, and must continually return upon our steps. Ballantrae had indeed collected what he could from Dutton; but it's hard to travel upon hearsay; and the estuary, which spreads into a vast irregular harbour, turned us off upon every side with a new stretch of water.

We were near beside ourselves, and already quite spent with running, when, coming to the top of a dune, we saw we were again cut off by another ramification of the bay. This was a creek, however, very different from those that had arrested us before; being set in rocks, and so precipitously deep that a small vessel was able to lie alongside, made fast with a hawser; and her crew had laid a plank to the shore. Here they had lighted a fire, and were sitting at their meal. As for the vessel herself, she was one of those they build in the Bermudas.

The love of gold and the great hatred that everybody has to pirates were motives of the most influential, and would certainly raise the country in our pursuit. Besides, it was now plain we were on some sort of straggling peninsula, like the fingers of a hand; and the wrist, or passage to the mainland, which we should have taken at the first, was by this time not improbably secured. These considerations put us on a bolder counsel. For as long as we dared, looking every moment to hear sounds of the chase, we lay among some bushes on the top of the dune; and having by this means secured a little breath and recomposed our appearance, we strolled down at last, with a great affectation of carelessness, to the party by the fire.

It was a trader and his negroes, belonging to Albany, in the province of New York, and now on the way home from the Indies with a cargo; his name I cannot recall. We were amazed to learn he had put in here from terror of the *Sarah*; for we had no thought our exploits had been so notorious. As soon as the Albanian heard she had been taken the day before, he jumped to his feet, gave us a cup of spirits for our good news, and sent his negroes to get sail on the Bermudan. On our side, we profited by the dram to become more confidential, and at last offered ourselves as passengers. He looked askance at our tarry clothes and pistols, and replied civilly enough that he had scarce accommodation for himself; nor could either our prayers or our offers of money, in which we advanced pretty far, avail to shake him.

'I see, you think ill of us,' says Ballantrae, 'but I will show you how well we think of you by telling you the truth. We are Jacobite fugitives, and there is a price upon our heads.'

At this, the Albanian was plainly moved a little. He asked us many questions as to the Scotch war, which Ballantrae very patiently answered. And then, with a wink, in a vulgar manner, 'I guess you and your Prince Charlie got more than you cared about,' said he.

'Bedad, and that we did,' said I. 'And, my dear man, I wish you would set a new example and give us just that much.'

This I said in the Irish way, about which there is allowed to be something very engaging. It's a remarkable thing, and a testimony to the love with which our nation is regarded, that this address scarce ever fails in a handsome fellow. I cannot tell how often I have seen a private soldier escape the horse, or a beggar wheedle out a good alms by a touch of the brogue. And, indeed, as soon as the Albanian had laughed at me I was pretty much at rest. Even then, however, he made many conditions, and—for one thing—took away our arms, before he suffered us aboard; which was the signal to cast off; so that in a moment after, we were gliding down the bay with a good breeze, and blessing the name of God for our deliverance. Almost in the mouth of the estuary, we passed the cruiser, and a little after the poor *Sarah* with her prize crew; and these were both sights to make us tremble. The Bermudas seemed a very safe place to be in, and our bold stroke to have been fortunately played, when we were thus reminded of the case of our companions. For all that, we had only exchanged traps, jumped out of the frying-pan into the fire, run from the yard-arm to the block, and escaped the open hostility of the man-of-war to lie at the mercy of the doubtful faith of our Albanian merchant.

From many circumstances, it chanced we were safer than we could have dared to hope. The town of Albany was at that time much concerned in contraband trade across the desert with the Indians and the French. This, as it was highly illegal, relaxed their loyalty, and as it brought them in relation with the politest people on the earth, divided even their sympathies. In short, they were like all the smugglers in the world, spies and agents ready-made for either party. Our Albanian, besides, was a very honest man indeed, and very greedy; and, to crown our luck, he conceived a great delight in our society. Before we had reached the town of New York we had come to a full agreement, that he should carry us as far as Albany upon his ship, and thence put us on a way to pass the boundaries and join the French. For all this we were to pay at a high rate; but beggars cannot be choosers, nor outlaws bargainers.

We sailed, then, up the Hudson River, which I protest is a very fine stream, and put up at the ' King's Arms ' in Albany. The town was full of the militia of the province, breathing slaughter against the French. Governor Clinton was there himself, a very busy man, and, by what I could learn, very near distracted by the factiousness of his Assembly. The Indians on both sides were on the war-path; we saw parties of them bringing in prisoners and (what was much worse) scalps, both male and female, for which they were paid at a fixed rate; and I assure you the sight was not encouraging. Altogether, we could scarce have come at a period more unsuitable for our designs; our position in the chief inn was dreadfully conspicuous; our Albanian fubbed us off with a thousand delays, and seemed upon the point of a retreat from his engagements; nothing but peril appeared to environ the poor fugitives, and for some time we drowned our concern in a very irregular course of living.

This, too, proved to be fortunate; and it's one of the remarks that fall to be made upon our escape, how providentially our steps were conducted to the very end. What a humiliation to the dignity of man! My philosophy, the extraordinary genius of Ballantrae, our valour, in which I grant that we were equal —all these might have proved insufficient without the Divine blessing on our efforts. And how true it is, as the Church tells us, that the Truths of Religion are, after all, quite applicable even to daily affairs! At least, it was in the course of our revelry that we made the acquaintance of a spirited youth by the name of Chew. He was one of the most daring of the Indian traders, very well acquainted with the secret paths of the wilderness, needy, dissolute, and, by a last good fortune, in some disgrace with his family. Him we persuaded to come to our relief; he privately provided what was needful for our flight, and one day we slipped out of Albany, without a word to our former friend, and embarked, a little above, in a canoe.

To the toils and perils of this journey, it would require a pen more elegant than mine to do full justice. The reader must conceive for himself the dreadful wilderness which we had now to tread; its thickets, swamps, precipitous rocks, impetuous rivers and amazing waterfalls. Among these barbarous scenes we must toil all day, now paddling, now carrying our canoe upon our shoulders; and at night we slept about a fire, surrounded by the howling of wolves and other savage animals. It was our design to mount the headwaters of the Hudson, to the neighbourhood of Crown Point, where the French had a strong place in the woods, upon Lake Champlain. But to have done this directly were too perilous; and it was accordingly gone upon by such a labyrinth of rivers, lakes, and portages as makes my head giddy to remember. These paths were in ordinary times entirely desert; but the country was now up, the tribes on the war-path, the woods full of Indian scouts. Again and again we came upon these parties when we least expected them; and one day, in particular, I shall never forget, how, as dawn was coming in, we were suddenly surrounded by five or six of these painted devils, uttering a very dreary sort of cry, and brandishing their hatchets. It passed off harmlessly, indeed, as did the rest of our encounters; for Chew was well known and highly valued among the different tribes. Indeed, he was a very gallant, respectable young man; but even with the advantage of his companionship, you must not think these meetings were without sensible peril. To prove friendship on our part, it was needful to draw upon our stock of rum—indeed, under whatever disguise, that is the true business of the Indian trader, to keep a travelling public-house in the forest; and when once the braves had got their bottle of *scaura* (as they call this beastly liquor), it behoved us to set forth and paddle for our scalps. Once they were a little drunk, good-bye to any sense or decency; they had but one thought, to get more *scaura*. They might easily take it in their heads to give us chase, and had we been overtaken, I had never written these memoirs.

We were come to the most critical portion of our course, where we might equally expect to fall into the hands of French or English, when a terrible calamity befell us. Chew was taken suddenly sick with symptoms like those of poison, and in the course of a few hours expired in the bottom of the canoe. We thus lost at once our guide, our interpreter, our boatman, and our passport, for he was all these in one; and found ourselves reduced, at a blow, to the most desperate and irremediable distress. Chew, who took a great pride in his knowledge, had indeed often lectured us on the geography; and Ballantrae, I believe, would listen. But for my part I have always found such information highly tedious; and beyond the fact that we were now in the country of the Adirondack Indians, and not so distant from our destination, could we but have found the way, I was entirely ignorant. The wisdom of my course was soon the more apparent; for with all his pains, Ballantrae was no further advanced than myself. He knew we must continue to go up one stream; then, by way of a portage, down another; and then up a third. But you are to consider, in a mountain country, how many streams came rolling in from every hand. And how is a gentleman, who is a perfect stranger in that part of the world, to tell any one of them from any other? Nor was this our only trouble. We were great novices, besides, in handling a canoe; the portages were almost beyond our strength, so that I have seen us sit down in despair for half an hour at a time without one word; and the appearance of a single Indian, since we had now no means of speaking to them, would have been in all probability the means of our destruction. There is altogether some excuse if Ballantrae showed something of a glooming disposition; his habit of imputing blame to others, quite as capable as himself, was less tolerable, and his language it was not always easy to accept. Indeed, he had contracted on board the pirate ship a manner of address which was in a high degree unusual between gentlemen; and now, when you might say he was in a fever, it increased upon him hugely.

The third day of these wanderings, as we were carrying the canoe up a rocky portage, she fell, and was entirely bilged. The portage was between two lakes, both pretty extensive; the track, such as it was, opened at both ends upon the water, and on both hands was enclosed by the unbroken woods; and the sides of the lakes were quite impassable with bog: so that we beheld ourselves not only condemned to go without our boat and the greater part of our provisions, but to plunge at once into impenetrable thickets and to desert what little guidance we still had—the course of the river. Each stuck his pistols in his belt, shouldered an axe, made a pack of his treasure and as much food as he could stagger under; and deserting the rest of our possessions, even to our swords, which would have much embarrassed us among the woods, we set forth on this deplorable adventure. The labours of Hercules, so finely described by Homer, were a trifle to what we now underwent. Some parts of the forest were perfectly dense down to the ground, so that we must cut our way like mites in a cheese. In some the bottom was full of deep swamp, and the whole wood entirely rotten. I have leapt on a great fallen log and sunk to the knees in touchwood; I have sought to stay myself, in falling, against what looked to be a solid trunk, and the whole thing has whiffed away at my touch like a sheet of paper. Stumbling, falling, bogging to the knees, hewing our way, our eyes almost put out with twigs and branches, our clothes plucked from our bodies, we laboured all day, and it is doubtful if we made two miles. What was worse, as we could rarely get a view of the country, and were perpetually justled from our path by obstacles, it was impossible even to have a guess in what direction we were moving.

A little before sundown, in an open place with a stream, and set about with barbarous mountains, Ballantrae threw down his pack. 'I will go no further,' said he, and bade me light the fire, damning my blood in terms not proper for a chairman.

I told him to try to forget he had ever been a pirate, and to remember he had been a gentleman.

'Are you mad?' he cried. 'Don't cross me here!' And then, shaking his fist at the hills, 'To think,' cries he, 'that I must leave my bones in this miserable wilderness! Would God I had died upon the scaffold like a gentleman!' This he said ranting like an actor; and then sat biting his fingers and staring on the ground, a most unchristian object.

I took a certain horror of the man, for I thought a soldier and a gentleman should confront his end with more philosophy. I made him no reply, therefore, in words; and presently the evening fell so chill that I was glad, for my own sake, to kindle a fire. And yet God knows, in such an open spot, and the country alive with savages, the act was little short of lunacy. Ballantrae seemed never to observe me; but at last, as I was about parching a little corn, he looked up.

'Have you ever a brother?' said he.

'By the blessing of Heaven,' said I, 'not less than five.'

'I have the one,' said he, with a strange voice; and then presently: 'He shall pay me for all this,' he added. And when I asked him what was his brother's part in our distress, 'What!' he cried, 'he sits in my place, he bears my name, he courts my wife; and I am here alone with a damned Irishman in this tooth-chattering desert! Oh, I have been a common gull!' he cried.

The explosion was in all ways so foreign to my friend's nature that I was daunted out of all my just susceptibility. Sure, an offensive expression, however vivacious, appears a wonderfully small affair in circumstances so extreme! But here there is a strange thing to be noted. He had only once before referred to the lady with whom he was contracted. That was when we came in view of the town of New York, when he had told me, if all had their rights, he was now in sight of his own property, for Miss Graeme enjoyed a large estate in the province. And this was certainly a natural occasion; but now here she was named a second time; and what is surely fit to be observed, in this very month, which was November, '47, and *I believe upon that very day as we sat among these barbarous mountains,* his brother and Miss Graeme were married. I am the least superstitious of men; but the hand of Providence is here displayed too openly not to be remarked.[1]

The next day, and the next, were passed in similar labours; Ballantrae often deciding on our course by the spinning of a coin; and once, when I expostulated on this childishness, he had an odd remark that I have never forgotten. 'I know no better way,' said he, 'to express my scorn of human reason.' I think it was the third day that we found the body of a Christian, scalped and most abominably mangled, and lying in a pudder of his blood; the birds of the desert screaming over him, as thick as flies. I cannot describe how dreadfully this sight affected us; but it robbed me of all strength and all hope for this world. The same day, and only a little after, we were scrambling over a part of the forest that had been burned, when Ballantrae, who was a little ahead, ducked suddenly behind a fallen trunk. I joined him in this shelter, whence we could look abroad without being seen ourselves; and in the bottom of the next vale, beheld a large war party of the savages going by across our line. There might be the value of a weak battalion present; all naked to the waist, blacked with grease and soot, and painted with white lead and vermilion, according to their beastly habits. They went one behind another like a string of geese, and at a quickish trot; so that they took but a little while to rattle by, and disappear again among the woods. Yet I suppose we endured a greater agony of hesitation and suspense in these few minutes than goes usually to a man's whole life. Whether they were French or English Indians, whether they desired scalps or prisoners, whether we should declare ourselves upon the chance, or lie quiet and continue the heart-breaking business of our journey: sure, I think these were questions to have puzzled the brains of Aristotle himself. Ballantrae turned to me with a face all wrinkled up and his teeth showing in his mouth, like what I have read of people starving; he said no word, but his whole appearance was a kind of dreadful question.

'They may be of the English side,' I whispered; 'and think!

---

1 *Note by Mr. Mackellar.* A complete blunder: there was at this date no word of the marriage: see above in my own narration.

the best we could then hope, is to begin this over again.'

'I know—I know,' he said. 'Yet it must come to a plunge at last.' And he suddenly plucked out his coin, shook it in his closed hands, looked at it, and then lay down with his face in the dust.

Addition by Mr. Mackellar.—I drop the Chevalier's narration at this point because the couple quarrelled and separated the same day; and the Chevalier's account of the quarrel seems to me (I must confess) quite incompatible with the nature of either of the men. Henceforth they wandered alone, undergoing extraordinary sufferings; until first one and then the other was picked up by a party from Fort St. Frederick. Only two things are to be noted. And first (as most important for my purpose) that the Master, in the course of his miseries buried his treasure, at a point never since discovered, but of which he took a drawing in his own blood on the lining of his hat. And second, that on his coming thus penniless to the Fort, he was welcomed like a brother by the Chevalier, who thence paid his way to France. The simplicity of Mr. Burke's character leads him at this point to praise the Master exceedingly; to an eye more worldly wise, it would seem it was the Chevalier alone that was to be commended. I have the more pleasure in pointing to this really very noble trait of my esteemed correspondent, as I fear I may have wounded him immediately before. I have refrained from comments on any of his extraordinary and (in my eyes) immoral opinions, for I know him to be jealous of respect. But his version of the quarrel is really more than I can reproduce; for I knew the Master myself, and a man more insusceptible of fear, is not conceivable. I regret this oversight of the Chevalier's, and all the more because the tenor of his narrative (set aside a few flourishes) strikes me as highly ingenuous.

4

Persecutions endured by Mr. Henry

You can guess on what part of his adventures the Colonel principally dwelled. Indeed, if we had heard it all, it is to be thought the current of this business had been wholly altered; but the pirate ship was very gently touched upon. Nor did I hear the Colonel to an end even of that which he was willing to disclose; for Mr. Henry, having for some while been plunged in a brown study, rose at last from his seat and (reminding the Colonel there were matters that he must attend to) bade me follow him immediately to the office.

Once there, he sought no longer to dissemble his concern, walking to and fro in the room with a contorted face, and passing his hand repeatedly upon his brow.

'We have some business,' he began at last; and there broke off, declared we must have wine, and sent for a magnum of the best. This was extremely foreign to his habitudes; and what was still more so, when the wine had come, he gulped down one glass upon another like a man careless of appearances. But the drink steadied him.

'You will scarce be surprised, Mackellar,' says he, 'when I tell you that my brother—whose safety we are all rejoiced to learn—stands in some need of money.'

I told him I had misdoubted as much; but the time was not very fortunate, as the stock was low.

'Not mine,' said he. 'There is the money for the mortgage.'

I reminded him it was Mrs. Henry's.

'I will be answerable to my wife,' he cried violently.

'And then,' said I, 'there is the mortgage.'

'I know,' said he; 'it is on that I would consult you.'

I showed him how unfortunate a time it was to divert this money from its destination; and how, by so doing, we must lose the profit of our past economies, and plunge back the estate into the mire. I even took the liberty to plead with him; and when he still opposed me with a shake of the head and a bitter dogged smile, my zeal quite carried me beyond my place. 'This is midsummer madness,' cried I; 'and I for one will be no party to it.'

'You speak as though I did it for my pleasure,' says he. 'But I have a child now; and, besides, I love order; and to say the honest truth, Mackellar, I had begun to take a pride in the estates.' He gloomed for a moment. 'But what would you have?' he went on. 'Nothing is mine, nothing. This day's news has knocked the bottom out of my life. I have only the name and the shadow of things—only the shadow; there is no substance in my rights.'

'They will prove substantial enough before a court,' said I.

He looked at me with a burning eye, and seemed to repress the word upon his lips; and I repented what I had said, for I saw that while he spoke of the estate he had still a side-thought to his marriage. And then, of a sudden, he twitched the letter from his pocket, where it lay all crumpled, smoothed it violently on the table, and read these words to me with a trembling

67

tongue:—'"My dear Jacob"—This is how he begins!' cried he—
'"My dear Jacob, I once called you so, you may remember;
and you have now done the business, and flung my heels as
high as Criffel." What do you think of that Mackellar,' says he,
'from an only brother? I declare to God I liked him very
well; I was always staunch to him; and this is how he writes!
But I will not sit down under the imputation '—walking to and
fro—'I am as good as he; I am a better man than he, I call
on God to prove it! I cannot give him all the monstrous sum he
asks; he knows the estate to be incompetent; but I will give
him what I have, and it is more than he expects. I have borne
all this too long. See what he writes further on; read it for
yourself: "I know you are a niggardly dog." A niggardly dog!
I niggardly? Is that true, Mackellar? You think it is?' I
really thought he would have struck me at that. 'Oh, you all
think so! Well, you shall see, and he shall see, and God shall see.
If I ruin the estate and go barefoot, I shall stuff this bloodsucker.
Let him ask all—all, and he shall have it! It is all his by rights.
Ah!' he cried, 'and I foresaw all this, and worse, when he would
not let me go.' He poured out another glass of wine, and was
about to carry it to his lips, when I made so bold as to lay a
finger on his arm. He stopped a moment. 'You are right,' said
he, and flung glass and all in the fireplace. 'Come, let us count
the money.'

I durst no longer oppose him; indeed, I was very much
affected by the sight of so much disorder in a man usually so
controlled; and we sat down together, counted the money, and
made it up in packets for the greater ease of Colonel Burke, who
was to be the bearer. This done, Mr. Henry returned to the hall,
where he and my old lord sat all night through with their guest.

A little before dawn I was called and set out with the Colonel.
He would scarce have liked a less responsible convoy, for he was
a man who valued himself; nor could we afford him one more
dignified, for Mr. Henry must not appear with the freetraders.
It was a very bitter morning of wind, and as we went down
through the long shrubbery the Colonel held himself muffled
in his cloak.

'Sir,' said I, 'this is a great sum of money that your friend
requires. I must suppose his necessities to be very great.'

'We must suppose so,' says he, I thought drily, but perhaps
it was the cloak about his mouth.

'I am only a servant of the family,' said I. 'You may deal
openly with me. I think we are likely to get little good by him?'

'My dear man,' said the Colonel, 'Ballantrae is a gentleman

of the most eminent natural abilities, and a man that I admire, and that I revere, to the very ground he treads on.' And then he seemed to me to pause like one in a difficulty.

'But for all that,' said I, 'we are likely to get little good by him?'

'Sure, and you can have it your own way, my dear man,' says the Colonel.

By this time we had come to the side of the creek, where the boat awaited him. 'Well,' said he, 'I am sure I am very much your debtor for your civility, Mr. Whatever-your-name-is; and just as a last word, and since you show so much intelligent interest, I will mention a small circumstance that may be of use to the family. For I believe my friend omitted to mention that he has the largest pension on the Scots Fund of any refugee in Paris; and it's the more disgraceful, sir,' cries the Colonel, warming, 'because there's not one dirty penny for myself.'

He cocked his hat at me, as if I had been to blame for this partiality; then changed again into his usual swaggering civility, shook me by the hand, and set off down to the boat, with the money under his arms, and whistling as he went the pathetic air of *Shule Aroon*. It was the first time I had heard that tune; I was to hear it again, words and all, as you shall learn, but I remember how that little stave of it ran in my head after the freetraders had bade him 'Wheesht, in the deil's name,' and the grating of the oars had taken its place, and I stood and watched the dawn creeping on the sea, and the boat drawing away, and the lugger lying with her foresail backed awaiting it.

The gap made in our money was a sore embarrassment, and, among other consequences, it had this: that I must ride to Edinburgh, and there raise a new loan, on very questionable terms to keep the old afloat; and was thus, for close upon three weeks, absent from the house of Durrisdeer.

What passed in the interval I had none to tell me, but I found Mrs. Henry, upon my return, much changed in her demeanour. The old talks with my lord for the most part pretermitted; a certain deprecation visible towards her husband, to whom I thought she addressed herself more often; and, for one thing, she was now greatly wrapped up in Miss Katharine. You would think the change was agreeable to Mr. Henry; no such matter! To the contrary, every circumstance of alteration was a stab to him; he read in each the avowal of her truant fancies. That constancy to the Master of which she was proud while she supposed him dead, she had to blush for now she knew he was alive, and these blushes were the hated spring of her new conduct. I am to conceal no truth; and I will here say plainly, I think this was the period in which Mr. Henry showed the worst. He contained himself, indeed, in public; but there was a deepseated irritation visible underneath. With me, from whom he had less concealment, he was often grossly unjust, and even for his wife he would sometimes have a sharp retort: perhaps when she had ruffled him with some unwonted kindness; perhaps upon no tangible occasion, the mere habitual tenor of the man's annoyance bursting spontaneously forth. When he would thus forget himself (a thing so strangely out of keeping with the terms of their relation), there went a shock through the whole company, and the pair would look upon each other in a kind of pained amazement.

All the time, too, while he was injuring himself by this defect of temper, he was hurting his position by a silence, of which I scarce know whether to say it was the child of generosity or pride. The freetraders came again and again, bringing messengers from the Master, and none departed empty-handed. I never durst reason with Mr. Henry; he gave what was asked of him in a kind of noble rage. Perhaps because he knew he was by nature inclining to the parsimonious, he took a backforemost pleasure in the recklessness with which he supplied his brother's exigence. Perhaps the falsity of the position would have spurred a humbler man into the same excess. But the estate (if I may say so) groaned under it; our daily expenses were shorn lower and lower; the stables were emptied, all but four roadsters; servants were discharged, which raised a dreadful murmuring in the country, and heated up the old disfavour upon Mr. Henry; and at last the yearly visit to Edinburgh must be discontinued.

This was in 1756. You are to suppose that for seven years this bloodsucker had been drawing the life's blood from Durrisdeer, and that all this time my patron had held his peace. It was an effect of devilish malice in the Master that he addressed Mr. Henry alone upon the matter of his demands, and there was never a word to my lord. The family had looked on, wondering at our economies. They had lamented, I have no doubt, that my patron had become so great a miser—a fault always despicable, but in the young abhorrent, and Mr. Henry was not yet thirty years of age. Still, he had managed the business of Durrisdeer almost from a boy; and they bore with these changes in a silence as proud and bitter as his own, until the copingstone of the Edinburgh visit.

At this time I believe my patron and his wife were rarely together, save at meals. Immediately on the back of Colonel

Burke's announcement Mrs. Henry made palpable advances; you might say she had laid a sort of timid court to her husband, different, indeed, from her former manner of unconcern and distance. I never had the heart to blame Mr. Henry because he recoiled from these advances; nor yet to censure the wife, when she was cut to the quick by their rejection. But the result was an entire estrangement, so that (as I say) they rarely spoke, except at meals. Even the matter of the Edinburgh visit was first broached at table, and it chanced that Mrs. Henry was that day ailing and querulous. She had no sooner understood her husband's meaning than the red flew in her face.

'At last,' she cried, 'this is too much! Heaven knows what pleasure I have in my life, that I should be denied my only consolation. These shameful proclivities must be trod down; we are already a mark and an eyesore in the neighbourhood. I will not endure this fresh insanity.'

'I cannot afford it,' says Mr. Henry.

'Afford?' she cried. 'For shame! But I have money of my own.'

'That is all mine, madam, by marriage,' he snarled, and instantly left the room.

My old lord threw up his hands to Heaven, and he and his daughter, withdrawing to the chimney, gave me a broad hint to be gone. I found Mr. Henry in his usual retreat, the steward's room, perched on the end of the table, and plunging his penknife in it with a very ugly countenance.

'Mr. Henry,' said I, 'you do yourself too much injustice, and it is time this should cease.'

'Oh!' cries he, 'nobody minds here. They think it only natural. I have shameful proclivities. I am a niggardly dog,' and he drove his knife up to the hilt. 'But I will show that fellow,' he cried with an oath, 'I will show him which is the more generous.'

'This is no generosity,' said I; 'this is only pride.'

'Do you think I want morality?' he asked.

I thought he wanted help, and I should give it him, willy-nilly; and no sooner was Mrs. Henry gone to her room than I presented myself at her door and sought admittance.

She openly showed her wonder. 'What do you want with me, Mr. Mackellar?' said she.

'The Lord knows, madam,' says I, 'I have never troubled you before with any freedoms; but this thing lies too hard upon my conscience, and it will out. Is it possible that two people can be so blind as you and my lord? and have lived all these years with a noble gentleman like Mr. Henry, and understand so little of his nature?'

'What does this mean?' she cried.

'Do you not know where his money goes to? his—and yours—and the money for the very wine he does not drink at table?' I went on. 'To Paris—to that man! Eight thousand pounds has he had of us in seven years, and my patron fool enough to keep it secret!'

'Eight thousand pounds!' she repeated. 'It is impossible; the estate is not sufficient.'

'God knows how we have sweated farthings to produce it,' said I. 'But eight thousand and sixty is the sum, beside odd shillings. And if you can think my patron miserly after that, this shall be my last interference.'

'You need say no more, Mr. Mackellar,' said she. 'You have done most properly in what you too modestly call your interference. I am much to blame; you must think me indeed a very unobservant wife' (looking upon me with a strange smile), 'but I shall put this right at once. The Master was always of a very thoughtless nature; but his heart is excellent; he is the soul of generosity. I shall write to him myself. You cannot think how you have pained me by this communication.'

'Indeed, madam, I had hoped to have pleased you,' said I, for I raged to see her still thinking of the Master.

'And pleased,' said she, 'and pleased me, of course.'

That same day (I will not say but what I watched) I had the satisfaction to see Mr. Henry come from his wife's room in a state most unlike himself; for his face was all bloated with weeping, and yet he seemed to me to walk upon the air. By this, I was sure his wife had made him full amends for once. 'Ah,' thought I to myself, 'I have done a brave stroke this day.'

On the morrow, as I was seated at my books, Mr. Henry came in softly behind me, took me by the shoulders, and shook me in a manner of playfulness. 'I find you are a faithless fellow after all,' says he, which was his only reference to my part; but the tone he spoke in was more to me than any eloquence of protestation. Nor was this all I had effected; for when the next messenger came (as he did not long afterwards) from the Master, he got nothing away with him but a letter. For some while back it had been I myself who had conducted these affairs; Mr. Henry not setting pen to paper, and I only in the dryest and most formal terms. But this letter I did not even see; it would scarce be pleasant reading, for Mr. Henry felt he had his wife behind him for once, and I observed, on the day it was despatched, he had a very gratified expression.

Things went better now in the family, though it could scarce be pretended they went well. There was now at least no misconception; there was kindness upon all sides; and I believe my patron and his wife might again have drawn together if he could but have pocketed his pride, and she forgot (what was the ground of all) her brooding on another man. It is wonderful how a private thought leaks out; it is wonderful to me now how we should all have followed the current of her sentiments; and though she bore herself quietly, and had a very even disposition, yet we should have known whenever her fancy ran to Paris. And would not anyone have thought that my disclosure must have rooted up that idol? I think there is a devil in women: all these years passed, never a sight of the man, little enough kindness to remember (by all accounts) even while she had him, the notion of his death intervening, his heartless rapacity laid bare to her; that all should not do, and she must still keep the best place in her heart for this accursed fellow, is a thing to make a plain man rage. I had never much natural sympathy for the passion of love; but this unreason in my patron's wife disgusted me outright with the whole matter. I remember checking a maid because she sang some bairnly kickshaw while my mind was thus engaged; and my asperity brought about my ears the enmity of all the petticoats about the house; of which I recked very little, but it amused Mr. Henry, who rallied me much upon our joint unpopularity. It is strange enough (for my own mother was certainly one of the salt of the earth, and my Aunt Dickson, who paid my fees at the University, a very notable woman), but I have never had much toleration for the female sex, possibly not much understanding; and being far from a bold man, I have ever shunned their company. Not only do I see no cause to regret this diffidence in myself, but have invariably remarked that most unhappy consequences follow those who were less wise. So much I thought proper to set down lest I show myself unjust to Mrs. Henry. And, besides, the remark arose naturally, on a re-perusal of the letter which was the next step in these affairs, and reached me, to my sincere astonishment, by a private hand, some week or so after the departure of the last messenger.

Letter from Colonel BURKE *(afterwards Chevalier) to* MR. MACKELLAR

TROYES IN CHAMPAGNE.
July 12, 1756.

MY DEAR SIR,—You will doubtless be surprised to receive a communication from one so little known to you; but on the occasion I had the good fortune to rencounter you at Durrisdeer, I remarked you for a young man of a solid gravity of character: a qualification which I profess I admire and revere next to natural genius or the bold chivalrous spirit of the soldier. I was, besides, interested in the noble family which you have the honour to serve, or (to speak more by the book) to be the humble and respected friend of; and a conversation I had the pleasure to have with you very early in the morning has remained much upon my mind.

Being the other day in Paris, on a visit from this famous city, where I am in garrison, I took occasion to inquire your name (which I profess I had forgot) at my friend, the Master of B.; and a fair opportunity occurring, I write to inform you of what's new.

The Master of B. (when we had last some talk of him together) was in receipt, as I think I then told you, of a highly advantageous pension on the Scots Fund. He next received a company, and was soon after advanced to a regiment of his own. My dear sir, I do not offer to explain this circumstance; any more than why I myself, who had rid at the right hand of Princes, should be fubbed off with a pair of colours and sent to rot in a hole at the bottom of the province. Accustomed as I am to Courts, I cannot but feel it is no atmosphere for a plain soldier; and I could never hope to advance by similar means, even could I stoop to the endeavour. But our friend has a particular aptitude to succeed by the means of ladies; and if all be true that I have heard, he enjoyed a remarkable protection. It is like this turned against him; for when I had the honour to shake him by the hand, he was but newly released from the Bastille, where he had been cast on a sealed letter; and, though now released, has both lost his regiment and his pension. My dear sir, the loyalty of a plain Irishman will ultimately succeed in the place of craft; as I am sure a gentleman of your probity will agree.

Now, sir, the Master is a man whose genius I admire beyond expression, and, besides, he is my friend; but I thought a little word of this revolution in his fortunes would not come amiss, for, in my opinion, the man's desperate. He spoke, when I saw him, of a trip to India (whither I am myself in some hope of accompanying my illustrious countryman, Mr. Lally); but for this he would require (as I understood) more money than was readily at his command. You may have heard a military proverb: that it is a good thing to make a bridge of gold to a flying enemy? I trust you will take my meaning, and I subscribe myself, with proper respects to my Lord Durrisdeer, to his son, and to the beauteous Mrs. Durie,

> My dear Sir,
>
> > Your obedient humble servant,
>
> > > FRANCIS BURKE.

This missive I carried at once to Mr. Henry; and I think there was but the one thought between the two of us: that it had come a week too late. I made haste to send an answer to Colonel Burke, in which I begged him, if he should see the Master, to assure him his next messenger would be attended to. But with all my haste I was not in time to avert what was impending; the arrow had been drawn, it must now fly. I could almost doubt the power of Providence (and certainly His will) to stay the issue of events; and it is a strange thought, how many of us had been storing up the elements of this catastrophe, for how long a time, and with how blind an ignorance of what we did.

From the coming of the Colonel's letter, I had a spy-glass in my room, began to drop questions to the tenant folk, and as there was no great secrecy observed, and the freetrade (in our part) went by force as much as stealth, I had soon got together a knowledge of the signals in use, and knew pretty well to an hour when any messenger might be expected. I say, I questioned the tenants; for with the traders themselves, desperate blades that went habitually armed, I could never bring myself to meddle willingly. Indeed, by what proved in the sequel an unhappy chance I was an object of scorn to some of these braggadocios; who had not only gratified me with a nickname, but catching me one night upon a by-path, and being all (as they would have said) somewhat merry, had caused me to dance for their diversion. The method employed was that of cruelly chipping at my toes with naked cutlasses, shouting at the same time ' Square Toes; ' and though they did me no bodily mischief,

I was none the less deplorably affected, and was indeed for several days confined to my bed: a scandal on the state of Scotland on which no comment is required.

It happened on the afternoon of November 7th, in this same unfortunate year, that I espied, during my walk, the smoke of a beacon fire upon the Muckleross. It was drawing near time for my return; but the uneasiness upon my spirits was that day so great that I must burst through the thicket to the edge of what they call the Craig Head. The sun was already down, but there was still a broad light in the west, which showed me some of the smugglers treading out their signal fire upon the Ross, and in the bay the lugger lying with her sails brailed up. She was plainly but new come to anchor, and yet the skiff was already lowered and pulling for the landing-place at the end of the long shrubbery. And this I knew could signify but one thing, the coming of a messenger for Durrisdeer.

I laid aside the remainder of my terrors, clambered down the brae—a place I had never ventured through before—and was hid among the shore-side thickets in time to see the boat touch. Captain Crail himself was steering, a thing not usual; by his side there sat a passenger; and the men gave way with difficulty, being hampered with near upon half a dozen portmanteaus, great and small. But the business of landing was briskly carried through; and presently the baggage was all tumbled on shore, the boat on its return voyage to the lugger, and the passenger standing alone upon the point of rock, a tall slender figure of a gentleman, habited in black, with a sword by his side and a walking-cane upon his wrist. As he so stood, he waved the cane to Captain Crail by way of salutation, with something both of grace and mockery that wrote the gesture deeply on my mind.

No sooner was the boat away with my sworn enemies than I took a sort of half courage, came forth to the margin of the thicket, and there halted again, my mind being greatly pulled about between natural diffidence and a dark foreboding of the truth. Indeed, I might have stood there swithering all night, had not the stranger turned, spied me through the mists, which were beginning to fall, and waved and cried on me to draw near. I did so with a heart like lead.

'Here, my good man,' said he, in the English accent, 'here are some things for Durrisdeer.'

I was now near enough to see him, a very handsome figure and countenance, swarthy, lean, long, with a quick, alert, black look, as of one who was a fighter, and accustomed to command;

upon one cheek he had a mole, not unbecoming; a large diamond sparkled on his hand; his clothes, although of the one hue, were of a French and foppish design; his ruffles, which he wore longer than common, of exquisite lace; and I wondered the more to see him in such a guise when he was but newly landed from a dirty smuggling lugger. At the same time he had a better look at me, toised me a second time sharply, and then smiled.

' I wager, my friend,' says he, ' that I know both your name and your nickname. I divined these very clothes upon your hand of writing, Mr. Mackellar.'

At these words I fell to shaking.

' Oh,' says he, ' you need not be afraid of me. I bear no malice for your tedious letters; and it is my purpose to employ you a good deal. You may call me Mr. Bally: it is the name I have assumed; or rather (since I am addressing so great a precisian) it is so I have curtailed my own. Come now, pick up that and that '—indicating two of the portmanteaus. ' That will be as much as you are fit to bear, and the rest can very well wait. Come, lose no time, if you please.'

His tone was so cutting that I managed to do as he bid by a sort of instinct, my mind being all the time quite lost. No sooner had I picked up the portmanteaus than he turned his back and marched off through the long shrubbery, where it began already to be dusk, for the wood is thick and evergreen. I followed behind, loaded almost to the dust, though I profess I was not conscious of the burthen; being swallowed up in the monstrosity of this return, and my mind flying like a weaver's shuttle.

On a sudden I set the portmanteaus to the ground and halted. He turned and looked back at me.

' Well ? ' said he.

' You are the Master of Ballantrae ? '

' You will do me the justice to observe,' says he, ' that I have made no secret with the astute Mackellar.'

' And in the name of God,' cries I, ' what brings you here? Go back, while it is yet time.'

' I thank you,' said he. ' Your master has chosen this way, and not I; but since he has made the choice, he (and you also) must abide by the result. And now pick up these things of mine, which you have set down in a very boggy place, and attend to that which I have made your business.'

But I had no thought now of obedience; I came straight up to him. ' If nothing will move you to go back,' said I; ' though, sure, under all the circumstances, any Christian or even any gentleman would scruple to go forward ...'

'These are gratifying expressions,' he threw in.

'If nothing will move you to go back,' I continued, 'there are still some decencies to be observed. Wait here with your baggage, and I will go forward and prepare your family. Your father is an old man; and ...' I stumbled ... 'there are decencies to be observed.'

'Truly,' said he, 'this Mackellar improves upon acquaintance. But look you here, my man, and understand it once for all— you waste your breath upon me, and I go my own way with inevitable motion.'

'Ah!' says I. 'Is that so? We shall see, then!'

And I turned and took to my heels for Durrisdeer. He clutched at me and cried out angrily, and then I believe I heard him laugh, and then I am certain he pursued me for a step or two, and (I suppose) desisted. One thing at least is sure, that I came but a few minutes later to the door of the great house, nearly strangled for the lack of breath, but quite alone. Straight up the stair I ran, and burst into the hall, and stopped before the family without the power of speech; but I must have carried my story in my looks, for they rose out of their places and stared on me like changelings.

'He has come,' I panted out at last.

'He?' said Mr. Henry.

'Himself,' said I.

'My son?' cried my lord. 'Imprudent, imprudent boy! Oh, could he not stay where he was safe!'

Never a word says Mrs. Henry; nor did I look at her, I scarce knew why.

'Well,' said Mr. Henry, with a very deep breath, 'and where is he?'

'I left him in the long shrubbery,' said I.

'Take me to him,' said he.

So we went out together, he and I, without another word from any one; and in the midst of the gravelled plot encountered the Master strolling up, whistling as he came, and beating the air with his cane. There was still light enough overhead to recognise, though not to read, a countenance.

'Ah! Jacob,' says the Master. 'So here is Esau back.'

'James,' says Mr. Henry, 'for God's sake, call me by my name. I will not pretend that I am glad to see you; but I would fain make you as welcome as I can in the house of our fathers.'

'Or in *my* house? or *yours*?' says the Master. 'Which were you about to say? But this is an old sore, and we need not rub it. If you would not share with me in Paris, I hope you will yet scarce deny your elder brother a corner of the fire at Durrisdeer?'

'That is very idle speech,' replied Mr. Henry. 'And you understand the power of your position excellently well.'

'Why, I believe I do,' said the other with a little laugh. And this, though they had never touched hands, was (as we may say) the end of the brothers' meeting; for at this the Master turned to me and bade me fetch his baggage.

I, on my side, turned to Mr. Henry for a confirmation; perhaps with some defiance.

'As long as the Master is here, Mr. Mackellar, you will very much oblige me by regarding his wishes as you would my own,' says Mr. Henry. 'We are constantly troubling you: will you be so good as send one of the servants?'—with an accent on the word.

If this speech were anything at all, it was surely a well-deserved reproof upon the stranger; and yet, so devilish was his impudence, he twisted it the other way.

'And shall we be common enough to say "Sneck up"?' inquires he softly, looking upon me sideways.

Had a kingdom depended on the act, I could not have trusted myself in words; even to call a servant was beyond me; I had rather serve the man myself than speak; and I turned away in silence and went into the long shrubbery, with a heart full of anger and despair. It was dark under the trees, and I walked before me and forgot what business I was come upon, till I near broke my shin on the portmanteaus. Then it was that I remarked a strange particular; for whereas I had before carried both and scarce observed it, it was now as much as I could do to manage one. And this, as it forced me to make two journeys, kept me the longer from the hall.

When I got there, the business of welcome was over long ago; the company was already at supper; and by an oversight that cut me to the quick, my place had been forgotten. I had seen one side of the Master's return; now I was to see the other. It was he who first remarked my coming in, standing back (as I did) in some annoyance. He jumped from his seat.

'And if I have not got the good Mackellar's place!' cries he. 'John, lay another for Mr. Bally; I protest he will disturb no one, and your table is big enough for all.'

I could scarce credit my ears, nor yet my senses, when he took me by the shoulders and thrust me, laughing, into my own place—such an affectionate playfulness was in his voice. And while John laid the fresh place for him (a thing on which he still insisted), he went and leaned on his father's chair and looked down upon him, and the old man turned about and looked upwards on his son, with such a pleasant mutual tenderness that I could have carried my hand to my head in mere amazement.

Yet all was of a piece. Never a harsh word fell from him, never a sneer showed upon his lip. He had laid aside even his cutting English accent, and spoke with the kindly Scots tongue, that set a value on affectionate words; and though his manners had a graceful elegance mighty foreign to our ways in Durrisdeer, it was still a homely courtliness, that did not shame but flattered us. All that he did throughout the meal, indeed, drinking wine with me with a notable respect, turning about for a pleasant word with John, fondling his father's hand, breaking into little merry tales of his adventures, calling up the past with happy reference—all he did was so becoming, and himself so handsome, that I could scarce wonder if my lord and Mrs. Henry sat about the board with radiant faces, or if John waited behind with dropping tears.

As soon as supper was over, Mrs. Henry rose to withdraw.

'This was never your way, Alison,' said he.

'It is my way now,' she replied: which was notoriously false, 'and I will give you a good-night, James, and a welcome—from the dead,' said she, and her voice dropped and trembled.

Poor Mr. Henry, who had made rather a heavy figure through the meal, was more concerned than ever; pleased to see his wife withdraw, and yet half displeased, as he thought upon the cause of it; and the next moment altogether dashed by the fervour of her speech.

On my part, I thought I was now one too many; and was stealing after Mrs. Henry, when the Master saw me.

'Now, Mr. Mackellar,' says he, 'I take this near on an unfriendliness. I cannot have you go: this is to make a stranger of the prodigal son; and let me remind you where—in his own father's house! Come, sit ye down, and drink another glass with Mr. Bally.'

'Ay, ay, Mr. Mackellar,' says my lord, 'we must not make a stranger either of him or you. I have been telling my son,' he added, his voice brightening as usual on the word, 'how much we valued all your friendly service.'

So I sat there, silent, till my usual hour; and might have been almost deceived in the man's nature but for one passage, in which his perfidy appeared too plain. Here was the passage;

of which, after what he knows of the brothers' meeting, the reader shall consider for himself. Mr. Henry sitting somewhat dully, in spite of his best endeavours to carry things before my lord, up jumps the Master, passes about the board, and claps his brother on the shoulder.

'Come, come, *Hairry lad*,' says he, with a broad accent such as they must have used together when they were boys, 'you must not be downcast because your brother has come home. All's yours, that's sure enough, and little I grudge it you. Neither must you grudge me my place beside my father's fire.'

'And that is too true, Henry,' says my old lord with a little frown, a thing rare with him. 'You have been the elder brother of the parable in the good sense; you must be careful of the other.'

'I am easily put in the wrong,' said Mr. Henry.

'Who puts you in the wrong?' cried my lord, I thought very tartly for so mild a man. 'You have earned my gratitude and your brother's many thousand times: you may count on its endurance; and let that suffice.'

'Ay, Harry, that you may,' said the Master; and I thought Mr. Henry looked at him with a kind of wildness in his eye.

On all the miserable business that now followed, I have four questions that I asked myself often at the time, and ask myself still:—Was the man moved by a particular sentiment against Mr. Henry? or by what he thought to be his interest? or by a mere delight in cruelty such as cats display and theologians tell us of the devil? or by what he would have called love? My common opinion halts among the three first; but perhaps there lay at the spring of his behaviour an element of all. As thus:—Animosity to Mr. Henry would explain his hateful usage of him when they were alone; the interests he came to serve would explain his very different attitude before my lord; that and some spice of a design of gallantry, his care to stand well with Mrs. Henry; and the pleasure of malice for itself, the pains he was continually at to mingle and oppose these lines of conduct.

Partly because I was a very open friend to my patron, partly because in my letters to Paris I have often given myself some freedom of remonstrance, I was included in his diabolical amusement. When I was alone with him, he pursued me with sneers; before the family he used me with the extreme of family condescension. This was not only painful in itself; not only did it put me continually in the wrong; but there was in it an element of insult indescribable. That he should thus leave me out in his dissimulation, as though even my testimony were too despicable to be considered, galled me to the blood. But what it was to me is not worth notice. I make but memorandum of it here; and chiefly for this reason, that it had one good result, and gave me the quicker sense of Mr. Henry's martyrdom.

It was on him the burthen fell. How was he to respond to the public advances of one who never lost a chance of gibing him in private? How was he to smile back on the deceiver and the insulter? He was condemned to seem ungracious. He was condemned to silence. Had he been less proud, had he spoken, who would have credited the truth? The acted calumny had done its work; my lord and Mrs. Henry were the daily witnesses of what went on; they could have sworn in court that the Master was a model of long-suffering good-nature, and Mr. Henry a pattern of jealousy and thanklessness. And ugly enough as these must have appeared in any one, they seemed tenfold uglier in Mr. Henry; for who could forget that the Master lay in peril of his life, and that he had already lost his mistress, his title, and his fortune?

'Henry, will you ride with me?' asks the Master one day.

And Mr. Henry who had been goaded by the man all morning, raps out: 'I will not.'

'I sometimes wish you would be kinder, Henry,' says the other, wistfully.

I give this for a specimen; but such scenes befell continually. Small wonder if Mr. Henry was blamed; small wonder if I fretted myself into something near upon a bilious fever; nay, and at the mere recollection feel a bitterness in my blood.

Sure, never in this world was a more diabolical contrivance: so perfidious, so simple, so impossible to combat. And yet I think again, and I think always, Mrs. Henry might have read between the lines; she might have had more knowledge of her husband's nature; after all these years of marriage she might have commanded or captured his confidence. And my old lord, too—that very watchful gentleman—where was all his observation? But, for one thing, the deceit was practised by a master hand, and might have gulled an angel. For another (in the case of Mrs. Henry), I have observed there are no persons so far away as those who are both married and estranged, so that they seem out of earshot or to have no common tongue. For a third (in the case of both of these spectators), they were blinded by old ingrained predilection. And for a fourth, the risk the Master was supposed to stand in (supposed, I say—you will soon hear why) made it seem the more ungenerous to criticise; and keeping them in a perpetual tender solicitude about his life, blinded them the more effectually to his faults.

It was during this time that I perceived most clearly the effect of manner, and was led to lament most deeply the plainness of my own. Mr. Henry had the essence of a gentleman; when he was moved, when there was any call of circumstance, he could play his part with dignity and spirit; but in the day's commerce (it is idle to deny it) he fell short of the ornamental. The Master (on the other hand) had never a movement but it commended him. So it befell that when the one appeared gracious and the other ungracious, every trick of their bodies seemed to call out confirmation. Not that alone: but the more deeply Mr. Henry floundered in his brother's toils, the more clownish he grew; and the more the Master enjoyed his spiteful entertainment, the more engagingly, the more smilingly, he went! So that the plot, by its own scope and progress, furthered and confirmed itself.

It was one of the man's arts to use the peril in which (as I say) he was supposed to stand. He spoke of it to those who loved him with a gentle pleasantry, which made it the more touching. To Mr. Henry he used it as a cruel weapon of offence. I remember his laying his finger on the clean lozenge of the painted window one day when we three were alone together in the hall. ' Here went your lucky guinea, Jacob,' said he. And when Mr. Henry only looked upon him darkly, ' Oh!' he added, ' you need not look such impotent malice, my good fly. You can be rid of your spider when you please. How long, O Lord? When are you to be wrought to the point of a denunciation, scrupulous brother? It is one of my interests, in this dreary hole. I ever loved experiment.' Still Mr. Henry only stared upon him with a glooming brow, and a changed colour; and at last the Master broke out in a laugh and clapped him on the shoulder, calling him a sulky dog. At this my patron leaped back with a gesture I thought very dangerous; and I must suppose the Master thought so too, for he looked the least in the world discountenanced, and I do not remember him again to have laid hands on Mr. Henry.

But though he had his peril always on his lips in the one way or the other, I thought his conduct strangely incautious, and began to fancy the Government—who had set a price upon his head—was gone sound asleep. I will not deny I was tempted with the wish to denounce him; but two thoughts withheld me: one, that if he were thus to end his life upon an honourable scaffold, the man would be canonised for good in the minds of his father and my patron's wife; the other, that if I was anyway mingled in the matter, Mr. Henry himself would scarce escape some glancings of suspicion. And in the meanwhile our enemy went in and out more than I could have thought possible, the fact that he was home again was buzzed about all the country-side, and yet he was never stirred. Of all these so-many and so-different persons who were acquainted with his presence, none had the least greed—as I used to say in my annoyance—or the least loyalty; and the man rode here and there—fully more welcome, considering the lees of old unpopularity, than Mr. Henry—and considering the freetraders, far safer than myself.

Not but what he had a trouble of his own; and this, as it brought about the gravest consequences, I must now relate. The reader will scarce have forgotten Jessie Broun; her way of life was much among the smuggling party; Captain Crail himself was of her intimates; and she had early word of Mr. Bally's presence at the house. In my opinion, she had long ceased to care two straws for the Master's person; but it was become her habit to connect herself continually with the Master's name; that was the ground of all her play-acting; and so now, when he was back, she thought she owed it to herself to grow a haunter of the neighbourhood of Durrisdeer. The Master could scarce go abroad but she was there in wait for him; a scandalous figure of a woman, not often sober; hailing him wildly as ' her bonny laddie,' quoting pedlar's poetry, and, as I receive the story, even seeking to weep upon his neck. I own I rubbed my hands over this persecution; but the Master, who laid so much upon others, was himself the least patient of men. There were strange scenes enacted in the policies. Some say he took his cane to her, and Jessie fell back upon her former weapons—stones. It is certain at least that he made a motion to Captain Crail to have the woman trepanned, and that the Captain refused the proposition with uncommon vehemence. And the end of the matter was victory for Jessie. Money was got together; an interview took place, in which my proud gentleman must consent to be kissed and wept upon; and the woman was set up in a public of her own, somewhere on Solway side (but I forget where), and, by the only news I ever had of it, extremely ill-frequented.

This is to look forward. After Jessie had been but a little while upon his heels, the Master comes to me one day in the steward's office, and with more civility than usual, ' Mackellar,' says he, ' there is a damned crazy wench comes about here. I cannot well move in the matter myself, which brings me to you. Be so good as to see to it; the men must have a strict injunction to drive the wench away.'

'Sir,' said I, trembling a little, 'you can do your own dirty errands for yourself.'

He said not a word to that, and left the room.

Presently came Mr. Henry. 'Here is news!' cried he. 'It seems all is not enough, and you must add to my wretchedness. It seems you have insulted Mr. Bally.'

'Under your kind favour, Mr. Henry,' said I, 'it was he that insulted me, and, as I think, grossly. But I may have been careless of your position when I spoke; and if you think so when you know all, my dear patron, you have but to say the word. For you I would obey in any point whatever, even to sin, God pardon me!' And thereupon I told him what had passed.

Mr. Henry smiled to himself; a grimmer smile I never witnessed. 'You did exactly well,' said he. 'He shall drink his Jessie Broun to the dregs.' And then, spying the Master outside, he opened the window, and crying to him by the name of Mr. Bally, asked him to step up and have a word.

'James,' said he, when our persecutor had come in and closed the door behind him, looking at me with a smile, as if he thought I was to be humbled, 'you brought me a complaint against Mr. Mackellar, into which I have inquired. I need not tell you I would always take his word against yours; for we are alone, and I am going to use something of your own freedom. Mr. Mackellar is a gentleman I value; and you must contrive, so long as you are under this roof, to bring yourself into no more collisions with one whom I will support at any possible cost to me or mine. As for the errand upon which you came to him, you must deliver yourself from the consequences of your own cruelty, and none of my servants shall be at all employed in such a case.'

'My father's servants, I believe,' says the Master.

'Go to him with this tale,' said Mr. Henry.

The Master grew very white. He pointed at me with his finger. 'I want that man discharged,' he said.

'He shall not be,' said Mr Henry.

'You shall pay pretty dear for this,' says the Master.

'I have paid so dear already for a wicked brother,' said Mr. Henry, 'that I am bankrupt even of fears. You have no place left where you can strike me.'

'I will show you about that,' says the Master, and went softly away.

'What will he do next, Mackellar?' cries Mr. Henry.

'Let me go away,' said I. 'My dear patron, let me go away; I am but the beginning of fresh sorrows.'

'Would you leave me quite alone?' said he.

85

We were not long in suspense as to the nature of the new assault. Up to that hour the Master had played a very close game with Mrs. Henry; avoiding pointedly to be alone with her, which I took at the time for an effect of decency, but now think to be a most insidious art; meeting her, you may say, at meal-time only; and behaving, when he did so, like an affectionate brother. Up to that hour, you may say he had scarce directly interfered between Mr. Henry and his wife; except in so far as he had manœuvred the one quite forth from the good graces of the other. Now all that was to be changed; but whether really in revenge, or because he was wearying of Durrisdeer and looked about for some diversion, who but the devil shall decide?

From that hour, at least, began the siege of Mrs. Henry; a thing so deftly carried on that I scarce know if she was aware of it herself, and that her husband must look on in silence. The first parallel was opened (as was made to appear) by accident. The talk fell, as it did often, on the exiles in France; so it glided to the matter of their songs.

'There is one,' says the Master, 'if you are curious in these matters, that has always seemed to me very moving. The poetry is harsh; and yet, perhaps because of my situation, it has always found the way to my heart. It is supposed to be sung, I should tell you, by an exile's sweetheart; and represents perhaps, not so much the truth of what she is thinking, as the truth of what she hopes of her, poor soul! in these far lands.' And here the Master sighed. 'I protest it is a pathetic sight when a score of rough Irish, all common sentinels, get to this song; and you may see, by their falling tears, how it strikes home to them. It goes thus, father,' says he, very adroitly taking my lord for his listener, 'and if I cannot get to the end of it, you must think it is a common case with us exiles.' And thereupon he struck up the same air as I had heard the Colonel whistle; but now to words, rustic indeed, yet most pathetically setting forth a poor girl's aspirations for an exiled lover; of which one verse indeed (or something like it) still sticks by me:—

O, I will dye my petticoat red,
With my dear boy I'll beg my bread,
Though all my friends should wish me dead,
    For Willie among the rushes, O!

He sang it well, even as a song; but he did better yet as a performer. I have heard famous actors, when there was not a dry eye in the Edinburgh theatre; a great wonder to behold: but no more wonderful than how the Master played upon that little ballad, and on those who heard him, like an instrument, and seemed now upon the point of failing, and now to conquer his distress, so that words and music seemed to pour out of his own heart and his own past, and to be aimed directly at Mrs. Henry. And his art went further yet; for all was so delicately touched, it seemed impossible to suspect him of the least design; and so far from making a parade of emotion, you would have sworn he was striving to be calm. When it came to an end, we all sat silent for a time; he had chosen the dusk of the afternoon, so that none could see his neighbour's face; but it seemed as if we held our breathing; only my old lord cleared his throat. The first to move was the singer, who got to his feet suddenly and softly, and went and walked softly to and fro in the low end of the hall, Mr. Henry's customary place. We were to suppose that he there struggled down the last of his emotion; for he presently returned and launched into a disquisition on the nature of the Irish (always so much miscalled, and whom he defended) in his natural voice; so that, before the lights were brought, we were in the usual course of talk. But even then, methought Mrs. Henry's face was a shade pale; and, for another thing, she withdrew almost at once.

The next sign was a friendship this insidious devil struck up with innocent Miss Katharine; so that they were always together, hand in hand, or she climbing on his knee, like a pair of children. Like all his diabolic acts, this cut in several ways. It was the last stroke to Mr. Henry, to see his own babe debauched against him; it made him harsh with the poor innocent; which brought him still a peg lower in his wife's esteem; and (to conclude) it was a bond of union between the lady and the Master. Under this influence their old reserve melted by daily stages. Presently there came walks in the long shrubbery, talks in the Belvedere, and I know not what tender familiarity. I am sure Mrs. Henry was like many a good woman; she had a whole conscience, but perhaps by the means of a little winking. For even to so dull an observer as myself, it was plain her kindness was of a more moving nature than the sisterly. The tones of her voice appeared more numerous; she had a light and softness in her eye; she was more gentle with all of us, even with Mr. Henry, even with myself; methought she breathed of some quiet melancholy happiness.

To look on at this, what a torment it was for Mr. Henry! And yet it brought our ultimate deliverance, as I am soon to tell.

The purport of the Master's stay was no more noble (gild it as they might) than to wring money out. He had some design of a fortune in the French Indies, as the Chevalier wrote me; and it was the sum required for this that he came seeking. For the rest of the family it spelled ruin; but my lord, in his incredible partiality, pushed ever for the granting. The family was now so narrowed down (indeed, there were no more of them than just the father and the two sons) that it was possible to break the entail and alienate a piece of land. And to this, at first by hints, and then by open pressure, Mr. Henry was brought to consent. He never would have done so, I am very well assured, but for the weight of the distress under which he laboured. But for his passionate eagerness to see his brother gone, he would not thus have broken with his own sentiment and the traditions of his house. And even so, he sold them his consent at a dear rate, speaking for once openly, and holding the business up in its own shameful colours.

'You will observe,' he said, 'this is an injustice to my son, if ever I have one.'

'But that you are not likely to have,' said my lord.

'God knows!' said Mr. Henry. 'And considering the cruel falseness of the position in which I stand to my brother, and that you, my lord, are my father, and have a right to command me, I set my hand to this paper. But one thing I will say first: I have been ungenerously pushed, and when next, my lord, you are tempted to compare your sons, I call on you to remember what I have done and what he has done. Acts are the fair test.'

My lord was the most uneasy man I ever saw; even in his old face the blood came up. 'I think this is not a very wisely chosen moment, Henry, for complaints,' said he. 'This takes away from the merit of your generosity.'

'Do not deceive yourself, my lord,' said Mr. Henry. 'This injustice is not done from generosity to him, but in obedience to yourself.'

'Before strangers...' begins my lord, still more unhappily affected.

'There is no one but Mackellar here,' said Mr. Henry; 'he is my friend. And, my lord, as you make him no stranger to your frequent blame, it were hard if I must keep him one to a thing so rare as my defence.'

Almost I believe my lord would have rescinded his decision; but the Master was on the watch.

'Ah! Henry, Henry,' says he, 'you are the best of us still. Rugged and true! Ah! man, I wish I was as good.'

And at that instance of his favourite's generosity my lord desisted from his hesitation, and the deed was signed.

As soon as it could be brought about, the land of Ochterhall was sold for much below its value, and the money paid over to our leech and sent by some private carriage into France. Or so he said; though I have suspected since it did not go so far. And now here was all the man's business brought to a successful head, and his pockets once more bulging with our gold; and yet the point for which we had consented to this sacrifice was still denied us, and the visitor still lingered on at Durrisdeer. Whether in malice, or because the time was not yet come for his adventure to the Indies, or because he had hopes of his design on Mrs. Henry, or from the orders of the Government, who shall say? but linger he did, and that for weeks.

You will observe I say: from the orders of Government; for about this time the man's disreputable secret trickled out.

The first hint I had was from a tenant, who commented on the Master's stay, and yet more on his security; for this tenant was a Jacobitish sympathiser, and had lost a son at Culloden, which gave him the more critical eye. 'There is one thing,' said he, 'that I cannot but think strange; and that is how he got to Cockermouth.'

'To Cockermouth?' said I, with a sudden memory of my first wonder on beholding the man disembark so *point-de-vice* after so long a voyage.

'Why, yes,' says the tenant, 'it was there he was picked up by Captain Crail. You thought he had come from France by sea? And so we all did.'

I turned this news a little in my head, and then carried it to Mr. Henry. 'Here is an odd circumstance,' said I, and told him.

'What matters how he came, Mackellar, so long as he is here?' groans Mr. Henry.

'No, no,' said I, 'but think again! Does not this smack a little of some Government connivance? You know how much we have wondered already at the man's security.'

'Stop,' said Mr. Henry. 'Let me think of this.' And as he thought there came that grim smile upon his face that was a little like the Master's. 'Give me paper,' said he. And he sat without another word and wrote to a gentleman of his acquaintance—I will name no unnecessary names, but he was one in a high place. This letter I despatched by the only hand I could depend upon in such a case—Macconochie's; and the old man rode hard, for he was back with the reply before even my eagerness had ventured to expect him. Again, as he read it, Mr. Henry had the same grim smile.

' This is the best you have done for me yet, Mackellar,' says he. ' With this in my hand I will give him a shog. Watch for us at dinner.'

At dinner accordingly Mr. Henry proposed some very public appearance for the Master; and my lord, as he had hoped, objected to the danger of the course.

' Oh! ' says Mr. Henry, very easily, ' you need no longer keep this up with me. I am as much in the secret as yourself.'

' In the secret? ' says my lord. ' What do you mean, Henry? I give you my word, I am in no secret from which you are excluded.'

The Master had changed countenance, and I saw he was struck in a joint of his harness.

' How? ' says Mr. Henry, turning to him with a huge appearance of surprise. ' I see you serve your masters very faithfully; but I had thought you would have been humane enough to set your father's mind at rest.'

' What are you talking of? I refuse to have my business publicly discussed. I order this to cease,' cries the Master very foolishly and passionately, and indeed more like a child than a man.

' So much discretion was not looked for at your hands, I can assure you,' continued Mr. Henry. ' For see what my correspondent writes ' —unfolding the paper—' " It is, of course, in the interests both of the Government and the gentleman whom we may perhaps best continue to call Mr. Bally, to keep this understanding secret; but it was never meant his own family should continue to endure the suspense you paint so feelingly; and I am pleased mine should be the hand to set these fears at rest. Mr. Bally is as safe in Great Britain as yourself." '

' Is this possible? ' cries my lord, looking at his son, with a great deal of wonder and still more of suspicion in his face.

' My dear father,' says the Master, already much recovered, ' I am overjoyed that this may be disclosed. My own instructions, direct from London, bore a very contrary sense, and I was charged to keep the indulgence secret from everyone, yourself not excepted, and indeed yourself expressly named—as I can show in black and white unless I have destroyed the letter. They must have changed their mind very swiftly, for the whole matter is still quite fresh; or rather, Henry's correspondent must have misconceived that part, as he seems to have misconceived the rest. To tell you the truth, sir,' he continued, getting visibly more easy, ' I had supposed this unexplained favour to a rebel was the effect of some application from yourself; and the injunction to secrecy among my family the result of a desire on your part to conceal your kindness. Hence I was the more careful to obey orders. It remains now to guess by what other channel indulgence can have flowed on so notorious an offender as myself; for I do not think your son need defend himself from what seems hinted at in Henry's letter. I have never yet heard of a Durrisdeer who was a turncoat or a spy,' says he proudly.

And so it seemed he had swum out of this danger unharmed; but this was to reckon without a blunder he had made, and without the pertinacity of Mr. Henry, who was now to show he had something of his brother's spirit.

' You say the matter is still fresh,' says Mr. Henry.

' It is recent,' says the Master, with a fair show of stoutness and yet not without a quaver.

' Is it so recent as that? ' asks Mr. Henry, like a man a little puzzled, and spreading his letter forth again.

In all the letter there was no word as to the date; but how was the Master to know that?

' It seemed to come late enough for me,' says he, with a laugh. And at the sound of that laugh, which rang false, like a cracked bell, my lord looked at him again across the table, and I saw his old lips draw together close.

' No,' said Mr. Henry, still glancing on his letter, ' but I remember your expression. You said it was very fresh.'

And here we had a proof of our victory, and the strongest instance yet of my lord's incredible indulgence; for what must he do but interfere to save his favourite from exposure!

' I think, Henry,' says he, with a kind of pitiful eagerness, ' I think we need dispute no more. We are all rejoiced at last to find your brother safe; we are all at one on that; and, as grateful subjects, we can do no less than drink to the king's health and bounty.'

Thus was the Master extricated; but at least he had been put to his defence, he had come lamely out, and the attraction of his personal danger was now publicly plucked away from him. My lord, in his heart of hearts, now knew his favourite to be a Government spy; and Mrs. Henry (however she explained the tale) was notably cold in her behaviour to the discredited hero of romance. Thus in the best fabric of duplicity, there is some weak point, if you can strike it, which will loosen all; and if, by this fortunate stroke, we had not shaken the idol, who can say how it might have gone with us at the catastrophe?

And yet at the time we seemed to have accomplished nothing. Before a day or two he had wiped off the ill-results of his discomfiture, and, to all appearance, stood as high as ever. As for my Lord Durrisdeer, he was sunk in parental partiality; it was not so much love, which should be an active quality, as an apathy and torpor of his other powers; and forgiveness (so to misapply a noble word) flowed from him in sheer weakness, like the tears of senility. Mrs. Henry's was a different case; and Heaven alone knows what he found to say to her, or how he persuaded her from her contempt. It is one of the worst things of sentiment, that the voice grows to be more important than the words, and the speaker than that which is spoken. But some excuse the Master must have found, or perhaps he had even struck upon some art to wrest this exposure to his own advantage; for after a time of coldness, it seemed as if things went worse than ever between him and Mrs. Henry. They were then constantly together. I would not be thought to cast one shadow of blame beyond what is due to a half-wilful blindness, on that unfortunate lady; but I do think, in these last days, she was playing very near the fire; and whether I be wrong or not in that, one thing is sure and quite sufficient: Mr. Henry thought so. The poor gentleman sat for days in my room, so great a picture of distress that I could never venture to address him; yet it is to be thought he found some comfort even in my presence and the knowledge of my sympathy. There were times, too, when we talked, and a strange manner of talk it was; there was never a person named, nor an individual circumstance referred to; yet we had the same matter in our minds, and we were each aware of it. It is a strange art that can thus be practised; to talk for hours of a thing, and never name nor yet so much as hint at it. And I remember I wondered if it was by some such natural skill that the Master made love to Mrs. Henry all day long (as he manifestly did), yet never startled her into reserve.

To show how far affairs had gone with Mr. Henry, I will give some words of his, uttered (as I have cause not to forget) upon the 26th of February, 1757. It was unseasonable weather, a cast back into winter: windless, bitter cold, the world all white with rime, the sky low and gray: the sea black and silent like a quarry-hole. Mr. Henry sat close by the fire and debated (as was now common with him) whether 'a man' should 'do things,' whether 'interference was wise,' and the like general propositions, which each of us particularly applied. I was by the window looking out, when there passed below me the Master, Mrs. Henry, and Miss Katharine, that now constant trio. The child was running to and fro, delighted with the frost; the Master spoke close in the lady's ear with what seemed (even from so far) a devilish grace of insinuation; and she on her part looked on the ground like a person lost in listening. I broke out of my reserve.

' If I were you, Mr. Henry,' said I, ' I would deal openly with my lord.'

' Mackellar, Mackellar,' said he, ' you do not see the weakness of my ground. I can carry no such base thoughts to anyone—to my father least of all; that would be to fall into the bottom of his scorn. The weakness of my ground,' he continued, ' lies in myself, that I am not one who engages love. I have their gratitude, they all tell me that; I have a rich estate of it! But I am not present in their minds; they are moved neither to think with me nor to think for me. There is my loss!' He got to his feet, and trod down the fire. ' But some method must be found, Mackellar,' said he, looking at me suddenly over his shoulder; ' some way must be found. I am a man of a great deal of patience—far too much—far too much. I begin to despise myself. And yet, sure, never was a man involved in such a toil!' He fell back to his brooding.

' Cheer up,' said I. ' It will burst of itself.'

' I am far past anger now,' says he, which had so little coherency with my own observation that I let both fall.

5

Account of all that passed on the night of February 27th, 1757

ON the evening of the interview referred to, the Master went abroad; he was abroad a great deal of the next day also, that fatal 27th; but where he went, or what he did, we never concerned ourselves to ask until next day. If we had done so, and by any chance found out, it might have changed all. But as all we did was done in ignorance, and should be so judged, I shall so narrate these passages as they appeared to us in the moment of their birth, and reserve all that I since discovered for the time of its discovery. For I have now come to one of the dark parts of my narrative, and must engage the reader's indulgence for my patron.

All the 27th that rigorous weather endured: a stifling cold;

the folk passing about like smoking chimneys; the wide hearth in the hall piled high with fuel; some of the spring birds that had already blundered north into our neighbourhood, besieging the windows of the house or trotting on the frozen turf like things distracted. About noon there came a blink of sunshine; showing a very pretty, wintry, frosty landscape of white hills and woods, with Crail's lugger waiting for a wind under the Craig Head, and the smoke mounting straight into the air from every farm and cottage. With the coming of night, the haze closed in overhead; it fell dark and still and starless, and exceeding cold: a night the most unseasonable, fit for strange events.

Mrs. Henry withdrew, as was now her custom, very early. We had set ourselves of late to pass the evening with a game of cards; another mark that our visitor was wearying mightily of the life at Durrisdeer; and we had not been long at this when my old lord slipped from his place beside the fire, and was off without a word to seek the warmth of bed. The three thus left together had neither love nor courtesy to share; not one of us would have sat up one instant to oblige another; yet from the influence of custom, and as the cards had just been dealt, we continued the form of playing out the round. I should say we were late sitters; and though my lord had departed earlier than was his custom, twelve was already gone some time upon the clock, and the servants long ago in bed. Another thing I should say, that although I never saw the Master anyway affected with liquor, he had been drinking freely, and was perhaps (although he showed it not) a trifle heated.

Anyway, he now practised one of his transitions; and so soon as the door closed behind my lord, and without the smallest change of voice, shifted from ordinary civil talk into a stream of insult.

'My dear Henry, it is yours to play,' he had been saying, and now continued: 'it is a very strange thing how, even in so small a matter as a game of cards, you display your rusticity. You play, Jacob, like a bonnet laird, or a sailor in a tavern. The same dulness, the same petty greed, *cette lenteur d'hébété qui me fait rager*; it is strange I should have such a brother. Even Square-toes has a certain vivacity when his stake is imperilled; but the dreariness of a game with you I positively lack language to depict.'

Mr. Henry continued to look at his cards, as though very maturely considering some play; but his mind was elsewhere.

'Dear God, will this never be done?' cries the Master. '*Quel lourdeau!* But why do I trouble you with French expressions,

which are lost on such an ignoramus? A *lourdeau*, my dear
brother, is as we might say a bumpkin, a clown, a clodpole: a
fellow without grace, lightness, quickness; any gift of pleasing,
any natural brilliancy: such a one as you shall see, when you
desire, by looking in the mirror. I tell you these things for your
good, I assure you; and besides, Square-toes' (looking at me
and stifling a yawn), 'it is one of my diversions in this very
dreary spot to toast you and your master at the fire like chestnuts.
I have great pleasure in your case, for I observe the nickname
(rustic as it is) has always the power to make you writhe. But
sometimes I have more trouble with this dear fellow here, who
seems to have gone to sleep upon his cards. Do you not see
the applicability of the epithet I have just explained, dear
Henry? Let me show you. For instance, with all those solid
qualities which I delight to recognise in you, I never knew a
woman who did not prefer me—nor, I think,' he continued,
with the most silken deliberation, 'I think—who did not continue to prefer me.'

Mr. Henry laid down his cards. He rose to his feet very softly
and seemed all the while like a person in deep thought. 'You
coward!' he said gently, as if to himself. And then, with neither
hurry nor any particular violence, he struck the Master in the
mouth.

The Master sprang to his feet like one transfigured; I had
never seen the man so beautiful. 'A blow!' he cried. 'I would
not take a blow from God Almighty!'

'Lower your voice,' said Mr. Henry. 'Do you wish my
father to interfere for you again?'

'Gentlemen, gentlemen,' I cried, and sought to come between
them.

The Master caught me by the shoulder, held me at arm's
length, and still addressing his brother: Do you know what
this means?' said he.

'It was the most deliberate act of my life,' says Mr. Henry.

'I must have blood, I must have blood for this,' says the
Master.

'Please God it shall be yours,' said Mr. Henry; and he went
to the wall and took down a pair of swords that hung there with
others, naked. These he presented to the Master by the points.
'Mackellar shall see us play fair,' said Mr. Henry. 'I think it
very needful.'

'You need insult me no more,' said the Master, taking
one of the swords at random. 'I have hated you all my
life.'

' My father is but newly gone to bed,' said Mr. Henry. ' We must go somewhere forth of the house.'

' There is an excellent place in the long shrubbery,' said the Master.

' Gentlemen,' said I, ' shame upon you both! Sons of the same mother, would you turn against the life she gave you?'

' Even so, Mackellar,' said Mr. Henry, with the same perfect quietude of manner he had shown throughout.

' It is what I will prevent,' said I.

And now here is a blot upon my life. At these words of mine the Master turned his blade against my bosom; I saw the light run along the steel; and I threw up my arms and fell to my knees before him on the floor. ' No, no,' I cried, like a baby.

' We shall have no more trouble with him,' said the Master. ' It is a good thing to have a coward in the house.'

' We must have light,' said Mr. Henry, as though there had been no interruption.

' This trembler can bring a pair of candles,' said the Master.

To my shame be it said, I was still so blinded with the flashing of that bare sword that I volunteered to bring a lantern.

' We do not need a l-l-lantern,' says the Master, mocking me. ' There is no breath of air. Come, get to your feet, take a pair of lights, and go before. I am close behind with this '—making the blade glitter as he spoke.

I took up the candlesticks and went before them, steps that I would give my hand to recall; but a coward is a slave at the best; and even as I went, my teeth smote each other in my mouth. It was as he had said: there was no breath stirring; a windless stricture of frost had bound the air; and as we went forth in the shine of the candles, the blackness was like a roof over our heads. Never a word was said; there was never a sound but the creaking of our steps along the frozen path. The cold of the night fell about me like a bucket of water; I shook as I went with more than terror; but my companions, bareheaded like myself, and fresh from the warm hall, appeared not even conscious of the change.

' Here is the place,' said the Master. ' Set down the candles.'

I did as he bid me, and presently the flames went up, as steady as in a chamber, in the midst of the frosted trees, and I beheld these two brothers take their places.

' The light is something in my eyes,' said the Master.

' I will give you every advantage,' replied Mr. Henry, shifting his ground, ' for I think you are about to die.' He spoke rather sadly than otherwise, yet there was a ring in his voice.

'Henry Durie,' said the Master, 'two words before I begin. You are a fencer, you can hold a foil; you little know what a change it makes to hold a sword! And by that I know you are to fall. But see how strong is my situation! If you fall, I shift out of this country to where my money is before me. If I fall, where are you? My father, your wife—who is in love with me, as you very well know—your child even, who prefers me to yourself:—how will these avenge me! Had you thought of that, dear Henry?' He looked at his brother with a smile; then made a fencing-room salute.

Never a word said Mr. Henry, but saluted too, and the swords rang together.

I am no judge of the play; my head, besides, was gone with cold and fear and horror; but it seems that Mr. Henry took and kept the upper hand from the engagement, crowding in upon his foe with a contained and glowing fury. Nearer and nearer he crept upon the man, till of a sudden the Master leaped back with a little sobbing oath; and I believe the movement brought the light once more against his eyes. To it they went again, on the fresh ground; but now methought closer, Mr. Henry pressing more outrageously, the Master beyond doubt with shaken confidence. For it is beyond doubt he now recognised himself for lost, and had some taste of the cold agony of fear; or he had never attempted the foul stroke. I cannot say I followed it, my untrained eye was never quick enough to seize details, but it appears he caught his brother's blade with his left hand, a practice not permitted. Certainly Mr. Henry only saved himself by leaping on one side; as certainly the Master, lunging in the air, stumbled on his knee, and before he could move the sword was through his body.

I cried out with a stifled scream, and ran in; but the body was already fallen to the ground, where it writhed a moment like a trodden worm, and then lay motionless.

'Look at his left hand,' said Mr. Henry.

'It is all bloody,' said I.

'On the inside?' said he.

'It is cut on the inside,' said I.

'I thought so,' said he, and turned his back.

I opened the man's clothes; the heart was quite still, it gave not a flutter.

'God forgive us, Mr. Henry!' said I. 'He is dead.'

'Dead?' he repeated, a little stupidly; and then with a rising tone, 'Dead? dead?' says he, and suddenly cast his bloody sword upon the ground.

'What must we do?' said I. 'Be yourself, sir. It is too late now: you must be yourself.'

He turned and stared at me. 'Oh, Mackellar!' says he, and put his face in his hands.

I plucked him by the coat. 'For God's sake, for all our sakes, be more courageous!' said I. 'What must we do?'

He showed me his face with the same stupid stare. 'Do?' says he. And with that his eye fell on the body, and 'Oh!' he cries out, with his hand to his brow, as if he had never remembered; and, turning from me, made off towards the house of Durrisdeer at a strange stumbling run.

I stood a moment mused; then it seemed to me my duty lay most plain on the side of the living; and I ran after him, leaving the candles on the frosty ground and the body lying in their light under the trees. But run as I pleased, he had the start of me, and was got into the house, and up to the hall, where I found him standing before the fire with his face once more in his hands, and as he so stood, he visibly shuddered.

'Mr. Henry, Mr. Henry,' I said, 'this will be the ruin of us all.'

'What is this that I have done?' cries he, and then looking upon me with a countenance that I shall never forget. 'Who is to tell the old man?' he said.

The word knocked at my heart; but it was no time for weakness. I went and poured him out a glass of brandy. 'Drink that,' said I, 'drink it down.' I forced him to swallow it like a child and, being still perished with the cold of the night, I followed his example.

'It has to be told, Mackellar,' said he. 'It must be told.' And he fell suddenly in a seat—my old lord's seat by the chimney-side—and was shaken with dry sobs.

Dismay came upon my soul. it was plain there was no help in Mr. Henry.

'Well,' said I, 'sit there, and leave all to me.' And taking a candle in my hand, I set forth out of the room in the dark house. There was no movement; I must suppose that all had gone unobserved; and I was now to consider how to smuggle through the rest with the like secrecy. It was no hour for scruples; and I opened my lady's door without so much as a knock, and passed boldly in.

'There is some calamity happened,' she cried, sitting up in bed.

'Madam,' said I, 'I will go forth again into the passage; and do you get as quickly as you can into your clothes. There is much to be done.'

She troubled me with no questions, nor did she keep me waiting. Ere I had time to prepare a word of that which I must say to her, she was on the threshold signing me to enter.

'Madam,' said I, 'if you cannot be very brave, I must go elsewhere; for if no one helps me to-night, there is an end of the house of Durrisdeer.'

'I am very courageous,' said she; and she looked at me with a sort of smile, very painful to see, but very brave too.

'It has come to a duel,' said I.

'A duel?' she repeated. 'A duel! Henry and—— '

'And the Master,' said I. 'Things have been borne so long, things of which you know nothing, which you would not believe if I should tell. But to-night it went too far, and when he insulted you—— '

'Stop,' said she. 'He? Who?'

'Oh! madam,' cried I, my bitterness breaking forth, 'do you ask me such a question? Indeed, then, I may go elsewhere for help; there is none here!'

'I do not know in what I have offended you,' said she. 'Forgive me; put me out of this suspense.'

But I dared not tell her yet; I felt not sure of her; and at the doubt, and under the sense of impotence it brought with it, I turned on the poor woman with something near to anger.

'Madam,' said I, 'we are speaking of two men; one of them insulted you, and you ask me which. I will help you to the answer. With one of these men you have spent all your hours: has the other reproached you? To one you have been always kind; to the other, as God sees me and judges between us two, I think not always: has his love ever failed you? To-night one of these two men told the other, in my hearing—the hearing of a hired stranger—that you were in love with him. Before I say one word, you shall answer your own question: Which was it? Nay, madam, you shall answer me another: If it has come to this dreadful end, whose fault is it?'

She stared at me like one dazzled. 'Good God!' she said once, in a kind of bursting exclamation; and then a second time in a whisper to herself: 'Great God!—In the name of mercy, Mackellar, what is wrong?' she cried. 'I am made up; I can hear all.'

'You are not fit to hear,' said I. 'Whatever it was, you shall say first it was your fault.'

'Oh!' she cried, with a gesture of wringing her hands, 'this man will drive me mad! Can you not put *me* out of your thoughts?'

' I think not once of you,' I cried. ' I think of none but my dear unhappy master.'

' Ah! ' she cried, with her hand to her heart, ' is Henry dead? '

' Lower your voice,' said I. ' The other.'

I saw her sway like something stricken by the wind; and I know not whether in cowardice or misery, turned aside and looked upon the floor. ' These are dreadful tidings,' said I at length, when her silence began to put me in some fear; ' and you and I behove to be the more bold if the house is to be saved.' Still she answered nothing. ' There is Miss Katharine, besides,' I added: ' unless we bring this matter through, her inheritance is like to be of shame.'

I do not know if it was the thought of her child or the naked word shame, that gave her deliverance; at least, I had no sooner spoken than a sound passed her lips, the like of it I never heard; it was as though she had lain buried under a hill and sought to move that burthen. And the next moment she had found a sort of voice.

' It was a fight,' she whispered. ' It was not——? ' and she paused upon the word.

' It was a fair fight on my dear master's part,' said I. ' As for the other, he was slain in the very act of a foul stroke.'

' Not now! ' she cried.

' Madam,' said I, ' hatred of that man glows in my bosom like a burning fire; ay, even now he is dead. God knows, I would have stopped the fighting, had I dared. It is my shame I did not. But when I saw him fall, if I could have spared one thought from pitying of my master, it had been to exult in that deliverance.'

I do not know if she marked; but her next words were, ' My lord? '

' That shall be my part,' said I.

' You will not speak to him as you have to me? ' she asked.

' Madam,' said I, ' have you not some one else to think of! Leave my lord to me.'

' Some one else? ' she repeated.

' Your husband,' said I. She looked at me with a countenance illegible. ' Are you going to turn your back on him? ' I asked.

Still she looked at me; then her hand went to her heart again. ' No,' said she.

' God bless you for that word! ' I said. ' Go to him now, where he sits in the hall; speak to him—it matters not what you say; give him your hand; say, " I know all; "—if God gives you grace enough, say, " Forgive me." '

'God strengthen you, and make you merciful,' said she. 'I will go to my husband.'

'Let me light you there,' said I, taking up the candle.

'I will find my way in the dark,' she said, with a shudder, and I think the shudder was at me.

So we separated—she downstairs to where a little light glimmered in the hall-door, I along the passage to my lord's room. It seems hard to say why, but I could not burst in on the old man as I could on the young woman; with whatever reluctance, I must knock. But his old slumbers were light, or perhaps he slept not; and at the first summons I was bidden enter.

He, too, sat up in bed; very aged and bloodless he looked; and whereas he had a certain largeness of appearance when dressed for daylight, he now seemed frail and little, and his face (the wig being laid aside) not bigger than a child's. This daunted me; nor less, the haggard surmise of misfortune in his eye. Yet his voice was even peaceful as he inquired my errand. I set my candle down upon a chair, leaned on the bed-foot, and looked at him.

'Lord Durrisdeer,' said I, 'it is very well known to you that I am a partisan in your family.'

'I hope we are none of us partisans,' said he. 'That you love my son sincerely, I have always been glad to recognise.'

'Oh! my lord, we are past the hour of these civilities,' I replied. 'If we are to save anything out of the fire, we must look the fact in its bare countenance. A partisan I am; partisans we have all been; it is as a partisan that I am here in the middle of the night to plead before you. Hear me; before I go, I will tell you why.'

'I would always hear you, Mr. Mackellar,' said he, 'and that at any hour, whether of the day or night, for I would be always sure you had a reason. You spoke once before to very proper purpose; I have not forgotten that.'

'I am here to plead the cause of my master,' I said. 'I need not tell you how he acts. You know how he is placed. You know with what generosity he has always met your other—met your wishes,' I corrected myself, stumbling at that name of son. 'You know—you must know—what he has suffered—what he has suffered about his wife.'

'Mr. Mackellar!' cried my lord, rising in bed like a bearded lion.

'You said you would hear me,' I continued. 'What you do not know, what you should know, one of the things I am here to speak of, is the persecution he must bear in private. Your back is not turned before one whom I dare not name to you falls upon him with the most unfeeling taunts; twits him—pardon me, my lord—twits him with your partiality, calls him Jacob, calls him clown, pursues him with ungenerous raillery, not to be borne by man. And let but one of you appear, instantly he changes; and my master must smile and courtesy to the man who has been feeding him with insults; I know, for I have shared in some of it, and I tell you the life is insupportable. All these months it has endured; it began with the man's landing; it was by the name of Jacob that my master was greeted the first night.'

My lord made a movement as if to throw aside the clothes and rise. ' If there be any truth in this—— ' said he.

' Do I look like a man lying? ' I interrupted, checking him with my hand.

' You should have told me at first,' he said.

' Ah, my lord! indeed I should, and you may well hate the face of this unfaithful servant! ' I cried.

' I will take order,' said he, ' at once.' And again he made the movement to rise.

Again I checked him. ' I have not done,' said I. ' Would God I had! All this my dear, unfortunate patron has endured without help or countenance. Your own best word, my lord, was only gratitude. Oh, but he was your son, too! He had no other father. He was hated in the country, God knows how unjustly. He had a loveless marriage. He stood on all hands without affection or support—dear, generous, ill-fated, noble heart! '

' Your tears do you much honour and me much shame,' says my lord, with a palsied trembling. ' But you do me some injustice. Henry has been ever dear to me, very dear. James (I do not deny it, Mr. Mackellar), James is perhaps dearer; you have not seen my James in quite a favourable light; he has suffered under his misfortunes; and we can only remember how great and how unmerited these were. And even now his is the more affectionate nature. But I will not speak of him. All that you say of Henry is most true; I do not wonder, I know him to be very magnanimous; you will say I trade upon the knowledge? It is possible; there are dangerous virtues: virtues that tempt the encroacher. Mr. Mackellar, I will make it up to him! I will take order with all this. I have been weak; and, what is worse, I have been dull.'

' I must not hear you blame yourself, my lord, with that which I have yet to tell upon my conscience,' I replied. ' You have not been weak; you have been abused by a devilish dissembler. You saw yourself how he had deceived you in the matter of his danger; he has deceived you throughout in every step of his career. I wish to pluck him from your heart; I wish to force your eyes upon your other son; ah, you have a son there!'

'No, no,' said he, 'two sons—I have two sons.'

I made some gesture of despair that struck him; he looked at me with a changed face. 'There is much worse behind?' he asked, his voice dying as it rose upon the question.

'Much worse,' I answered. 'This night he said these words to Mr. Henry: "I have never known a woman who did not prefer me to you, and I think who did not continue to prefer me."'

'I will hear nothing against my daughter,' he cried; and from his readiness to stop me in this direction, I conclude his eyes were not so dull as I had fancied, and he had looked not without anxiety upon the siege of Mrs. Henry.

'I think not of blaming her,' cried I. 'It is not that. These words were said in my hearing to Mr. Henry; and if you find them not yet plain enough, these others but a little after: "Your wife, who is in love with me."'

'They have quarrelled?' he said.

I nodded.

'I must fly to them,' he said, beginning once again to leave his bed.

'No, no!' I cried, holding forth my hands.

'You do not know,' said he. 'These are dangerous words.'

'Will nothing make you understand, my lord?' said I.

His eyes besought me for the truth.

I flung myself on my knees by the bedside. 'Oh, my lord,' cried I, 'think on him you have left; think of this poor sinner whom you begot, whom your wife bore to you, whom we have none of us strengthened as we could; think of him, not of yourself; he is the other sufferer—think of him! That is the door for sorrow—Christ's door, God's door: oh! it stands open. Think of him, even as he thought of you. "*Who is to tell the old man?*" these were his words. It was for that I came; that is why I am here pleading at your feet.'

'Let me get up,' he cried, thrusting me aside, and was on his feet before myself. His voice shook like a sail in the wind, yet he spoke with a good loudness; his face was like the snow, but his eyes were steady and dry. 'Here is too much speech,' said he. 'Where was it?'

'In the shrubbery,' said I.

'And Mr. Henry?' he asked. And when I had told him he knotted his old face in thought.

'And Mr. James?' says he.

'I have left him lying,' said I, 'beside the candles.'

'Candles?' he cried. And with that he ran to the window, opened it, and looked abroad. 'It might be spied from the road.'

'Where none goes by at such an hour,' I objected.

'It makes no matter,' he said. 'One might. Hark!' cries he. 'What is that?'

It was the sound of men very guardedly rowing in the bay; and I told him so.

'The freetraders,' said my lord. 'Run at once, Mackellar; put these candles out. I will dress in the meanwhile; and when you return we can debate on what is wisest.'

I groped my way downstairs, and out at the door. From quite a far way off a sheen was visible, making points of brightness in the shrubbery; in so black a night it might have been remarked for miles; and I blamed myself bitterly for my incaution. How much more sharply when I reached the place! One of the candlesticks was overthrown, and that taper quenched. The other burned steadily by itself, and made a broad space of light upon the frosted ground. All within that circle seemed, by the force of contrast and the overhanging blackness, brighter than by day. And there was the bloodstain in the midst; and a little farther off Mr. Henry's sword, the pommel of which was of silver; but of the body, not a trace. My heart thumped upon my ribs, the hair stirred upon my scalp, as I stood there staring —so strange was the sight, so dire the fears it wakened. I looked right and left; the ground was so hard, it told no story. I stood and listened till my ears ached, but the night was hollow about me like an empty church; not even a ripple stirred upon the shore; it seemed you might have heard a pin drop in the county.

I put the candle out, and the blackness fell about me groping dark; it was like a crowd surrounding me; and I went back to the house of Durrisdeer, with my chin upon my shoulder, startling, as I went, with craven suppositions. In the door a figure moved to meet me, and I had near screamed with terror ere I recognised Mrs. Henry.

'Have you told him?' says she.

'It was he who sent me,' said I. 'It is gone. But why are you here?'

'It is gone!' she repeated. 'What is gone?'

'The body,' said I. 'Why are you not with your husband?'

'Gone?' said she. 'You cannot have looked. Come back.'

'There is no light now,' said I. 'I dare not.'

'I can see in the dark. I have been standing here so long —so long,' said she. 'Come, give me your hand.'

We returned to the shrubbery hand in hand, and to the fatal place.

'Take care of the blood,' said I.

'Blood?' she cried, and started violently back.

'I suppose it will be,' said I. 'I am like a blind man.'

'No,' said she, 'nothing! Have you not dreamed?'

'Ah, would to God we had!' cried I.

She spied the sword, picked it up, and seeing the blood, let it fall again with her hands thrown wide. 'Ah!' she cried. And then, with an instant courage, handled it the second time, and thrust it to the hilt into the frozen ground. 'I will take it back and clean it properly,' says she, and again looked about her on all sides. 'It cannot be that he was dead?' she added.

'There was no flutter of his heart,' said I, and then remembering: 'Why are you not with your husband?'

'It is no use,' said she; 'he will not speak to me.'

'Not speak to you?' I repeated. 'Oh! you have not tried.'

'You have a right to doubt me,' she replied, with a gentle dignity.

At this, for the first time, I was seized with sorrow for her. 'God knows, madam,' I cried, 'God knows I am not so hard as I appear; on this dreadful night who can veneer his words? But I am a friend to all who are not Henry Durie's enemies.'

'It is hard, then, you should hesitate about his wife,' said she.

I saw all at once, like the rending of a veil, how nobly she had borne this unnatural calamity, and how generously my reproaches.

'We must go back and tell this to my lord,' said I.

'Him I cannot face,' she cried.

'You will find him the least moved of all of us,' said I.

'And yet I cannot face him,' said she.

'Well,' said I, 'you can return to Mr. Henry; I will see my lord.'

As we walked back, I bearing the candlesticks, she the sword —a strange burthen for that woman—she had another thought. 'Should we tell Henry?' she asked.

'Let my lord decide,' said I.

My lord was nearly dressed when I came to his chamber. He heard me with a frown. 'The freetraders,' said he. 'But whether dead or alive?'

'I thought him——' said I, and paused, ashamed of the word.

'I know; but you may very well have been in error. Why should they remove him if not living?' he asked. 'Oh! here is a great door of hope. It must be given out that he departed —as he came—without any note of preparation. We must save all scandal.'

I saw he had fallen, like the rest of us, to think mainly of the house. Now that all the living members of the family were plunged in irremediable sorrow, it was strange how we turned to that conjoint abstraction of the family itself, and sought to bolster up the airy nothing of its reputation: not the Duries only, but the hired steward himself.

'Are we to tell Mr. Henry?' I asked him.

'I will see,' said he. 'I am going first to visit him; then I go forth with you to view the shrubbery and consider.'

We went downstairs into the hall. Mr. Henry sat by the table with his head upon his hand, like a man of stone. His wife stood a little back from him, her hand at her mouth; it was plain she could not move him. My old lord walked very steadily to where his son was sitting; he had a steady countenance, too, but methought a little cold. When he was quite come up, he held both his hands and said, 'My son!'

With a broken, strangled cry, Mr. Henry leaped up and fell on his father's neck, crying and weeping, the most pitiful sight that ever a man witnessed. 'Oh! father,' he cried, 'you know I loved him; you know I loved him in the beginning; I could have died for him—you know that! I would have given my life for him and you. Oh! say you know that. Oh! say you can forgive me. O father, father, what have I done—what have I done? And we used to be bairns together!' and wept and sobbed, and fondled the old man, and clutched him about the neck, with the passion of a child in terror.

And then he caught sight of his wife (you would have thought for the first time), where she stood weeping to hear him, and in a moment had fallen at her knees. And 'O my lass,' he cried, 'you must forgive me too! Not your husband—I have only been the ruin of your life. But you knew me when I was a lad; there was no harm in Henry Durie then; he meant aye to be a friend to you. It's him—it's the old bairn that played with you—oh, can ye never, never forgive him?'

Throughout all this my lord was like a cold, kind spectator with his wits about him. At the first cry, which was indeed enough to call the house about us, he had said to me over his shoulder, ' Close the door.' And now he nodded to himself.

' We may leave him to his wife now,' says he. ' Bring a light, Mr. Mackellar.'

Upon my going forth again with my lord, I was aware of a strange phenomenon; for though it was quite dark, and the night not yet old, methought I smelt the morning. At the same time there went a tossing through the branches of the evergreens, so that they sounded like a quiet sea, and the air puffed at times against our faces, and the flame of the candle shook. We made the more speed, I believe, being surrounded by this bustle; visited the scene of the duel, where my lord looked upon the blood with stoicism; and passing farther on toward the landing-place, came at last upon some evidences of the truth. For, first of all, where there was a pool across the path, the ice had been trodden in, plainly by more than one man's weight; next, and but a little farther, a young tree was broken, and down by the landing-place, where the traders' boats were usually beached, another stain of blood marked where the body must have been infallibly set down to rest the bearers.

This stain we set ourselves to wash away with the sea-water, carrying it in my lord's hat; and as we were thus engaged there came up a sudden moaning gust and left us instantly benighted.

' It will come to snow,' says my lord; ' and the best thing that we could hope. Let us go back now; we can do nothing in the dark.'

As we went houseward, the wind being again subsided, we were aware of a strong pattering noise about us in the night; and when we issued from the shelter of the trees, we found it raining smartly.

Throughout the whole of this my lord's clearness of mind, no less than his activity of body, had not ceased to minister to my amazement. He set the crown upon it in the council we held on our return. The freetraders had certainly secured the Master, though whether dead or alive we were still left to our conjectures; the rain would, long before day, wipe out all marks of the transaction; by this we must profit. The Master had unexpectedly come after the fall of night; it must now be given out he had as suddenly departed before the break of day; and, to make all this plausible, it now only remained for me to mount into the man's chamber, and pack and conceal his baggage. True, we still lay at the discretion of the traders; but that was the incurable weakness of our guilt.

I heard him, as I said, with wonder, and hastened to obey. Mr. and Mrs. Henry were gone from the hall; my lord, for

warmth's sake, hurried to his bed; there was still no signs of
stir among the servants, and as I went up the tower stair, and
entered the dead man's room, a horror of solitude weighed upon
my mind. To my extreme surprise, it was all in the disorder
of departure. Of his three portmanteaus, two were already locked;
the third lay open and near full. At once there flashed upon
me some suspicion of the truth. The man had been going, after
all; he had but waited upon Crail, as Crail waited upon the
wind; early in the night the seamen had perceived the weather
changing; the boat had come to give notice of the change and
call the passenger aboard, and the boat's crew had stumbled
on him lying in his blood. Nay, and there was more behind.
This pre-arranged departure shed some light upon his inconceivable insult of the night before; it was a parting shot, hatred
being no longer checked by policy. And, for another thing, the
nature of that insult, and the conduct of Mrs. Henry, pointed
to one conclusion, which I have never verified, and can now never
verify until the great assize—the conclusion that he had at last
forgotten himself, had gone too far in his advances, and had been
rebuffed. It can never be verified, as I say; but as I thought
of it that morning among his baggage, the thought was sweet
to me like honey.

Into the open portmanteau I dipped a little ere I closed it.
The most beautiful lace and linen, many suits of those fine plain
clothes in which he loved to appear; a book or two, and those
of the best, Cæsar's 'Commentaries,' a volume of Mr. Hobbes,
the 'Henriade,' of M. de Voltaire, a book upon the Indies, one
on the mathematics, far beyond where I have studied: these
were what I observed with very mingled feelings. But in the
open portmanteau, no papers of any description. This set me
musing. It was possible the man was dead; but, since the traders
had carried him away, not likely. It was possible he might still
die of his wound; but it was also possible he might not. And
in this latter case I was determined to have the means of some
defence.

One after another I carried his portmeanteaus to a loft in
the top of the house which we kept locked; went to my own
room for my keys, and, returning to the loft, had the gratification
to find two that fitted pretty well. In one of the portmanteaus
there was a shagreen letter-case, which I cut open with my
knife; and thenceforth (so far as my credit went) the man was
at my mercy. Here was a vast deal of gallant correspondence,
chiefly of his Paris days; and, what was more to the purpose,
here were the copies of his own reports to the English Secretary,

and the originals of the Secretary's answers: a most damning series: such as to publish would be to wreck the Master's honour and to set a price upon his life. I chuckled to myself as I ran through the documents; I rubbed my hands, I sang aloud in my glee. Day found me at the pleasing task; nor did I then remit my diligence, except in so far as I went to the window—looked out for a moment, to see the frost quite gone, the world turned black again, and the rain and the wind driving in the bay—and to assure myself that the lugger was gone from its anchorage, and the Master (whether dead or alive) now tumbling on the Irish Sea.

It is proper I should add in this place the very little I have subsequently angled out upon the doings of that night. It took me a long while to gather it: for we dared not openly ask, and the freetraders regarded me with enmity, if not with scorn. It was near six months before we even knew for certain that the man survived; and it was years before I learned from one of Crail's men, turned publican on his ill-gotten gain, some particulars which smack to me of truth. It seems the traders found the Master struggled on one elbow, and now staring round him, and now gazing at the candle or at his hand which was all bloodied, like a man stupid. Upon their coming, he would seem to have found his mind, bade them carry him aboard, and hold their tongues; and on the captain asking how he had come in such a pickle, replied with a burst of passionate swearing, and incontinently fainted. They held some debate, but they were momently looking for a wind, they were highly paid to smuggle him to France, and did not care to delay. Besides which, he was well enough liked by these abominable wretches: they supposed him under capital sentence, knew not in what mischief he might have got his wound, and judged it a piece of good nature to remove him out of the way of danger. So he was taken aboard, recovered on the passage over, and was set ashore a convalescent at the Havre de Grace. What is truly notable: he said not a word to anyone of the duel, and not a trader knows to this day in what quarrel, or by the hand of what adversary, he fell. With any other man I should have set this down to natural decency; with him, to pride. He could not bear to avow, perhaps even to himself, that he had been vanquished by one whom he had so much insulted and whom he so cruelly despised.

6

Summary of events during the Master's second absence

OF the heavy sickness which declared itself next morning I can think with equanimity, as of the last unmingled trouble that befell my master; and even that was perhaps a mercy in disguise; for what pain of the body could equal the miseries of his mind? Mrs. Henry and I had the watching by the bed. My old lord called from time to time to take the news, but would not usually pass the door. Once, I remember, when hope was nigh gone, he stepped to the bedside, looked awhile in his son's face, and turned away with a singular gesture of the head and hand thrown up, that remains upon my mind as something tragic; such grief and such a scorn of sublunary things were there expressed. But the most of the time Mrs. Henry and I had the room to ourselves, taking turns by night, and bearing each other company by day, for it was dreary watching. Mr. Henry, his shaven head bound in a napkin, tossed to and fro without remission, beating the bed with his hands. His tongue never lay; his voice ran continuously like a river, so that my heart was weary with the sound of it. It was notable, and to me inexpressibly mortifying, that he spoke all the while on matters of no import: comings and goings, horses—which he was ever calling to have saddled, thinking perhaps (the poor soul!) that he might ride away from his discomfort—matters of the garden, the salmon nets, and (what I particularly raged to hear) continually of his affairs, cyphering figures and holding disputation with the tenantry. Never a word of his father or his wife, nor of the Master, save only for a day or two, when his mind dwelled entirely in the past, and he supposed himself a boy again and upon some innocent child's play with his brother. What made this the more affecting: it appeared the Master had then run some peril of his life, for there was a cry—'Oh! Jamie will be drowned—Oh, save Jamie!' which he came over and over with a great deal of passion.

This, I say, was affecting both to Mrs. Henry and myself; but the balance of my master's wanderings did him little justice. It seemed he had set out to justify his brother's calumnies; as though he was bent to prove himself a man of a dry nature, immersed in money-getting. Had I been there alone, I would not have troubled my thumb; but all the while, as I listened, I was estimating the effect on the man's wife, and telling myself that he fell lower every day. I was the one person on the surface of the globe that comprehended him, and I was bound there should be yet another. Whether he was to die there and his virtues perish: or whether he should save his days and come back to that inheritance of sorrows, his right memory: I was bound he should be heartily lamented in the one case, and unaffectedly welcomed in the other, by the person he loved the most, his wife.

Finding no occasion of free speech, I bethought me at last of a kind of documentary disclosure; and for some nights, when I was off duty and should have been asleep, I gave my time to the preparation of that which I may call my budget. But this I found to be the easiest portion of my task, and that which remained—namely, the presentation to my lady—almost more than I had fortitude to overtake. Several days I went about with my papers under my arm, spying for some juncture of talk to serve as introduction. I will not deny but that some offered; only when they did my tongue clove to the roof of my mouth; and I think I might have been carrying about my packet till this day, had not a fortunate accident delivered me from all my hesitations. This was at night, when I was once more leaving the room, the thing not yet done, and myself in despair at my own cowardice.

'What do you carry about with you, Mr. Mackellar?' she asked. 'These last days, I see you always coming in and out witht the same armful.'

I returned upon my steps without a word, laid the papers before her on the table, and left her to her reading. Of what that was, I am now to give you some idea; and the best will be to reproduce a letter of my own which came first in the budget and of which (according to an excellent habitude) I have preserved the scroll. It will show, too, the moderation of my part in these affairs, a thing which some have called recklessly in question.

'Durrisdeer.
'1757.

'HONOURED MADAM,

'I trust I would not step out of my place without occasion; but I see how much evil has flowed in the past to all of your noble house from that unhappy and secretive fault of reticency, and the papers on which I venture to call your attention are family papers, and all highly worthy your acquaintance.

'I append a schedule with some necessary observations, And am, Honoured Madam,

'Your ladyship's obliged, obedient servant,

'EPHRAIM MACKELLAR.

'*Schedule of Papers.*

'A. Scroll of ten letters from Ephraim Mackellar to the Hon. James Durie, Esq., by courtesy Master of Ballantrae during the latter's residence in Paris: under dates . . . ' (*follow the dates*) . . . '*Nota*: to be read in connection with B. and C.

'B. Seven original letters from the said M^r of Ballantrae to the said E. Mackellar, under dates . . . ' (*follow the dates.*)

'C. Three original letters from the said M^r of Ballantrae to the Hon. Henry Durie, Esq., under dates . . . ' (*follow the dates*) . . . '*Nota*: given me by Mr. Henry to answer: copies of my answers A4, A5, and A9 of these productions. The purport of Mr. Henry's communications, of which I can find no scroll, may be gathered from those of his unnatural brother.

'D. A correspondence, original and scroll, extending over a period of three years till January of the current year, between the said M^r of Ballantrae and —— ——, Under Secretary of State; twenty-seven in all. *Nota*: found among the Master's papers.'

Weary as I was with watching and distress of mind, it was impossible for me to sleep. All night long I walked in my chamber, revolving what should be the issue, and sometimes repenting the temerity of my immixture in affairs so private; and with the first peep of morning I was at the sick-room door. Mrs. Henry had thrown open the shutters and even the window, for the temperature was mild. She looked steadfastly before her; where was nothing to see, or only the blue of the morning creeping among woods. Upon the stir of my entrance she did not so much as turn about her face: a circumstance from which I augured very ill.

'Madam,' I began; and then again, 'Madam;' but could make no more of it. Nor yet did Mrs. Henry come to my assistance with a word. In this pass I began gathering up the papers where they lay scattered on the table; and the first thing that struck me, their bulk appeared to have diminished. Once I ran them through, and twice; but the correspondence with the Secretary of State, on which I had reckoned so much against the future, was nowhere to be found. I looked in the chimney; amid the smouldering embers, black ashes of papers fluttered in the draught; and at that my timidity vanished.

'Good God, madam,' cried I, in a voice not fitting for a sick-room. 'Good God, madam, what have you done with my papers?'

'I have burned them,' said Mrs. Henry, turning about. 'It is enough, it is too much, that you and I have seen them.'

'This is a fine night's work that you have done!' cried I. 'And all to save the reputation of a man that ate bread by the shedding of his comrade's blood, as I do by the shedding of ink.'

'To save the reputation of that family in which you are a servant, Mr. Mackellar,' she returned, 'and for which you have already done so much.'

'It is a family I will not serve much longer,' I cried, 'for I am driven desperate. You have stricken the sword out of my hands; you have left us all defenceless. I had always these letters I could shake over his head; and now—what is to do? We are so falsely situate we dare not show the man the door; the country would fly on fire against us; and I had this one hold upon him —and now it is gone—now he may come back to-morrow, and we must all sit down with him to dinner, go for a stroll with him on the terrace, or take a hand at cards, of all things, to divert his leisure! No, madam! God forgive you, if He can find it in His heart, for I cannot find it in mine.'

'I wonder to find you so simple, Mr. Mackellar,' said Mrs. Henry. 'What does this man value reputation? But he knows how high we prize it; he knows we would rather die than make these letters public; and do you suppose he would not trade upon the knowledge? What you call your sword, Mr. Mackellar, and which had been one indeed against a man of any remnant of propriety, would have been but a sword of paper against him. He would smile in your face at such a threat. He stands upon his degradation, he makes that his strength: it is in vain to struggle with such characters.' She cried out this last a little desperately, and then with more quiet: 'No, Mr. Mackellar; I have thought upon this matter all night, and there is no way out of it. Papers or no papers, the door of this house stands open for him; he is the rightful heir, forsooth! If we sought to exclude him, all would redound against poor Henry, and I should see him stoned again upon the streets. Ah! if Henry dies, it is a different matter? They have broke the entail for their own good purposes; the estate goes to my daughter; and I shall see who sets a foot upon it. But if Henry lives, my poor Mr. Mackellar, and that man returns, we must suffer: only this time it will be together.'

On the whole I was well pleased with Mrs. Henry's attitude of mind; nor could I even deny there was some cogency in that which she advanced about the papers.

'Let us say no more about it,' said I. 'I can only be sorry I trusted a lady with the originals, which was an unbusinesslike proceeding at the best. As for what I said of leaving the service of the family, it was spoken with the tongue only; and you may set your mind at rest. I belong to Durrisdeer, Mrs. Henry, as if I had been born there.'

I must do her the justice to say she seemed perfectly relieved; so that we began this morning, as we were to continue for so many years, on a proper ground of mutual indulgence and respect.

The same day, which was certainly prededicate to joy, we observed the first signal of recovery in Mr. Henry; and about three of the following afternoon he found his mind again, re-cognising me by name with the strongest evidences of affection. Mrs. Henry was also in the room, at the bedfoot; but it did not appear that he observed her. And indeed (the fever being gone) he was so weak that he made but the one effort and sank again into lethargy. The course of his restoration was now slow but equal; every day his appetite improved; every week we were able to remark an increase both of strength and flesh; and before the end of the month he was out of bed and had even begun to be carried in his chair upon the terrace.

It was perhaps at this time that Mrs. Henry and I were the most uneasy in mind. Apprehension for his days was at an end; and a worse fear succeeded. Every day we drew consciously nearer to a day of reckoning; and the days passed on, and still there was nothing. Mr. Henry bettered in strength, he held long talks with us on a great diversity of subjects, his father came and sat with him and went again; and still there was no reference to the late tragedy or to the former troubles which had brought it on. Did he remember, and conceal his dreadful knowledge? or was the whole blotted from his mind? This was the problem that kept us watching and trembling all day when we were in his company and held us awake at night when we were in our lonely beds. We knew not even which alternative to hope for, both appearing so unnatural and pointing so directly to an unsound brain. Once this fear offered, I observed his conduct with sedulous particularity. Something of the child he exhibited: a cheerfulness quite foreign to his previous character, an interest readily aroused, and then very tenacious, in small matters which he had heretofore despised. When he was stricken down, I was his only confidant, and I may say his only friend, and he was on terms of division with his wife; upon his recovery, all was changed, the past forgotten, the wife first and even single in his thoughts. He turned to her with all his emotions, like a child to its mother, and seemed secure of sympathy; called her in all his needs with something of that querulous familiarity that marks a certainty of indulgence; and I must say, in justice to the woman, he was never disappointed. To her, indeed, this changed behaviour was inexpressibly affecting; and I think she felt it secretly as a reproach; so that I have seen her, in early days, escape out of the room that she might indulge herself in weeping. But to me the change appeared not natural; and viewing it along with all the rest, I began to wonder, with many head-shakings, whether his reason was perfectly erect.

As this doubt stretched over many years, endured indeed until my master's death, and clouded all our subsequent relations, I may well consider of it more at large. When he was able to resume some charge of his affairs, I had many opportunities to try him with precision. There was no lack of understanding, nor yet of authority; but the old continuous interest had quite departed; he grew readly fatigued, and fell to yawning; and he carried into money relations, where it is certainly out of place, a facility that bordered upon slackness. True, since we had no longer the exactions of the Master to contend against, there was the less occasion to raise strictness into principle or do battle for a farthing. True, again, there was nothing excessive in these relaxations, or I would have been no party to them. But the whole thing marked a change, very slight yet very perceptible; and though no man could say my master had gone at all out of his mind, no man could deny that he had drifted from his character. It was the same to the end, with his manner and appearance. Some of the heat of the fever lingered in his veins: his movements a little hurried, his speech notably more voluble, yet neither truly amiss. His whole mind stood open to happy impressions, welcoming these and making much of them; but the smallest suggestion of trouble or sorrow he received with visible impatience and dismissed again with immediate relief. It was to this temper that he owed the felicity of his later days; and yet here it was, if anywhere, that you could call the man insane. A great part of this life consists in contemplating what we cannot cure; but Mr. Henry, if he could not dismiss solicitude by an effort of the mind, must instantly and at whatever cost annihilate the cause of it; so that he played alternately the ostrich and the bull. It is to this strenuous cowardice of pain that I have to set down all the unfortunate and excessive steps of his subsequent career. Certainly this was the reason of his beating McManus, the groom, a thing so much out of all his former practice, and which awakened so much comment at the time. It is to this, again, that I must lay the total loss of near upon two hundred pounds, more than the half of which I could have saved if his impatience would have suffered me. But he preferred loss or any desperate extreme to a continuance of mental suffering.

All this has led me far from our immediate trouble: whether he remembered or had forgotten his late dreadful act; and if he remembered, in what light he viewed it. The truth burst upon us suddenly, and was indeed one of the chief surprises of my life. He had been several times abroad, and was now beginning to walk a little with an arm, when it chanced I should be left alone with him upon the terrace. He turned to me with a singular furtive smile, such as schoolboys use when in fault; and says he, in a private whisper and without the least preface: 'Where have you buried him?'

I could not make one sound in answer.

'Where have you buried him?' he repeated. 'I want to see his grave.'

I conceived I had best take the bull by the horns. 'Mr. Henry,' said I, 'I have news to give that will rejoice you exceedingly. In all human likelihood, your hands are clear of blood. I reason from certain indices; and by these it should appear your brother was not dead, but was carried in a swound on board the lugger. But now he may be perfectly recovered.'

What there was in his countenance I could not read. 'James?' he asked.

'Your brother James,' I answered, 'I would not raise a hope that may be found deceptive, but in my heart I think it very probable he is alive.'

'Ah!' says Mr. Henry; and suddenly rising from his seat with more alacrity than he had yet discovered, set one finger on my breast, and cried at me in a kind of screaming whisper, 'Mackellar'—these were his words—'nothing can kill that man. He is not mortal. He is bound upon my back to all eternity—to all God's eternity!' says he, and, sitting down again, fell upon a stubborn silence.

A day or two after, with the same secret smile, and first looking about as if to be sure we were alone, 'Mackellar,' said he, 'when you have any intelligence, be sure and let me know. We must keep an eye upon him, or he will take us when we least expect.'

'He will not show face here again,' said I.

'Oh, yes, he will,' said Mr. Henry. 'Wherever I am, there will he be.' And again he looked all about him.

'You must not dwell upon this thought, Mr. Henry,' said I.

'No,' said he, 'that is very good advice. We will never think of it, except when you have news. And we do not know yet,' he added; 'he may be dead.'

The manner of his saying this convinced me thoroughly of what I had scarce ventured to suspect: that, so far from suffering any penitence for the attempt, he did but lament his failure. This was a discovery I kept to myself, fearing it might do him a prejudice with his wife. But I might have saved myself the trouble; she had divined it for herself, and found the sentiment quite natural. Indeed, I could not but say that there were three of us, all of the same mind; nor could any news have reached Durrisdeer, more generally welcome than tidings of the Master's death.

This brings me to speak of the exception, my old lord. As soon as my anxiety for my own master began to be relaxed, I was aware of a change in the old gentleman, his father, that seemed to threaten mortal consequences.

His face was pale and swollen; as he sat in the chimney-side with his Latin, he would drop off sleeping and the book roll in the ashes; some days he would drag his foot, others stumble in speaking. The amenity of his behaviour appeared more extreme; full of excuses for the least trouble, very thoughtful for all; to myself, of a most flattering civility. One day, that he had sent for his lawyer and remained a long while private, he met me as he was crossing the hall with painful footsteps and took me kindly by the hand, 'Mr. Mackellar,' said he, 'I have had many occasions to set a proper value on your services; and to-day, when I re-cast my will, I have taken the freedom to name you for one of my executors. I believe you bear love enough to our house to render me this service.' At that very time he passed the greater portion of his days in slumber, from which it was very often difficult to rouse him; seemed to have lost all count of years, and had several times (particularly on waking) called for his wife and for an old servant whose very gravestone was now green with moss. If I had been put to my oath, I must have declared he was incapable of testing; and yet there was never a will drawn more sensible in every trait, or showing a more excellent judgment both of persons and affairs.

His dissolution, though it took not very long, proceeded by infinitesimal gradations. His faculties decayed together steadily; the power of his limbs was almost gone, he was extremely deaf, his speech had sunk into mere mumblings; and yet to the end he managed to discover something of his former courtesy and kindness, pressing the hand of any that helped him, presenting me with one of his Latin books, in which he had laboriously traced my name, and in a thousand ways reminding us of the greatness of that loss which it might almost be said we had already suffered. To the end, the power of articulation returned to him in flashes; it seemed he had only forgotten the art of speech as a child forgets his lesson, and at times he would call some part of it to mind. On the last night of his life he suddenly broke silence with these words from Virgil: ' Gnatique patrisque, alma, precor, mise-rere,' perfectly uttered, and with a fitting accent. At the sudden clear sound of it we started from our several occupations; but it was in vain we turned to him; he sat there silent, and, to all appearance, fatuous. A little later he was had to bed with more difficulty than ever before; and some time in the night, without any mortal violence, his spirit fled.

At a far later period I chanced to speak of these particulars with a doctor of medicine, a man of so high a reputation that I scruple to adduce his name. By his view of it father and son both suffered from the same affection: the father from the strain of his unnatural sorrows—the son perhaps in the excitation of the fever; each had ruptured a vessel on the brain, and there was probably (my doctor added) some predisposition in the family to accidents of that description. The father sank, the son recovered all the externals of a healthy man; but it is like there was some destruction in those delicate tissues where the soul resides and does her earthly business; her heavenly, I would fain hope, cannot be thus obstructed by material accidents. And yet, upon a more mature opinion, it matters not one jot; for He who shall pass judgment on the records of our life is the same that formed us in frailty.

The death of my old lord was the occasion of a fresh surprise to us who watched the behaviour of his successor. To any considering mind, the two sons had between them slain their father, and he who took the sword might be even said to have slain him with his hand; but no such thought appeared to trouble my new lord. He was becomingly grave; I could scarce say sor-rowful, or only with a pleasant sorrow; talking of the dead with a regretful cheerfulness, relating old examples of his charac-ter, smiling at them with a good conscience; and when the day of the funeral came round, doing the honours with exact pro-priety. I could perceive, besides, that he found a solid gratifi-cation in his accession to the title: the which he was punctilious in exacting.

And now there came upon the scene a new character, and one that played his part, too, in the story; I mean the present lord,

Alexander, whose birth (17th July, 1757) filled the cup of my poor master's happiness. There was nothing then left him to wish for; nor yet leisure to wish for it. Indeed, there never was a parent so fond and doting as he showed himself. He was continually uneasy in his son's absence. Was the child abroad? the father would be watching the clouds in case it rained. Was it night? he would rise out of his bed to observe its slumbers. His conversation grew even wearyful to strangers, since he talked of little but his son. In matters relating to the estate, all was designed with a particular eye to Alexander; and it would be: ' Let us put it in hand at once, that the wood may be grown against Alexander's majority; ' or ' This will fall in again handsomely for Alexander's marriage.' Every day this absorption of the man's nature became more observable, with many touching and some very blameworthy particulars. Soon the child could walk abroad with him, at first on the terrace, hand in hand, and afterward at large about the policies; and this grew to be my lord's chief occupation. The sound of their two voices (audible a great way off, for they spoke loud) became familiar in the neighbourhood; and for my part I found it more agreeable than the sound of birds. It was pretty to see the pair returning, full of briars, and the father as flushed and sometimes as bemuddied as the child, for they were equal sharers in all sorts of boyish entertainment, digging in the beach, damming of streams, and what not; and I have seen them gaze through a fence at cattle with the same childish contemplation.

The mention of these rambles brings me to a strange scene of which I was a witness. There was one walk I never followed myself without emotion, so often had I gone there upon miserable errands, so much had there befallen against the house of Durrisdeer. But the path lay handy from all points beyond the Muckle Ross; and I was driven, although much against my will, to take my use of it perhaps once in the two months. It befell when Mr. Alexander was of the age of seven or eight, I had some business on the far side in the morning, and entered the shrubbery, on my homeward way, about nine of a bright forenoon. It was that time of year when the woods are all in their spring colours, the thorns all in flower, and the birds in the high season of their singing. In contrast to this merriment, the shrubbery was only the more sad, and I the more oppressed by its associations. In this situation of spirit it struck me disagreeably to hear voices a little way in front, and to recognise the tones of my lord and Mr. Alexander. I pushed ahead, and came presently into their view. They stood together in the open space where the duel was, my lord with his hand on his son's shoulder, and speaking with some gravity. At least, as he raised his head upon my coming, I thought I could perceive his countenance to lighten.

'Ah!' says he, 'here comes the good Mackellar. I have just been telling Sandie the story of this place, and how there was a man whom the devil tried to kill, and how near he came to kill the devil instead.'

I had thought it strange enough he should bring the child into that scene; that he should actually be discoursing of his act, passed measure. But the worst was yet to come; for he added, turning to his son—'You can ask Mackellar; he was here and saw it.'

'Is it true, Mr. Mackellar?' asked the child. 'And did you really see the devil?'

'I have not heard the tale,' I replied; 'and I am in a press of business.' So far I said a little sourly, fencing with the embarrassment of the position; and suddenly the bitterness of the past, and the terror of that scene by candlelight, rushed in upon my mind. I bethought me that, for the difference of a second's quickness in parade, the child before me might have never seen the day; and the emotion that always fluttered round my heart in that dark shrubbery burst forth in words. 'But so much is true,' I cried, 'that I have met the devil in these woods, and seen him foiled here. Blessed be God that we escaped with life—blessed be God that one stone yet stands upon another in the walls of Durrisdeer! And, oh! Mr. Alexander, if ever you come by this spot, though it was a hundred years hence, and you came with the gayest and the highest in the land, I would step aside and remember a bit prayer.'

My lord bowed his head gravely. 'Ah!' says he, 'Mackellar is always in the right. Come, Alexander, take your bonnet off.' And with that he uncovered, and held out his hand. 'O Lord,' says he, 'I thank Thee, and my son thanks Thee, for Thy manifold great mercies. Let us have peace for a little; defend us from the evil man. Smite him, O Lord, upon the lying mouth!' The last broke out of him like a cry; and at that, whether remembered anger choked his utterance, or whether he perceived this was a singular sort of prayer, at least he suddenly came to a full stop; and, after a moment, set back his hat upon his head.

'I think you have forgot a word, my lord,' said I. '"Forgive us our trespasses, as we forgive them that trespass against us. For Thine is the kingdom, and the power, and the glory, for ever and ever. Amen."'

'Ah! that is easy saying,' said my lord. 'That is very easy

saying, Mackellar. But for me to forgive!—I think I would cut a very silly figure if I had the affectation to pretend it.'

' The bairn, my lord! ' said I, with some severity, for I thought his expressions little fitted for the ears of children.

' Why, very true,' said he. ' This is dull work for a bairn. Let's go nesting.'

I forget if it was the same day, but it was soon after, my lord, finding me alone, opened himself a little more on the same head.

' Mackellar,' he said, ' I am now a very happy man.'

' I think so indeed, my lord,' said I, ' and the sight of it gives me a light heart.'

' There is an obligation in happiness—do you not think so? ' says he, musingly.

' I think so indeed,' says I, ' and one in sorrow, too. If we are not here to try to do the best, in my humble opinion the sooner we are away the better for all parties.'

' Ay, but if you were in my shoes, would you forgive him? ' asks my lord.

The suddenness of the attack a little gravelled me. ' It is a duty laid upon us strictly,' said I.

' Hut! ' said he. ' These are expressions! Do you forgive the man yourself? '

' Well—no! ' said I. ' God forgive me, I do not.'

' Shake hands upon that! ' cries my lord, with a kind of joviality.

' It is an ill sentiment to shake hands upon,' said I, ' for Christian people. I think I will give you mine on some more evangelical occasion.'

This I said, smiling a little; but as for my lord, he went from the room laughing aloud.

For my lord's slavery to the child, I can find no expression adequate. He lost himself in that continual thought: business, friends, and wife being all alike forgotten, or only remembered with a painful effort, like that of one struggling with a posset. It was most notable in the matter of his wife. Since I had known Durrisdeer, she had been the burthen of his thought and the loadstone of his eyes; and now she was quite cast out. I have seen him come to the door of a room, look round, and pass my lady over as though she were a dog before the fire. It would be Alexander he was seeking, and my lady knew it well. I have heard him speak to her so ruggedly that I nearly found it in my heart to intervene: the cause would still be the same, that she had in some way thwarted Alexander. Without doubt this was in the nature of a judgment upon my lady. Without doubt she had the tables turned upon her, as only Providence can do it; she who had been cold so many years to every mark of tenderness, it was her part now to be neglected: the more praise to her that she played it well.

An odd situation resulted: that we had once more two parties in the house, and that now I was of my lady's. Not that ever I lost the love I bore my master. But, for one thing, he had the less use for my society. For another, I could not but compare the case of Mr. Alexander with that of Miss Katharine; for whom my lord had never found the least attention. And for a third, I was wounded by the change he discovered to his wife, which struck me in the nature of an infidelity. I could not but admire, besides, the constancy and kindness she displayed. Perhaps her sentiment of my lord, as it had been founded from the first in pity, was that rather of a mother than of a wife; perhaps it pleased her—if I may so say—to behold her two children so happy in each other; the more as one had suffered so unjustly in the past. But for all that, and though I could never trace in her one spark of jealousy, she must fall back for society on poor neglected Miss Katharine; and I, on my part, came to pass my spare hours more and more with the mother and daughter. It would be easy to make too much of this division, for it was a pleasant family, as families go; still the thing existed; whether my lord knew it or not, I am in doubt. I do not think he did; he was bound up so entirely in his son; but the rest of us knew it, and in a manner suffered from the knowledge.

What troubled us most, however, was the great and growing danger to the child. My lord was his father over again; it was to be feared the son would prove a second Master. Time has proved these fears to have been quite exaggerate. Certainly there is no more worthy gentleman to-day in Scotland than the seventh Lord Durrisdeer. Of my own exodus from his employment it does not become me to speak, above all in a memorandum written only to justify his father. . . .

[*Editor's Note. Five pages of Mr. Mackellar's MS. are here omitted. I have gathered from their perusal an impression that Mr. Mackellar, in his old age, was rather an exacting servant. Against the seventh Lord Durrisdeer (with whom, at any rate, we have no concern) nothing material is alleged—R. L. S.*].

. . . But our fear at the time was lest he should turn out, in the person of his son, a second edition of his brother. My lady had tried to interject some wholesome discipline; she had been glad to give that up, and now looked on with secret dismay; sometimes she even spoke of it by hints; and sometimes, when there was brought to her knowledge some monstrous instance of my lord's indulgence, she would betray herself in a gesture or perhaps an exclamation. As for myself, I was haunted by the thought both day and night: not so much for the child's sake as for the father's. The man had gone to sleep, he was dreaming a dream, and any rough wakening must infallibly prove mortal. That he should survive its death was inconceivable; and the fear of its dishonour made me cover my face.

It was this continual preoccupation that screwed me up at last to a remonstrance; a matter worthy to be narrated in detail. My lord and I sat one day at the same table upon some tedious business of detail; I have said that he had lost his former interest in such occupations; he was plainly itching to be gone, and he looked fretful, weary, and methought older than I had ever previously observed. I suppose it was the haggard face that put me suddenly upon my enterprise.

' My lord,' said I, with my head down, and feigning to continue my occupation—' or, rather, let me call you again by the name of Mr. Henry, for I fear your anger and want you to think upon old times—— '

' My good Mackellar! ' said he; and that in tones so kindly that I had near forsook my purpose. But I called to mind that I was speaking for his good, and stuck to my colours.

' Has it never come in upon your mind what you are doing? ' I asked.

' What I am doing? ' he repeated; ' I was never good at guessing riddles.'

' What you are doing with your son? ' said I.

' Well,' said he, with some defiance in his tone, ' and what am I doing with my son? '

' Your father was a very good man,' says I, straying from the direct path. ' But do you think he was a wise father? '

There was a pause before he spoke, and then, ' I say nothing against him,' he replied. ' I had the most cause, perhaps; but I say nothing.'

' Why, there it is,' said I. ' You had the cause at least. And yet your father was a good man; I never knew a better, save on the one point, nor yet a wiser. Where he stumbled, it is highly possible another man should fall. He had the two sons—— '

My lord rapped suddenly and violently on the table.

' What is this? ' cried he. ' Speak out! '

'I will, then,' said I, my voice almost strangled with the thumping of my heart. 'If you continue to indulge Mr. Alexander, you are following in your father's footsteps. Beware, my lord, lest (when he grows up) your son should follow in the Master's.'

I had never meant to put the thing so crudely; but in the extreme of fear there comes a brutal kind of courage, the most brutal indeed of all; and I burnt my ships with that plain word. I never had the answer. When I lifted my head, my lord had risen to his feet, and the next moment he fell heavily on the floor. The fit or seizure endured not very long; he came to himself vacantly, put his hand to his head, which I was then supporting, and says he, in a broken voice: 'I have been ill,' and a little after: 'Help me.' I got him to his feet, and he stood pretty well, though he kept hold of the table. 'I have been ill, Mackellar,' he said again. 'Something broke, Mackellar—or was going to break, and then all swam away. I think I was very angry. Never you mind, Mackellar; never you mind, my man. I wouldnae hurt a hair upon your head. Too much has come and gone. It's a certain thing between us two. But I think, Mackellar, I will go to Mrs. Henry—I think I will go to Mrs. Henry,' said he, and got pretty steadily from the room, leaving me overcome with penitence.

Presently the door flew open, and my lady swept in with flashing eyes. 'What is all this?' she cried. 'What have you done to my husband? Will nothing teach you your position in this house? Will you never cease from making and meddling?'

'My lady,' said I, 'since I have been in this house I have had penty of hard words. For a while they were my daily diet, and I swallowed them all. As for to-day, you may call me what you please; you will never find the name hard enough for such a blunder. And yet I meant it for the best.'

I told her all with ingenuity, even as it is written here; and when she had heard me out she pondered, and I could see her animosity fall. 'Yes,' she said, 'you meant well indeed. I have had the same thought myself, or the same temptation rather, which makes me pardon you. But, dear God, can you not understand that he can bear no more. He can bear no more!' she cried. 'The cord is stretched to snapping. What matters the future if he have one or two good days?'

'Amen,' said I. 'I will meddle no more. I am pleased enough that you should recognise the kindness of my meaning.'

'Yes,' said my lady; 'but when it came to the point, I have to suppose your courage failed you; for what you said was said cruelly.' She paused, looking at me; then suddenly, smiled a little and said a singular thing: 'Do you know what you are, Mr. Mackellar? You are an old maid.'

No more incident of any note occurred in the family until the return of that ill-starred man the Master. But I have to place here a second extract from the memoirs of Chevalier Burke, interesting in itself, and highly necessary for my purpose. It is our only sight of the Master on his Indian travels; and the first word in these pages of Secundra Dass. One fact, it is to observe, appears here very clearly, which if we had known some twenty years ago, how many calamities and sorrows had been spared!— that Secundra Dass spoke English.

7

Adventure of Chevalier Burke in India:
Extracted from his Memoirs

... HERE was I, therefore, on the streets of that city, the name of which I cannot call to mind, while even then I was so ill-acquainted with its situation that I knew not whether to go south or north. The alert being sudden, I had run forth without shoes or stockings; my hat had been struck from my head in the mellay; my kit was in the hands of the English; I had no companion but the cipaye, no weapon but my sword, and the devil a coin in my pocket. In short, I was for all the world like one of those calenders with whom Mr. Galland has made us acquainted in his elegant tales. These gentlemen, you will remember, were for ever falling in with extraordinary incidents; and I was myself upon the brink of one so astonishing that I protest I cannot explain it to this day.

The cipaye was a very honest man; he had served many years with the French colours, and would have let himself be cut to pieces for any of the brave countrymen of Mr. Lally. It is the same fellow (his name has quite escaped me) of whom I have narrated already a suprising instance of generosity of mind —when he found Mr. de Fessac and myself upon the ramparts, entirely overcome with liquor, and covered us with straw while the commandant was passing by. I consulted him, therefore, with perfect freedom. It was a fine question what to do; but we decided at last to escalade a garden wall, where we could certainly sleep in the shadow of the trees, and might perhaps

125

find an occasion to get hold of a pair of slippers and a turban. In that part of the city we had only the difficulty of the choice, for it was a quarter consisting entirely of walled gardens, and the lanes which divided them were at that hour of the night deserted. I gave the cipaye a back, and we had soon dropped into a large enclosure full of trees. The place was soaking with dew, which, in that country is exceedingly unwholesome, above all to whites; yet my fatigue was so extreme that I was already half asleep, when the cipaye recalled me to my senses. In the far end of the enclosure a bright light had suddenly shone out, and continued to burn steadily among the leaves. It was a circumstance highly unusual in such a place and hour; and, in our situation, it behoved us to proceed with some timidity. The cipaye was sent to reconnoitre, and pretty soon returned with the intelligence that we had fallen extremely amiss, for the house belonged to a white man, who was in all likelihood English.

'Faith,' says I, 'if there is a white man to be seen, I will have a look at him; for, the Lord be praised! there are more sorts than the one!'

The cipaye led me forward accordingly to a place from which I had a clear view upon the house. It was surrounded with a wide verandah; a lamp, very well trimmed, stood upon the floor of it, and on either side of the lamp there sat a man, cross-legged, after the Oriental manner. Both, besides, were bundled up in muslin like two natives; and yet one of them was not only a white man, but a man very well known to me and the reader, being indeed that very Master of Ballantrae of whose gallantry and genius I have had to speak so often. Word had reached me that he was come to the Indies, though we had never met at least, and I heard little of his occupations. But, sure, I had no sooner recognised him, and found myself in the arms of so old a comrade, than I supposed my tribulations were quite done. I stepped plainly forth into the light of the moon, which shone exceeding strong, and hailing Ballantrae by name, made him in a few words master of my grievous situation. He turned, started the least thing in the world, looked me fair in the face while I was speaking, and when I had done addressed himself to his companion in the barbarous native dialect. The second person, who was of an extraordinary delicate appearance, with legs like walking canes and fingers like the stalk of a tobacco pipe[1], now rose to his feet.

'The Sahib,' says he, 'understands no English language. I understand it myself, and I see you make some small mistake—

[1] *Note by Mr. Mackellar.* Plainly Secundra Dass.—E. McK.

oh! which may happen very often. But the Sahib would be glad to know how you come in a garden.'

'Ballantrae!' I cried, 'have you the damned impudence to deny me to my face?'

Ballantrae never moved a muscle, staring at me like an image in a pagoda.

'The Sahib understands no English language,' says the native, as glib as before. 'He be glad to know how you come in a garden.'

'Oh! the divil fetch him,' says I. 'He would be glad to know how I come in a garden, would he? Well, now, my dear man, just have the civility to tell the Sahib, with my kind love, that we are two soldiers here whom he never met and never heard of, but the cipaye is a broth of a boy, and I am a broth of a boy myself; and if we don't get a full meal of meat, and a turban, and slippers, and the value of a gold mohur in small change as a matter of convenience, bedad, my friend, I could lay my finger on a garden where there is going to be trouble.'

They carried their comedy so far as to converse awhile in Hindustanee; and then says the Hindu, with the same smile, but sighing as if he were tired of the repetition, 'The Sahib would be glad to know how you come in a garden.'

'Is that the way of it?' says I, and laying my hand on my sword-hilt I bade the cipaye draw.

Ballantrae's Hindu, still smiling, pulled out a pistol from his bosom, and though Ballantrae himself never moved a muscle I knew him well enough to be sure he was prepared.

'The Sahib thinks you better go away,' says the Hindu.

Well, to be plain, it was what I was thinking myself; for the report of a pistol would have been, under Providence, the means of hanging the pair of us.

'Tell the Sahib I consider him no gentleman,' says I, and turned away with a gesture of contempt.

I was not gone three steps when the voice of the Hindu called me back. 'The Sahib would be glad to know if you are a dam low Irishman,' says he; and at the words Ballantrae smiled and bowed very low.

'What is that?' says I.

'The Sahib say you ask your friend Mackellar,' says the Hindu. 'The Sahib he cry quits.'

'Tell the Sahib I will give him a cure for the Scots fiddle when next we meet,' cried I.

The pair were still smiling as I left.

There is little doubt some flaws may be picked in my own

behaviour; and when a man, however gallant, appeals to posterity with an account of his exploits, he must almost certainly expect to share the fate of Cæsar and Alexander, and to meet with some detractors. But there is one thing that can never be laid at the door of Francis Burke: he never turned his back on a friend. . . .

(Here follows a passage which the Chevalier Burke has been at the pains to delete before sending me his manuscript. Doubtless it was some very natural complaint of what he supposed to be an indiscretion on my part; though, indeed, I can call none to mind. Perhaps Mr. Henry was less guarded; or it is just possible the Master found the means to examine my correspondence, and himself read the letter from Troyes: in revenge for which this cruel jest was perpetrated on Mr. Burke in his extreme necessity. The Master, for all his wickedness, was not without some natural affection; I believe he was sincerely attached to Mr. Burke in the beginning; but the thought of treachery dried up the springs of his very shallow friendship, and his detestable nature appeared naked.—E. McK.)

8

The enemy in the house

IT is a strange thing that I should be at a stick for a date —the date, besides, of an incident that changed the very nature of my life, and sent us all into foreign lands. But the truth is, I was stricken out of all my habitudes, and find my journals very ill redd-up,[1] the day not indicated sometimes for a week or two together, and the whole fashion of the thing like that of a man near desperate. It was late in March at least, or early in April, 1764. I had slept heavily, and awakened with a premonition of some evil to befall. So strong was this upon my spirit that I hurried downstairs in my shirt and breeches, and my hand (I remember) shook upon the rail. It was a cold, sunny morning, with a thick white frost; the blackbirds sang exceeding sweet and loud about the house of Durrisdeer, and there was a noise of the sea in all the chambers. As I came by the doors of the hall, another sound arrested me—of voices talking. I drew nearer, and stood like a man dreaming. Here was certainly a human voice, and that in my own master's house, and yet I knew it not; certainly human speech, and that in

[1] Ordered.

my native land; and yet, listen as I pleased, I could not catch one syllable. An old tale started up in my mind of a fairy wife (or perhaps only a wandering stranger), that came to the place of my fathers some generations back, and stayed the matter of a week, talking often in a tongue that signified nothing to the hearers; and went again, as she had come, under cloud of night, leaving not so much as a name behind her. A little fear I had, but more curiosity; and I opened the hall-door, and entered.

The supper-things still lay upon the table; the shutters were still closed, although day peeped in the divisions; and the great room lighted only with a single taper and some lurching reverberation of the fire. Close in the chimney sat two men. The one that was wrapped in a cloak and wore boots, I knew at once: it was the bird of ill omen back again. Of the other, who was set close to the red embers, and made up into a bundle like a mummy, I could but see that he was an alien, of a darker hue than any man of Europe, very frailly built, with a singular tall forehead, and a secret eye. Several bundles and a small valise were on the floor; and to judge by the smallness of this luggage, and by the condition of the Master's boots, grossly patched by some unscrupulous country cobbler, evil had not prospered.

He rose upon my entrance; our eyes crossed; and I know not why it should have been, but my courage rose like a lark on a May morning.

'Ha!' said I, 'is this you?'—and I was pleased with the unconcern of my own voice.

'It is even myself, worthy Mackellar,' says the Master.

'This time you have brought the black dog visibly upon your back,' I continued.

'Referring to Secundra Dass?' asked the Master. 'Let me present you. He is a native gentleman of India.'

'Hum!' said I. 'I am no great lover either of you or your friends, Mr. Bally. But I will let a little daylight in, and have a look at you.' And so saying, I undid the shutters of the eastern window.

By the light of the morning I could perceive the man was changed. Later, when we were all together, I was more struck to see how lightly time had dealt with him; but the first glance was otherwise.

'You are getting an old man,' said I.

A shade came upon his face. 'If you could see yourself,' said he, 'you would perhaps not dwell upon the topic.'

'Hut!' I returned, 'old age is nothing to me. I think I

have been always old; and I am now, I thank God, better known and more respected. It is not every one that can say that, Mr. Bally! The lines in *your* brow are calamities: your life begins to close in upon you like a prison; death will soon be rapping at the door: and I see not from what source you are to draw your consolations.'

Here the Master addressed himself to Secundra Dass in Hindustanee, from which I gathered (I freely confess, with a high degree of pleasure) that my remarks annoyed him. All this while, you may be sure, my mind had been busy upon other matters, even while I rallied my enemy; and chiefly as to how I should communicate secretly and quickly with my lord. To this, in the breathing-space now given me, I turned all the forces of my mind; when, suddenly shifting my eyes, I was aware of the man himself standing in the doorway, and, to all appearance, quite composed. He had no sooner met my looks than he stepped across the threshold. The Master heard him coming, and advanced upon the other side; about four feet apart, these brothers came to a full pause, and stood exchanging steady looks, and then my lord smiled, bowed a little forward, and turned briskly away.

'Mackellar,' says he, 'we must see to breakfast for these travellers.'

It was plain the Master was a trifle disconcerted; but he assumed the more impudence of speech and manner. 'I am as hungry as a hawk,' says he. 'Let it be something good, Henry.'

My lord turned to him with the same hard smile. 'Lord Durrisdeer,' says he.

'Oh! never in the family,' returned the Master.

'Every one in this house renders me my proper title,' says my lord. 'If it please you to make an exception, I will leave you to consider what appearance it will bear to strangers, and whether it may not be translated as an effect of impotent jealousy.'

I could have clapped my hands together with delight: the more so as my lord left no time for any answer, but bidding me with a sign to follow him, went straight out of the hall.

'Come quick,' says he; 'we have to sweep vermin from the house.' And he sped through the passages, with so swift a step that I could scarce keep up with him, straight to the door of John Paul, the which he opened without summons and walked in. John was, to all appearance, sound asleep, but my lord made no pretence of waking him.

'John Paul,' said he, speaking as quietly as ever I heard him, 'you served my father long, or I would pack you from the house like a dog. If in half an hour's time I find you gone, you shall continue to receive your wages in Edinburgh. If you linger here or in St. Bride's—old man, old servant, and altogether—I shall find some very astonishing way to make you smart for your disloyalty. Up and begone. The door you let them in by will serve for your departure. I do not choose my son shall see your face again.'

'I am rejoiced to find you bear the thing so quietly,' said I, when we were forth again by ourselves.

'Quietly?' cries he, and put my hand suddenly against his heart, which struck upon his bosom like a sledge.

At this revelation I was filled with wonder and fear. There was no constitution could bear so violent a strain—his least of all, that was unhinged already; and I decided in my mind that we must bring this monstrous situation to an end.

'It would be well, I think, if I took word to my lady,' said I. Indeed, he should have gone himself, but I counted—not in vain—on his indifference.

'Ay,' says he, 'do. I will hurry breakfast: we must all appear at the table, even Alexander; it must appear we are untroubled.'

I ran to my lady's room, and with no preparatory cruelty disclosed my news.

'My mind was long ago made up,' said she. 'We must make our packets secretly to-day, and leave secretly to-night. Thank heaven, we have another house! The first ship that sails shall bear us to New York.'

'And what of him?' I asked.

'We leave him Durrisdeer,' she cried. 'Let him work his pleasure upon that.'

'Not so, by your leave,' said I. 'There shall be a dog at his heels that can hold fast. Bed he shall have, and board, and a horse to ride upon, if he behave himself; but the keys—if you think well of it, my lady—shall be left in the hands of one Mackellar. There will be good care taken; trust him for that.'

'Mr. Mackellar,' she cried, 'I thank you for that thought. All shall be left in your hands. If we must go into a savage country, I bequeath it to you to take our vengeance. Send Macconochie to St. Bride's to arrange privately for horses and to call the lawyer. My lord must leave procuration.'

At that moment my lord came to the door, and we opened our plan to him.

'I will never hear of it,' he cried; 'he would think I feared him. I will stay in my own house, please God, until I die. There lives not the man can beard me out of it. Once and for all, here I am, and here I stay, in spite of all the devils in hell.' I can give no idea of the vehemency of his words and utterance; but we both stood aghast, and I in particular, who had been a witness of his former self-restraint.

My lady looked at me with an appeal that went to my heart and recalled me to my wits. I made her a private sign to go, and when my lord and I were alone, went up to him where he was racing to and fro in one end of the room like a half-lunatic, and set my hand firmly on his shoulder.

'My lord,' says I, 'I am going to be the plain-dealer once more; if for the last time, so much the better, for I am grown weary of the part.'

'Nothing will change me,' he answered. 'God forbid I should refuse to hear you; but nothing will change me.' This he said firmly, with no signal of the former violence, which already raised my hopes.

'Very well,' said I. 'I can afford to waste my breath.' I pointed to a chair, and he sat down and looked at me. 'I can remember a time when my lady very much neglected you,' said I.

'I never spoke of it while it lasted,' returned my lord, with a high flush of colour; 'and it is all changed now.'

'Do you know how much?' I said. 'Do you know how much it is all changed? The tables are turned, my lord! It is my lady that now courts you for a word, a look—ay, and courts you in vain. Do you know with whom she passes her days while you are out gallivanting in the policies? My lord, she is glad to pass them with a certain dry old grieve[1] of the name of Ephraim Mackellar; and I think you may be able to remember what that means, for I am the more in a mistake or you were once driven to the same company yourself.'

'Mackellar!' cries my lord, getting to his feet. 'O my God, Mackellar!'

'It is neither the name of Mackellar nor the name of God that can change the truth,' said I; 'and I am telling you the fact. Now for you, that suffered so much, to deal out the same suffering to another, is that the part of any Christian? But you are so swallowed up in your new friend that the old are all forgotten. They are all clean vanished from your memory. And yet they stood by you at the darkest; my lady not the least. And does my lady ever cross your mind? Does it ever cross your

[1] Land steward.

mind what she went through that night?—or what manner of a wife she has been to you thenceforward?—or in what kind of a position she finds herself to-day? Never. It is your pride to stay and face him out, and she must stay along with you. Oh! my lord's pride—that's the great affair! And yet she is the woman, and you are a great hulking man! She is the woman that you swore to protect; and, more betoken, the own mother of that son of yours!'

'You are speaking very bitterly, Mackellar,' said he; 'but, the Lord knows, I fear you are speaking very true. I have not proved worthy of my happiness. Bring my lady back.'

My lady was waiting near at hand to learn the issue. When I brought her in, my lord took a hand of each of us, and laid them both upon his bosom. 'I have had two friends in my life,' said he. 'All the comfort ever I had, it came from one or other. When you two are in a mind, I think I would be an ungrateful dog——' He shut his mouth very hard, and looked on us with swimming eyes. 'Do what ye like with me,' says he, 'only don't think——' He stopped again. 'Do what ye please with me: God knows I love and honour you.' And dropping our two hands, he turned his back and went and gazed out of the window. But my lady ran after, calling his name, and threw herself upon his neck in a passion of weeping.

I went out and shut the door behind me, and stood and thanked God from the bottom of my heart.

At the breakfast board, according to my lord's design, we were all met. The Master had by that time plucked off his patched boots and made a toilet suitable to the hour; Secundra Dass was no longer bundled up in wrappers, but wore a decent plain black suit, which misbecame him strangely; and the pair were at the great window, looking forth, when the family entered. They turned; and the black man (as they had already named him in the house) bowed almost to his knees, but the Master was for running forward like one of the family. My lady stopped him, curtseying low from the far end of the hall, and keeping her children at her back. My lord was a little in front: so there were the three cousins of Durrisdeer face to face. The hand of time was very legible on all; I seemed to read in their changed faces a *memento mori*; and what affected me still more, it was the wicked man that bore his years the handsomest. My lady was quite transfigured into the matron, a becoming woman for the head of a great tableful of children and dependents. My lord was grown slack in his limbs; he stooped; he walked with a running motion, as though he had learned again from Mr. Alexander; his face was drawn; it seemed a trifle longer than of old; and it wore at times a smile very singularly mingled, and which (in my eyes) appeared both bitter and pathetic. But the Master still bore himself erect, although perhaps with effort; his brow barred about the centre with imperious lines, his mouth set as for command. He had all the gravity and something of the splendour of Satan in the 'Paradise Lost.' I could not help but see the man with admiration, and was only surprised that I saw him with so little fear.

But indeed (as long as we were at the table) it seemed as if his authority were quite vanished and his teeth all drawn. We had known him a magician that controlled the elements; and here he was, transformed into an ordinary gentleman, chatting like his neighbours at the breakfast-board. For now the father was dead, and my lord and lady reconciled, in what ear was he to pour his calumnies? It came upon me in a kind of vision how hugely I had overrated the man's subtlety. He had his malice still; he was false as ever; and, the occasion being gone that made his strength, he sat there impotent; he was still the viper, but now spent his venom on a file. Two more thoughts occurred to me while yet we sat at breakfast: the first, that he was abashed—I had almost said, distressed—to find his wickedness quite unavailing; the second, that perhaps my lord was in the right, and we did amiss to fly from our dismasted enemy. But my poor master's leaping heart came in my mind, and I remembered it was for his life we played the coward.

When the meal was over, the Master followed me to my room, and, taking a chair (which I had never offered him), asked me what was to be done with him.

'Why, Mr. Bally,' said I, 'the house will still be open to you for a time.'

'For a time?' says he. 'I do not know if I quite take your meaning.'

'It is plain enough,' said I. 'We keep you for our reputation; as soon as you shall have publicly disgraced yourself by some of your misconduct, we shall pack you forth again.'

'You are become an impudent rogue,' said the Master, bending his brows at me dangerously.

'I learned in a good school,' I returned. 'And you must have perceived yourself that with my old lord's death your power is quite departed. I do not fear you now, Mr. Bally; I think even—God forgive me—that I take a certain pleasure in your company.'

He broke out in a burst of laughter, which I clearly saw to be assumed.

' I have come with empty pockets,' says he, after a pause.

' I do not think there will be any money going,' I replied. ' I would advise you not to build on that.'

' I shall have something to say on the point,' he returned.

' Indeed? ' said I. ' I have not a guess what it will be, then.'

' Oh! you affect confidence,' said the Master. ' I have still one strong position—that you people fear a scandal, and I enjoy it.'

' Pardon me, Mr. Bally,' says I. ' We do not in the least fear a scandal against you.'

He laughed again. ' You have been studying repartee,' he said. ' But speech is very easy, and sometimes very deceptive. I warn you fairly: you will find me vitriol in the house. You would do wiser to pay money down and see my back.' And with that he waved his hand to me and left the room.

A little after, my lord came with the lawyer, Mr. Carlyle; a bottle of old wine was brought, and we all had a glass before we fell to business. The necessary deeds were then prepared and executed, and the Scotch estates made over in trust to Mr. Carlyle and myself.

' There is one point, Mr. Carlyle,' said my lord, when these affairs had been adjusted, ' on which I wish that you would do us justice. This sudden departure coinciding with my brother's return will be certainly commented on. I wish you would discourage any conjunction of the two.'

' I will make a point of it, my lord,' said Mr. Carlyle. ' The Mas—Mr. Bally does not, then, accompany you? '

' It is a point I must approach,' said my lord. ' Mr. Bally remains at Durrisdeer, under the care of Mr. Mackellar; and I do not mean that he shall even know our destination.'

' Common report, however—— ' began the lawyer.

' Ah! but, Mr. Carlyle, this is to be a secret quite among ourselves,' interrupted my lord. ' None but you and Mackellar are to be made acquainted with my movements.'

' And Mr. Bally stays here? Quite so,' said Mr. Carlyle. ' The powers you leave—— ' Then he broke off again. ' Mr. Mackellar, we have a rather heavy weight upon us.'

' No doubt, sir,' said I.

' No doubt,' said he. ' Mr. Bally will have no voice? '

' He will have no voice,' said my lord; ' and I hope no influence. Mr. Bally is not a good adviser.'

' I see,' said the lawyer. ' By the way, has Mr. Bally means? '

' I understand him to have nothing,' replied my lord. ' I give him table, fire, and candle in this house.'

' And in the matter of an allowance? If I am to share the responsibility, you will see how highly desirable it is that I should understand your views,' said the lawyer. ' On the question of an allowance? '

' There will be no allowance,' said my lord. ' I wish Mr. Bally to live very private. We have not always been gratified with his behaviour.'

' And in the matter of money,' I added, ' he has shown himself an infamous bad husband. Glance your eye upon that docket, Mr. Carlyle, where I have brought together the different sums the man has drawn from the estate in the last fifteen or twenty years. The total is pretty.'

Mr. Carlyle made the motion of whistling. ' I had no guess of this,' said he. ' Excuse me once more, my lord, if I appear to push you; but it is really desirable that I should penetrate your intentions. Mr. Mackellar may die, when I should find myself alone upon this trust. Would it not be rather your lordship's preference that Mr. Bally should—ahem—should leave the country? '

My lord looked at Mr. Carlyle. ' Why do you ask that? ' said he.

' I gather, my lord, that Mr. Bally is not a comfort to his family,' says the lawyer with a smile.

My lord's face became suddenly knotted. ' I wish he was in hell! ' cried he, and filled himself a glass of wine, but with a hand so tottering that he spilled the half into his bosom. This was the second time that, in the midst of the most regular and wise behaviour, his animosity had spirted out. It startled Mr. Carlyle, who observed my lord henceforth with covert curiosity; and to me it restored the certainty that we were acting for the best in view of my lord's health and reason.

Except for this explosion the interview was very successfully conducted. No doubt Mr. Carlyle would talk, as lawyers do, little by little. We could thus feel we had laid the foundations of a better feeling in the country, and the man's own misconduct would certainly complete what we had begun. Indeed, before his departure, the lawyer showed us there had already gone abroad some glimmerings of the truth.

' I should perhaps explain to you, my lord,' said he, pausing, with his hat in his hand, ' that I have not been altogether surprised with your lordship's dispositions in the case of Mr. Bally. Something of this nature oozed out when he was last in Durrisdeer.

There was some talk of a woman at St. Bride's, to whom you had behaved extremely handsome, and Mr. Bally with no small degree of cruelty. There was the entail, again, which was much controverted. In short, there was no want of talk, back and forward; and some of our wiseacres took up a strong opinion. I remained in suspense, as became one of my cloth; but Mr. Mackellar's docket here has finally opened my eyes. I do not think, Mr. Mackellar, that you and I will give him that much rope.'

The rest of that important day passed prosperously through. It was our policy to keep the enemy in view, and I took my turn to be his watchman with the rest. I think his spirits rose as he perceived us to be so attentive, and I know that mine insensibly declined. What chiefly daunted me was the man's singular dexterity to worm himself into our troubles. You may have felt (after a horse accident) the hand of a bone-setter artfully divide and interrogate the muscles, and settle strongly on the injured place? It was so with the Master's tongue, that was so cunning to question; and his eyes, that were so quick to observe. I seemed to have said nothing, and yet to have let all out. Before I knew where I was the man was condoling with me on my lord's neglect of my lady and myself, and his hurtful indulgence to his son. On this last point I perceived him (with panic fear) to return repeatedly. The boy had displayed a certain shrinking from his uncle; it was strong in my mind that his father had been fool enough to indoctrinate the same, which was no wise beginning: and when I looked upon the man before me, still so handsome, so apt a speaker, with so great a variety of fortunes to relate, I saw he was the very personage to captivate a boyish fancy. John Paul had left only that morning; it was not to be supposed he had been altogether dumb upon his favourite subject: so that here would be Mr. Alexander in the part of Dido, with a curiosity inflamed to hear; and there would be the Master, like a diabolical Æneas, full of matter the most pleasing in the world to any youthful ear, such as battles, sea-disasters, flights, the forests of the West, and (since his later voyage) the ancient cities of the Indies. How cunningly these baits might be employed, and what an empire might be so founded, little by little, in the mind of any boy, stood obviously clear to me. There was no inhibition, so long as the man was in the house, that would be strong enough to hold these two apart; for if it be hard to charm serpents, it is no very difficult thing to cast a glamour on a little chip of manhood not very long in breeches. I recalled an ancient sailor-man who dwelt in a lone house beyond the Figgate Whins (I believe, he called it after Portobello), and how the boys would troop out of Leith on a Saturday, and sit and listen to his swearing tales, as thick as crows about a carrion: a thing I often remarked as I went by, a young student, on my own more meditative holiday diversion. Many of these boys went, no doubt, in the face of an express command; many feared and even hated the old brute of whom they made their hero; and I have seen them flee from him when he was tipsy, and stone him when he was drunk. And yet there they came each Saturday! How much more easy would a boy like Mr. Alexander fall under the influence of a high-looking, high-spoken gentleman-adventurer, who should conceive the fancy to entrap him; and, the influence gained, how easy to employ it for the child's perversion!

I doubt if our enemy had named Mr. Alexander three times before I perceived which way his mind was aiming—all this train of thought and memory passed in one pulsation through my own—and you may say I started back as though an open hole had gaped across a pathway. Mr. Alexander: there was the weak point, there was the Eve in our perishable paradise; and the serpent was already hissing on the trail.

I promise you, I went the more heartily about the preparations; my last scruple gone, the danger of delay written before me in huge characters. From that moment forth I seem not to have sat down or breathed. Now I would be at my post with the Master and his Indian; now in the garret, buckling a valise; now sending forth Macconochie by the side postern and the wood-path to bear it to the trysting-place; and, again, snatching some words of counsel with my lady. This was the *verso* of our life in Durrisdeer that day; but on the *recto* all appeared quite settled, as of a family at home in its paternal seat; and what perturbation may have been observable, the Master would set down to the blow of his unlooked-for coming, and the fear he was accustomed to inspire.

Supper went creditably off, cold salutations passed, and the company trooped to their respective chambers. I attended the Master to the last. We had put him next door to his Indian, in the north wing; because that was the most distant and could be severed from the body of the house with doors. I saw he was a kind friend or good master (whichever it was) to his Secundra Dass—seeing to his comfort; mending the fire with his own hand, for the Indian complained of cold; inquiring as to the rice on which the stranger made his diet; talking with him pleasantly in the Hindustanee, while I stood by, my candle in my hand, and affected to be overcome with slumber. At length the Master observed my signals of distress. 'I perceive,' says he, 'that you have all your ancient habits: early to bed and early to rise. Yawn yourself away!'

Once in my own room, I made the customary motions of undressing, so that I might time myself; and when the cycle was complete, set my tinder-box ready, and blew out my taper. The matter of an hour afterward I made a light again, put on my shoes of list that I had worn by my lord's sick-bed, and set forth into the house to call the voyagers. All were dressed and waiting—my lord, my lady, Miss Katharine, Mr. Alexander, my lady's woman Christie; and I observed the effect of secrecy even upon quite innocent persons, that one after another showed in the chink of the door a face as white as paper. We slipped out of the side postern into a night of darkness, scarce broken by a star or two; so that at first we groped and stumbled and fell among the bushes. A few hundred yards up the wood-path Macconochie was awaiting us with a great lantern; so the rest of the way we went easy enough, but still in a kind of guilty silence. A little beyond the abbey the path debouched on the main road; and some quarter of a mile farther, at the place called Engles, where the moors begin, we saw the lights of the two carriages stand shining by the wayside. Scarce a word or two was uttered at our parting, and these regarded business: a silent grasping of hands, a turning of faces aside, and the thing was over; the horses broke into a trot, the lamp-light sped like Will-o'-the-Wisp upon the broken moorland, it dipped beyond Stony Brae; and there were Macconochie and I alone with our lantern on the road. There was one thing more to wait for, and that was the reappearance of the coach upon Cartmore. It seems they must have pulled up upon the summit, looked back for a last time, and seen our lantern not yet moved away from the place of separation. For a lamp was taken from a carriage, and waved three times up and down by way of a farewell. And then they were gone indeed, having looked their last on the kind roof of Durrisdeer, their faces toward a barbarous country. I never knew before, the greatness of that vault of night in which we two poor serving-men—the one old and the one elderly—stood for the first time deserted; I had never felt before my own dependency upon the countenance of others. The sense of isolation burned in my bowels like a fire. It seemed that we who remained at home were the true exiles, and that Durrisdeer and Solwayside, and all that made my country native, its air good to me, and its language welcome, had gone forth and was far over the sea with my old masters.

The remainder of that night I paced to and fro on the smooth highway, reflecting on the future and the past. My thoughts, which at first dwelled tenderly on those who were just gone, took a more manly temper as I considered what remained for me to do. Day came upon the inland mountain-tops, and the fowls began to cry, and the smoke of homesteads to arise in the brown bosom of the moors, before I turned my face homeward, and went down the path to where the roof of Durrisdeer shone in the morning by the sea.

At the customary hour I had the Master called, and awaited his coming in the hall with a quiet mind. He looked about him at the empty room and the three covers set.

'We are a small party,' said he. 'How comes that?'

'This is the party to which we must grow accustomed,' I replied.

He looked at me with a sudden sharpness. 'What is all this?' said he.

'You and I and your friend Mr. Dass are now all the company,' I replied. 'My lord, my lady, and the children, are gone upon a voyage.'

'Upon my word!' said he. 'Can this be possible? I have indeed fluttered your Volscians in Corioli! But this is no reason why our breakfast should go cold. Sit down, Mr. Mackellar, if you please'—taking, as he spoke, the head of the table, which I had designed to occupy myself—'and as we eat, you can give me the details of this evasion.'

I could see he was more affected than his language carried, and I determined to equal him in coolness. 'I was about to ask you to take the head of the table,' said I; 'for though I am now thrust into the position of your host, I could never forget that you were, after all, a member of the family.'

For a while he played the part of entertainer, giving directions to Macconochie, who received them with an evil grace, and attending specially upon Secundra. 'And where has my good family withdrawn to?' he asked carelessly.

'Ah! Mr. Bally, that is another point,' said I. 'I have no orders to communicate their destination.'

'To me,' he corrected.

'To any one,' said I.

'It is the less pointed,' said the Master; '*c'est de bon ton*: my brother improves as he continues. And I, dear Mr. Mackellar?'

'You will have bed and board, Mr. Bally,' said I. 'I am permitted to give you the run of the cellar, which is pretty reasonably stocked. You have only to keep well with me, which is no very difficult matter, and you shall want neither for wine nor a saddle-horse.'

He made an excuse to send Macconochie from the room.

'And for money?' he inquired. 'Have I to keep well with my good friend Mackellar for my pocket-money also? This is a pleasing return to the principles of boyhood.'

'There was no allowance made,' said I; 'but I will take it on myself to see you are supplied in moderation.'

'In moderation,' he repeated. 'And you will take it on yourself?' He drew himself up, and looked about the hall at the dark rows of portraits. 'In the name of my ancestors, I thank you,' says he; and then, with a return to irony, 'But there must certainly be an allowance for Secundra Dass?' he said. 'It is not possible they have omitted that?'

'I will make a note of it, and ask instructions when I write,' said I.

And he, with a sudden change of manner, and leaning forward with an elbow on the table—'Do you think this entirely wise?'

'I execute my orders, Mr. Bally,' said I.

'Profoundly modest,' said the Master; 'perhaps not equally ingenuous. You told me yesterday my power was fallen with my father's death. How comes it, then, that a peer of the realm flees under cloud of night out of a house in which his fathers have stood several sieges? that he conceals his address, which must be a matter of concern to his Gracious Majesty and to the whole republic? and that he should leave me in possession, and under the paternal charge of his invaluable Mackellar? This smacks to me of a very considerable and genuine apprehension.'

I sought to interrupt him with some not very truthful denegation; but he waved me down, and pursued his speech.

'I say, it smacks of it,' he said; 'but I will go beyond that, for I think the apprehension grounded. I came to this house with some reluctance. In view of the manner of my last departure, nothing but necessity could have induced me to return. Money, however, is that which I must have. You will not give with a good grace; well, I have the power to force it from you. Inside of a week, without leaving Durrisdeer, I will find out where these fools are fled to. I will follow; and when I have run my quarry down, I will drive a wedge into that family, that shall once more burst it into shivers. I shall see then whether my Lord Durrisdeer ' (said with indescribable scorn and rage) 'will choose to buy my absence; and you will all see whether, by that time, I decide for profit or revenge.'

I was amazed to hear the man so open. The truth is, he was consumed with anger at my lord's successful flight, felt himself to figure as a dupe, and was in no humour to weigh language.

'Do you consier *this* entirely wise?' said I, copying his words.

'These twenty years I have lived by my poor wisdom,' he answered with a smile that seemed almost foolish in its vanity.

'And come out a beggar in the end,' said I, 'if beggar be a strong enough word for it.'

'I would have you to observe, Mr. Mackellar,' cried he, with a sudden imperious heat, in which I could not but admire him, 'that I am scrupulously civil: copy me in that, and we shall be the better friends.'

Throughout this dialogue I had been incommoded by the observation of Secundra Dass. Not one of us, since the first word, had made a feint of eating: our eyes were in each other's faces— you might say, in each other's bosoms; and those of the Indian troubled me with a certain changing brightness, as of comprehension. But I brushed the fancy aside, telling myself once more he understood no English; only, from the gravity of both voices, and the occasional scorn and anger in the Master's, smelled out there was something of import in the wind.

For the matter of three weeks we continued to live together in the house of Durrisdeer: the beginning of that most singular chapter of my life—what I must call my intimacy with the Master. At first he was somewhat changeable in his behaviour: now civil, now returning to his old manner of flouting me to my face; and in both I met him half-way. Thanks be to Providence, I had now no measure to keep with the man; and I was never afraid of black brows, only of naked swords. So that I found a certain entertainment in these bouts of incivility, and was not always ill-inspired in my rejoinders. At last (it was at supper) I had a droll expression that entirely vanquished him. He laughed again and again; and 'Who would have guessed,' he cried, 'that this old wife had any wit under his petticoats?'

'It is no wit, Mr. Bally,' said I: 'a dry Scot's humour, and something of the driest.' And, indeed, I never had the least pretension to be thought a wit.

From that hour he was never rude with me, but all passed between us in a manner of pleasantry. One of our chief times of daffing[1] was when he required a horse, another bottle, or some money. He would approach me then after the manner of a schoolboy and I would carry it on by way of being his father: on both sides, with an infinity of mirth. I could not but perceive that he thought more of me, which tickled that poor part of mankind, the vanity. He dropped, besides (I must suppose unconsciously), into a manner that was not only familiar, but even friendly; and this on the part of one who had so long detested me, I found the more insidious. He went little abroad; sometimes even refusing invitations. 'No,' he would say, 'what do I care for these thick-headed bonnet-lairds. I will stay at home, Mackellar; and we shall share a bottle quietly, and have one of our good talks.' And, indeed, meal-time at Durrisdeer must have been a delight to any one, by reason of the brilliancy of the discourse. He would often express wonder at his former indifference to my society. 'But you see,' he would add, 'we were upon opposite sides. And so we are to-day; but let us never speak of that. I would think much less of you if you were not staunch to your employer.' You are to consider he seemed to me quite impotent for any evil; and how it is a most engaging form of flattery when (after many years) tardy justice is done to a man's character and parts. But I have no thought to excuse myself. I was to blame; I let him cajole me, and, in short, I think the watch-dog was going sound asleep, when he was suddenly aroused.

I should say the Indian was continually travelling to and fro in the house. He never spoke, save in his own dialect and with the Master; walked without sound; and was always turning up where you would least expect him, fallen into a deep abstraction, from which he would start (upon your coming) to mock you with one of his grovelling obeisances. He seemed so quiet, so frail, and so wrapped in his own fancies, that I came to pass him over without much regard, or even to pity him for a harmless exile from his country. And yet without doubt the creature was still eavesdropping; and without doubt it was through his stealth and my security that our secret reached the Master.

It was one very wild night, after supper, and when we had been making more than usually merry, that the blow fell on me.

'This is all very fine,' says the Master, 'but we should do better to be buckling our valise.'

'Why so?' I cried. 'Are you leaving?'

'We are all leaving to-morrow in the morning,' said he. 'For the port of Glasgow first, thence for the province of New York.'

1 Fooling.

I suppose I must have groaned aloud.

'Yes,' he continued, 'I boasted; I said a week, and it has taken me near twenty days. But never mind; I shall make it up; I will go the faster.'

'Have you the money for this voyage?' I asked.

'Dear and ingenuous personage, I have,' said he. 'Blame me, if you choose, for my duplicity; but while I have been wringing shillings from my daddy, I had a stock of my own put by against a rainy day. You will pay for your own passage, if you choose to accompany us on our flank march; I have enough for Secundra and myself, but not more—enough to be dangerous, not enough to be generous. There is, however, an outside seat upon the chaise which I will let you have upon a moderate commutation; so that the whole menagerie can go together— the housedog, the monkey, and the tiger.'

'I go with you,' said I.

'I count upon it,' said the Master. 'You have seen me foiled; I mean you shall see me victorious. To gain that I will risk wetting you like a sop in this wild weather.'

'And at least,' I added, 'you know very well you could not throw me off.'

'Not easily,' said he. 'You put your finger on the point with your usual excellent good sense. I never fight with the inevitable.'

'I suppose it is useless to appeal to you?' said I.

'Believe me, perfectly,' said he.

'And yet, if you would give me time, I could write——' I began.

'And what would be my Lord Durrisdeer's answer?' asks he.

'Ay,' said I, 'that is the rub.'

'And, at any rate, how much more expeditious that I should go myself!' says he. 'But all this is quite a waste of breath. At seven to-morrow the chaise will be at the door. For I start from the door, Mackellar; I do not skulk through woods and take my chaise upon the wayside—shall we say, at Engles?'

My mind was now thoroughly made up. 'Can you spare me a quarter of an hour at St. Bride's?' said I. 'I have a little necessary business with Carlyle.'

'An hour, if you prefer,' said he. 'I do not seek to deny that the money for your seat is an object to me; and you could always get the first to Glasgow with saddle-horses.'

'Well,' said I, 'I never thought to leave old Scotland.'

'It will brisken you up,' says he.

'This will be an ill journey for some one,' I said. 'I think, sir, for you. Something speaks in my bosom; and so much it says plain—that this is an ill-omened journey.'

' If you take to prophecy,' says he, ' listen to that.'

There came up a violent squall off the open Solway, and the rain was dashed on the great windows.

' Do ye ken what that bodes, warlock? ' said he, in a broad accent: ' that there'll be a man Mackellar unco' sick at sea.'

When I got to my chamber, I sat there under a painful excitation, hearkening to the turmoil of the gale, which struck full upon that gable of the house. What with the pressure on my spirits, the eldritch cries of the wind among the turret-tops, and the perpetual trepidation of the masoned house, sleep fled my eyelids utterly. I sat by my taper, looking on the black panes of the window, where the storm appeared continually on the point of bursting in its entrance; and upon that empty field I beheld a perspective of consequences that made the hair to rise upon my scalp. The child corrupted, the home broken up, my master dead or worse than dead, my mistress plunged in desolation—all these I saw before me painted brightly on the darkness; and the outcry of the wind appeared to mock at my inaction.

9

Mr. Mackellar's journey with the Master

THE chaise came to the door in a strong drenching mist. We took our leave in silence: the house of Durrisdeer standing with dropping gutters and windows closed, like a place dedicate to melancholy. I observed the Master kept his head out, looking back on these splashed walls and glimmering roofs, till they were suddenly swallowed in the mist; and I must suppose some natural sadness fell upon the man at this departure; or was it some pre-vision of the end? At least, upon our mounting the long brae from Durrisdeer, as we walked side by side in the wet, he began first to whistle and then to sing the saddest of our country tunes, which sets folk weeping in a tavern, *Wandering Willie*. The set of words he used with it I have not heard elsewhere, and could never come by any copy; but some of them which were the most appropriate to our departure linger in my memory. One verse began—

Home was home then, my dear, full of kindly faces;
Home was home then, my dear, happy for the child.

And ended somewhat thus—

> Now, when day dawns on the brow of the moorland,
>   Lone stands the house, and the chimney-stone is cold.
> Lone let it stand, now the folks are all departed,
>   The kind hearts, the true hearts, that loved the place of old.

I could never be a judge of the merit of these verses; they were so hallowed by the melancholy of the air, and were sung (or rather 'soothed') to me by a master-singer at a time so fitting. He looked in my face when he had done, and saw that my eyes watered.

'Ah! Mackellar,' said he, 'do you think I have never a regret?'

'I do not think you could be so bad a man,' said I, 'if you had not all the machinery to be a good one.'

'No, not all,' says he: 'not all. You are there in error. The malady of not wanting, my evangelist.' But methought he sighed as he mounted again into the chaise.

All day long we journeyed in the same miserable weather: the mist besetting us closely, the heavens incessantly weeping on my head. The road lay over moorish hills, where was no sound but the crying of moor-fowl in the wet heather and the pouring of the swollen burns. Sometimes I would doze off in slumber, when I would find myself plunged at once in some foul and ominous nightmare, from the which I would awake strangling. Sometimes, if the way was steep and the wheels turning slowly, I would overhear the voices from within, talking in that tropical tongue which was to me as inarticulate as the piping of the fowls. Sometimes, at a longer ascent, the Master would set foot to ground and walk by my side, mostly without speech. And all the time, sleeping or waking, I beheld the same black perspective of approaching ruin; and the same pictures rose in my view, only they were now painted upon hillside mist. One, I remember, stood before me with the colours of a true illusion. It showed me my lord seated at a table in a small room; his head, which was at first buried in his hands, he slowly raised, and turned upon me a countenance from which hope had fled. I saw it first on the black window-panes, my last night in Durrisdeer; it haunted and returned upon me half the voyage through; and yet it was no effect of lunacy, for I have come to a ripe old age with no decay of my intelligence; nor yet (as I was then tempted to suppose) a heaven-sent warning of the future, for all manner of calamities befell, not that calamity—and I saw many pitiful sights, but never that one.

It was decided we should travel on all night; and it was singular, once the dusk had fallen, my spirits somewhat rose. The bright lamps, shining forth into the mist and on the smoking horses and the hodding post-boy, gave me perhaps an outlook intrinsically more cheerful than what day had shown; or perhaps my mind had become wearied of its melancholy. At least, I spent some waking hours, not without satisfaction in my thoughts, although wet and weary in my body; and fell at last into a natural slumber without dreams. Yet I must have been at work even in the deepest of my sleep; and at work with at least a measure of intelligence. For I started broad awake, in the very act of crying out to myself

Home was home then, my dear, happy for the child,

stricken to find in it an appropriateness, which I had not yesterday observed, to the Master's detestable purpose in the present journey.

We were then close upon the city of Glasgow, where we were soon breakfasting together at an inn, and where (as the devil would have it) we found a ship in the very article of sailing. We took our places in the cabin; and, two days after, carried our effects on board. Her name was the *Nonesuch*, a very ancient ship and very happily named. By all accounts this should be her last voyage; people shook their heads upon the quays, and I had several warnings offered me by strangers in the street to the effect that she was rotten as a cheese, too deeply loaden, and must infallibly founder if we met a gale. From this it fell out we were the only passengers; the Captain, McMurtrie, was a silent, absorbed man, with the Glasgow or Gaelic accent; the mates ignorant rough seafarers, come in through the hawsehole; and the Master and I were cast upon each other's company.

The *Nonesuch* carried a fair wind out of the Clyde, and for near upon a week we enjoyed bright weather and a sense of progress. I found myself (to my wonder) a born seaman, in so far at least as I was never sick; yet I was far from tasting the usual serenity of my health. Whether it was the motion of the ship on the billows, the confinement, the salted food, or all of these together, I suffered from a blackness of spirit and a painful strain upon my temper. The nature of my errand on that ship perhaps contributed; I think it did no more; the malady (whatever it was) sprang from my environment; and if the ship were not to blame, then it was the Master. Hatred and fear are ill bedfellows; but (to my shame be it spoken) I have tasted those in other places, lain down and got up with them, and eaten and drunk with them, and yet never before, nor after, have I been so poisoned through and through, in soul and body, as I was on board the *Nonesuch*. I freely confess my enemy set me a fair example of forbearance; in our worst days displayed the most patient geniality, holding me in conversation as long as I would suffer, and when I had rebuffed his civility, stretching himself on deck to read. The book he had on board with him was Mr. Richardson's famous *Clarissa*, and among other small attentions he would read me passages aloud; nor could any elocutionist have given with greater potency the pathetic portions of that work. I would retort upon him with passages out of the Bible, which was all my library—and very fresh to me, my religious duties (I grieve to say it) being always and even to this day extremely neglected. He tasted the merits of the work like the connoisseur he was; and would sometimes take it from my hand, turn the leaves over like a man that knew his way, and give me, with his fine declamation, a Roland for my Oliver. But it was singular how little he applied his reading to himself; it passed high above his head like summer thunder: Lovelace and Clarissa, the tales of David's generosity, the psalms of his penitence, the solemn questions of the book of Job, the touching poetry of Isaiah—they were to him a source of entertainment only, like the scraping of a fiddle in a change-house. This outer sensibility and inner toughness set me against him; it seemed of a piece with that impudent grossness which I knew to underlie the veneer of his fine manners; and sometimes my gorge rose against him as though he were deformed—and sometimes I would draw away as though from something partly spectral. I had moments when I thought of him as of a man of pasteboard—as though, if one should strike smartly through the buckram of his countenance, there would be found a mere vacuity within. This horror (not merely fanciful, I think), vastly increased my detestation of his neighbourhood; I began to feel something shiver within me on his drawing near; I had at times a longing to cry out; there were days when I thought I would have struck him. This frame of mind was doubtless helped by shame, because I had dropped during our last days at Durrisdeer into a certain toleration of the man; and if any one had then told me I should drop into it again, I must have laughed in his face. It is possible he remained unconscious of this extreme fever of my resentment; yet I think he was too quick; and rather that he had fallen, in a long life of idleness, into a positive need of company, which obliged him to confront and tolerate my unconcealed aversion. Certain, at least, that he loved the note of his own tongue, as, indeed, he entirely loved all the parts and properties of himself; a sort of imbecility which almost necessarily attends on wickedness. I have seen him driven, when I proved recalcitrant, to long discourses with the skipper; and this, although the man plainly testified his weariness, fiddling miserably with both hand and foot, and replying only with a grunt.

After the first week out we fell in with foul winds and heavy weather. The sea was high. The *Nonesuch*, being an old-fashioned ship and badly loaden, rolled beyond belief; so that the skipper trembled for his masts, and I for my life. We made no progress on our course. An unbearable ill-humour settled on the ship: men, mates, and masters, girding at one another all day long. A saucy word on the one hand, and a blow on the other, made a daily incident. There were times when the whole crew refused their duty; and we of the afterguard were twice got under arms —being the first time that ever I bore weapons—in the fear of mutiny.

In the midst of our evil season sprang up a hurricane of wind; so that all supposed she must go down. I was shut in the cabin from noon of one day till sundown of the next: the Master was somewhere lashed on deck. Secundra had eaten of some drug and lay insensible; so you may say I passed these hours in an unbroken solitude. At first I was terrified beyond motion, and almost beyond thought, my mind appearing to be frozen. Presently there stole in on me a ray of comfort. If the *Nonesuch* foundered, she would carry down with her into the deeps of that unsounded sea the creature whom we all so feared and hated; there would be no more Master of Ballantrae; the fish would sport among his ribs; his schemes all brought to nothing, his harmless enemies at peace. At first, I have said, it was but a ray of comfort; but it had soon grown to be broad sunshine. The thought of the man's death, of his deletion from this world, which he embittered for so many, took possession of my mind. I hugged it, I found it sweet in my belly. I conceived the ship's last plunge, the sea bursting upon all sides into the cabin, the brief mortal conflict there, all by myself, in that closed place; I numbered the horrors, I had almost said with satisfaction; I felt I could bear all and more, if the *Nonesuch* carried down with her, overtook by the same ruin, the enemy of my poor master's house. Towards noon of the second day the screaming of the wind abated; the ship lay not so perilously over, and it began to be clear to me that we were past the height of the tempest. As I hope for mercy, I was singly disappointed. In the selfishness of that vile, absorbing passion of hatred, I forgot the case of our innocent shipmates, and thought but of myself and my enemy. For myself, I was already old; I had never been young, I was not formed for the world's pleasures I had few affections; it mattered not the toss of a silver tester whether I was drowned there and then in the Atlantic, or dribbled out a few more years, to die, perhaps no less terribly, in a deserted sick-bed. Down I went upon my knees—holding on by the locker, or else I had been instantly dashed across the tossing cabin—and, lifting up my voice in the midst of that clamour of the abating hurricane, impiously prayed for my own death. ' O God! ' I cried, ' I would be liker a man if I rose and struck this creature down; but Thou madest me a coward from my mother's womb. O Lord, Thou madest me so, Thou knowest my weakness, Thou knowest that any face of death will set me shaking in my shoes. But, lo! here is Thy servant ready, his mortal weakness laid aside. Let me give my life for this creature's; take the two of them, Lord! take the two, and have mercy on the innocent! ' In some such words as these, only yet more irreverent and with more sacred adjurations, I continued to pour forth my spirit. God heard me not, I must suppose in mercy; and I was still absorbed in my agony of supplication when some one, removing the tarpaulin cover, let the light of the sunset pour into the cabin. I stumbled to my feet ashamed and was seized with surprise to find myself totter and ache like one that had been stretched upon the rack. Secundra Dass, who had slept off the effects of his drug, stood in a corner not far off, gazing at me with wild eyes; and from the open skylight the captain thanked me for my supplications.

' It's you that's saved the ship, Mr. Mackellar,' says he. ' There is no craft of seamanship that could have kept her floating: well may we say, " Except the Lord the city keep, the watchmen watch in vain! " '

I was abashed by the captain's error; abashed, also, by the surprise and fear with which the Indian regarded me at first, and the obsequious civilities with which he soon began to cumber me. I know now that he must have overheard and comprehended the peculiar nature of my prayers. It is certain, of course, that he at once disclosed the matter to his patron; and looking back with greater knowledge, I can now understand what so much puzzled me at the moment, those singular and (so to speak) approving smiles with which the Master honoured me. Similarly, I can understand a word that I remember to have

fallen from him in conversation that same night; when, holding
up his hand and smiling, 'Ah! Mackellar,' said he, 'not every
man is so great a coward as he thinks he is—nor yet so good a
Christian.' He did not guess how true he spoke! For the fact
is, the thoughts which had come to me in the violence of the
storm retained their hold upon my spirit; and the words that
rose to my lips unbidden in the instancy of prayer continued to
sound in my ears: with what shameful consequences it is fitting
I should honestly relate; for I could not support a part of such
disloyalty as to describe the sins of others and conceal my own.

The wind fell, but the sea hove ever the higher. All night the
Nonesuch rolled outrageously; the next day dawned, and the
next, and brought no change. To cross the cabin was scarce possible; old experienced seamen were cast down upon the deck,
and one cruelly mauled in the concussion; every board and block
in the old ship cried out aloud; and the great bell by the anchor-
bitts continually and dolefully rang. One of these days the Master
and I sate alone together at the break of the poop. I should say
the *Nonesuch* carried a high-raised poop. About the top of it
ran considerable bulwarks, which made the ship unweatherly;
and these, as they approached the front on each side, ran down
in a fine, old-fashioned, carven scroll to join the bulwarks of the
waist. From this disposition, which seems designed rather for
ornament than use, it followed there was a discontinuance of
protection: and that, besides, at the very margin of the elevated
part where (in certain movements of the ship) it might be the
most needful. It was here we were sitting: our feet hanging down,
the Master betwixt me and the side, and I holding on with both
hands to the grating of the cabin skylight; for it struck me it
was a dangerous position, the more so as I had continually before
my eyes a measure of our evolutions in the person of the Master,
which stood out in the break of the bulwarks against the sun.
Now his head would be in the zenith and his shadow fall quite
beyond the *Nonesuch* on the farther side; and now he would
swing down till he was underneath my feet, and the line of the
sea leaped high above him like the ceiling of a room. I looked
on upon this with a growing fascination, as birds are said to
look on snakes. My mind, besides, was troubled with an astonishing diversity of noises; for now that we had all sails spread in
the vain hope to bring her to the sea, the ship sounded like a
factory with their reverberations. We spoke first of the mutiny
with which we had been threatened; this led us on to the topic
of assassination; and that offered a temptation to the Master
more strong than he was able to resist. He must tell me a tale,

and show me at the same time how clever he was and how wicked. It was a thing he did always with affectation and display; generally with a good effect. But this tale, told in a high key in the midst of so great a tumult, and by a narrator who was one moment looking down at me from the skies and the next peering up from under the soles of my feet—this particular tale, I say, took hold upon me in a degree quite singular.

'My friend the count,' it was thus that he began his story, 'had for an enemy a certain German baron, a stranger in Rome. It matters not what was the ground of the count's enmity; but as he had a firm design to be revenged, and that with safety to himself, he kept it secret even from the baron. Indeed, that is the first principle of vengeance; and hatred betrayed is hatred impotent. The count was a man of a curious, searching mind; he had something of the artist; if anything fell for him to do, it must always be done with an exact perfection, not only as to the result, but in the very means and instruments, or he thought the thing miscarried. It chanced he was one day riding in the outer suburbs, when he came to a disused by-road branching off into the moor which lies about Rome. On the one hand was an ancient Roman tomb; on the other a deserted house in a garden of evergreen trees. This road brought him presently into a field of ruins, in the midst of which, in the side of a hill, he saw an open door, and, not far off, a single stunted pine no greater than a currant-bush. The place was desert and very secret; a voice spoke in the count's bosom that there was something here to his advantage. He tied his horse to the pine-tree, took his flint and steel in his hand to make a light, and entered into the hill. The doorway opened on a passage of old Roman masonry, which shortly after branched in two. The count took the turning to the right, and followed it, groping forward in the dark, till he was brought up by a kind of fence, about elbow high, which extended quite across the passage. Sounding forward with his foot, he found an edge of polished stone, and then vacancy. All his curiosity was now awakened, and, getting some rotten sticks that lay about the floor, he made a fire. In front of him was a profound well; doubtless some neighbouring peasant had once used it for his water, and it was he that had set up the fence. A long while the count stood leaning on the rail and looking down into the pit. It was of Roman foundation, and, like all that nation set their hands to, built as for eternity; the sides were still straight, and the joints smooth; to a man who should fall in no escape was possible. "Now," the count was thinking, " a strong impulsion brought me to this place. What for? what

have I gained? why should I be sent to gaze into this well?"
when the rail of the fence gave suddenly under his weight, and
he came within an ace of falling headlong in. Leaping back to
save himself, he trod out the last flicker of his fire, which gave
him thenceforward no more light, only an incommoding smoke.
"Was I sent here to my death?" says he, and shook from head to
foot. And then a thought flashed in his mind. He crept forth
on hands and knees to the brink of the pit, and felt above him
in the air. The rail had been fast to a pair of uprights; it had
only broken from the one, and still depended from the other.
The count set it back again as he had found it, so that the place
meant death to the first comer, and groped out of the catacomb
like a sick man. The next day, riding in the Corso with the baron,
he purposely betrayed a stronger preoccupation. The other (as
he had designed) inquired into the cause; and he, after some
fencing, admitted that his spirits had been dashed by an unusual
dream. This was calculated to draw on the baron—a superstitious man, who affected the scorn of superstition. Some
rallying followed, and then the count, as if suddenly carried
away, called on his friend to beware, for it was of him that he had
dreamed. You know enough of human nature, my excellent
Mackellar, to be certain of one thing: I mean that the baron did
not rest till he had heard the dream. The count, sure that he
would never desist, kept him in play till his curiosity was highly
inflamed, and then suffered himself, with seeming reluctance, to
be overborne. "I warn you," says he, "evil will come of it;
something tells me so. But since there is to be no peace either
for you or me except on this condition, the blame be on your
own head! This was the dream: I beheld you riding, I know
not where, yet I think it must have been near Rome, for on
your one hand was an ancient tomb, and on the other a garden
of evergreen trees. Methought I cried and cried upon you to
come back in a very agony of terror; whether you heard me I
know not, but you went doggedly on. The road brought you
to a desert place among ruins, where was a door in a hillside,
and hard by the door a misbegotten pine. Here you dismounted
(I still crying on you to beware), tied your horse to the pine-tree,
and entered resolutely in by the door. Within, it was dark; but
in my dream I could still see you and still besought you to hold
back. You felt your way along the right-hand wall, took a
branching passage to the right, and came to a little chamber,
where was a well with a railing. At this—I know not why—my
alarm for you increased a thousandfold, so that I seemed to
scream myself hoarse with warnings, crying it was still time, and

bidding you begone at once from that vestibule. Such was the word I used in my dream, and it seemed then to have a clear significancy; but to-day, and awake, I profess I know not what it means. To all my outcry you rendered not the least attention, leaning the while upon the rail and looking down intently in the water. And then there was made to you a communication; I do not think I even gathered what it was, but the fear of it plucked me clean out of my slumber, and I awoke shaking and sobbing. And now," continues the count, " I thank you from my heart for your insistency. This dream lay on me like a load; and now I have told it in plain words and in the broad daylight, it seems no great matter."—" I do not know," says the baron. " It is in some points strange. A communication, did you say? Oh, it is an odd dream. It will make a story to amuse our friends." —" I am not sure," says the count. " I am sensible of some reluctancy. Let us rather forget it."—" By all means," says the baron. And (in fact) the dream was not again referred to. Some days after the count proposed a ride in the fields, which the baron (since they were daily growing faster friends) very readily accepted. On the way back to Rome, the count led them insensibly by a particular route. Presently he reined in his horse, clapped his hand before his eyes, and cried out aloud. Then he showed his face again (which was now quite white, for he was a consummate actor), and stared upon the baron. " What ails you? " cries the baron. " What is wrong with you? "—" Nothing," cries the count. " It is nothing. A seizure, I know not what. Let us hurry back to Rome." But in the meanwhile the baron had looked about him, and there, on the left hand side of the way as they went back to Rome, he saw a dusty by-road with a tomb upon the one hand and a garden of evergreen trees upon the other.—" Yes," says he, with a changed voice. " Let us by all means hurry back to Rome. I fear you are not well in health." —" Oh, for God's sake! " cries the count, shuddering, " back to Rome and let me get to bed." They made their return with scarce a word; and the count, who should by rights have gone into society, took to his bed and gave out he had a touch of country fever. The next day the baron's horse was found tied to the pine, but himself was never heard of from that hour.—And, now, was that a murder? ' says the Master, breaking sharply off.

' Are you sure he was a count? ' I asked.

' I am not certain of the title,' said he, ' but he was a gentleman of family: and the Lord deliver you, Mackellar, from an enemy so subtile! '

These last words he spoke down at me, smiling, from high

above; the next, he was under my feet. I continued to follow his evolutions with a childish fixity; they made me giddy and vacant, and I spoke as in a dream.

'He hated the baron with a great hatred?' I asked.

'His belly moved when the man came near him,' said the Master.

'I have felt that same,' said I.

'Verily!' cries the Master. 'Here is news indeed! I wonder—do I flatter myself? or am I the cause of these ventral perturbations?'

He was quite capable of choosing out a graceful posture, even with no one to behold him but myself, and all the more if there were any element of peril. He sat now with one knee flung across the other, his arms on his bosom, fitting the swing of the ship with an exquisite balance, such as a featherweight might overthrow. All at once I had the vision of my lord at the table, with his head upon his hands: only now, when he showed me his countenance, it was heavy with reproach. The words of my own prayer—*I were liker a man if I struck this creature down*—shot at the same time into my memory. I called my energies together and (the ship then heeling downward toward my enemy) thrust at him swiftly with my foot. It was written I should have the guilt of this attempt without the profit. Whether from my own uncertainty or his incredible quickness, he escaped the thrust, leaping to his feet and catching hold at the same moment of a stay.

I do not know how long a time passed by: I lying where I was upon the deck, overcome with terror and remorse and shame: he standing with the stay in his hand, backed against the bulwarks, and regarding me with an expression singularly mingled. At last he spoke.

'Mackellar,' said he, 'I make no reproaches, but I offer you a bargain. On your side, I do not suppose you desire to have this exploit made public; on mine, I own to you freely I do not care to draw my breath in a perpetual terror of assassination by the man I sit at meat with. Promise me—but no,' says he, breaking off, 'you are not yet in the quiet possession of your mind; you might think I had extorted the promise from your weakness; and I would leave no door open for casuistry to come in—that dishonesty of the conscientious. Take time to meditate.'

With that he made off up the sliding deck like a squirrel, and plunged into the cabin. About half an hour later he returned—I still lying as he had left me.

'Now,' says he, 'will you give me your troth as a Christian, and a faithful servant of my brother's, that I shall have no more to fear from your attempts?'

'I give it you,' said I.

'I shall require your hand upon it,' says he.

'You have the right to make conditions,' I replied, and we shook hands.

He sat down at once in the same place and the old perilous attitude.

'Hold on!' cried I, covering my eyes. 'I cannot bear to see you in that posture. The least irregularity of the sea might plunge you overboard.'

'You are highly inconsistent,' he replied, smiling, but doing as I asked. 'For all that, Mackellar, I would have you to know you have risen forty feet in my esteem. You think I cannot set a price upon fidelity? But why do you suppose I carry that Secundra Dass about the world with me? Because he would die or do murder for me to-morrow; and I love him for it. Well, you may think it odd, but I like you the better for this afternoon's performance. I thought you were magnetised with the Ten Commandments; but no—God damn my soul!'—he cries, 'the old wife has blood in his body after all! Which does not change the fact,' he continued, smiling again, 'that you have done well to give your promise; for I doubt if you would ever shine in your new trade.'

'I suppose,' said I, 'I should ask your pardon and God's for my attempt. At any rate, I have passed my word, which I will keep faithfully. But when I think of those you persecute —— ' I paused.

'Life is a singular thing,' said he, 'and mankind a very singular people. You suppose yourself to love my brother. I assure you, it is merely custom. Interrogate your memory; and when first you came to Durrisdeer, you will find you considered him a dull, ordinary youth. He is as dull and ordinary now, though not so young. Had you instead fallen in with me, you would to-day be as strong upon my side.'

'I would never say you were ordinary, Mr. Bally,' I returned; 'but here you prove yourself dull. You have just shown your reliance on my word. In other terms, that is my conscience—the same which starts instinctively back from you, like the eye from a strong light.'

'Ah!' says he, 'but I mean otherwise. I mean, had I met you in my youth. You are to consider I was not always as I am to-day; nor (had I met in with a friend of your description) should I have ever been so.'

'But, Mr. Bally,' says I, 'you would have made a mock of me; you would never have spent ten civil words on such a Square-toes.'

But he was now fairly started on his new course of justification, with which he wearied me throughout the remainder of the passage. No doubt in the past he had taken pleasure to paint himself unnecessarily black, and made a vaunt of his wickedness, bearing it for a coat-of-arms. Nor was he so illogical as to abate one item of his old confessions. 'But now that I know you are a human being,' he would say, 'I can take the trouble to explain myself. For I assure you I am human, too, and have my virtues, like my neighbours.' I say, he wearied me, for I had only the one word to say in answer: twenty times I must have said it. 'Give up your present purpose and return with me to Durrisdeer; then I will believe you.'

Thereupon he would shake his head at me. 'Ah! Mackellar, you might live a thousand years and never understand my nature,' he would say. 'This battle is now committed, the hour of reflection quite past, the hour for mercy not yet come. It began between us when we span a coin in the hall of Durrisdeer, now twenty years ago; we have had our ups and downs, but never either of us dreamed of giving in; and as for me, when my glove is cast, life and honour go with it.'

'A fig for your honour!' I would say. 'And by your leave, these warlike similitudes are something too high-sounding for the matter in hand. You want some dirty money; there is the bottom of your contention; and as for your means, what are they? to stir up sorrow in a family that never harmed you, to debauch (if you can) your own nephew, and to wring the heart of your born brother! A footpad that kills an old granny in a woollen-mutch with a dirty bludgeon, and that for a shilling-piece and a paper of snuff—there is all the warrior that you are.'

When I would attack him thus (or somewhat thus) he would smile, and sigh like a man misunderstood. Once, I remember, he defended himself more at large, and had some curious sophistries, worth repeating, for a light upon his character.

'You are very like a civilian to think war consists in drums and banners,' said he. 'War (as the ancients said very wisely) is *ultima ratio*. When we take our advantage unrelentingly, then we make war. Ah! Mackellar, you are a devil of a soldier in the steward's room at Durrisdeer, or the tenants do you sad injustice.'

'I think little of what war is or is not,' I replied. 'But you weary me with claiming my respect. Your brother is a good man, and you are a bad one—neither more nor less.'

'Had I been Alexander——' he began.

'It is so we all dupe ourselves,' I cried. 'Had I been St. Paul, it would have been all one; I would have made the same hash of that career, that you now see me making of my own.'

'I tell you,' he cried, bearing down my interruption; 'had I been the least petty chieftain in the Highlands, had I been the least king of naked negroes in the African desert, my people would have adored me. A bad man, am I? Ah! but I was born for a good tyrant! Ask Secundra Dass; he will tell you I treat him like a son. Cast in your lot with me to-morrow, become my slave, my chattel, a thing I can command as I command the powers of my own limbs and spirit—you will see no more that dark side that I turn upon the world in anger. I must have all or none. But where all is given, I give it back with usury. I have a kingly nature: there is my loss!'

'It has been hitherto rather the loss of others,' I remarked, 'which seems a little on the hither side of royalty.'

'Tilly-vally!' cried he. 'Even now, I tell you, I would spare that family in which you take so great an interest: yes, even now —to-morrow I would leave them to their petty warfare, and disappear in that forest of cut-throats and thimble-riggers that we call the world. I would do it to-morrow!' says he. 'Only— only——'

'Only what?' I asked.

'Only they must beg it on their bended knees. I think in public too,' he added, smiling. 'Indeed, Mackellar, I doubt if there be a hall big enough to serve my purpose for that act of reparation.'

'Vanity, vanity!' I moralised. 'To think that this great force for evil should be swayed by the same sentiment that sets a lassie mincing to her glass!'

'Oh! there are double words for everything: the word that swells, the word that belittles; you cannot fight me with a word!' said he. 'You said the other day that I relied on your conscience: were I in your humour of detraction, I might say I built upon your vanity. It is your pretension to be *un homme de parole*; 'tis mine not to accept defeat. Call it vanity, call it virtue, call it greatness of soul—what signifies the expression? But recognise in each of us a common strain: that we both live for an idea.'

It will be gathered from so much familiar talk, and so much patience on both sides, that we now lived together upon excellent terms. Such was again the fact, and this time more seriously than before. Apart from disputations such as that which I have tried to reproduce, not only consideration reigned, but, I am tempted to say, even kindness. When I fell sick (as I did shortly after our great storm), he sat by my berth to entertain me with his conversation, and treated me with excellent remedies, which I accepted with security. Himself commented on the circumstance. ' You see,' says he, ' you begin to know me better. A very little while ago, upon this lonely ship, where no one but myself has any smattering of science, you would have made sure I had designs upon your life. And, observe, it is since I found you had designs upon my own, that I have shown you most respect. You will tell me if this speaks of a small mind.' I found little to reply. In so far as regarded myself, I believed him to mean well; I am, perhaps, the more a dupe of his dissimulation, but I believed (and I still believe) that he regarded me with genuine kindness. Singular and sad fact. so soon as this change began, my animosity abated, and these haunting visions of my master passed utterly away. So that, perhaps, there was truth in the man's last vaunting word to me, uttered on the second day of July, when our long voyage was at last brought almost to an end, and we lay becalmed at the sea end of the vast harbour of New York, in a gasping heat, which was presently exchanged for a surprising waterfall of rain. I stood on the poop, regarding the green shores near at hand, and now and then the light smoke of the little town, our destination. And as I was even then devising how to steal a march on my familiar enemy, I was conscious of a shade of embarrassment when he approached me with his hand extended.

' I am now to bid you farewell,' said he, ' and that for ever. For now you go among my enemies, where all your former prejudices will revive. I never yet failed to charm a person when I wanted; even you, my good friend—to call you so for once— even you have now a very different portrait of me in your memory, and one that you will never quite forget. The voyage has not lasted long enough, or I should have wrote the impression deeper. But now all is at an end, and we are again at war. Judge by this little interlude how dangerous I am; and tell those fools,'—pointing with his finger to the town—' to think twice and thrice before they set me at defiance.'

I have mentioned I was resolved to steal a march upon the Master; and this, with the complicity of Captain McMurtrie, was mightily easily effected: a boat being partly loaded on the one side of our ship and the Master placed on board of it, the while a skiff put off from the other, carrying me alone. I had no more trouble in finding a direction to my lord's house, whither I went at top speed, and which I found to be on the outskirts of the place, a very suitable mansion, in a fine garden, with an extraordinary large barn, byre, and stable, all in one. It was here my lord was walking when I arrived; indeed, it had become his chief place of frequentation, and his mind was now filled with farming. I burst in upon him breathless, and gave him my news: which was, indeed, no news at all, several ships having outsailed the *Nonesuch* in the interval.

'We have been expecting you long,' said my lord; 'and indeed, of late days, ceased to expect you any more. I am glad to take your hand again, Mackellar. I thought you had been at the bottom of the sea.'

'Ah! my lord, would God I had!' cried I. 'Things would have been better for yourself.'

'Not in the least,' says he, grimly. 'I could not ask better. There is a long score to pay, and now—at last—I can begin to pay it.'

I cried out against his security.

'Oh!' says he, 'this is not Durrisdeer, and I have taken my precautions. His reputation awaits him; I have prepared a welcome for my brother. Indeed, fortune has served me; for I found here a merchant of Albany who knew him after the '45 and had mighty convenient suspicions of a murder: some one of the name of Chew it was, another Albanian. No one here will be surprised if I deny him my door; he will not be suffered to address my children, nor even to salute my wife: as for myself, I make so much exception for a brother that he may speak to me. I should lose my pleasure else,' says my lord, rubbing his palms.

Presently he bethought himself, and set men off running, with billets, to summon the magnates of the province. I cannot recall what pretext he employed; at least, it was successful; and when our ancient enemy appeared upon the scene, he found my lord pacing in front of his house under some trees of shade, with the

Governor upon one hand, and various notables upon the
other. My lady, who was seated in the verandah, rose with
a very pinched expression and carried her children into the
house.

The Master, well dressed and with an elegant walking-sword,
bowed to the company in a handsome manner and nodded to
my lord with familiarity. My lord did not accept the salutation
but looked upon his brother with bended brows.

' Well, sir,' says he, at last, ' what ill wind brings you hither
of all places, where (to our common disgrace) your reputation
has preceded you? '

' Your lordship is pleased to be civil,' cries the Master, with
a fine start.

' I am pleased to be very plain,' returned my lord; ' because
it is needful you should clearly understand your situation. At
home, where you were so little known, it was still possible to
keep appearances; that would be quite vain in this province;
and I have to tell you that I am quite resolved to wash my hands
of you. You have already ruined me almost to the door, as you
ruined my father before me—whose heart you also broke. Your
crimes escape the law; but my friend the Governor has promised
protection to my family. Have a care, sir! ' cries my lord, shaking
his cane at him; ' if you are observed to utter two words to any
of my innocent household, the law shall be stretched to make
you smart for it.'

' Ah! ' says the Master, very slowly. ' And so this is the
advantage of a foreign land! These gentlemen are unacquainted
with our story, I perceive. They do not know that I am the Lord
Durrisdeer; they do not know you are my younger brother,
sitting in my place under a sworn family compact; they do not
know (or they would not be seen with you in familiar correspondence) that every acre is mine before God Almighty—and
every doit of the money you withhold from me, you do it as a
thief, a perjurer, and a disloyal brother! '

' General Clinton,' I cried, ' do not listen to his lies. I am
the steward of the estate, and there is not one word of truth in
it. The man is a forfeited rebel turned into a hired spy: there
is his story in two words.'

It was thus that (in the heat of the moment) I let slip his
infamy.

' Fellow,' said the Governor, turning his face sternly on the
Master, ' I know more of you than you think for. We have
some broken ends of your adventures in the provinces, which
you will do very well not to drive me to investigate. There is

the disappearance of Mr. Jacob Chew with all his merchandise; there is the matter of where you came ashore from with so much money and jewels, when you were picked up by a Bermudan out of Albany. Believe me, if I let these matters lie, it is in commiseration for your family and out of respect for my valued friend, Lord Durrisdeer.'

There was a murmur of applause from the provincials.

' I should have remembered how a title would shine out in such a hole as this,' says the Master, white as a sheet: ' no matter how unjustly come by. It remains for me, then, to die at my lord's door, where my dead body will form a very cheerful ornament.'

' Away with your affectations!' cries my lord. ' You know very well I have no such meaning; only to protect myself from calumny, and my home from your intrusion. I offer you a choice. Either I shall pay your passage home on the first ship, when you may perhaps be able to resume your occupations under Government, although God knows I would rather see you on the highway! Or, if that likes you not, stay here and welcome! I have inquired the least sum on which body and soul can be decently kept together in New York; so much you shall have, paid weekly; and if you cannot labour with your hands to better it, high time you should betake yourself to learn. The condition is—that you speak with no member of my family except myself,' he added.

I do not think I have ever seen any man so pale as was the Master; but he was erect and his mouth firm.

' I have been met here with some very unmerited insults,' said he, ' from which I have certainly no idea to take refuge by flight. Give me your pittance; I take it without shame, for it is mine already—like the shirt upon your back; and I choose to stay until these gentlemen shall understand me better. Already they must spy the cloven hoof, since with all your pretended eagerness for the family honour, you take a pleasure to degrade it in my person.'

' This is all very fine,' says my lord: ' but to us who know you of old, you must be sure it signifies nothing. You take that alternative out of which you think that you can make the most. Take it, if you can, in silence; it will serve you better in the long run, you may believe me, than this ostentation of ingratitude.'

' Oh, gratitude, my lord,' cries the Master, with a mounting intonation and his forefinger very conspicuously lifted up. ' Be at rest: it will not fail you. It now remains that I should salute these gentlemen whom we have wearied with our family affairs.'

And he bowed to each in succession, settled his walking-sword, and took himself off, leaving everyone amazed at his behaviour, and me not less so at my lord's.

We were now to enter on a changed phase of this family division. The Master was by no manner of means so helpless as my lord supposed, having at his hand, and entirely devoted to his service, an excellent artist in all sorts of goldsmith work. With my lord's allowance, which was not so scanty as he had described it, the pair could support life; and all the earnings of Secundra Dass might be laid upon one side for any future purpose. That this was done, I have no doubt. It was in all likelihood the Master's design to gather a sufficiency, and then proceed in quest of that treasure which he had buried long before among the mountains; to which, if he had confined himself, he would have been more happily inspired. But unfortunately for himself and all of us, he took counsel of his anger. The public disgrace of his arrival—which I sometimes wonder he could manage to survive—rankled in his bones; he was in that humour when a man—in the words of the old adage—will cut off his nose to spite his face; and he must make himself a public spectacle in the hopes that some of the disgrace might spatter on my lord.

He chose, in a poor quarter of the town, a lonely, small house of boards, overhung with some acacias. It was furnished in front with a sort of hutch opening, like that of a dog's kennel, but about as high as a table from the ground, in which the poor man that built it had formerly displayed some wares; and it was this which took the Master's fancy and possibly suggested his proceedings. It appears, on board the pirate ship he had acquired some quickness with the needle—enough, at least, to play the part of tailor in the public eye; which was all that was required by the nature of his vengeance. A placard was hung above the hutch, bearing these words in something of the following disposition:

JAMES DURIE,
FORMERLY MASTER OF BALLANTRAE.
CLOTHES NEATLY CLOUTED.

———

SECUNDRA DASS,
DECAYED GENTLEMAN OF INDIA.
FINE GOLDSMITH WORK.

Underneath this, when he had a job, my gentleman sat within-side tailorwise and busily stitching. I say, when he had a job; but such customers as came were rather for Secundra, and the

Master's sewing would be more in the manner of Penelope's. He could never have designed to gain even butter to his bread by such a means of livelihood: enough for him that there was the name of Durie dragged in the dirt on the placard, and the sometime heir of that proud family set up cross-legged in public for a reproach upon his brother's meanness. And in so far his device succeeded that there was murmuring in the town and a party formed highly inimical to my lord. My lord's favour with the Governor laid him more open on the other side; my lady (who was never so well received in the colony) met with painful innuendoes; in a party of women, where it would be the topic most natural to introduce, she was almost debarred from the naming of needle-work; and I have seen her return with a flushed countenance and avow that she would go abroad no more.

In the meanwhile my lord dwelled in his decent mansion, immersed in farming; a popular man with his intimates, and careless or unconscious of the rest. He laid on flesh; had a bright, busy face; even the heat seemed to prosper with him; and my lady—in despite of her own annoyances—daily blessed Heaven her father should have left her such a paradise. She had looked on from a window upon the Master's humiliation; and from that hour appeared to feel at ease. I was not so sure myself; as time went on there seemed to me a something not quite wholesome in my lord's condition. Happy he was, beyond a doubt, but the grounds of this felicity were secret; even in the bosom of his family he brooded with manifest delight upon some private thought; and I conceived at last the suspicion (quite unworthy of us both) that he kept a mistress somewhere in the town. Yet he went little abroad, and his day was very fully occupied; indeed, there was but a single period, and that pretty early in the morning, while Mr. Alexander was at his lesson-book, of which I was not certain of the disposition. It should be borne in mind, in the defence of that which I now did, that I was always in some fear my lord was not quite justly in his reason; and with our enemy sitting so still in the same town with us, I did well to be upon my guard. Accordingly I made a pretext, had the hour changed at which I taught Mr. Alexander the foundation of cyphering and the mathematic, and set myself instead to dog my master's footsteps.

Every morning, fair or foul, he took his gold-headed cane, set his hat on the back of his head—a recent habitude, which I thought to indicate a burning brow—and betook himself to make a certain circuit. At the first his way was among pleasant trees and beside a graveyard, where he would sit awhile, if the day were fine, in meditation. Presently the path turned down to the waterside, and came back along the harbour-front and past the Master's booth. As he approached this second part of his circuit, my Lord Durrisdeer began to pace more leisurely, like a man delighted with the air and scene; and before the booth, half-way between that and the water's edge, would pause a little, leaning on his staff. It was the hour when the Master sate within upon his board and plied his needle. So these two brothers would gaze upon each other with hard faces; and then my lord move on again, smiling to himself.

It was but twice that I must stoop to that ungrateful necessity of playing spy. I was then certain of my lord's purpose in his rambles and of the secret source of his delight. Here was his mistress: it was hatred and not love that gave him healthful colours. Some moralists might have been relieved by the discovery; I confess that I was dismayed. I found this situation of two brethren not only odious in itself, but big with possibilities of further evil; and I made it my practice, in so far as many occupations would allow, to go by a shorter path and be secretly present at their meeting. Coming down one day a little late, after I had been near a week prevented, I was struck with surprise to find a new development. I should say there was a bench against the Master's house, where customers might sit to parley with the shopman; and here I found my lord, seated, nursing his cane and looking pleasantly forth upon the bay. Not three feet from him sate the Master, stitching. Neither spoke; nor (in this new situation) did my lord so much as cast a glance upon his enemy. He tasted his neighbourhood, I must suppose, less indirectly in the bare proximity of person; and, without doubt, drank deep of hateful pleasures.

He had no sooner come away than I openly joined him.

' My lord, my lord,' said I, ' this is no manner of behaviour.'

' I grow fat upon it,' he replied; and not merely the words, which were strange enough, but the whole character of his expression shocked me.

' I warn you, my lord, against this indulgency of evil feeling,' said I. ' I know not to which it is more perilous, the soul or the reason; but you go the way to murder both.'

' You cannot understand,' said he. ' You had never such mountains of bitterness upon your heart.'

' And if it were no more,' I added, ' you will surely goad the man to some extremity.'

' To the contrary; I am breaking his spirit,' says my lord.

Every morning for hard upon a week my lord took his same place upon the bench. It was a pleasant place, under the green acacias, with a sight upon the bay and shipping, and a sound (from some way off) of mariners singing at their employ. Here the two sate without speech or any external movement, beyond that of the needle or the Master biting off a thread, for he still clung to his pretence of industry; and here I made a point to join them, wondering at myself and my companions. If any of my lord's friends went by, he would hail them cheerfully, and cry out he was there to give some good advice to his brother, who was now (to his delight) grown quite industrious. And even this the Master accepted with a steady countenance; what was in his mind, God knows, or perhaps Satan only.

All of a sudden, on a still day of what they call the Indian Summer, when the woods were changed into gold and pink and scarlet, the Master laid down his needle and burst into a fit of merriment. I think he must have been preparing it a long while in silence, for the note in itself was pretty naturally pitched; but breaking suddenly from so extreme a silence, and in circumstances so averse from mirth, it sounded ominously on my ear.

'Henry,' said he, 'I have for once made a false step, and for once you have had the wit to profit by it. The farce of the cobbler ends to-day; and I confess to you (with my compliments) that you have had the best of it. Blood will out; and you have certainly a choice idea of how to make yourself unpleasant.'

Never a word said my lord; it was just as though the Master had not broken silence.

'Come,' resumed the Master, 'do not be sulky; it will spoil your attitude. You can now afford (believe me) to be a little gracious; for I have not merely a defeat to accept. I had meant to continue this performance till I had gathered enough money for a certain purpose; I confess ingenuously, I have not the courage. You naturally desire my absence from this town; I have come round by another way to the same idea. And I have a proposition to make; or, if your lordship prefers, a favour to ask.'

'Ask it,' says my lord.

'You may have heard that I had once in this country a considerable treasure,' returned the Master; 'it matters not whether or no—such is the fact; and I was obliged to bury it in a spot of which I have sufficient indications. To the recovery of this, has my ambition now come down; and, as it is my own, you will not grudge it me.'

'Go and get it,' says my lord. 'I make no opposition.'

'Yes,' said the Master; 'but to do so, I must find men and carriage. The way is long and rough, and the country infested with wild Indians. Advance me only so much as shall be needful: either as a lump sum, in lieu of my allowance; or, if you prefer it, as a loan, which I shall repay on my return. And then, if you so decide, you may have seen the last of me.'

My lord stared him steadily in the eyes; there was a hard smile upon his face, but he uttered nothing.

'Henry,' said the Master, with a formidable quietness, and drawing at the same time somewhat back—'Henry, I had the honour to address you.'

'Let us be stepping homeward,' says my lord to me, who was plucking at his sleeve; and with that he rose, stretched himself, settled his hat, and still without a syllable of response, began to walk steadily along the shore.

I hesitated awhile between the two brothers, so serious a climax did we seem to have reached. But the Master had resumed his occupation, his eyes lowered, his hand seemingly as deft as ever; and I decided to pursue my lord.

'Are you mad?' I cried, so soon as I had overtook him. 'Would you cast away so fair an opportunity?'

'Is it possible you should still believe in him?' inquired my lord, almost with a sneer.

'I wish him forth of this town!' I cried. 'I wish him anywhere and anyhow but as he is.'

'I have said my say,' returned my lord, 'and you have said yours. There let it rest.'

But I was bent on dislodging the Master. That sight of him patiently returning to his needlework was more than my imagination could digest. There was never a man made, and the Master the least of any, that could accept so long a series of insults. The air smelt blood to me. And I vowed there should be no neglect of mine if, through any chink of possibility, crime could be yet turned aside. That same day, therefore, I came to my lord in his business room, where he sat upon some trivial occupation.

'My lord,' said I, 'I have found a suitable investment for my small economies. But these are unhappily in Scotland; it will take some time to lift them, and the affair presses. Could your lordship see his way to advance me the amount against my note?'

He read me awhile with keen eyes. 'I have never inquired into the state of your affairs, Mackellar,' says he. 'Beyond the amount of your caution, you may not be worth a farthing for what I know.'

'I have been a long while in your service, and never told a lie, nor yet asked a favour for myself,' said I, 'until to-day.'

'A favour for the Master,' he returned, quietly. 'Do you take me for a fool, Mackellar? Understand it once and for all, I treat this beast in my own way; fear nor favour shall not move me; and before I am hoodwinked, it will require a trickster less transparent than yourself. I ask service, loyal service; not that you should make and mar behind my back, and steal my own money to defeat me.'

'My lord,' said I, 'these are very unpardonable expressions.'

'Think once more, Mackellar,' he replied; 'and you will see they fit the fact. It is your own subterfuge that is unpardonable. Deny (if you can) that you designed this money to evade my orders with, and I will ask your pardon freely. If you cannot, you must have the resolution to hear your conduct go by its own name.'

'If you think I had any design but to save you——' I began.

'Oh! my old friend,' said he, 'you know very well what I think! Here is my hand to you with all my heart; but of money, not one rap.'

Defeated upon this side, I went straight to my room, wrote a letter, ran with it to the harbour, for I knew a ship was on the point of sailing; and came to the Master's door a little before dusk. Entering without the form of any knock, I found him sitting with his Indian at a simple meal of maize porridge with some milk. The house within was clean and poor; only a few books upon a shelf distinguished it, and (in one corner) Secundra's little bench.

'Mr. Bally,' said I, 'I have near five hundred pounds laid by in Scotland, the economies of a hard life. A letter goes by yon ship to have it lifted. Have so much patience till the return ship comes in, and it is all yours, upon the same condition you offered to my lord this morning.'

He rose from the table, came forward, took me by the shoulders, and looked me in the face, smiling.

'And yet you are very fond of money!' said he. 'And yet you love money beyond all things else, except my brother!'

'I fear old age and poverty,' said I, 'which is another matter.'

'I will never quarrel for a name. Call it so,' he replied. 'Ah, Mackellar, Mackellar, if this were done from any love to me, how gladly would I close upon your offer!'

'And yet,' I eagerly answered—'I say it to my shame, but

I cannot see you in this poor place without compunction. It is not my single thought, nor my first; and yet it's there! I would gladly see you delivered. I do not offer it in love, and far from that; but, as God judges me—and I wonder at it too!—quite without enmity.'

' Ah! ' says he, still holding my shoulders, and now gently shaking me, ' you think of me more than you suppose. " And I wonder at it too," ' he added, repeating my expression and, I suppose, something of my voice. ' You are an honest man, and for that cause I spare you.'

' Spare me? ' I cried.

' Spare you,' he repeated, letting me go and turning away. And then, fronting me once more: ' You little know what I would do with it, Mackellar! Did you think I had swallowed my defeat indeed? Listen: my life has been a series of unmerited cast-backs. That fool, Prince Charlie, mismanaged a most promising affair: there fell my first fortune. In Paris I had my foot once more high upon the ladder: that time it was an accident: a letter came to the wrong hand, and I was bare again. A third time, I found my opportunity; I built up a place for myself in India with an infinite patience; and then Clive came, my rajah was swallowed up, and I escaped out of the convulsion, like another Æneas, with Secundra Dass upon my back. Three times I have had my hand upon the highest station: and I am not yet three-and-forty. I know the world as few men know it when they come to die—Court and camp, the East and the West; I know where to go, I see a thousand openings. I am now at the height of my resources, sound of health, of inordinate ambition. Well, all this I resign; I care not if I die and the world never hear of me; I care only for one thing, and that I will have. Mind yourself; lest, when the roof falls, you, too, should be crushed under the ruins.'

As I came out of his house, all hope of intervention quite destroyed, I was aware of a stir on the harbour side, and, raising my eyes, there was a great ship newly come to anchor. It seems strange I could have looked upon her with so much indifference, for she brought death to the brothers of Durrisdeer. After all the desperate episodes of this contention, the insults, the opposing interests, the fraternal duel in the shrubbery, it was reserved for some poor devil in Grub Street, scribbling for his dinner, and not caring what he scribbled, to cast a spell across four thousand miles of the salt sea, and send forth both these brothers into savage and wintry deserts, there to die. But such a thought was distant from my mind; and while all the provincials were fluttered about me by the unusual animation of their port, I passed throughout their midst on my return homeward, quite absorbed in the recollection of my visit and the Master's speech.

The same night there was brought to us from the ship a little packet of pamphlets. The next day my lord was under engagement to go with the Governor upon some party of pleasure; the time was nearly due, and I left him for a moment alone in his room and skimming through the pamphlets. When I returned, his head had fallen upon the table, his arms lying abroad amongst the crumpled papers.

'My lord, my lord!' I cried as I ran forward, for I supposed he was in some fit.

He sprang up like a figure upon wires, his countenance deformed with fury, so that in a strange place I should scarce have known him. His hand at the same time flew above his head, as though to strike me down. 'Leave me alone!' he screeched, and I fled, as fast as my shaking legs would bear me, for my lady. She, too, lost no time; but when we returned, he had the door locked within, and only cried to us from the other side to leave him be. We looked in each other's faces, very white—each supposing the blow had come at last.

'I will write to the Governor to excuse him,' says she. 'We must keep our strong friends.' But when she took up the pen, it flew out of her finger. 'I cannot write,' said she. 'Can you?'

'I will make a shift, my lady,' said I.

She looked over me as I wrote. 'That will do,' she said, when I had done. 'Thank God, Mackellar, I have you to lean upon! But what can it be now? What, what can it be?'

In my own mind, I believed there was no explanation possible, and none required; it was my fear that the man's madness had now simply burst forth its way, like the long-smothered flames of a volcano; but to this (in mere mercy to my lady) I durst not give expression.

'It is more to the purpose to consider our own behaviour,' said I. 'Must we leave him there alone?'

'I do not dare disturb him,' she replied. 'Nature may know best; it may be Nature that cries to be alone; and we grope in the dark. Oh, yes, I would leave him as he is.'

'I will, then, despatch this letter, my lady, and return here, if you please, to sit with you,' said I.

'Pray do,' cries my lady.

All afternoon we sat together, mostly in silence, watching my lord's door. My own mind was busy with the scene that had just passed, and its singular resemblance to my vision. I must say a word upon this, for the story has gone abroad with great exaggeration, and I have even seen it printed, and my own name referred to for particulars. So much was the same: here was my lord in a room, with his head upon the table, and when he raised his face, it wore such an expression as distressed me to the soul. But the room was different, my lord's attitude at the table not all the same, and his face, when he disclosed it, expressed a painful degree of fury instead of that haunting despair which had always (except once, already referred to) characterised it in the vision. There is the whole truth at last before the public; and if the differences be great, the coincidence was yet enough to fill me with uneasiness. All afternoon, as I say, I sat and pondered upon this quite to myself; for my lady had trouble of her own, and it was my last thought to vex her with fancies. About the midst of our time of waiting, she conceived an ingenious scheme, had Mr. Alexander fetched, and bid him knock at his father's door. My lord sent the boy about his business, but without the least violence, whether of manner or expression; so that I began to entertain a hope the fit was over.

At last, as the night fell and I was lighting a lamp that stood there trimmed, the door opened and my lord stood within upon the threshold. The light was not so strong that we could read his countenance; when he spoke, methought his voice a little altered but yet perfectly steady.

' Mackellar,' said he, ' carry this note to its destination with your own hand. It is highly private. Find the person alone when you deliver it.'

' Henry,' says my lady, ' you are not ill? '

' No, no,' says he, querulously, ' I am occupied. Not at all; I am only occupied. It is a singular thing a man must be supposed to be ill when he has any business! Send me supper to this room, and a basket of wine: I expect the visit of a friend. Otherwise I am not to be disturbed.'

And with that he once more shut himself in.

The note was addressed to one Captain Harris, at a tavern on the portside. I knew Harris (by reputation) for a dangerous adventurer, highly suspected of piracy in the past, and now following the rude business of an Indian trader. What my lord should have to say to him, or he to my lord, it passed my imagination to conceive: or yet how my lord had heard of him, unless by a disgraceful trial from which the man was recently escaped. Altogether I went upon the errand with reluctance, and from the little I saw of the Captain, returned from it with sorrow.

I found him in a foul-smelling chamber, sitting by a guttering candle and an empty bottle; he had the remains of a military carriage, or rather perhaps it was an affectation, for his manners were low.

'Tell my lord, with my service, that I will wait upon his lordship in the inside of half an hour,' says he, when he had read the note; and then had the servility, pointing to his empty bottle, to propose that I should buy him liquor.

Although I returned with my best speed, the Captain followed close upon my heels, and he stayed late into the night. The cock was crowing a second time when I saw (from my chamber window) my lord lighting him to the gate, both men very much affected with their potations, and sometimes leaning one upon the other to confabulate. Yet the next morning my lord was abroad again early with a hundred pounds of money in his pocket. I never supposed that he returned with it; and yet I was quite sure it did not find its way to the Master, for I lingered all morning within view of the booth. That was the last time my Lord Durrisdeer passed his own enclosure till we left New York; he walked in his barn, or sat and talked with his family, all much as usual; but the town saw nothing of him, and his daily visits to the Master seemed forgotten. Nor yet did Harris reappear; or not until the end.

I was now much oppressed with a sense of the mysteries in which we had begun to move. It was plain, if only from his change of habitude, my lord had something on his mind of a grave nature; but what it was, whence it sprang, or why he should now keep the house and garden, I could make no guess at. It was clear, even to probation, the pamphlets had some share in this revolution; I read all I could find, and they were all extremely insignificant, and of the usual kind of party scurrility; even to a high politician, I could spy out no particular matter of offence, and my lord was a man rather indifferent on public questions. The truth is, the pamphlet which was the spring of this affair, lay all the time on my lord's bosom. There it was that I found it at last, after he was dead, in the midst of the north wilderness: in such a place, in such dismal circumstances, I was to read for the first time these idle, lying words of a Whig pamphleteer, declaiming against indulgency to Jacobites:—
'Another notorious Rebel, the M——r of B——e, is to have his Title restored,' the passage ran. 'This Business has been long in hand, since he rendered some very disgraceful Services in Scotland and France. His Brother, L——d D——r, is known to be no better than himself in Inclination; and the supposed

Heir, who is now to be set aside, was bred up in the most detestable Principles. In the old Phrase, it is *six of the one and half a dozen of the other*; but the Favour of such a Reposition is too extreme to be passed over.' A man in his right wits could not have cared two straws for a tale so manifestly false; that Government should ever entertain the notion, was inconceivable to any reasoning creature, unless possibly the fool that penned it; and my lord, though never brilliant, was ever remarkable for sense. That he should credit such a rodomontade, and carry the pamphlet on his bosom and the words in his heart, is the clear proof of the man's lunacy. Doubtless the mere mention of Mr. Alexander, and the threat directly held out against the child's succession, precipitated that which had so long impended. Or else my master had been truly mad for a long time, and we were too dull or too much used to him, and did not perceive the extent of his infirmity.

About a week after the day of the pamphlets I was late upon the harbour-side, and took a turn towards the Master's, as I often did. The door opened, a flood of light came forth upon the road, and I beheld a man taking his departure with friendly salutations. I cannot say how singularly I was shaken to recognise the adventurer Harris. I could not but conclude it was the hand of my lord that had brought him there; and prolonged my walk in very serious and apprehensive thought. It was late when I came home, and there was my lord making up his portmanteau for a voyage.

' Why do you come so late? ' he cried. ' We leave to-morrow for Albany, you and I together; and it is high time you were about your preparations.'

' For Albany, my lord? ' I cried. ' And for what earthly purpose? '

' Change of scene,' said he.

And my lady, who appeared to have been weeping, gave me the signal to obey without more parley. She told me a little later (when we found occasion to exchange some words) that he had suddenly announced his intention after a visit from Captain Harris, and her best endeavours, whether to dissuade him from the journey, or to elicit some explanation of its purpose, had alike proved unavailing.

11

The journey in the Wilderness

WE made a prosperous voyage up that fine river of the Hudson, the weather grateful, the hills singularly beautified with the colours of the autumn. At Albany we had our residence at an inn, where I was not so blind and my lord not so cunning but what I could see he had some design to hold me prisoner. The work he found for me to do was not so pressing that we should transact it apart from necessary papers in the chamber of an inn; nor was it of such importance that I should be set upon as many as four or five scrolls of the same document. I submitted in appearance; but I took private measures on my own side, and had the news of the town communicated to me daily by the politeness of our host. In this way I received at last a piece of intelligence for which, I may say, I had been waiting. Captain Harris (I was told) with ' Mr. Mountain, the trader,' had gone up the river in a boat. I would have feared the landlord's eye, so strong the sense of some complicity upon my master's part oppressed me. But I made out to say I had some knowledge of the Captain, although none of Mr. Mountain, and to inquire who else was of the party. My informant knew not; Mr. Mountain had come ashore upon some needful purchases; had gone round the town buying, drinking, and prating; and it seemed the party went upon some likely venture, for he had spoken much of great things he would do when he returned. No more was known, for none of the rest had come ashore, and it seemed they were pressed for time to reach a certain spot before the snow should fall.

And sure enough, the next day, there fell a sprinkle even in Albany; but it passed as it came, and was but a reminder of what lay before us. I thought of it lightly then, knowing so little as I did of that inclement province: the retrospect is different; and I wonder at times if some of the horror of these events which I must now rehearse flowed not from the foul skies and savage winds to which we were exposed, and the agony of cold that we must suffer.

The boat having passed by, I thought at first we should have left the town. But no such matter. My lord continued his stay in Albany, where he had no ostensible affairs, and kept me by him, far from my due employment, and making a pretence of occupation. It is upon this passage I expect, and perhaps deserve, censure. I was not so dull but what I had my own thoughts.

I could not see the Master entrust himself into the hands of Harris, and not expect some underhand contrivance. Harris bore a villainous reputation, and he had been tampered with in private by my lord; Mountain, the trader, proved, upon inquiry, to be another of the same kidney; the errand they were all gone upon being the recovery of ill-gotten treasures, offered in itself a very strong incentive to foul play; and the character of the country where they journeyed promised impunity to deeds of blood. Well: it is true I had all these thoughts and fears, and guesses of the Master's fate. But you are to consider I was the same man that sought to dash him from the bulwarks of a ship in the mid-sea; the same that, a little before, very impiously but sincerely offered God a bargain, seeking to hire God to be my bravo. It is true again that I had a good deal melted towards our enemy. But this I always thought of as a weakness of the flesh and even culpable; my mind remaining steady and quite bent against him. True, yet again, that it was one thing to assume on my own shoulders the guilt and danger of a criminal attempt, and another to stand by and see my lord imperil and besmirch himself. But this was the very ground of my inaction. For (should I anyway stir in the business) I might fail indeed to save the Master, but I could not miss to make a byword of my lord.

Thus it was that I did nothing; and upon the same reasons, I am still strong to justify my course. We lived meanwhile in Albany, but though alone together in a strange place, had little traffic beyond formal salutations. My lord had carried with him several introductions to chief people of the town and neighbourhood; others he had before encountered in New York: with this consequence, that he went much abroad, and I am sorry to say was altogether too convivial in his habits. I was often in bed, but never asleep, when he returned; and there was scarce a night when he did not betray the influence of liquor. By day he would still lay upon me endless tasks, which he showed considerable ingenuity to fish up and renew, in the manner of Penelope's web. I never refused, as I say, for I was hired to do his bidding; but I took no pains to keep my penetration under a bushel, and would sometimes smile in his face.

' I think I must be the devil and you Michael Scott,' I said to him one day. ' I have bridged the Tweed and split the Eildons; and now you set me to the rope of sand.'

He looked at me with shining eyes, and looked away again, his jaw chewing, but without words.

'Well, well, my lord,' said I, 'your will is my pleasure. I will do this thing for the fourth time; but I would beg of you to invent another task against to-morrow, for by my troth, I am weary of this one.'

'You do not know what you are saying,' returned my lord, putting on his hat and turning back to me. 'It is a strange thing you should take a pleasure to annoy me. A friend—but that is a different affair. It is a strange thing. I am a man that has had ill-fortune all my life through. I am still surrounded by contrivances. I am always treading into plots,' he burst out. ' The whole world is banded against me.'

'I would not talk wicked nonsense if I were you,' said I: ' but I will tell you what I *would* do—I would put my head in cold water, for you had more last night than you could carry.'

'Do ye think that?' said he, with a manner of interest highly awakened. 'Would that be good for me? It's a thing I never tried.'

'I mind the days when you had no call to try, and I wish, my lord, that they were back again,' said I. 'But the plain truth is, if you continue to exceed, you will do yourself a mischief.'

'I don't appear to carry drink the way I used to,' said my lord. 'I get overtaken, Mackellar. But I will be more upon my guard.'

'That is what I would ask of you,' I replied. 'You are to bear in mind that you are Mr. Alexander's father: give the bairn a chance to carry his name with some responsibility.'

'Ay, ay,' said he. 'Ye're a very sensible man, Mackellar, and have been long in my employ. But I think, if you have nothing more to say to me I will be stepping. If you have nothing more to say?' he added, with that burning, childish eagerness that was now so common with the man.

'No, my lord, I have nothing more,' said I, drily enough.

'Then I think I will be stepping,' says my lord, and stood and looked at me, fidgeting with his hat, which he had taken off again. 'I suppose you will have no errands. No? I am to meet Sir William Johnson, but I will be more upon my guard.' He was silent for a time, and then, smiling: 'Do you call to mind a place, Mackellar—it's a little below Engles—where the burn runs very deep under a wood of rowans. I mind being there when I was a lad—dear, it comes over me like an old song! I was after the fishing, and I made a bonny cast. Eh, but I was happy. I wonder, Mackellar, why I am never happy now?'

'My lord,' said I, 'if you would drink with more moderation

you would have the better chance. It is an old byword that the bottle is a false consoler.'

' No doubt,' said he, ' no doubt. Well, I think I will be going.'

' Good-morning, my lord,' said I.

' Good-morning, good-morning,' said he, and so got himself at last from the apartment.

I give that for a fair specimen of my lord in the morning; and I must have described my patron very ill if the reader does not perceive a notable falling off. To behold the man thus fallen: to know him accepted among his companions for a poor, muddled toper, welcome (if he were welcome at all) for the bare consideration of his title; and to recall the virtues he had once displayed against such odds of fortune; was not this a thing at once to rage and to be humbled at?

In his cups, he was more excessive. I will give but the one scene, close upon the end, which is strongly marked upon my memory to this day, and at the time affected me almost with horror.

I was in bed, lying there awake, when I heard him stumbling on the stair and singing. My lord had no gift of music, his brother had all the graces of the family, so that when I say singing, you are to understand a manner of high, carolling utterance, which was truly neither speech nor song. Something not unlike is to be heard upon the lips of children, ere they learn shame; from those of a man grown elderly, it had a strange effect. He opened the door with noisy precaution; peered in, shading his candle; conceived me to slumber; entered, set his light upon the table, and took off his hat. I saw him very plain; a high, feverish exultation appeared to boil in his veins, and he stood and smiled and smirked upon the candle. Presently he lifted up his arm, snapped his fingers, and fell to undress. As he did so, having once more forgot my presence, he took back to his singing; and now I could hear the words, which were those from the old song of the *Twa Corbies* endlessly repeated:

And over his banes when they are bare
The wind sall blaw for evermair!

I have said there was no music in the man. His strains had no logical succession except in so far as they inclined a little to the minor mode; but they exercised a rude potency upon the feelings, and followed the words, and signified the feelings of the singer with barbaric fitness. He took it first in the time and manner of a rant; presently this ill-favoured gleefulness abated, he began to dwell upon the notes more feelingly, and sank at last into a degree of maudlin pathos that was to me scarce bearable. By equal steps, the original briskness of his acts declined; and when he was stripped to his breeches, he sat on the bedside and fell to whimpering. I know nothing less respectable than the tears of drunkenness, and turned my back impatiently on this poor sight.

But he had started himself (I am to suppose) on that slippery descent of self-pity; on the which, to a man unstrung by old sorrows and recent potations there is no arrest except exhaustion. His tears continued to flow, and the man to sit there, three parts naked, in the cold air of the chamber. I twitted myself alternately with inhumanity and sentimental weakness, now half rising in my bed to interfere, now reading myself lessons of indifference and courting slumber, until, upon a sudden, the *quantum mutatus ab illo* shot into my mind; and calling to remembrance his old wisdom, constancy, and patience, I was overborne with a pity almost approaching the passionate, not for my master alone but for the sons of man.

At this I leaped from my place, went over to his side and laid a hand on his bare shoulder, which was cold as stone. He uncovered his face and showed it me all swollen and begrutten[1] like a child's; and at the sight my impatience partially revived.

'Think shame to yourself,' said I. 'This is bairnly conduct. I might have been snivelling myself, if I had cared to swill my belly with wine. But I went to my bed sober like a man. Come: get into yours, and have done with this pitiable exhibition.'

'Oh, Mackellar,' said he, 'my heart is wae!'

'Wae?' cried I. 'For a good cause, I think. What words were these you sang as you came in? Show pity to others, we then can talk of pity to yourself. You can be the one thing or the other, but I will be no party to half-way houses. If you're a striker, strike, and if you're a bleater, bleat!'

'Cry!' cries he, with a burst, 'that's it—strike! that's talking! Man, I've stood it all too long. But when they laid a hand upon the child, when the child's threatened '—his momentary vigour whimpering off—'my child, my Alexander!'—and he was at his tears again.

I took him by the shoulders and shook him. 'Alexander!' said I. 'Do you ever think of him? Not you! Look yourself in the face like a brave man, and you'll find you're but a self-deceiver. The wife, the friend, the child, they're all equally forgot, and you sunk in a mere log of selfishness.'

'Mackellar,' said he, with a wonderful return to his old man-

[1] Tear-marked.

ner and appearance, ' you may say what you will of me, but one thing I never was—I was never selfish.'

' I will open your eyes in your despite,' said I. ' How long have we been here? and how often have you written to your family? I think this is the first time you were ever separate: have you written at all? Do they know if you are dead or living? '

I had caught him here too openly; it braced his better nature; there was no more weeping, he thanked me very penitently, got to bed and was soon fast asleep; and the first thing he did the next morning was to sit down and begin a letter to my lady: a very tender letter it was too, though it was never finished. Indeed all communication with New York was transacted by myself; and it will be judged I had a thankless task of it. What to tell my lady and in what words, and how far to be false and how far cruel, was a thing that kept me often from my slumber.

All this while, no doubt, my lord waited with growing impatiency for news of his accomplices. Harris, it is to be thought, had promised a high degree of expedition; the time was already overpast when word was to be looked for; and suspense was a very evil counsellor to a man of an impaired intelligence. My lord's mind throughout this interval dwelled almost wholly in the Wilderness, following that party with whose deeds he had so much concern. He continually conjured up their camps and progresses, the fashion of the country, the perpetration in a thousand different manners of the same horrid fact, and that consequent spectacle of the Master's bones lying scattered in the wind. These private guilty considerations I would continually observe to peep forth in the man's talk, like rabbits from a hill. And it is the less wonder if the scene of his meditations began to draw him bodily.

It is well known what pretext he took. Sir William Johnson had a diplomatic errand in these parts: and my lord and I (from curiosity, as was given out) went in his company. Sir William was well attended and liberally supplied. Hunters brought us venison, fish was taken for us daily in the streams, and brandy ran like water. We proceeded by day and encamped by night in the military style; sentinels were set and changed; every man had his named duty; and Sir William was the spring of all. There was much in this that might at times have entertained me; but for our misfortune, the weather was extremely harsh, the days were in the beginning open, but the nights frosty from the first. A painful keen wind blew most of the time, so that we sat in the boat with blue fingers, and at night, as we scorched our faces at the fire, the clothes upon our back appeared to be of paper. A dreadful solitude surrounded our steps; the land was quite dispeopled, there was no smoke of fires, and save for a single boat of merchants on the second day, we met no travellers. The season was indeed late, but this desertion of the waterways impressed Sir William himself; and I have heard him more than once express a sense of intimidation. ' I have come too late, I fear; they must have dug up the hatchet,' he said; and the future proved how justly he had reasoned.

I could never depict the blackness of my soul upon this journey. I have none of those minds that are in love with the unusual; to see the winter coming and to lie in the field so far from any house, oppressed me like a nightmare; it seemed, indeed, a kind of awful braving of God's power; and this thought, which I daresay only writes me down a coward, was greatly exaggerated by my private knowledge of the errand we were come upon. I was besides encumbered by my duties to Sir William, whom it fell upon me to entertain; for my lord was quite sunk into a state bordering on *pervigilium*, watching the woods with a rapt eye, sleeping scarce at all, and speaking sometimes not twenty words in a whole day. That which he said was still coherent; but it turned almost invariably upon the party for whom he kept his crazy lookout. He would tell Sir William often, and always as if it were a new communication, that he had ' a brother somewhere in the woods,' and beg that the sentinels should be directed ' to inquire for him.' ' I am anxious for news of my brother,' he would say. And sometimes, when we were under way, he would fancy he spied a canoe far off upon the water or a camp on the shore, and exhibit painful agitation. It was impossible but Sir William should be struck with these singularities; and at last he led me aside, and hinted his uneasiness. I touched my head and shook it; quite rejoiced to prepare a little testimony against possible disclosures.

' But in that case,' cries Sir William, ' is it wise to let him go at large? '

' Those that know him best,' said I, ' are persuaded that he should be humoured.'

' Well, well,' replied Sir William, ' it is none of my affairs. But if I had understood, you would never have been here.'

Our advance into this savage country had thus uneventfully proceeded for about a week, when we encamped for a night at a place where the river ran among considerable mountains clothed in wood. The fires were lighted on a level space at the water's edge; and we supped and lay down to sleep in the customary fashion. It chanced the night fell murderously cold; the stringency of the frost seized and bit me through my coverings, so that pain kept me wakeful; and I was afoot again before the peep of day, crouching by the fires or trotting to and fro at the stream's edge, to combat the aching of my limbs. At last dawn began to break upon hoar woods and mountains, the sleepers rolled in their robes, and the boisterous river dashing among spears of ice. I stood looking about me, swaddled in my stiff coat of a bull's fur, and the breath smoking from my scorched nostrils, when, upon a sudden, a singular, eager cry rang from the borders of the wood. The sentries answered it, the sleepers sprang to their feet; one pointed, the rest followed his direction with their eyes, and there, upon the edge of the forest and betwixt two trees, we beheld the figure of a man reaching forth his hands like one in ecstasy. The next moment he ran forward, fell on his knees at the side of the camp, and burst in tears.

This was John Mountain, the trader, escaped from the most horrid perils; and his first word, when he got speech, was to ask if we had seen Secundra Dass.

' Seen what? ' cries Sir William.

' No,' said I, ' we have seen nothing of him. Why? '

' Nothing? ' says Mountain. ' Then I was right after all.' With that he struck his palm upon his brow. ' But what takes him back? ' he cried. ' What takes the man back among dead bodies? There is some damned mystery here.'

This was a word which highly aroused our curiosity, but I shall be more perspicacious, if I narrate these incidents in their true order. Here follows a narrative which I have compiled out of three sources, not very consistent in all points:

First, a written statement by Mountain, in which everything criminal is cleverly smuggled out of view;

Second, two conversations with Secundra Dass; and

Third, many conversations with Mountain himself, in which he was pleased to be entirely plain; for the truth is he regarded me as an accomplice.

Narrative of the Trader, Mountain

The crew that went up the river under the joint command of Captain Harris and the Master numbered in all nine persons, of whom (if I except Secundra Dass) there was not one that had not merited the gallows. From Harris downwards the voyagers were notorious in that colony for desperate, bloody-minded miscreants; some were reputed pirates, the most hawkers of rum;

all ranters and drinkers; all fit associates, embarking together without remorse upon this treacherous and murderous design. I could not hear there was much discipline or any set captain in the gang; but Harris and four others, Mountain himself, two Scotchmen—Pinkerton and Hastie—and a man of the name of Hicks, a drunken shoemaker, put their heads together and agreed upon the course. In a material sense, they were well enough provided, and the Master in particular brought with him a tent where he might enjoy some privacy and shelter.

Even this small indulgence told against him in the minds of his companions. But indeed he was in a position so entirely false (and even ridiculous) that all his habit of command and arts of pleasing were here thrown away. In the eyes of all, except Secundra Dass, he figured as a common gull and designated victim; going unconsciously to death; yet he could not but suppose himself the contriver and the leader of the expedition; he could scarce help but so conduct himself; and at the least hint of authority or condescension, his deceivers would be laughing in their sleeves. I was so used to see and to conceive him in a high, authoritative attitude, that when I had conceived his position on this journey, I was pained and could have blushed. How soon he may have entertained a first surmise, we cannot know; but it was long, and the party had advanced into the Wilderness beyond the reach of any help, ere he was fully awakened to the truth.

It fell thus. Harris and some others had drawn apart into the woods for consultation, when they were startled by a rustling in the brush. They were all accustomed to the arts of Indian warfare, and Mountain had not only lived and hunted, but fought and earned some reputation, with the savages. He could move in the woods without noise, and follow a trail like a hound; and upon the emergence of this alert, he was deputed by the rest to plunge into the thicket for intelligence. He was soon convinced there was a man in his close neighbourhood, moving with precaution but without art among the leaves and branches; and coming shortly to a place of advantage, he was able to observe Secundra Dass crawling briskly off with many backward glances. At this he knew not whether to laugh or cry; and his accomplices, when he had returned and reported, were in much the same dubiety. There was now no danger of an Indian onslaught; but on the other hand, since Secundra Dass was at the pains to spy upon them, it was highly probable he knew English, and if he knew English it was certain the whole of their design was in the Master's knowledge. There was one singularity in the position. If Secundra Dass knew and concealed his knowledge of English, Harris was a proficient in several of the tongues of India, and as his career in that part of the world had been a great deal worse than profligate, he had not thought proper to remark upon the circumstance. Each side had thus a spy-hole on the counsels of the other. The plotters, so soon as this advantage was explained, returned to camp; Harris, hearing the Hindustani was once more closeted with his master, crept to the side of the tent; and the rest, sitting about the fire with their tobacco, awaited his report with impatience. When he came at last, his face was very black. He had overheard enough to confirm the worst of his suspicions. Secundra Dass was a good English scholar; he had been some days creeping and listening, the Master was now fully informed of the conspiracy, and the pair proposed on the morrow to fall out of line at a carrying place and plunge at a venture in the woods; preferring the full risk of famine, savage beasts, and savage men to their position in the midst of traitors.

What, then, was to be done? Some were for killing the Master on the spot; but Harris assured them that would be a crime without profit, since the secret of the treasure must die along with him that buried it. Others were for desisting at once from the whole enterprise and making for New York; but the appetising name of treasure, and the thought of the long way they had already travelled, dissuaded the majority. I imagine they were dull fellows for the most part. Harris, indeed, had some acquirements, Mountain was no fool, Hastie was an educated man; but even these had manifestly failed in life, and the rest were the dregs of colonial rascality. The conclusion they reached, at least, was more the offspring of greed and hope, than reason. It was to temporise, to be wary and watch the Master, to be silent and supply no further aliment to his suspicions, and to depend entirely (as well as I make out) on the chance that their victim was as greedy, hopeful, and irrational as themselves, and might, after all, betray his life and treasure.

Twice in the course of the next day Secundra and the Master must have appeared to themselves to have escaped; and twice they were circumvented. The Master, save that the second time he grew a little pale, displayed no sign of disappointment, apologised for the stupidity with which he had fallen aside, thanked his recapturers as for a service, and rejoined the caravan with all his usual gallantry and cheerfulness of mien and bearing. But it is certain he had smelled a rat; for from thenceforth he and Secundra spoke only in each other's ear, and Harris listened and shivered by the tent in vain. The same night it was announced they were to leave the boats and proceed by foot, a circumstance which (as it put an end to the confusion of the portages) greatly lessened the chances of escape.

And now there began between the two sides a silent contest, for life on the one hand, for riches on the other. They were now near that quarter of the desert in which the Master himself must begin to play the part of guide; and using this for a pretext of persecution, Harris and his men sat with him every night about the fire, and laboured to entrap him into some admission. If he let slip his secret, he knew well it was the warrant for his death; on the other hand, he durst not refuse their questions, and must appear to help them to the best of his capacity or he practically published his mistrust. And yet Mountain assures me the man's brow was never ruffled. He sat in the midst of these jackals, his life depending by a thread, like some easy, witty householder at home by his own fire; an answer he had for everything—as often as not a jesting answer; avoided threats, evaded insults; talked, laughed, and listened with an open countenance; and, in short, conducted himself in such a manner as must have disarmed suspicion, and went near to stagger knowledge. Indeed, Mountain confessed to me they would soon have disbelieved the Captain's story, and supposed their designated victim still quite innocent of their designs; but for the fact that he continued (however ingeniously) to give the slip to questions, and the yet stronger confirmation of his repeated efforts to escape. The last of these, which brought things to a head, I am now to relate. And first I should say that by this time the temper of Harris's companions was utterly worn out; civility was scarce pretended; and for one very insignificant circumstance, the Master and Secundra had been (on some pretext) deprived of weapons. On their side, however, the threatened pair kept up the parade of friendship handsomely; Secundra was all bows, the Master all smiles; and on the last night of the truce he had even gone so far as to sing for the diversion of the company. It was observed that he had also eaten with unusual heartiness and drank deep, doubtless from design.

At least, about three in the morning, he came out of the tent into the open air, audibly mourning and complaining, with all the manner of a sufferer from surfeit. For some while, Secundra publicly attended on his patron, who at last became more easy, and fell asleep on the frosty ground behind the tent, the Indian returning within. Some time after, the sentry was changed; had the Master pointed out to him, where he lay in what is called a robe of buffalo: and thenceforth kept an eye upon him (he declared) without remission. With the first of the dawn, a draught of wind came suddenly and blew open one side of the corner of the robe; and with the same puff, the Master's hat whirled in the air and fell some yards away. The sentry thinking it remarkable the sleeper should not awaken, thereupon drew near; and the next moment, with a great shout, informed the camp their prisoner was escaped. He had left behind his Indian, who (in the first vivacity of the surprise) came near to pay the forfeit of his life, and was, in fact, inhumanly mishandled; but Secundra, in the midst of threats and cruelties, stuck to it with extraordinary loyalty, that he was quite ignorant of his master's plans, which might indeed be true, and of the manner of his escape, which was demonstrably false. Nothing was therefore left to the conspirators but to rely entirely on the skill of Mountain. The night had been frosty, the ground quite hard; and the sun was no sooner up than a strong thaw set in. It was Mountain's boast that few men could have followed that trail, and still fewer (even of the native Indians) found it. The Master had thus a long start before his pursuers had the scent, and he must have travelled with surprising energy for a pedestrian so unused, since it was near noon before Mountain had a view of him. At this conjuncture the trader was alone, all his companions following, at his own request, several hundred yards in the rear; he knew the Master was unarmed; his heart was besides heated with the exercise and lust of hunting; and seeing the quarry so close, so defenceless, and seeming so fatigued, he vain-gloriously determined to effect the capture with his single hand. A step or two farther brought him to one margin of a little clearing; on the other, with his arms folded and his back to a huge stone, the Master sat. It is possible Mountain may have made a rustle, it is certain, at least, the Master raised his head and gazed directly at that quarter of the thicket where his hunter lay; ' I could not be sure he saw me,' Mountain said; ' he just looked my way like a man with his mind made up, and all the courage ran out of me like rum out of a bottle.' And presently, when the Master looked away again, and appeared to resume those meditations in which he had sat immersed before the trader's coming, Mountain slunk stealthily back and returned to seek the help of his companions.

And now began the chapter of surprises, for the scout had scarce informed the others of his discovery, and they were yet preparing their weapons for a rush upon the fugitive, when the man himself appeared in their midst, walking openly and quietly, with his hands behind his back.

'Ah, men!' says he, on his beholding them. 'Here is a fortunate encounter. Let us get back to camp.'

Mountain had not mentioned his own weakness or the Master's disconcerting gaze upon the thicket, so that (with all the rest) his return appeared spontaneous. For all that, a hubbub arose; oaths flew, fists were shaken, and guns pointed.

'Let us get back to camp,' said the Master. 'I have an explanation to make, but it must be laid before you all. And in the meanwhile I would put up these weapons, one of which might very easily go off and blow away your hopes of treasure. I would not kill,' says he, smiling, 'the goose with the golden eggs.'

The charm of his superiority once more triumphed; and the party, in no particular order, set off on their return. By the way, he found occasion to get a word or two apart with Mountain.

'You are a clever fellow and a bold,' says he, 'but I am not so sure that you are doing yourself justice. I would have you to consider whether you would not do better, ay, and safer, to serve me instead of serving so commonplace a rascal as Mr. Harris. Consider of it,' he concluded, dealing the man a gentle tap upon the shoulder, 'and don't be in haste. Dead or alive, you will find me an ill man to quarrel with.'

When they were come back to the camp, where Harris and Pinkerton stood guard over Secundra, these two ran upon the Master like viragoes, and were amazed out of measure when they were bidden by their comrades to 'stand back and hear what the gentleman had to say.' The Master had not flinched before their onslaught; nor, at this proof of the ground he had gained, did he betray the least sufficiency.

'Do not let us be in haste,' says he. 'Meat first and public speaking after.'

With that they made a hasty meal; and as soon as it was done, the Master, leaning on one elbow, began his speech. He spoke long, addressing himself to each except Harris, finding for each (with the same exception) some particular flattery. He called them 'bold, honest blades,' declared he had never seen a more jovial company, work better done, or pains more merrily supported. 'Well, then,' says he, 'some one asks me, Why the devil I ran away? But that is scarce worth answer, for I think you all know pretty well. But you know only pretty well: that is a point I shall arrive at presently, and be you ready to remark it when it comes. There is a traitor here: a double traitor: I will give you his name before I am done; and let that suffice for now. But here comes some other gentleman and asks me, " Why, in the devil, I came back? " Well, before I answer that question, I have one to put to you. It was this cur here, this Harris, that speaks Hindustani? ' cries he, rising on one knee and pointing fair at the man's face, with a gesture indescribably menacing; and when he had been answered in the affirmative, ' Ah! ' says he, ' then are all my suspicions verified, and I did rightly to come back. Now, men, hear the truth for the first time.' Thereupon he launched forth in a long story, told with extraordinary skill, how he had all along suspected Harris, how he had found the confirmation of his fears, and how Harris must have misrepresented what passed between Secundra and himself. At this point he made a bold stroke with excellent effect. ' I suppose,' says he, ' you think you are going shares with Harris, I suppose you think you will see to that yourselves; you would naturally not think so flat a rogue could cozen you. But have a care! These half idiots have a sort of cunning, as the skunk has its stench; and it may be news to you that Harris has taken care of himself already. Yes, for him the treasure is all money in the bargain. You must find it or go starve. But he has been paid beforehand; my brother paid him to destroy me; look at him, if you doubt—look at him, grinning and gulping, a detected thief! ' Thence, having made this happy impression, he explained how he had escaped, and thought better of it, and at last concluded to come back, lay the truth before the company, and take his chance with them once more: persuaded as he was, they would instantly depose Harris and elect some other leader. ' There is the whole truth,' said he: ' and with one exception, I put myself entirely in your hands. What is the exception? There he sits,' he cried pointing once more to Harris; ' a man that has to die! Weapons and conditions are all one to me; put me face to face with him, and if you give me nothing but a stick, in five minutes I will show you a sop of broken carrion, fit for dogs to roll in.'

It was dark night when he made an end; they had listened in almost perfect silence; but the firelight scarce permitted anyone to judge, from the look of his neighbours, with what result of persuasion or conviction. Indeed, the Master had set himself in the brightest place, and kept his face there, to be the centre of men's eyes: doubtless on a profound calculation. Silence followed for a while, and presently the whole party became involved in disputation: the Master lying on his back, with his hands knit under his head and one knee flung across the other, like a person unconcerned in the result. And here, I daresay, his bravado carried him too far and prejudiced his case. At least, after a cast or two back and forward, opinion settled itself finally against him. It's possible he hoped to repeat the business of the pirate ship, and be himself, perhaps, on hard enough conditions, elected leader; and things went so far that way, that Mountain actually threw out the proposition. But the rock he split upon was Hastie. This fellow was not well liked, being sour and slow, with an ugly, glowering disposition, but he had studied some time for the church at Edinburgh College, before ill conduct had destroyed his prospects, and he now remembered and applied what he had learned. Indeed he had not proceeded very far, when the Master rolled carelessly upon one side, which was done (in Mountain's opinion) to conceal the beginnings of despair upon his countenance. Hastie dismissed the most of what they had heard as nothing to the matter: what they wanted was the treasure. All that was said of Harris might be true, and they would have to see to that in time. But what had that to do with the treasure? They had heard a vast of words; but the truth was just this, that Mr. Durie was damnably frightened and had several times run off. Here he was—whether caught or come back was all one to Hastie: the point was to make an end of the business. As for the talk of deposing and electing captains, he hoped they were all free men and could attend to their own affairs. That was dust flung in their eyes, and so was the proposal to fight Harris. ' He shall fight no one in this camp, I can tell him that,' said Hastie. ' We had trouble enough to get his arms away from him, and we should look pretty fools to give them back again. But if it's excitement the gentleman is after, I can supply him with more than perhaps he cares about. For I have no intention to spend the remainder of my life in these mountains; already I have been too long; and I propose that he should immediately tell us where that treasure is, or else immediately be shot. And there,' says he, producing his weapon, ' there is the pistol that I mean to use.'

' Come, I call you a man,' cries the Master, sitting up and looking at the speaker with an air of admiration.

' I didn't ask you to call me anything,' returned Hastie; ' which is it to be?'

' That's an idle question,' said the Master. ' Needs must when the devil drives. The truth is we are within easy walk of the place, and I will show it you to-morrow.'

With that, as if all were quite settled, and settled exactly to his mind, he walked off to his tent, whither Secundra had preceded him.

I cannot think of these last turns and wriggles of my old enemy except with admiration; scarce even pity is mingled with the sentiment, so strongly the man supported, so boldly resisted his misfortunes. Even at that hour, when he perceived himself quite lost, when he saw he had but effected an exchange of enemies, and overthrown Harris to set Hastie up, no sign of weakness appeared in his behaviour, and he withdrew to his tent, already determined (I must suppose) upon affronting the incredible hazard of his last expedient, with the same easy, assured, genteel expression and demeanour as he might have left a theatre withal to join a supper of the wits. But doubtless within, if we could see there, his soul trembled.

Early in the night, word went about the camp that he was sick; and the first thing the next morning he called Hastie to his side, and inquired most anxiously if he had any skill in medicine. As a matter of fact, this was a vanity of that fallen divinity student's, to which he had cunningly addressed himself. Hastie examined him; and being flattered, ignorant, and highly suspicious, knew not in the least whether the man was sick or malingering. In this state he went forth again to his companions; and (as the thing which would give himself most consequence either way) announced that the patient was in a fair way to die.

'For all that,' he added with an oath, 'and if he bursts by the wayside, he must bring us this morning to the treasure.'

But there were several in the camp (Mountain among the number) whom this brutality revolted. They would have seen the Master pistolled, or pistolled him themselves, without the smallest sentiment of pity; but they seemed to have been touched by his gallant fight and unequivocal defeat the night before; perhaps, too, they were even already beginning to oppose themselves to their new leader; at least, they now declared that (if the man was sick) he should have a day's rest in spite of Hastie's teeth.

The next morning he was manifestly worse, and Hastie himself began to display something of humane concern, so easily does even the pretence of doctoring awaken sympathy. The third day the Master called Mountain and Hastie to the tent, announced himself to be dying, gave them full particulars as to the position of the cache, and begged them to set out incontinently on the quest, so that they might see if he deceived them, and (if they were at first unsuccessful) he should be able to correct their error.

But here arose a difficulty on which he doubtless counted.

None of these men would trust another, none would consent to stay behind. On the other hand, although the Master seemed extremely low, spoke scarce above a whisper, and lay much of the time insensible, it was still possible it was a fraudulent sickness; and if all went treasure-hunting, it might prove they had gone upon a wild-goose chase, and return to find their prisoner flown. They concluded, therefore, to hang idling round the camp, alleging sympathy to their reason; and certainly, so mingled are our dispositions, several were sincerely (if not very deeply) affected by the natural peril of the man whom they callously designed to murder. In the afternoon Hastie was called to the bedside to pray: the which (incredible as it must appear) he did with unction; about eight at night, the wailing of Secundra announced that all was over; and before ten, the Indian, with a link stuck in the ground, was toiling at the grave. Sunrise of next day beheld the Master's burial, all hands attending with great decency of demeanour; and the body was laid in the earth, wrapped in a fur robe, with only the face uncovered; which last was of a waxy whiteness, and had the nostrils plugged according to some Oriental habit of Secundra's. No sooner was the grave filled than the lamentations of the Indian once more struck concern to every heart; and it appears this gang of murderers, so far from resenting his outcries, although both distressful and (in such a country) perilous to their own safety, roughly but kindly endeavoured to console him.

But if human nature is even in the worst of men occasionally kind, it is still, and before all things, greedy; and they soon turned from the mourner to their own concerns. The cache of the treasure being hard by, although yet unidentified, it was concluded not to break camp; and the day passed, on the part of the voyagers, in unavailing exploration of the woods, Secundra the while lying on his master's grave. That night they placed no sentinel, but lay altogether about the fire in the customary woodman fashion, the heads outward, like the spokes of a wheel. Morning found them in the same disposition; only Pinkerton, who lay on Mountain's right, between him and Hastie, had (in the hours of darkness) been secretly butchered, and there lay, still wrapped as to his body in his mantle, but offering above that ungodly and horrific spectacle of the scalped head. The gang were that morning as pale as a company of phantoms, for the pertinacity of Indian war (or to speak more correctly, Indian murder) was well known to all. But they laid the chief blame on their unsentinelled posture; and fired with the neighbourhood of the treasure, determined to continue where they were. Pinkerton was buried hard by the Master; the survivors again passed the day in exploration, and returned in a mingled humour of anxiety and hope, being partly certain they were now close on the discovery of what they sought, and on the other hand (with the return of darkness) were infected with the fear of Indians. Mountain was the first sentry; he declares he neither slept nor yet sat down, but kept his watch with a perpetual and straining vigilance, and it was even with unconcern that (when he saw by the stars his time was up) he drew near the fire to awaken his successor. This man (it was Hicks the shoemaker) slept on the lee side of the circle, something farther off in consequence than those to windward, and in a place darkened by the blowing smoke. Mountain stooped and took him by the shoulder; his hand was at once smeared by some adhesive wetness; and (the wind at the moment veering) the firelight shone upon the sleeper, and showed him, like Pinkerton, dead and scalped.

It was clear they had fallen in the hands of one of those matchless Indian bravos, that will sometimes follow a party for days, and in spite of indefatigable travel, and unsleeping watch, continue to keep up with their advance, and steal a scalp at every resting-place. Upon this discovery, the treasure-seekers, already reduced to a poor half dozen, fell into mere dismay, seized a few necessaries, and deserting the remainder of their goods, fled outright into the forest. Their fire they left still burning, and their dead comrade unburied. All day they ceased not to flee, eating by the way, from hand to mouth; and since they feared to sleep, continued to advance at random even in the hours of darkness. But the limit of man's endurance is soon reached; when they rested at last it was to sleep profoundly; and when they woke, it was to find that the enemy was still upon their heels, and death and mutilation had once more lessened and deformed their company.

By this they had become light-headed, they had quite missed their path in the wilderness, their stores were already running low. With the further horrors, it is superfluous that I should swell this narrative, already too prolonged. Suffice it to say that when at length a night passed by innocuous, and they might breathe again in the hope that the murderer had at last desisted from pursuit, Mountain and Secundra were alone. The trader is firmly persuaded their unseen enemy was some warrior of his own acquaintance, and that he himself was spared by favour. The mercy extended to Secundra he explains on the ground that the East Indian was thought to be insane; partly from the fact that, through all the horrors of the flight and while others were casting away their very food and weapons, Secundra continued to stagger forward with a mattock on his shoulder, and partly because, in the last days and with a great degree of heat and fluency, he perpetually spoke with himself in his own language. But he was sane enough when it came to English.

'You think he will be gone quite away?' he asked, upon their blest awakening in safety.

'I pray God so, I believe so, I dare to believe so,' Mountain had replied almost with incoherence, as he described the scene to me.

And indeed he was so much distempered that until he met us, the next morning, he could scarce be certain whether he had dreamed, or whether it was a fact, that Secundra had thereupon turned directly about and returned without a word upon their footprints, setting his face for these wintry and hungry solitudes, along a path whose every stage was mile-stoned with a mutilated corpse.

12

The journey in the Wilderness (continued)

MOUNTAIN's story, as it was laid before Sir William Johnson and my lord, was shorn, of course, of all the earlier particulars, and the expedition described to have proceeded uneventfully, until the Master sickened. But the latter part was very forcibly related, the speaker visibly thrilling to his recollections; and our then situation, on the fringe of the same desert, and the private interests of each, gave him an audience prepared to share in his emotions. For Mountain's intelligence not only changed the world for my Lord Durrisdeer, but materially affected the designs of Sir William Johnson.

These I find I must lay more at length before the reader. Word had reached Albany of dubious import; it had been rumoured some hostility was to be put in act; and the Indian diplomatist had, thereupon, sped into the wilderness, even at the approach of winter, to nip that mischief in the bud. Here, on the borders, he learned that he was come too late; and a difficult choice was thus presented to a man (upon the whole) not any more bold than prudent. His standing with the painted braves may be compared to that of my Lord President Culloden among the chiefs of our own Highlanders at the 'Forty-five; that is as much as to say, he was, to these men, reason's only speaking trumpet, and counsels of peace and moderation, if they were to prevail at all, must prevail singly through his influence. If, then, he should return, the province must lie open to all the abominable tragedies of Indian war—the houses blaze, the wayfarer be cut off, and the men of the woods collect their usual disgusting spoil of human scalps. On the other side, to go farther north, to risk so small a party deeper in the desert, to carry words of peace among warlike savages already rejoicing to return to war: here was an extremity from which it was easy to perceive his mind revolted.

'I have come too late,' he said more than once, and would fall into a deep consideration, his head bowed in his hands, his foot patting the ground.

At length he raised his face and looked upon us, that is to say upon my lord, Mountain, and myself, sitting close round a small fire, which had been made for privacy in one corner of the camp.

'My lord, to be quite frank with you, I find myself in two minds,' said he. 'I think it very needful I should go on, but not at all proper I should any longer enjoy the pleasure of your company. We are here still upon the water side; and I think the risk to southward no great matter. Will not yourself and Mr. Mackellar take a single boat's crew and return to Albany?'

My lord, I should say, had listened to Mountain's narrative, regarding him throughout with a painful intensity of gaze; and since the tale concluded, had sat as in a dream. There was something very daunting in his look; something to my eyes not rightly human; the face, lean, and dark, and aged, the mouth painful, the teeth disclosed in a perpetual rictus; the eyeball swimming clear of the lids upon a field of blood-shot white. I could not behold him myself without a jarring irritation, such as, I believe, is too frequently the uppermost feeling on the sickness of those dear to us. Others, I could not but remark, were scarce able to support his neighbourhood—Sir William eviting to be near him, Mountain dodging his eye, and, when he met it, blenching and halting in his story. At this appeal, however, my lord appeared to recover his command upon himself.

'To Albany?' said he, with a good voice.

'Nor short of it, at least,' replied Sir William. 'There is no safety nearer hand.'

'I would be very sweir[1] to return,' says my lord. 'I am not afraid—of Indians,' he added, with a jerk.

[1] Unwilling.

'I wish that I could say so much,' returned Sir William, smiling; 'although, if any man durst say it, it should be myself. But you are to keep in view my responsibility, and that as the voyage has now become highly dangerous, and your business—if you ever had any,' says he, 'brought quite to a conclusion by the distressing family intelligence you have received, I should be hardly justified if I even suffered you to proceed, and run the risk of some obloquy if anything regrettable should follow.'

My lord turned to Mountain. 'What did he pretend he died of?' he asked.

'I don't think I understand your honour,' said the trader, pausing like a man very much affected, in the dressing of some cruel frostbites.

For a moment my lord seemed at a full stop· and then, with some irritation, 'I ask you what he died of. Surely that's a plain question,' said he.

'Oh! I don't know,' said Mountain. 'Hastie even never knew. He seemed to sicken natural, and just pass away.'

'There it is, you see!' concluded my lord, turning to Sir William.

'Your lordship is too deep for me,' replied Sir William.

'Why,' says my lord, 'this is a matter of succession; my son's title may be called in doubt; and the man being supposed to be dead of nobody can tell what, a great deal of suspicion would be naturally roused.'

'But, God damn me, the man's buried!' cried Sir William.

'I will never believe that,' returned my lord, painfully trembling. 'I'll never believe it!' he cried again, and jumped to his feet. 'Did he *look* dead?' he asked of Mountain.

'Look dead?' repeated the trader. 'He looked white. Why, what would he be at? I tell you, I put the sods upon him.'

My lord caught Sir William by the coat with a hooked hand. 'This man has the name of my brother,' says he, 'but it's well understood that he was never canny.'

'Canny?' says Sir William. 'What is that?'

'He's not of this world,' whispered my lord, 'neither him nor the black deil that serves him. I have struck my sword throughout his vitals,' he cried; 'I have felt the hilt dirl[1] on his breastbone, and the hot blood spirt in my very face, time and again, time and again!' he repeated, with a gesture indescribable. 'But he was never dead for that,' said he, and I sighed aloud. 'Why should I think he was dead now? No, not till I see him rotting,' says he.

1 Ring.

Sir William looked across at me with a long face. Mountain forgot his wounds, staring and gaping.

'My lord,' said I, 'I wish you would collect your spirits.' But my throat was so dry, and my own wits so scattered, I could add no more.

'No,' says my lord, 'it's not to be supposed that he would understand me. Mackellar does, for he kens all, and has seen him buried before now. This is a very good servant to me, Sir William, this man Mackellar; he buried him with his own hands—he and my father—by the light of two siller candlesticks. The other man is a familiar spirit; he brought him from Coromandel. I would have told ye this long syne, Sir William, only it was in the family.' These last remarks he made with a kind of melancholy composure, and his time of aberration seemed to pass away. 'You can ask yourself what it all means,' he proceeded. 'My brother falls sick, and dies, and is buried, as so they say; and all seems very plain. But why did the familiar go back? I think ye must see for yourself it's a point that wants some clearing.'

'I will be at your service, my lord, in half a minute,' said Sir William, rising. 'Mr. Mackellar, two words with you;' and he led me without the camp, the frost crunching in our steps, the trees standing at our elbow, hoar with frost, even as on that night in the Long Shrubbery. 'Of course, this is midsummer madness,' said Sir William, as soon as we were gotten out of hearing.

'Why, certainly,' said I. 'The man is mad. I think that manifest.'

'Shall I seize and bind him?' asked Sir William. 'I will upon your authority. If these are all ravings, that should certainly be done.'

I looked down upon the ground, back at the camp, with its bright fires and the folk watching us, and about me on the woods and mountains; there was just the one way that I could not look, and that was in Sir William's face.

'Sir William,' said I at last, 'I think my lord not sane, and have long thought him so. But there are degrees in madness; and whether he should be brought under restraint—Sir William, I am no fit judge,' I concluded.

'I will be the judge,' said he. 'I ask for facts. Was there, in all that jargon, any word of truth or sanity? Do you hesitate?' he asked. 'Am I to understand you have buried this gentleman before?'

'Not buried,' said I; and then, taking up courage at last,

'Sir William,' said I, 'unless I were to tell you a long story, which much concerns a noble family (and myself not in the least), it would be impossible to make this matter clear to you. Say the word, and I will do it, right or wrong. And, at any rate, I will say so much, that my lord is not so crazy as he seems. This is a strange matter, into the tail of which you are unhappily drifted.'

'I desire none of your secrets,' replied Sir William; 'but I will be plain at the risk of incivility, and confess that I take little pleasure in my present company.'

'I would be the last to blame you,' said I, 'for that.'

'I have not asked either for your censure or your praise, sir,' returned Sir William. 'I desire simply to be quit of you: and to that effect I put a boat and complement of men at your disposal.'

'This is fairly offered,' said I, after reflection. 'But you must suffer me to say a word upon the other side. We have a natural curiosity to learn the truth of this affair; I have some of it myself; my lord (it is very plain) has but too much. The matter of the Indian's return is enigmatical.'

'I think so myself,' Sir William interrupted, 'and I propose (since I go in that direction) to probe it to the bottom. Whether or not the man has gone like a dog to die upon his master's grave, his life, at least, is in great danger, and I propose, if I can, to save it. There is nothing against his character?'

'Nothing, Sir William,' I replied.

'And the other?' he said. 'I have heard my lord, of course; but, from the circumstances of his servant's loyalty, I must suppose he had some noble qualities.'

'You must not ask that!' I cried. 'Hell may have noble flames. I have known him a score of years, and always hated, and always admired, and always slavishly feared him.'

'I appear to intrude again upon your secrets,' said Sir William, 'believe me, inadvertently. Enough that I will see the grave, and (if possible) rescue the Indian. Upon these terms, can you persuade your master to return to Albany?'

'Sir William,' said I, 'I will tell you how it is. You do not see my lord to advantage; it will seem even strange to you that I should love him; but I do, and I am not alone. If he goes back to Albany, it must be by force, and it will be the death-warrant of his reason, and perhaps his life. That is my sincere belief; but I am in your hands, and ready to obey, if you will assume so much responsibility as to command.'

'I will have no shred of responsibility; it is my single endeavour to avoid the same,' cried Sir William. 'You insist upon following this journey up; and be it so! I wash my hands of the whole matter.'

With which word, he turned upon his heel and gave the order to break camp; and my lord, who had been hovering near by, came instantly to my side.

' Which is it to be? ' said he.

' You are to have your way,' I answered. ' You shall see the grave.'

The situation of the Master's grave was, between guides, easily described; it lay, indeed, beside a chief landmark of the wilderness, a certain range of peaks, conspicuous by their design and altitude, and the source of many brawling tributaries to that inland sea, Lake Champlain. It was therefore possible to strike for it direct, instead of following back the blood-stained trail of the fugitives, and to cover, in some sixteen hours of march, a distance which their perturbed wanderings had extended over more than sixty. Our boats we left under a guard upon the river; it was, indeed, probable we should return to find them frozen fast; and the small equipment with which we set forth upon the expedition, included not only an infinity of furs to protect us from the cold, but an arsenal of snow-shoes to render travel possible, when the inevitable snow should fall. Considerable alarm was manifested at our departure; the march was conducted with soldierly precaution, the camp at night sedulously chosen and patrolled; and it was a consideration of this sort that arrested us, the second day, within not many hundred yards of our destination—the night being already imminent, the spot in which we stood well qualified to be a strong camp for a party of our numbers; and Sir William, therefore, on a sudden thought, arresting our advance.

Before us was the high range of mountains toward which we had been all day deviously drawing near. From the first light of the dawn, their silver peaks had been the goal of our advance across a tumbled lowland forest, thrid with rough streams, and strewn with monstrous boulders; the peaks (as I say) silver, for already at the higher altitudes the snow fell nightly; but the woods and the low ground only breathed upon with frost. All day heaven had been charged with ugly vapours in the which the sun swam and glimmered like a shilling piece; all day the wind blew on our left cheek barbarous cold, but very pure to breathe. With the end of the afternoon, however, the wind fell; the clouds, being no longer reinforced, were scattered or drunk up; the sun set behind us with some wintry splendour, and the white brow of the mountains shared its dying glow.

It was dark ere we had supper; we ate in silence, and the meal was scarce despatched before my lord slunk from the fireside to the margin of the camp; whither I made haste to follow him. The camp was on high ground, overlooking a frozen lake, perhaps a mile in its longest measurement; all about us, the forest lay in heights and hollows; above rose the white mountains; and higher yet, the moon rode in a fair sky. There was no breath of air; nowhere a twig creaked; and the sounds of our own camp were hushed and swallowed up in the surrounding stillness. Now that the sun and the wind were both gone down, it appeared almost warm, like a night of July; a singular illusion of the sense, when earth, air, and water were strained to bursting with the extremity of frost.

My lord (or what I still continued to call by his loved name) stood with his elbow in one hand, and his chin sunk in the other, gazing before him on the surface of the wood. My eyes followed his, and rested almost pleasantly upon the frosted contexture of the pines rising in moonlit hillocks, or sinking in the shadow of small glens. Hard by, I told myself, was the grave of our enemy, now gone where the wicked cease from troubling, the earth heaped for ever on his once so active limbs. I could not but think of him as somehow fortunate to be thus done with man's anxiety and weariness, the daily expense of spirit, and that daily river of circumstance to be swum through, at any hazard, under the penalty of shame or death. I could not but think how good was the end of that long travel; and with that, my mind swung at a tangent to my lord. For was not my lord dead also? a maimed soldier, looking vainly for discharge, lingering derided in the line of battle? A kind man, I remembered him; wise, with a decent pride, a son perhaps too dutiful, a husband only too loving, one that could suffer and be silent, one whose hand I loved to press. Of a sudden, pity caught in my windpipe with a sob; I could have wept aloud to remember and behold him; and standing thus by his elbow, under the broad moon, I prayed fervently either that he should be released, or I strengthened to persist in my affection.

' Oh God,' said I, ' this was the best man to me and to himself, and now I shrink from him. He did no wrong, or not till he was broke with sorrows; these are but his honourable wounds that we begin to shrink from. Oh, cover them up, oh, take him away, before we hate him!'

I was still so engaged in my own bosom, when a sound broke suddenly upon the night. It was neither very loud, nor very near; yet, bursting as it did from so profound and so prolonged a silence, it startled the camp like an alarm of trumpets. Ere I had taken breath, Sir William was beside me, the main part of the voyagers clustered at his back, intently giving ear. Methought, as I glanced at them across my shoulder, there was a whiteness, other than moonlight, on their cheeks; and the rays of the moon reflected with a sparkle on the eyes of some, and the shadows lying black under the brows of others (according as they raised or bowed their head to listen) gave to the group a strange air of animation and anxiety. My lord was to the front, crouching a little forth, his hand raised as for silence: a man turned to stone. And still the sounds continued breathlessly renewed with a precipitate rhythm.

Suddenly Mountain spoke in a loud, broken whisper, as of a man relieved. ' I have it now,' he said; and, as we all turned to hear him, ' the Indian must have known the cache,' he added. ' That is he—he is digging out the treasure.'

' Why, to be sure! ' exclaimed Sir William. ' We were geese not to have supposed so much.'

' The only thing is,' Mountain resumed, ' the sound is very close to our old camp. And, again, I do not see how he is there before us, unless the man had wings! '

' Greed and fear are wings,' remarked Sir William. ' But this rogue has given us an alert, and I have a notion to return the compliment. What say you, gentlemen, shall we have a moonlight hunt ? '

It was so agreed; dispositions were made to surround Secundra at his task; some of Sir William's Indians hastened in advance; and a strong guard being left at our headquarters, we set forth along the uneven bottom of the forest; frost crackling, ice sometimes loudly splitting under foot; and overhead the blackness of pinewoods, and the broken brightness of the moon. Our way led down into a hollow of the land; and as we descended, the sounds diminished and had almost died away. Upon the other slope it was more open, only dotted with a few pines, and several vast and scattered rocks that made inky shadows in the moonlight. Here the sounds began to reach us more distinctly; we could now perceive the ring of iron, and more exactly estimate the furious degree of haste with which the digger plied his instrument. As we neared the top of the ascent, a bird or two winged aloft and hovered darkly in the moonlight; and the next moment we were gazing through a fringe of trees upon a singular picture.

A narrow plateau, overlooked by the white mountains, and

encompassed nearer hand by woods, lay bare to the strong radiance of the moon. Rough goods, such as make the wealth of foresters, were sprinkled here and there upon the gound in meaningless disarray. About the midst, a tent stood, silvered with frost: the door open, gaping on the black interior. At the one end of this small stage lay what seemed the tattered remnants of a man. Without doubt we had arrived upon the scene of Harris's encampment; there were the goods scattered in the panic of flight; it was in yon tent the Master breathed his last; and the frozen carrion that lay before us was the body of the drunken shoemaker. It was always moving to come upon the theatre of any tragic incident; to come upon it after so many days, and to find it (in the seclusion of a desert) still unchanged, must have impressed the mind of the most careless. And yet it was not that which struck us into pillars of stone; but the sight (which yet we had been half expecting) of Secundra ankle deep in the grave of his late Master. He had cast the main part of his raiment by, yet his frail arms and shoulders glistened in the moonlight with a copious sweat; his face was contracted with anxiety and expectation; his blows resounded on the grave, as thick as sobs; and behind him, strangely deformed and ink-black upon the frosty ground, the creature's shadow repeated and parodied his swift gesticulations. Some night birds arose from the boughs upon our coming, and then settled back; but Secundra, absorbed in his toil, heard or heeded not at all.

I heard Mountain whisper to Sir William, 'Good God! it's the grave! He's digging him up!' It was what we had all guessed, and yet to hear it put in language thrilled me. Sir William violently started.

'You damned sacrilegious hound!' he cried. 'What's this?'

Secundra leaped in the air, a little breathless cry escaped him, the tool flew from his grasp, and he stood one instant staring at the speaker. The next, swift as an arrow, he sped for the woods upon the farther side; and the next again, throwing up his hands with a violent gesture of resolution, he had begun already to retrace his steps.

'Well, then, you come, you help—— ' he was saying. But by now my lord had stepped beside Sir William; the moon shone fair upon his face, and the words were still upon Secundra's lips, when he beheld and recognised his master's enemy. 'Him!' he screamed, clasping his hands, and shrinking on himself.

'Come, come!' said Sir William. 'There is none here to do you harm, if you be innocent; and if you be guilty, your escape is quite cut off. Speak, what do you here among the graves of the dead and the remains of the unburied?'

'You no murder?' inquired Secundra. 'You true man? You see me safe?'

'I will see you safe, if you be innocent,' returned Sir William. 'I have said the thing, and I see not wherefore you should doubt it.'

'There all murderers,' cried Secundra, 'that is why! He kill— murderer,' pointing to Mountain; 'there two hire-murderers,' pointing to my lord and myself—'all gallows-murderers! Ah! I see you all swing in a rope. Now I go save the sahib; he see you swing in a rope. The sahib,' he continued, pointing to the grave, 'he not dead. He bury, he not dead.'

My lord uttered a little noise, moved nearer to the grave, and stood and stared in it.

'Buried and not dead?' exclaimed Sir William. 'What kind of rant is this?'

'See, sahib,' said Secundra. 'The sahib and I alone with murderers; try all way to escape, no way good. Then try this way: good way in warm climate, good way in India; here, in this dam cold place, who can tell? I tell you pretty good hurry: you help, you light a fire, help rub.'

'What is the creature talking of?' cried Sir William. 'My head goes round.'

'I tell you I bury him alive,' said Secundra. 'I teach him swallow his tongue. Now dig him up pretty good hurry, and he not much worse. You light a fire.'

Sir William turned to the nearest of his men. 'Light a fire,' said he. 'My lot seems to be cast with the insane.'

'You good man,' returned Secundra. 'Now I go dig the sahib up.'

He returned as he spoke to the grave, and resumed his former toil. My lord stood rooted, and I at my lord's side, fearing I knew not what.

The frost was not yet very deep, and presently the Indian threw aside his tool, and began to scoop the dirt by handfuls. Then he disengaged a corner of a buffalo robe; and then I saw hair catch among his fingers: yet a moment more, and the moon shone on something white. Awhile Secundra crouched upon his knees, scraping with delicate fingers, breathing with puffed lips; and when he moved aside I beheld the face of the Master wholly disengaged. It was deadly white, the eyes closed, the ears and nostrils plugged, the cheeks fallen, the nose sharp as if in death; but for all he had lain so many days under the sod, corruption had not approached him, and (what strangely affected all of us) his lips and chin were mantled with a swarthy beard.

'My God!' cried Mountain, 'he was as smooth as a baby when we laid him there!'

'They say hair grows upon the dead,' observed Sir William; but his voice was thick and weak.

Secundra paid no heed to our remarks, digging swift as a terrier in the loose earth. Every moment the form of the Master, swathed in his buffalo robe, grew more distinct in the bottom of that shallow trough; the moon shining strong, and the shadows of the standersby, as they drew forward and back, falling and flitting over his emergent countenance. The sight held us with a horror not before experienced. I dared not look my lord in the face; but for as long as it lasted, I never observed him to draw breath; and a little in the background one of the men (I know not whom) burst into a kind of sobbing.

'Now,' said Secundra, 'you help me lift him out.'

Of the flight of time, I have no idea; it may have been three hours, and it may have been five, that the Indian laboured to reanimate his master's body. One thing only I know, that it was still night, and the moon was not yet set, although it had sunk low, and now barred the plateau with long shadows, when Secundra uttered a small cry of satisfaction; and, leaning swiftly forth, I thought I could myself perceive a change upon the icy countenance of the unburied. The next moment I beheld his eyelids flutter; the next they rose entirely, and the week-old corpse looked me for a moment in the face.

So much display of life I can myself swear to. I have heard from others that he visibly strove to speak, that his teeth showed in his beard, and that his brow was contorted as with an agony of pain and effort. And this may have been; I know not, I was otherwise engaged. For at that first disclosure of the dead man's eyes, my Lord Durrisdeer fell to the ground, and when I raised him up, he was a corpse.

Day came, and still Secundra could not be persuaded to desist from his unavailing efforts. Sir William, leaving a small party under my command, proceeded on his embassy with the first light; and still the Indian rubbed the limbs and breathed in the mouth of the dead body. You would think such labours might have vitalised a stone; but, except for that one moment (which was my lord's death), the black spirit of the Master held aloof from its discarded clay; and by about the hour of noon, even the faithful servant was at length convinced. He took it with unshaken quietude.

'Too cold,' said he, 'good way in India, no good here.' And, asking for some food, which he ravenously devoured as soon as it was set before him, he drew near to the fire and took his place at my elbow. In the same spot, as soon as he had eaten, he stretched himself out, and fell into a childlike slumber, from which I must arouse him, some hours afterwards, to take his part as one of the mourners at the double funeral. It was the same throughout; he seemed to have outlived at once, and with the same effort, his grief for his master and his terror of myself and Mountain.

One of the men left with me was skilled in stone-cutting; and before Sir William returned to pick us up, I had chiselled on a boulder this inscription, with a copy of which I may fitly bring my narrative to a close:

J. D.,
HEIR TO A SCOTTISH TITLE,
A MASTER OF THE ARTS AND GRACES,
ADMIRED IN EUROPE, ASIA, AMERICA,
IN WAR AND PEACE,
IN THE TENTS OF SAVAGE HUNTERS AND THE
CITADELS OF KINGS, AFTER SO MUCH
ACQUIRED, ACCOMPLISHED, AND
ENDURED, LIES HERE FOR-
GOTTEN.

———

H. D.,
HIS BROTHER,
AFTER A LIFE OF UNMERITED DISTRESS,
BRAVELY SUPPORTED,
DIED ALMOST IN THE SAME HOUR,
AND SLEEPS IN THE SAME GRAVE
WITH HIS FRATERNAL ENEMY.

———

THE PIETY OF HIS WIFE AND ONE OLD
SERVANT RAISETH THIS STONE
TO BOTH.

WEIR OF HERMISTON

TO
MY WIFE

I saw rain falling and the rainbow drawn
On Lammermuir. Hearkening I heard again
In my precipitous city beaten bells
Winnow the keen sea wind. And here afar,
Intent on my own race and place, I wrote.

Take thou the writing: thine it is. For who
Burnished the sword, blew on the drowsy coal,
Held still the target higher, chary of praise
And prodigal of counsel—who but thou?
So now, in the end, if this the least be good,
If any deed be done, if any fire
Burn in the imperfect page, the praise be thine.

R. L. S.

CONTENTS

INTRODUCTION

A NOVEL with a story to tell has become almost uncommon. Much of the fiction of our immediate day is concerned only with a glimpse of character or the presentment of a passing mood. Robert Louis Stevenson remains and endures as the Teller of Tales, as his dusky friends in Samoa were so quick to realise.

There are some stories that are conceived and narrated in cold blood. Stevenson could only be inspired by something which burned into his imagination and demanded transcript—sometimes almost in words of fire.

This is especially so of that greatest work of his which never found completion. *Weir of Hermiston* is the crown and summit of Stevenson's genius as a novelist. There is no shadow of doubt about the bigness of the theme and the mastery of its handling. One of the major tragedies of literature is that the writer was gripped by the hand of death and torn from the world of living men when he had, with triumphant surety, planned and (one is sure) mentally perfected his great task. Broken *Weir of Hermiston* ends with the words: ' It seemed unprovoked, a wilful convulsion of brute nature—— '

The words are an unconscious indictment of the greedy Reaper.

In the whole range of Scottish literature, there is no stronger and finer portrait of a man, with all the vices and some of the virtues of his race, than Hermiston. If the author of *The House with the Green Shutters*, George Douglas Brown, had depicted such a character as the Lord Justice-Clerk, his callous cruelty would have been insisted on. He would have appeared—as indeed Weir did seem to the fastidious—a boorish vulgarian, who flouted with his ribald mirth the niceties of his associates, and jeered at every decent human instinct.

Stevenson does his man justice. It may be that he does so because he had always a kindly eye for a ruffian who was not a hypocrite. We know that Weir had risen to his lofty position not through favour or the cringing that often climbs to power, but by his own gifts as a man who has mastered the law and who, at his own caprice, is prepared to bend it to cruel uses. R. L. S. tells us of the judge's gusto in lashing a man with his bitter, boisterous, fleering tongue while he was condemning him to the gallows. He recounts how the Lord Justice-Clerk insults those about him and makes mockery of decency and gentlehood. But he does convey to us the fearless honesty of the man, his hatred of shams, and his determination to tell the truth and shame the devil.

He is no bad family man, Adam Weir, though an unco' ill person to live with. Take his treatment of his exasperating, pietistical, marrowless wife who could never rule a house or keep a cook. Everything that appears on his table is uneatable, and, with a hearty curse or two he calls for bread and cheese. The feeble lady has an appropriate epitaph in her lord's expression when he heard on the threshold of his house that this ineffectual helpmate had breathed her last. ' Well, it's something of the suddenest. But she was a dwaibly body from the first.'

One is inclined to sympathise with Lord Hermiston over his son who is so horrified by his father's summing-up against the murderer, Duncan Jopp, that he makes a public denunciation of the hanging. One sympathises with Archie Weir too, in a way, and realises that his gorge did rise when sentence was being passed, but, after all, one must have certain loyalties, and Weir himself had a great love for his disappointing son hidden deep down in that harsh soul of his.

If it were not for that innate tenderness for his only child, that terrible climax Stevenson was leading up to—of the Lord Justice-Clerk sentencing his son to death for the murder of Frank Innes, the friend who had betrayed him with Christina—would be sheerly intolerable through its inhumanity. It would have failed in that redeeming horror—that high tragedy—which makes *Weir of Hermiston* a mighty thing even in its unfinished state.

It has been said again and again that Stevenson never knew how to depict a woman. The charge is met and dismissed in the presentation of Kirstie Elliott, that big-framed, golden-headed, frustrate, middle-aged lover of Archie Weir, who will never dare to admit to herself that the boy is anything but a beloved nephew to her. Big Kirstie is a fitting companion picture for burly, arrogant Weir of Hermiston himself.

What shall we say, too, of Kirstie the younger, who would be called Christina? If ever human girl appeared between covers, it is this. One sees Christina in the flesh and pities her for that false chivalry of her lover, Archie Weir, which throws her into the arms of so poor a creature as Frank Innes.

It detracts not one iota from the high merits of *Weir of Hermiston* that its main character is taken from History. Robert Macqueen, Lord Braxfield, from whom Stevenson painted his Lord Justice-Clerk, has been as Sir Sydney Colvin says, the subject of a hundred Edinburgh tales and anecdotes.

The whole hundred put together can give no such portrait

of a man as Robert Louis Stevenson has done in his fiction. Lord Hermiston indeed, as lovingly limned by Stevenson, stands among the world's immortals, whereas Lord Braxfield is esteemed only in Scotland.

Of the portion of *Heathercat*, the third of the unfinished stories in this edition, this tale of the Killing-Time is mostly preamble. Stevenson was very fond of giving the exact territory of his characters and telling you all about their forbears. In this he markedly resembles Scott.

The boy, Francie Traquair, son of Montroymont, was called Heathercat by his playmates because there was scarcely any spot but what he could leave it or approach it unseen. We see him at eleven years of age, secret and shy and rather cowardly. Francie's early days were to be identified with the harrying of the Covenanters, and then he was to go on a treasure quest to Darien.

The Young Chevalier, of which there is presented only a prologue and a small portion of its first chapter, was based on a suggestion of Andrew Lang, who had come upon an account of Prince Charles Edward and his adventures in the city of Avignon, after he had been expelled from France and grown weary of Rome.

The real hero was to be, not the Prince—Stevenson had no great love or respect for Charles Edward—but Francis Blair of Balmile, the Jacobite Lord Gladsmuir. The other characters are The Master of Ballantrae, an innkeeper, Paradou, ' built more like a bullock than a man,' and his wife Marie-Madeleine, who was a coquettish beauty. She adored Balmile, natheless the clumsy brutal jealousy of her formidable husband.

We are whipped away from Paradou's wine shop to a high apartment in which the Prince drinks and pities himself. The break-off of the chapter will tantalise every reader:—

' From two rooms beyond, the sudden sound of a raised voice attracted him.

' By . . .

Probably Robert Louis Stevenson himself, notwithstanding his fondness for the idea of ' The Great North Road,' was inclined to call it ' tushery.'

It has a boyishness about it, appealing in a way. He admits of the tale that he intended to turn it off like Treasure Island ' for coin,' but he says also that it kept growing under his hands. The fact that he completed eight short chapters of it is proof that he was engrossed by this theme. He evidently kept on writing for his own pleasure. It is a dashing piece of romance, but appears to contain no element of abiding literature. Nance Holdaway is just the ordinary pretty soubrette of tavern days. Her Uncle Jonathan, who has failed as an innkeeper and would become a highwayman if he possessed the courage, is not a very likeable kind of man. The mysterious young Mr. Archer, who has the courage to become a gentleman of the High Toby— and evidently does so—is a horse of a different colour.

The Story of a Recluse, in its four short pages, opens with vivacity. A young gentleman who has lost his money at gambling overnight, wakes to find himself in a strange bed and beside it a personable young woman viewing him with bewilderment, anger and disgust.

Of the three very short fragments, *The Owl*, *Cannonmils*, and *Mr. Baskerville and his Ward*, the first was to be a story of the Breton Revolution and of an apostate aristocrat faced by one of the Old Rock; the second merely introduces us to the Fordyce family at breakfast; and the third recounts how young Robin Rutledge left the village of Singleton St. Mary's after he had been severely whipped by his guardian, Mr. Baskerville, for telling a lie. It was to deal with Jacobite times. . . .

Very fascinating are the three chapters of the unfinished *Adventures of Henry Shovel*. Originally Stevenson conceived of a novel to cover half a dozen generations and to be called *The Shovels of Newton French*. Later he added to his suggested title: *Including Memories of Henry Shovel, a Private in the Peninsular War*. The fiction was to begin in 1664 and end about 1832.

The novel was to include in its characters Judge Jeffreys, Wellington and Townsend the Runner. One would give much to possess Stevenson's impression of the Iron Duke and of the red-robed, callous director of the Bloody Assize.

In the portion written it is obvious that Robert Louis Stevenson was devoting his best care and cunning to the characterisation of the First Shovel. Told in the first person it conveys, in direct narrative form, a clear impression of a froward boy, likely to fall into every error that insolent inexperience can subject him to.

Already, in the very opening of the novel, two most vivid little dramas are played in Henry's refusal to apologise to his uncle's guest whom he hates, and in the boy's cruel treatment of the wretched teacher, Mr. Bryce. Scottish lovers of Stevenson will not take too seriously his description of Bryce as: ' A diminutive, gray-faced creature with a ridiculous Scotch accent (I have always disliked that nation).' This is only the fun of a man who never entirely lost touch with the mockeries of boyhood.

INTRODUCTION

Here, then, is a book of fragments, but it can be read with as much delight as one brings to many completed stories. These unfinished castings are tantalising in a way, but they are never tiresome. Every page has a merit of its own. High above all the other experiments in prose stands the great torso of *Weir of Hermiston.*

LOUIS J. MCQUILLAND

INTRODUCTORY

IN the wild end of a moorland parish, far out of the sight of any house, there stands a cairn among the heather, and a little by east of it, in the going down of the braeside, a monument with some verses half defaced. It was here that Claverhouse shot with his own hand the Praying Weaver of Balweary, and the chisel of Old Mortality has clinked on that lonely gravestone. Public and domestic history have thus marked with a bloody finger this hollow among the hills; and since the Cameronian gave his life there, two hundred years ago, in a glorious folly, and without comprehension or regret, the silence of the moss has been broken once again by the report of firearms and the cry of the dying.

The Deil's Hags was the old name. But the place is now called Francie's Cairn. For a while it was told that Francie walked. Aggie Hogg met him in the gloaming by the cairnside, and he spoke to her, with chattering teeth, so that his words were lost. He pursued Rob Todd (if any one could have believed Robbie) for the space of half a mile with pitiful entreaties. But the age is one of incredulity; these superstitious decorations speedily fell off; and the facts of the story itself, like the bones of a giant buried there and half dug up, survived, naked and imperfect, in the memory of the scattered neighbours. To this day of winter nights, when the sleet is on the window and the cattle are quiet in the byre, there will be told again, amid the silence of the young and the additions and corrections of the old, the tale of the Justice-Clerk and of his son, young Hermiston, that vanished from men's knowledge; of the Two Kirsties and the Four Black Brothers of the Cauldstaneslap; and of Frank Innes, ' the young fool advocate,' that came into these moorland parts to find his destiny.

Life and death of Mrs. Weir

THE Lord Justice-Clerk was a stranger in that part of the
country; but his lady wife was known there from a child,
as her race had been before her. The old ' riding Rutherfords
of Hermiston,' of whom she was the last descendant, had been
famous men of yore, ill neighbours, ill subjects, and ill husbands
to their wives though not their properties. Tales of them were
rife for twenty miles about; and their name was even printed
in the page of our Scots histories, not always to their credit.
One bit the dust at Flodden; one was hanged at his peel door
by James the Fifth; another fell dead in a carouse with Tom
Dalyell; while a fourth (and that was Jean's own father) died
presiding at a Hell-Fire Club, of which he was the founder.
There were many heads shaken in Crossmichael at that judgment; the more so as the man had a villainous reputation
among high and low, and both with the godly and the worldly.
At that very hour of his demise, he had ten going pleas before
the session, eight of them oppressive. And the same doom
extended even to his agents; his grieve, that had been his right
hand in many a left-hand business, being cast from his horse
one night and drowned in a peat-hag on the Kye-skairs; and
his very doer (although lawyers have long spoons) surviving
him not long, and dying on a sudden in a bloody flux.

In all these generations, while a male Rutherford was in the
saddle with his lads, or brawling in a change-house, there would
be always a white-faced wife immured at home in the old peel
or the later mansion-house. It seemed this succession of martyrs
bided long, but took their vengeance in the end, and that was
in the person of the last descendant, Jean. She bore the name of
the Rutherfords, but she was the daughter of their trembling wives.
At the first, she was not wholly without charm. Neighbours
recalled in her, as a child, a strain of elfin wilfulness, gentle little
mutinies, sad little gaieties, even a morning gleam of beauty that
was not to be fulfilled. She withered in the growing, and (whether
it was the sins of her sires or the sorrows of her mothers) came to
her maturity depressed, and, as it were, defaced; no blood of
life in her, no grasp or gaiety; pious, anxious, tender, tearful,
and incompetent.

It was a wonder to many that she had married—seeming so

wholly of the stuff that makes old maids. But chance cast her in the path of Adam Weir, then the new Lord Advocate, a recognised, risen man, the conqueror of many obstacles, and thus late in the day beginning to think upon a wife. He was one who looked rather to obedience than beauty, yet it would seem he was struck with her at the first look. 'Wha's she?' he said, turning to his host; and, when he had been told, 'Ay,' says he, 'she looks menseful. She minds me——'; and then, after a pause (which some have been daring enough to set down to sentimental recollections), 'Is she releegious?' he asked, and was shortly after, at his own request, presented. The acquaintance, which it seems profane to call a courtship, was pursued with Mr. Weir's accustomed industry, and was long a legend, or rather a source of legends in the Parliament House. He was described coming, rosy with much port, into the drawing room, walking direct up to the lady, and assailing her with pleasantries, to which the embarrassed fair one responded, in what seemed a kind of agony, 'Eh, Mr. Weir!' or 'O, Mr. Weir!' or 'Keep me, Mr. Weir!' On the very eve of their engagement it was related that one had drawn near to the tender couple, and had overheard the lady cry out, with the tones of one who talked for the sake of talking, 'Keep me, Mr. Weir, and what became of him?' and the profound accents of the suitor's reply, 'Haangit, mem, haangit.' The motives upon either side were much debated. Mr. Weir must have supposed his bride to be somehow suitable; perhaps he belonged to that class of men who think a weak head the ornament of women—an opinion invariably punished in this life. Her descent and her estate were beyond question. Her wayfaring ancestors and her litigious father had done well by Jean. There was ready money and there were broad acres, ready to fall wholly to the husband, to lend dignity to his descendants, and to himself a title, when he should be called upon the Bench. On the side of Jean, there was perhaps some fascination of curiosity as to this unknown male animal that approached her with the roughness of a ploughman and the *aplomb* of an advocate. Being so trenchantly opposed to all she knew, loved, or undertood, he may well have seemed to her the extreme, if scarcely the ideal, of his sex. And besides, he was an ill man to refuse. A little over forty at the period of his marriage, he looked already older, and to the force of manhood added the senatorial dignity of years; it was, perhaps, with an unreverend awe, but he was awful. The Bench, the Bar, and the most experienced and reluctant witness, bowed to his authority—and why not Jeannie Rutherford?

The heresy about foolish women is always punished, I have said, and Lord Hermiston began to pay the penalty at once. His house in George Square was wretchedly ill-guided; nothing answerable to the expense of maintenance but the cellar, which was his own private care. When things went wrong at dinner, as they continually did, my lord would look up the table at his wife: ' I think these broth would be better to sweem in than to sup.' Or else to the butler: ' Here, M'Killop, awa' wi' this Raadical gigot—tak' it to the French, man, and bring me some puddocks! It seems rather a sore kind of business that I should be all day in Court haanging Raadicals, and get nawthing to my denner.' Of course this was but a manner of speaking and he had never hanged a man for being a Radical in his life; the law, of which he was the faithful minister, directing otherwise. And of course these growls were in the nature of pleasantry, but it was of a recondite sort; and uttered as they were in his resounding voice, and commented on by that expression which they called in the Parliament House ' Hermiston's hanging face '— they struck mere dismay into the wife. She sat before him speechless and fluttering; at each dish, as at a fresh ordeal, her eye hovered toward my lord's countenance and fell again; if he but ate in silence, unspeakable relief was her portion; if there were complaint, the world was darkened. She would seek out the cook, who was always her *sister in the Lord*. ' O my dear, this is the most dreidful thing that my lord can never be contented in his own house!' she would begin; and weep and pray with the cook; and then the cook would pray with Mrs. Weir; and the next day's meal would never be a penny the better—and the next cook (when she came) would be worse if anything, but just as pious. It was often wondered that Lord Hermiston bore it as he did; indeed he was a stoical old voluptuary, contented with sound wine and plenty of it. But there were moments when he overflowed. Perhaps half a dozen times in the history of his married life—' Here! tak' it awa', and bring me a piece of bread and kebbuck!' he had exclaimed, with an appalling explosion of his voice and rare gestures. None thought to dispute or to make excuses; the service was arrested; Mrs. Weir sat at the head of the table whimpering without disguise; and his lordship opposite munched his bread and cheese in ostentatious disregard. Once only Mrs. Weir had ventured to appeal. He was passing her chair on his way into the study.

' O, Edom!' she wailed, in a voice tragic with tears, and reaching out to him both hands, in one of which she held a sopping pocket-handkerchief.

He paused and looked upon her with a face of wrath, into which there stole, as he looked, a twinkle of humour.

'Noansense!' he said. 'You and your noansense! What do I want with a Christian faim'ly? I want Christian broth! Get me a lass that can plain-boil a potato, if she was a whüre off the streets.' And with these words, which echoed in her tender ears like blasphemy, he had passed on to his study and shut the door behind him.

Such was the housewifery in George Square. It was better at Hermiston, where Kirstie Elliott, the sister of a neighbouring bonnet-laird, and an eighteenth cousin of the lady's, bore the charge of all, and kept a trim house and a good country table. Kirstie was a woman in a thousand, clean, capable, notable; once a moorland Helen, and still comely as a blood horse and healthy as the hill wind. High in flesh and voice and colour, she ran the house with her whole intemperate soul, in a bustle, not without buffets. Scarce more pious than decency in those days required, she was the cause of many an anxious thought and many a tearful prayer to Mrs. Weir. Housekeeper and mistress renewed the parts of Martha and Mary; and though with a pricking conscience Mary reposed on Martha's strength as on a rock. Even Lord Hermiston held Kirstie in a particular regard. There were few with whom he unbent so gladly, few whom he favoured with so many pleasantries. 'Kirstie and me maun have our joke,' he would declare, in high good-humour, as he buttered Kirstie's scones and she waited at table. A man who had no need either of love or of popularity, a keen reader of men and of events, there was perhaps only one truth for which he was quite unprepared: he would have been quite unprepared to learn that Kirstie hated him. He thought maid and master were well matched; hard, handy, healthy, broad Scots folk, without a hair of nonsense to the pair of them. And the fact was that she made a goddess and an only child of the effete and tearful lady; and even as she waited at table her hands would sometimes itch for my lord's ears.

Thus, at least, when the family were at Hermiston, not only my lord, but Mrs. Weir too, enjoyed a holiday. Free from the dreadful looking-for of the miscarried dinner, she would mind her seam, read her piety books, and take her walk (which was my lord's orders), sometimes by herself, sometimes with Archie, the only child of that scarce natural union. The child was her next bond to life. Her frosted sentiment bloomed again, she breathed deep of life, she let loose her heart, in that society. The miracle of her motherhood was ever new to her. The sight of the little man at her skirt intoxicated her with the sense of power, and froze her with the consciousness of her responsibility. She looked forward, and, seeing him in fancy grow up and play his diverse part on the world's theatre, caught in her breath and lifted up her courage with a lively effort. It was only with the child that she forgot herself and was at moments natural; yet it was only with the child that she had conceived and managed to pursue a scheme of conduct. Archie was to be a great man and a good; a minister if possible, a saint for certain. She tried to engage his mind upon her favourite books, Rutherford's ' Letters,' Scougal's ' Grace Abounding,' and the like. It was a common practice of hers (and strange to remember now) that she would carry the child to the Deil's Hags, sit with him on the Praying Weaver's stone and talk of the Covenanters till their tears ran down. Her view of history was wholly artless, a design in snow and ink; upon the one side, tender innocents with psalms upon their lips; upon the other the persecutors, booted, bloody-minded, flushed with wine: a suffering Christ, a raging Beelzebub. *Persecutor* was a word that knocked upon the woman's heart; it was her highest thought of wickedness, and the mark of it was on her house. Her great-great-grandfather had drawn the sword against the Lord's anointed on the field of Rullion Green, and breathed his last (*tradition said*) in the arms of the detestable Dalyell. Nor could she blind herself to this, that had they lived in those old days, Hermiston himself would have been numbered alongside of Bloody Mackenzie and the politic Lauderdale and Rothes, in the band of God's immediate enemies. The sense of this moved her to the more fervour; she had a voice for that name of *persecutor* that thrilled in the child's marrow; and when one day the mob hooted and hissed them all in my lord's travelling carriage, and cried, ' Down with the persecutor! down with Hanging Hermiston!' and mamma covered her eyes and wept, and papa let down the glass and looked out upon the rabble with his droll formidable face, bitter and smiling, as they said he sometimes looked when he gave sentence, Archie was for the moment too much amazed to be alarmed, but he had scarce got his mother by herself before his shrill voice was raised demanding an explanation: Why had they called papa a persecutor?

' Keep me, my precious! ' she exclaimed. ' Keep me, my dear! this is poleetical. Ye must never ask me anything poleetical, Erchie. Your faither is a great man, my dear, and it's no for me or you to be judging him. It would be telling us all, if we behaved ourselves in our several stations the way your faither

221

does in his high office; and let me hear no more of any such disrespectful and undutiful questions! No that you meant to be undutiful, my lamb; your mother kens that—she kens it well, dearie!' and so slid off to safer topics, and left on the mind of the child an obscure but ineradicable sense of something wrong.

Mrs. Weir's philosophy of life was summed in one expression —tenderness. In her view of the universe, which was all lighted up with a glow out of the doors of hell, good people must walk there in a kind of ecstasy of tenderness. The beasts and plants had no souls; they were here but for a day, and let their day pass gently! And as for the immortal men, on what black, downward path were many of them wending, and to what a horror of an immortality! 'Are not two sparrows,' 'Whosoever shall smite thee,' 'God sendeth His rain,' 'Judge not that ye be not judged '—these texts made her body of divinity; she put them on in the morning with her clothes and lay down to sleep with them at night; they haunted her like a favourite air, they clung about her like a favourite perfume. Their minister was a marrowy expounder of the law, and my lord sat under him with relish; but Mrs. Weir respected him from afar off; heard him (like the cannon of a beleaguered city) usefully booming outside on the dogmatic ramparts; and meanwhile, within and out of shot, dwelt in her private garden, which she watered with grateful tears. It seems strange to say of this colourless and ineffectual woman, but she was a true enthusiast, and might have made the sunshine and the glory of a cloister. Perhaps none but Archie knew she could be eloquent; perhaps none but he had seen her—her colour raised, her hands clasped or quivering—glow with gentle ardour. There is a corner of the policy of Hermiston, where you come suddenly in view of the summit of Black Fell, sometimes like the mere grass top of a hill, sometimes (and this is her own expression) like a precious jewel in the heavens. On such days, upon the sudden view of it, her hand would tighten on the child's fingers, her voice rise like a song. 'I to the hills!' she would repeat. 'And O, Erchie, arena these like the hills of Naphtali?' and her easy tears would flow.

Upon an impressionable child the effect of this continual and pretty accompaniment to life was deep. The woman's quietism and piety passed on to his different nature undiminished; but whereas in her it was a native sentiment, in him it was only an implanted dogma. Nature and the child's pugnacity at times revolted. A cad from the Potterrow once struck him in the mouth; he struck back, the pair fought it out in the back stable lane towards the Meadows, and Archie returned with a considerable decline in the number of his front teeth, and unregenerately boasting of the losses of the foe. It was a sore day for Mrs. Weir; she wept and prayed over the infant backslider until my lord was due from Court, and she must resume that air of tremulous composure with which she always greeted him. The judge was that day in an observant mood, and remarked upon the absent teeth.

'I am afraid Erchie will have been fechting with some of they blagyard lads,' said Mrs. Weir.

My lord's voice rang out as it did seldom in the privacy of his own house. 'I'll have nonn of that, sir!' he cried. 'Do you hear me?—nonn of that! No son of mine shall be speldering in the glaur with any dirty raibble.'

The anxious mother was grateful for so much support; she had even feared the contrary. And that night when she put the child to bed—'Now, my dear, ye see!' she said, 'I told you what your faither would think of it, if he heard ye had fallen into this dreidful sin; and let you and me pray to God that ye may be keepit from the like temptation or stren'thened to resist it!'

The womanly falsity of this was thrown away. Ice and iron cannot be welded; and the points of view of the Justice-Clerk and Mrs. Weir were not less unassimilable. The character and position of his father had long been a stumbling-block to Archie, and with every year of his age the difficulty grew more instant. The man was mostly silent; when he spoke at all, it was to speak of the things of the world, always in a worldly spirit, often in language that the child had been schooled to think coarse, and sometimes with words that he knew to be sins in themselves. Tenderness was the first duty, and my lord was invariably harsh. God was love; the name of my lord (to all who knew him) was fear. In the world, as schematised for Archie by his mother, the place was marked for such a creature. There were some whom it was good to pity and well (though very likely useless) to pray for; they were named reprobates, goats, God's enemies, brands for the burning; and Archie tallied every mark of identification, and drew the inevitable private inference that the Lord Justice-Clerk was the chief of sinners.

The mother's honesty was scarce complete. There was one influence she feared for the child and still secretly combated; that was my lord's; and half unconsciously, half in a wilful blindness, she continued to undermine her husband with his son. As long as Archie remained silent, she did so ruthlessly, with a single eye to heaven and the child's salvation; but the day came when

Archie spoke. It was 1801, and Archie was seven, and beyond his years for curiosity and logic, when he brought the case up openly. If judging were sinful and forbidden, how came papa to be a judge? to have that sin for a trade? to bear the name of it for a distinction?

'I can't see it,' said the little Rabbi, and wagged his head.

Mrs. Weir abounded in commonplace replies.

'No, I canna see it,' reiterated Archie. 'And I'll tell you what, mamma, I don't think you and me's justifeed in staying with him.'

The woman awoke to remorse; she saw herself disloyal to her man, sovereign and bread-winner, in whom (with what she had of worldliness) she took a certain subdued pride. She expatiated in reply on my lord's honour and greatness; his useful services in this world of sorrow and wrong, and the place in which he stood, far above where babes and innocents could hope to see or criticise. But she had builded too well—Archie had his answers pat: Were not babes and innocents the type of the kingdom of heaven? Were not honour and greatness the badges of the world? And at any rate, how about the mob that had once seethed about the carriage?

'It's all very fine,' he concluded, 'but in my opinion, papa has no right to be it. And it seems that's not the worst yet of it. It seems he's called " the Hanging Judge "—it seems he's crooool. I'll tell you what it is, mamma, there's a tex' borne in upon me: It were better for that man if a milestone were bound upon his back and him flung into the deepestmost pairts of the sea.'

'O my lamb, ye must never say the like of that!' she cried. 'Ye're to honour faither and mother, dear, that your days may be long in the land. It's Atheists that cry out against him— French Atheists, Erchie! Ye would never surely even yourself down to be saying the same thing as French Atheists? It would break my heart to think that of you. And O, Erchie, here arena *you* setting up to *judge*? And have ye no' forgot God's plain command—the First with Promise, dear? Mind you upon the beam and the mote!'

Having thus carried the war into the enemy's camp, the terrified lady breathed again. And no doubt it is easy thus to circumvent a child with catchwords, but it may be questioned how far it is effectual. An instinct in his breast detects the quibble, and a voice condemns it. He will instantly submit, privately hold the same opinion. For even in this simple and antique relation of the mother and the child, hypocrisies are multiplied.

When the Court rose that year and the family returned to Hermiston, it was a common remark in all the country that the lady was sore failed. She seemed to lose and seize again her touch with life, now sitting inert in a sort of durable bewilderment, anon waking to feverish and weak activity. She dawdled about the lasses at their work, looking stupidly on; she fell to rummaging in old cabinets and presses, and desisted when half through; she would begin remarks with an air of animation and drop them without a struggle. Her common appearance was of one who has forgotten something and is trying to remember; and when she overhauled, one after another, the worthless and touching mementoes of her youth, she might have been seeking the clue to that lost thought. During this period she gave many gifts to the neighbours and house lassies, giving them with a manner of regret that embarrassed the recipients.

The last night of all she was busy on some female work, and toiled upon it with so manifest and painful a devotion that my lord (who was not often curious) inquired as to its nature.

She blushed to the eyes, ' O, Edom, it's for you! ' she said. ' It's slippers. I—I hae never made ye any.'

' Ye daft auld wife! ' returned his lordship. ' A bonny figure I would be, palmering about in bauchles! '

The next day, at the hour of her walk, Kirstie interfered. Kirstie took this decay of her mistress very hard; bore her a grudge, quarrelled with and railed upon her, the anxiety of a genuine love wearing the disguise of temper. This day of all days she insisted disrespectfully, with rustic fury, that Mrs. Weir should stay at home. But, ' No, no,' she said, ' it's my lord's orders,' and set forth as usual. Archie was visible in the acre bog, engaged upon some childish enterprise, the instrument of which was mire; and she stood and looked at him a while like one about to call; then thought otherwise, sighed, and shook her head, and proceeded on her rounds alone. The house lasses were at the burnside washing, and saw her pass with her loose, weary, dowdy gait.

' She's a terrible feckless wife, the mistress! ' said the one.

' Tut,' said the other, ' the wumman's seeck.'

' Weel, I canna see nae differ in her,' returned the first. ' A füshionless quean, a feckless carline.'

The poor creature thus discussed rambled a while in the grounds without a purpose. Tides in her mind ebbed and flowed, and carried her to and fro like seaweed. She tried a path, paused, returned, and tried another; questing, forgetting her quest; the spirit of choice extinct in her bosom, or devoid of sequency. On a sudden, it appeared as though she had remembered, or had formed a resolution, wheeled about, returned with hurried steps, and appeared in the dining-room, where Kirstie was at the cleaning, like one charged with an important errand.

'Kirstie!' she began, and paused; and then with conviction, 'Mr. Weir isna speeritually minded, but he has been a good man to me.'

It was perhaps the first time since her husband's elevation that she had forgotten the handle to his name, of which the tender, inconsistent woman was not a little proud. And when Kirstie looked up at the speaker's face, she was aware of a change.

'Goodsake, what's the maitter wi' ye, mem?' cried the housekeeper, starting from the rug.

'I do not ken,' answered her mistress, shaking her head. 'But he is not speeritually minded, my dear.'

'Here, sit down with ye! Godsake, what ails the wife?' cried Kirstie, and helped and forced her into my lord's own chair by the cheek of the hearth.

'Keep me, what's this?' she gasped. 'Kirstie, what's this? I'm frich'ened.'

They were her last words.

It was the lowering nightfall when my lord returned. He had the sunset in his back, all clouds and glory; and before him, by the wayside, spied Kirstie Elliott waiting. She was dissolved in tears, and addressed him in the high, false note of barbarous mourning, such as still lingers modified among Scots heather.

'The Lord peety ye, Hermiston! the Lord prepare ye!' she keened out. 'Weary upon me, that I should have to tell it!'

He reined in his horse and looked upon her with the hanging face.

'Has the French landit?' cried he.

'Man, man,' she said, 'is that a' ye can think of? The Lord prepare ye, the Lord comfort and support ye!'

'Is onybody deid?' says his lordship. 'It's no Erchie?'

'Bethankit, no!' exclaimed the woman, startled into a more natural tone. 'Na, na, it's no sae bad as that. It's the mistress, my lord; she just fair flittit before my e'en. She just gi'ed a sab and was by wi' it. Eh, my bonny Miss Jeannie, that I mind sae weel!' And forth again upon that pouring tide of lamentation in which women of her class excel and over-abound.

Lord Hermiston sat in the saddle, beholding her. Then he seemed to recover command upon himself.

'Weel, it's something of the suddenest,' said he. 'But she was a dwaibly body from the first.'

And he rode home at a precipitate amble with Kirstie at his horse's heels.

Dressed as she was for her last walk, they had laid the dead lady on her bed. She was never interesting in life; in death she was not impressive; and as her husband stood before her, with his hands crossed behind his powerful back, that which he looked upon was the very image of the insignificant.

'Her and me were never cut out for one another,' he remarked at last. 'It was a daftlike marriage.' And then, with a most unusual gentleness of tone, 'Puir bitch,' said he, 'puir bitch!' Then suddenly: 'Where's Erchie?'

Kirstie had decoyed him to her room and given him 'a jeely-piece.'

'Ye have some kind of gumption, too,' observed the Judge, and considered his housekeeper grimly. 'When all's said,' he added, 'I micht have done waur—I micht have been marriet upon a skirling Jezebel like you!'

'There's naebody thinking of you, Hermiston!' cried the offended woman. 'We think of her that's out of her sorrows. And could *she* have done waur? Tell me that, Hermiston— tell me that before her clay-cauld corp!'

'Weel, there's some of them gey an' ill to please,' observed his lordship.

2

Father and Son

My Lord Justice-Clerk was known to many; the man Adam Weir perhaps to none. He had nothing to explain or to conceal; he sufficed wholly and silently to himself; and that part of our nature which goes out (too often with false coin) to acquire glory or love, seemed in him to be omitted. He did not try to be loved, he did not care to be; it is probable the very thought of it was a stranger to his mind. He was an admired lawyer, a highly unpopular judge; and he looked down upon those who were his inferiors in either distinction, who were lawyers of less grasp or judges not so much detested. In all the rest of his days and doings, not one trace of vanity appeared; and he went on through life with a mechanical movement, as of the unconscious, that was almost august.

He saw little of his son. In the childish maladies with which the boy was troubled, he would make daily inquiries and daily pay him a visit, entering the sick-room with a facetious and appalling countenance, letting off a few perfunctory jests, and going again swiftly, to the patient's relief. Once, a Court holiday falling opportunely, my lord had his carriage, and drove the child himself to Hermiston, the customary place of convalescence. It is conceivable he had been more than usually anxious, for that journey always remained in Archie's memory as a thing apart, his father having related to him from beginning to end, and with much detail, three authentic murder cases. Archie went the usual round of other Edinburgh boys, the high school and the college; and Hermiston looked on, or rather looked away, with scarce an affectation of interest in his progress. Daily, indeed, upon a signal after dinner, he was brought in, given nuts and a glass of port, regarded sardonically, sarcastically questioned. 'Well, sir, and what have you donn with your book to-day?' my lord might begin, and set him posers in law Latin. To a child just stumbling into Corderius, Papinian and Paul proved quite invincible. But papa had memory of no other. He was not harsh to the little scholar, having a vast fund of patience learned upon the bench, and was at no pains whether to conceal or to express his disaapointment. 'Well, ye have a long jaunt before ye yet!' he might observe, yawning, and fall back on his own thoughts (as like as not) until the time came for separation, and my lord would take the decanter and the glass, and be off to the back chamber looking on the Meadows, where he toiled on his cases till the hours were small. There was no 'fuller man' on the Bench; his memory was marvellous, though wholly legal; if he had to 'advise' extempore, none did it better; yet there was none who more earnestly prepared. As he thus watched in the night, or sat at table and forgot the presence of his son, no doubt but he tasted deeply of recondite pleasures. To be wholly devoted to some intellectual exercise is to have succeeded in life; and perhaps only in law and the higher mathematics may this devotion be maintained, suffice to itself without reaction, and find continual rewards without excitement. This atmosphere of his father's sterling industry was the best of Archie's education. Assuredly it did not attract him; assuredly it rather rebutted and depressed. Yet it was still present, unobserved like the ticking of a clock, an arid ideal, a tasteless stimulant in the boy's life.

But Hermiston was not all of one piece. He was, besides, a mighty toper; he could sit at wine until the day dawned, and pass directly from the table to the Bench with a steady hand and a clear head. Beyond the third bottle, he showed the plebeian in a larger print; the low, gross accent, the low, foul mirth, grew broader and commoner; he became less formidable and infinitely more disgusting. Now, the boy had inherited from Jean Rutherford a shivering delicacy, unequally mated with potential violence. In the playing-fields, and amongst his own companions, he repaid a coarse expression with a blow; at his father's table (when the time came for him to join these revels) he turned pale and sickened in silence. Of all the guests whom he there encountered, he had toleration for only one: David Keith Carnegie, Lord Glenalmond. Lord Glenalmond was tall and emaciated, with long features and long delicate hands. He was often compared with the statue of Forbes of Culloden in the Parliament House; and his blue eye, at more than sixty, preserved some of the fire of youth. His exquisite disparity with any of his fellow-guests, his appearance as of an artist and an aristocrat stranded in rude company, riveted the boy's attention; and as curiosity and interest are the things in the world that are the most immediately and certainly rewarded, Lord Glenalmond was attracted to the boy.

'And so this is your son, Hermiston?' he asked, laying his hand on Archie's shoulder. 'He's getting a big lad.'

'Hout!' said the gracious father, 'just his mother over again—daurna say boo to a goose!'

But the stranger retained the boy, talked to him, drew him out, found in him a taste for letters, and a fine, ardent, modest, youthful soul; and encouraged him to be a visitor on Sunday evenings in his bare, cold, lonely dining-room, where he sat and read in the isolation of a bachelor grown old in refinement. The beautiful gentleness and grace of the old Judge, and the delicacy of his person, thoughts, and language, spoke to Archie's heart in its own tongue. He conceived the ambition to be such another; and, when the day came for him to choose a profession, it was in emulation of Lord Glenalmond, not of Lord Hermiston, that he chose the Bar. Hermiston looked on at this friendship with some secret pride, but openly with the intolerance of scorn. He scarce lost an opportunity to put them down with a rough jape; and, to say truth, it was not difficult, for they were neither of them quick. He had a word of contempt for the whole crowd of poets, painters, fiddlers, and their admirers, the bastard race of amateurs, which was continually on his lips. 'Signor Feedle-eerie!' he would say. 'Oh, for Goad's sake, no more of the Signor!'

'You and my father are great friends, are you not?' asked Archie once.

'There is no man that I more respect, Archie,' replied Lord

Glenalmond. ' He is two things of price. He is a great lawyer, and he is upright as the day.'

' You and he are so different,' said the boy, his eyes dwelling on those of his old friend, like a lover's on his mistress's.

' Indeed so,' replied the Judge; ' very different. And so I fear are you and he. Yet I would like it very ill if my young friend were to misjudge his father. He has all the Roman virtues: Cato and Brutus were such; I think a son's heart might well be proud of such an ancestry of one.'

' And I would sooner he were a plaided herd,' cried Archie, with sudden bitterness.

' And that is neither very wise, nor I believe entirely true,' returned Glenalmond. ' Before you are done you will find some of these expressions rise on you like a remorse. They are merely literary and decorative; they do not aptly express your thought, nor is your thought clearly apprehended, and no doubt your father (if he were here) would say " Signor Feedle-eerie! " '

With the infinitely delicate sense of youth, Archie avoided the subject from that hour. It was perhaps a pity. Had he but talked—talked freely—let himself gush out in words (the way youth loves to do and should), there might have been no tale to write upon the Weirs of Hermiston. But the shadow of a threat of ridicule sufficed; in the slight tartness of these words he read a prohibition; and it is likely that Glenalmond meant it so.

Besides the veteran, the boy was without confidant or friend. Serious and eager, he came through school and college, and moved among a crowd of the indifferent, in the seclusion of his shyness. He grew up handsome, with an open, speaking countenance, with graceful, youthful ways; he was clever, he took prizes, he shone in the Speculative Society.[1] It should seem he must become the centre of a crowd of friends; but something that was in part the delicacy of his mother, in part the austerity of his father, held him aloof from all. It is a fact, and a strange one, that among his contemporaries Hermiston's son was thought to be a chip of the old block. ' You're a friend of Archie Weir's? ' said one to Frank Innes; and Innes replied, with his usual flippancy and more than his usual insight: ' I know Weir, but I never met Archie.' No one had met Archie, a malady most incident to only sons. He flew his private signal, and none heeded it; it seemed he was abroad in a world from which the very hope of intimacy was banished; and he looked round about him on the concourse of his fellow-students, and forward

1 A famous debating society of the students of Edinburgh University.

to the trivial days and acquaintances that were to come, without hope of interest.

As time went on, the tough and rough old sinner felt himself drawn to the son of his loins and sole continuator of his new family, with softnesses of sentiment that he could hardly credit and was wholly impotent to express. With a face, voice, and manner trained through forty years to terrify and repel, Rhadamanthus may be great, but he will scarce be engaging. It is a fact that he tried to propitiate Archie, but a fact that cannot be too lightly taken; the attempt was so unconspicuously made, the failure so stoically supported. Sympathy is not due to these steadfast iron natures. If he failed to gain his son's friendship, or even his son's toleration, on he went up the great, bare staircase of his duty, uncheered and undepressed. There might have been more pleasure in his relations with Archie, so much he may have recognised at moments; but pleasure was a by-product of the singular chemistry of life which only fools expected.

An idea of Archie's attitude, since we are all grown up and have forgotten the days of our youth, it is more difficult to convey. He made no attempt whatsoever to understand the man with whom he dined and breakfasted. Parsimony of pain, glut of pleasure, these are the two alternating ends of youth; and Archie was of the parsimonious. The wind blew cold out of a certain quarter—he turned his back upon it; stayed as little as was possible in his father's presence; and when there, averted his eyes as much as was decent from his father's face. The lamp shone for many hundred days upon these two at table—my lord ruddy, gloomy, and unreverent; Archie with a potential brightness that was always dimmed and veiled in that society; and there were not, perhaps, in Christendom two men more radically strangers. The father, with a grand simplicity, either spoke of what interested himself, or maintained an unaffected silence. The son turned in his head for some topic that should be quite safe, that would spare him fresh evidences either of my lord's inherent grossness or of the innocence of his inhumanity; treading gingerly the ways of intercourse, like a lady gathering up her skirts in a by-path. If he made a mistake, and my lord began to abound in matter of offence, Archie drew himself up, his brow grew dark, his share of the talk expired; but my lord would faithfully and cheerfully continue to pour out the worst of himself before his silent and offended son.

'Well, it's a poor hert that never rejoices,' he would say, at the conclusion of such a nightmare interview. 'But I must get to me plew-stilts.' And he would seclude himself as usual in the back room, and Archie go forth into the night and the city, quivering with animosity and scorn.

3

In the matter of the hanging of Duncan Jopp

IT chanced in the year 1813 that Archie strayed one day into the Judiciary Court. The macer made room for the son of the presiding judge. In the dock, the centre of men's eyes, there stood a whey-coloured, misbegotten caitiff, Duncan Jopp, on trial for his life. His story, as it was raked out before him in that public scene, was one of disgrace and vice and cowardice, the very nakedness of crime; and the creature heard and it seemed at times as though he understood—as if at times he forgot the horror of the place he stood in, and remembered the shame of what had brought him there. He kept his head bowed and his hands clutched upon the rail; his hair dropped in his eyes and at times he flung it back; and now he glanced about the audience in a sudden fellness of terror, and now looked in the face of his judge and gulped. There was pinned about his throat a piece of dingy flannel; and this it was perhaps that turned the scale in Archie's mind between disgust and pity. The creature stood in a vanishing point; yet a little while, and he was still a man, and had eyes and apprehension; yet a little longer, and with a last sordid piece of pageantry, he would cease to be. And here, in the meantime, with a trait of human nature that caught at the beholder's breath, he was tending a sore throat.

Over against him, my Lord Hermiston occupied the bench in the red robes of criminal jurisdiction, his face framed in the white wig. Honest all through, he did not affect the virtue of impartiality; this was no case for refinement; there was a man to be hanged, he would have said, and he was hanging him. Nor was it possible to see his lordship, and acquit him of gusto in the task. It was plain he gloried in the exercise of his trained faculties, in the clear sight which pierced at once into the joint of fact, in the rude, unvarnished gibes with which he demolished every figment of defence. He took his ease and jested, unbending in that solemn place with some of the freedom of the tavern; and the rag of man with the flannel round his neck was hunted gallowsward with jeers.

Duncan had a mistress, scarce less forlorn and greatly older than himself, who came up, whimpering and curtseying, to add the weight of her betrayal. My lord gave her the oath in his most roaring voice, and added an intolerant warning.

' Mind what ye say now, Janet,' said he. ' I have an e'e upon ye; I'm ill to jest with.'

Presently, after she was tremblingly embarked on her story, ' And what made ye do this, ye auld runt? ' the Court interposed. ' Do ye mean to tell me ye was the panel's mistress? '

' If you please, ma loard,' whined the female.

' Godsake! ye made a bonny couple,' observed his lordship; and there was something so formidable and ferocious in his scorn that not even the galleries thought to laugh.

The summing up contained some jewels.

' These two peetiable creatures seem to have made up thegither, it's not for us to explain why.'—' The panel, who (whatever else he may be) appears to be equally ill set-out in mind and boady.' —' Neither the panel nor yet the old wife appears to have had so much common sense as even to tell a lie when it was necessary.' And in the course of sentencing, my lord had this *obiter dictum*: ' I have been the means, under God, of haanging a great number, but never just such a disjaskit rascal as yourself.' The words were strong in themselves: the light and heat and detonation of their delivery, and the savage pleasure of the speaker in his task, made them tingle in the ears.

When all was over, Archie came forth again into a changed world. Had there been the least redeeming greatness in the crime, any obscurity, any dubiety, perhaps he might have understood. But the culprit stood, with his sore throat, in the sweat of his mortal agony, without defence or excuse; a thing to cover up with blushes; a being so much sunk beneath the zones of sympathy that pity might seem harmless. And the judge had pursued him with a monstrous, relishing gaiety, horrible to be conceived, a trait for nightmares. It is one thing to spear a tiger, another to crush a toad; there are æsthetics even of the slaughter-house; and the loathsomeness of Duncan Jopp enveloped and infected the image of his judge.

Archie passed by his friends in the High Street with incoherent words and gestures. He saw Holyrood in a dream, remembrance of its romance awoke in him and faded; he had a vision of the old radiant stories, of Queen Mary and Prince Charlie, of the hooded stag, of the splendour and crime, the velvet and bright iron of the past; and dismissed them with a cry of pain. He lay and moaned in the Hunter's Bog, and the heavens were dark above him and the grass of the field an offence. 'This is my father,' he said. 'I draw my life from him; the flesh upon my bones is his, the bread I am fed with is the wages of these horrors.' He recalled his mother, and ground his forehead in the earth. He thought of flight, and where was he to flee to? of other lives, but was there any life worth living in this den of savage and jeering animals?

The interval before the execution was like a violent dream. He met his father; he would not look at him, he could not speak to him. It seemed there was no living creature but must have been swift to recognise that imminent animosity; but the hide of the Lord Justice-Clerk remained impenetrable. Had my lord been talkative, the truce could never have subsisted; but he was by fortune in one of his humours of sour silence; and under the very guns of his broadside. Archie nursed the enthusiasm of rebellion. It seemed to him, from the top of his nineteen years' experience, as if he were marked at birth to be the perpetrator of some signal action, to set back fallen Mercy, to overthrow the usurping devil that sat, horned and hoofed, on her throne. Seductive Jacobin figments, which he had often refuted at the Speculative, swam up in his mind and startled him as with voices; and he seemed to himself to walk accompanied by an almost tangible presence of new beliefs and duties.

On the named morning he was at the place of execution. He saw the fleering rabble, the flinching wretch produced. He looked on for a while at a certain parody of devotion, which seemed to strip the wretch of his last claim to manhood. Then followed the brutal instant of extinction, and the paltry dangling of the remains like a broken jumping jack. He had been prepared for something terrible, not for this tragic meanness. He stood a moment silent, and then—'I denounce this God-defying murder,' he shouted; and his father, if he must have disclaimed the sentiment, might have owned the stentorian voice with which it was uttered.

Frank Innes dragged him from the spot. The two handsome lads followed the same course of study and recreation, and felt a certain mutual attraction, founded mainly on good looks. It had never gone deep; Frank was by nature a thin, jeering creature, not truly susceptible whether of feeling or inspiring friendship; and the relation between the pair was altogether on the outside, a thing of common knowledge and the pleasantries that spring from a common acquaintance. The more credit to Frank that he was appalled by Archie's outburst, and at least conceived the design of keeping him in sight, and, if possible, in hand for the day. But Archie, who had just defied—was it God or Satan?—would not listen to the word of a college companion.

'I will not go with you,' he said. 'I do not desire your company, sir; I would be alone.'

'Here, Weir, man, don't be absurd,' said Innes, keeping a tight hold upon his sleeve. 'I will not let you go until I know what you mean to do with yourself; it's no use brandishing that staff.' For indeed at that moment Archie had made a sudden—perhaps a warlike—movement. 'This has been the most insane affair; you know it has. You know very well that I'm playing the good Samaritan. All I wish is to keep you quiet.'

'If quietness is what you wish, Mr. Innes,' said Archie, 'and you will promise to leave me entirely to myself, I will tell you so much, that I am going to walk in the country and admire the beauties of nature.'

'Honour bright?' asked Frank.

'I am not in the habit of lying, Mr. Innes,' retorted Archie. 'I have the honour of wishing you good-day.'

'You won't forget the Spec.?' asked Innes.

'The Spec.?' said Archie. 'Oh no, I won't forget the Spec.'

And the one young man carried his tortured spirit forth of the city and all the day long, by one road and another, in an endless pilgrimage of misery; while the other hastened smilingly to spread the news of Weir's access of insanity, and to drum up for that night a full attendance at the Speculative, where further eccentric developments might certainly be looked for. I doubt if Innes had the least belief in his prediction: I think it flowed rather from a wish to make the story as good and the scandal as great as possible; not from any ill-will to Archie—from the mere pleasure of beholding interested faces. But for all that his words were prophetic. Archie did not forget the Spec.; he put in an appearance there at the due time, and, before the evening was over, had dealt a memorable shock to his companions. It chanced he was the president of the night. He sat in the same room where the Society still meets—only the portraits were not there; the men who afterwards sat for them were then but beginning their career. The same lustre of many tapers shed its light over the meeting· the same chair, perhaps, supported him that so many of us have sat in since. At times he seemed to forget the business of the evening, but even in these periods he sat with a great air of energy and determination. At times he meddled bitterly and launched with defiance those fines which are the precious and rarely used artillery of the president. He little thought, as he did so, how he resembled his father, but his friends remarked upon it, chuckling. So far, in his high place above his fellow-students, he seemed set beyond the possibility of any scandal; but his mind was made up—he was determined to fulfil the sphere of his offence. He signed to Innes (whom he had just fined, and who had just impeached his ruling) to succeed him in the chair, stepped down from the platform, and took his place by the chimney-piece, the shine of many wax tapers from above illuminating his pale face, the glow of the great red fire relieving from behind his slim figure. He had to propose, as an amendment to the next subject in the case-book, ' Whether capital punishment be consistent with God's will or man's policy? '

A breath of embarrassment, of something like alarm, passed round the room, so daring did these words appear upon the lips of Hermiston's only son. But the amendment was not seconded; the previous question was promptly moved and unanimously voted, and the momentary scandal smuggled by. Innes triumphed in the fulfilment of his prophecy. He and Archie were now become the heroes of the night; but whereas every one crowded about Innes, when the meeting broke up, but one of all his companions came to speak to Archie.

' Weir, man! that was an extraordinary raid of yours! ' observed this courageous member, taking him confidentially by the arm as they went out.

' I don't think it a raid,' said Archie grimly. ' More like a war. I saw that poor brute hanged this morning, and my gorge rises at it yet.'

' Hut-tut! ' returned his companion, and, dropping his arm like something hot, he sought the less tense society of others.

Archie found himself alone. The last of the faithful—or was it only the boldest of the curious? had fled. He watched the black huddle of his fellow-students draw off down and up the street, in whispering or boisterous gangs. And the isolation of the moment weighed upon him like an omen and an emblem of his destiny in life. Bred up in unbroken fear of himself, among trembling servants, and in a house which (at the least ruffle in the master's voice) shuddered into silence, he saw himself on the brink of the red valley of war, and measured the danger and length of it with awe. He made a détour in the glimmer and shadow of the streets, came into the back stable lane, and watched for a long while the light burn steady in the Judge's room. The longer he gazed upon that illuminated window-blind, the more blank became the picture of the man who sat behind it, endlessly turning over sheets of process, pausing to sip a glass of port, or rising and passing heavily about his book-lined walls to verify some reference. He could not combine the brutal judge and the industrious, dispassionate student; the connecting link escaped him; from such a dual nature, it was impossible he should predict behaviour; and he asked himself if he had done well to plunge into a business of which the end could not be foreseen; and presently after, with a sickening decline of confidence, if he had done loyally to strike his father. For he had struck him—defied him twice over and before a cloud of witnesses —struck him a public buffet before crowds. Who had called him to judge his father in these precarious and high questions? The office was usurped. It might have become a stranger; in a son—there was no blinking it—in a son, it was disloyal. And now, between these two natures so antipathetic, so hateful to each other, there was depending an unpardonable affront: and the providence of God alone might foresee the manner in which it would be resented by Lord Hermiston.

These misgivings tortured him all night and arose with him in the winter's morning; they followed him from class to class, they made him shrinkingly sensitive to every shade of manner in his companions, they sounded in his ears through the current voice of the professor; and he brought them home with him at night unabated and indeed increased. The cause of this increase lay in a chance encounter with the celebrated Dr. Gregory. Archie stood looking vaguely in the lighted window of a book shop, trying to nerve himself for the approaching ordeal. My lord and he had met and parted in the morning as they had now done for long, with scarcely the ordinary civilities of life; and it was plain to the son that nothing had yet reached the father's ears. Indeed, when he recalled the awful countenance of my lord, a timid hope sprang up in him that perhaps there would be found no one bold enough to carry tales. If this were so, he asked himself, would he begin again? and he found no answer. It was at this moment that a hand was laid upon his arm, and a voice said in his ear, 'My dear Mr. Archie, you had better come and see me.'

He started, turned around, and found himself face to face with Dr. Gregory. 'And why should I come to see you?' he asked, with the defiance of the miserable.

'Because you are looking exceeding ill,' said the doctor, 'and you very evidently want looking after, my young friend. Good folk are scarce, you know; and it is not every one that would be quite so much missed as yourself. It is not every one that Hermiston would miss.'

And with a nod and a smile, the doctor passed on.

A moment after, Archie was in pursuit, and had in turn, but more roughly, seized him by the arm.

'What do you mean? what did you mean by saying that? What makes you think that Hermis——my father would have missed me?'

The doctor turned about and looked him all over with clinical eye. A far more stupid man than Dr. Gregory might have guessed the truth; but ninety-nine out of a hundred, even if they had been equally inclined to kindness, would have blundered by some touch of charitable exaggeration. The doctor was better inspired. He knew the father well; in that white face of intelligence and suffering, he divined something of the son; and he told, without apology or adornment, the plain truth.

'When you had the measles, Mr. Archibald, you had them gey and ill; and I thought you were going to slip between my fingers,' he said. 'Well, your father was anxious. How did I know it? says you. Simply because I am a trained observer. The sign that I saw him make ten thousand would have missed; and perhaps—*perhaps*, I say, because he's a hard man to judge of—but perhaps he never made another. A strange thing to consider! It was this. One day I came to him: "Hermiston," said I, "there's a change." He never said a word, just glowered at me (if ye'll pardon the phrase) like a wild beast. "A change for the better," said I. And I distinctly heard him take his breath.'

The doctor left no opportunity for anti-climax; nodding his cocked hat (a piece of antiquity to which he clung) and repeating 'Distinctly' with raised eyebrows, he took his departure, and left Archie speechless in the street.

The anecdote might be called infinitely little, and yet its meaning for Archie was immense. 'I did not know the old man had so much blood in him.' He had never dreamed this sire of his, this aboriginal antique, this adamantine Adam, had even so much of a heart as to be moved in the least degree for another—and that other himself, who had insulted him! With the generosity of youth, Archie was instantly under arms upon the other side; had instantly created a new image of Lord Hermiston, that of a man who was all iron without and all sensibility within. The mind of the vile jester, the tongue that had pursued Duncan Jopp with unmanly insults, the unbeloved countenance that he had known and feared for so long, were all forgotten; and he hastened home, impatient to confess his misdeeds, impatient to throw himself on the mercy of this imaginary character.

He was not to be long without a rude awakening. It was in the gloaming when he drew near the doorstep of the lighted house, and was aware of the figure of his father approaching from the opposite side. Little daylight lingered; but on the door being opened, the strong yellow shine of the lamp gushed out upon the landing and shone full on Archie, as he stood, in the old-fashioned observance of respect, to yield precedence. The Judge came without haste, stepping stately and firm; his chin raised, his face (as he entered the lamplight) strongly illumined, his mouth set hard. There was never a wink of change in his expresssion; without looking to the right or left, he mounted the stair, passed close to Archie, and entered the house. Instinctively, the boy, upon the first coming, had made a movement to meet him; instinctively, he recoiled against the railing, as the old man swept by him in a pomp of indignation. Words were needless; he knew all—perhaps more than all—and the hour of judgment was at hand.

It is possible that, in this sudden revulsion of hope and before these symptoms of impending danger, Archie might have fled. But not even that was left to him. My lord, after hanging up his cloak and hat, turned round in the lighted entry, and made him an imperative and silent gesture with his thumb, and with the strange instinct of obedience, Archie followed him into the house.

All dinner time there reigned over the Judge's table a palpable silence, and as soon as the solids were despatched he rose to his feet.

'M'Killop, tak' the wine into my room,' said he; and then to his son: 'Archie, you and me has to have a talk.'

It was at this sickening moment that Archie's courage, for the first and last time, entirely deserted him. 'I have an appointment,' said he.

'It'll have to be broken, then,' said Hermiston, and led the way into his study.

The lamp was shaded, the fire trimmed to a nicety, the table covered deep with orderly documents, the backs of law books made a frame upon all sides that was only broken by the window and the doors.

For a moment Hermiston warmed his hands at the fire, presenting his back to Archie; then suddenly disclosed on him the terrors of the Hanging Face.

'What's this I hear of ye?' he asked.

There was no answer possible to Archie.

'I'll have to tell ye, then,' pursued Hermiston. 'It seems

ye've been skirling against the father that begot ye, and one of His Maijesty's Judges in this land; and that in the public street, and while an order of the Court was being executit. Forbye which, it would appear that ye've been airing your opeenions in a Coallege Debatin' Society;' he paused a moment: and, then, with extraordinary bitterness, added: ' Ye damned eediot.'

' I had meant to tell you,' stammered Archie. ' I see you are well informed.'

' Muckle obleeged to ye,' said his lordship, and took his usual seat. ' And so you disapprove of Caapital Punishment?' he added.

' I am sorry, sir, I do,' said Archie.

' I am sorry, too,' said his lordship. ' And now, if you please, we shall approach this business with a little parteecularity. I hear that at the hanging of Duncan Jopp—and, man! ye had a fine client there—in the middle of all the riffraff of the ceety, ye thought fit to cry out, " This is a damned murder, and my gorge rises at the man that haangit him." '

' No, sir, these were not my words,' said Archie.

' What were yer words, then?' asked the judge.

' I believe I said, " I denounce it as a murder!"' said the son, ' I beg your pardon—a God-defying murder. I have no wish to conceal the truth,' he added, and looked his father for a moment in the face.

' God, it would only need that of it next!' cried Hermiston. ' There was nothing about your gorge rising, then?'

' That was afterwards, my lord, as I was leaving the Speculative. I said I had been to see the miserable creature hanged, and my gorge rose at it.'

' Did ye, though?' said Hermiston. ' And I suppose ye knew who haangit him?'

' I was present at the trial; I ought to tell you that, I ought to explain. I ask your pardon beforehand for any expression that may seem undutiful. The position in which I stand is wretched,' said the unhappy hero, now fairly face to face with the business he had chosen. ' I have been reading some of your cases. I was present while Jopp was tried. It was a hideous business. Father, it was a hideous thing! Grant he was vile, why should you hunt him with a vileness equal to his own? It was done with glee—that is the word—you did it with glee, and I looked on, God help me! with horror.'

' You're a young gentleman that doesna approve of Caapital Punishment,' said Hermiston. ' Weel, I'm an auld man that does. I was glad to get Jopp haangit, and what for would I pretend I wasna? You're all for honesty, it seems; you couldna even steik your mouth on the public street. What for should I steik mines upon the bench, the King's officer, bearing the sword, a dreid to evil-doers, as I was from the beginning, and as I will be to the end! Mair than enough of it! Heedious! I never gave twa thoughts to heediousness, I have no call to be bonny. I'm a man that gets through with my day's business, and let that suffice.'

The ring of sarcasm had died out of his voice as he went on; the plain words became invested with some of the dignity of the Justice-seat.

' It would be telling you if you could say as much,' the speaker resumed. ' But ye cannot. Ye've been reading some of my cases, ye say. But it was not for the law in them, it was to spy out your faither's nakedness, a fine employment in a son. You're splairging; you're running at lairge in life like a wild nowt. It's impossible you should think any longer of coming to the Bar. You're not fit for it; no splairger is. And another thing: son of mines or no son of mines, you have flung fylement in public on one of the Senators of the Coallege of Justice, and I would make it my business to see that ye were never admitted there yourself. There is a kind of a decency to be observit. Then comes the next of it—what am I to do with ye next? Ye'll have to find some kind of a trade, for I'll never support ye in idleset. What do ye fancy ye'll be fit for? The pulpit? Na, they could never get diveenity into that bloackhead. Him that the law of man whammles is no' likely to do muckle better by the law of God. What would ye make of hell? Wouldna your gorge rise at that? Na, there's no room for splairgers under the fower quarters of John Calvin. What else is there? Speak up. Have ye got nothing of your own? '

' Father, let me go to the Peninsula,' said Archie. ' That's all I'm fit for—to fight.'

' All? quo' he! ' returned the Judge. ' And it would be enough too, if I thought it. But I'll never trust ye so near the French, you that's so Frenchifeed.'

' You do me injustice there, sir,' said Archie. ' I am loyal; I will not boast; but any interest I may have ever felt in the French—— '

' Have ye been so loyal to me? ' interrupted his father.

There came no reply.

' I think not,' continued Hermiston. ' And I would send no man to be a servant of the King, God bless him! that has proved such a shauchling son to his own faither. You can splairge here on Edinburgh street, and where's the hairm? It doesna play buff on me! And if there were twenty thousand eediots like yourself, sorrow a Duncan Jopp would hang the fewer. But there's no splairging possible in a camp; and if you were to go to it, you would find out for yourself whether Lord Well'n'ton approves of caapital punishment or not. You a sodger!' he cried, with a sudden burst of scorn. 'Ye auld wife, the sodgers would bray at ye like cuddies!'

As at the drawing of a curtain, Archie was aware of some illogicality in his position, and stood abashed. He had a strong impression, besides, of the essential valour of the old gentleman before him, how conveyed it would be hard to say.

'Well, have ye no other proposeetion?' said my lord again.

'You have taken this so calmly, sir, that I cannot but stand ashamed,' began Archie.

'I'm nearer voamiting, though, than you would fancy,' said my lord.

The blood rose to Archie's brow.

'I beg your pardon, I should have said that you had accepted my affront. . . . I admit it was an affront; I did not think to apologise, but I do, I ask your pardon; it will not be so again, I pass you my word of honour. . . . I should have said that I admired your magnanimity with—this—offender,' Archie concluded with a gulp.

'I have no other son, ye see,' said Hermiston. 'A bonny one I have gotten! But I must just do the best I can wi' him, and what am I to do? If ye had been younger, I would have wheepit ye for this rideeculous exhibeetion. The way it is, I have just to grin and bear. But one thing is to be clearly understood. As a faither, I must grin and bear it; but if I had been the Lord Advocate instead of the Lord Justice-Clerk, son or no son, Mr. Erchibald Weir would have been in a jyle the night.'

Archie was now dominated. Lord Hermiston was coarse and cruel; and yet the son was aware of a bloomless nobility, an ungracious abnegation of the man's self in the man's office. At every word this sense of the greatness of Lord Hermiston's spirit struck more home; and along with it that of his own impotence, who had struck—and perhaps basely struck— at his own father, and not reached so far as to have even nettled him.

'I place myself in your hands without reserve,' he said.

'That's the first sensible word I've had of ye the night,' said Hermiston. 'I can tell ye, that would have been the end of it, the one way or the other; but it's better ye should come there yourself, than what I would have had to hirstle ye. Weel, by my way of it—and my way is the best—there's just the one thing it's possible that ye might be with decency, and that's a laird. Ye'll be out of hairm's way at the least of it. If ye have to rowt, ye can rowt amang the kye; and the maist feck of the caapital punishment ye're like to come across'll be guddling trouts. Now, I'm for no idle lairdies; every man has to work, if it's only at peddling ballants; to work, or to be wheepit, or to be haangit. If I set ye down at Hermiston, I'll have to see you work that place the way it has never been workit yet; ye must ken about the sheep like a herd; ye must be my grieve there, and I'll see that I gain by ye. Is that understood?'

' I will do my best,' said Archie.

' Well, then, I'll send Kirstie word the morn, and ye can go yourself the day after,' said Hermiston. ' And just try to be less of an eediot!' he concluded, with a freezing smile, and turned immediately to the papers on his desk.

4

Opinions of the bench

LATE the same night, after a disordered walk, Archie was admitted into Lord Glenalmond's dining-room where he sat, with a book upon his knee, beside three frugal coals of fire. In his robes upon the bench, Glenalmond had a certain air of burliness: plucked of these, it was a maypole of a man that rose unsteadily from his chair to give his visitor welcome. Archie had suffered much in the last days, he had suffered again that evening; his face was white and drawn, his eyes wild and dark. But Lord Glenalmond greeted him without the least mark of surprise or curiosity.

' Come in, come in,' said he. ' Come in and take a seat. Carstairs ' (to his servant), ' make up the fire, and then you can bring a bit of supper,' and again to Archie, with a very trivial accent: ' I was half expecting you,' he added.

' No supper,' said Archie. ' It is impossible that I should eat.'

' Not impossible,' said the tall old man, laying his hand upon his shoulder, ' and, if you will believe me, necessary.'

' You know what brings me?' said Archie, as soon as the servant had left the room.

' I have a guess, I have a guess,' replied Glenalmond. ' We will talk of it presently—when Carstairs has come and gone,

243

and you have had a piece of my good Cheddar cheese and a pull at the porter tankard: not before.'

'It is impossible I should eat,' repeated Archie.

'Tut, tut!' said Lord Glenalmond. 'You have eaten nothing to-day, and, I venture to add, nothing yesterday. There is no case that may not be made worse; this may be a very disagreeable business, but if you were to fall sick and die, it would be still more so, and for all concerned—for all concerned.'

'I see you must know all,' said Archie. 'Where did you hear it?'

'In the mart of scandal, in the Parliament House,' said Glenalmond. 'It runs riot below among the bar and the public, but it sifts up to us upon the bench, and rumour has some of her voices even in the divisions.'

Carstairs returned at this moment, and rapidly laid out a little supper; during which Lord Glenalmond spoke at large and a little vaguely on indifferent subjects, so that it might be rather said of him that he made a cheerful noise, than that he contributed to human conversation; and Archie sat upon the other side, not heeding him, brooding over his wrongs and errors.

But so soon as the servant was gone, he broke forth again at once. 'Who told my father? Who dared to tell him? Could it have been you?'

'No, it was not me,' said the Judge; 'although—to be quite frank with you, and after I had seen and warned you—it might have been me. I believe it was Glenkindie.'

'That shrimp!' cried Archie.

'As you say, that shrimp,' returned my lord; 'although really it is scarce a fitting mode of expression for one of the Senators of the College of Justice. We were hearing the parties in a long, crucial case, before the fifteen; Creech was moving at some length for an infeftment; when I saw Glenkindie lean forward to Hermiston with his hand over his mouth and make him a secret communication. No one could have guessed its nature from your father; from Glenkindie, yes, his malice sparked out of him a little grossly. But your father, no. A man of granite. The next moment he pounced upon Creech. "Mr. Creech," says he, "I'll take a look of that sasine," and for thirty minutes after,' said Glenalmond, with a smile. 'Messrs. Creech and Co. were fighting a pretty uphill battle, which resulted, I need hardly add, in their total rout. The case was dismissed. No, I doubt if ever I heard Hermiston better inspired. He was literally rejoicing *in apicibus juris*.'

Archie was able to endure no longer. He thrust his plate away and interrupted the deliberate and insignificant stream of talk. 'Here,' he said, 'I have made a fool of myself, if I have not made something worse. Do you judge between us—judge between a father and a son. I can speak to you; it is not like. . . . I will tell you what I feel and what I mean to do; and you shall be the judge,' he repeated.

'I decline jurisdiction,' said Glenalmond, with extreme seriousness. 'But, my dear boy, it if will do you any good to talk, and if it will interest you at all to hear what I may choose to say when I have heard you, I am quite at your command. Let an old man say it, for once, and not need to blush: I love you like a son.'

There came a sudden sharp sound in Archie's throat. 'Ay,' he cried, 'and there it is! Love! Like a son! And how do you think I love my father?'

'Quietly, quietly,' says my lord.

'I will be very quiet,' replied Archie. 'And I will be baldly frank. I do not love my father; I wonder sometimes if I do not hate him. There's my shame; perhaps my sin; at least, and in the sight of God, not my fault. How was I to love him? He has never spoken to me, never smiled upon me; I do not think he ever touched me. You know the way he talks? You do not talk so, yet you can sit and hear him without shuddering, and I cannot. My soul is sick when he begins with it; I could smite him in the mouth. And all that's nothing. I was at the trial of this Jopp. You were not there, but you must have heard him often; the man's notorious for it, for being—look at my position! he's my father and this is how I have to speak of him—notorious for being a brute and cruel and a coward. Lord Glenalmond, I give you my word, when I came out of that Court, I longed to die—the shame of it was beyond my strength: but I—I—— ' he rose from his seat and began to pace the room in a disorder. 'Well, who am I? A boy, who have never been tried, have never done anything except this twopenny impotent folly with my father. But I tell you, my lord, and I know myself, I am at least that kind of a man—or that kind of a boy, if you prefer it——that I could die in torments rather than that any one should suffer as that scoundrel suffered. Well, and what have I done? I see it now. I have made a fool of myself, as I said in the beginning; and I have gone back, and asked my father's pardon, and placed myself wholly in his hands—and he has sent me to Hermiston,' with a wretched smile, 'for life, I suppose—and what can I say? he strikes me as having done quite right, and let me off better than I had deserved.'

'My poor, dear boy!' observed Glenalmond. 'My poor, dear and, if you will allow me to say so, very foolish boy! You are only discovering where you are; to one of your temperament, or of mine, a painful discovery. The world was not made for us; it was made for ten hundred millions of men, all different from each other and from us; there's no royal road there, we just have to sclamber and tumble. Don't think that I am at all disposed to be surprised; don't suppose that I ever think of blaming you; indeed I rather admire! But there fall to be offered one or two observations on the case which occur to me and which (if you will listen to them dispassionately) may be the means of inducing you to view the matter more calmly. First of all, I cannot acquit you of a good deal of what is called intolerance. You seem to have been very much offended because your father talks a little sculduddery after dinner, which it is perfectly licit for him to do, and which (although I am not very fond of it myself) appears to be entirely an affair of taste. Your father, I scarcely like to remind you, since it is so trite a commonplace, is older than yourself. At least, he is *major* and *sui juris*, and may please himself in the matter of his conversation. And, do you know, I wonder if he might not have as good an answer against you and me? We say we sometimes find him *coarse*, but I suspect he might retort that he finds us always dull. Perhaps a relevant exception.'

He beamed on Archie, but no smile could be elicited.

'And now,' proceeded the Judge, 'for "Archibald on Capital Punishment." This is a very plausible academic opinion; of course I do not and I cannot hold it; but that's not to say that many able and excellent persons have not done so in the past. Possibly, in the past, also, I may have a little dipped myself in the same heresy. My third client, or possibly my fourth, was the means of a return in my opinions. I never saw the man I more believed in; I would have put my hand in the fire, I would have gone to the cross for him; and when it came to trial he was gradually pictured before me, by undeniable probation, in the light of so gross, so cold-blooded, and so black-hearted a villain, that I had a mind to have cast my brief upon the table. I was then boiling against the man with even a more tropical temperature than I had been boiling for him. But I said to myself: "No, you have taken up his case; and because you have changed your mind it must not be suffered to let drop. All that rich tide of eloquence that you prepared last night with so much enthusiasm is out of place, and yet you must not desert him, you must say something." So I said something, and I got him off. It made my reputation. But an experience of that kind is formative. A man must not bring his passions to the bar—or to the bench.'

This story had slightly rekindled Archie's interest. ' I could never deny,' he began—' I mean I can conceive that some men would be better dead. But who are we to know all the springs of God's unfortunate creatures? Who are we to trust ourselves where it seems that God himself must think twice before He treads, and to do it with delight? Yes, with delight. *Tigris ut aspera*.'

' Perhaps not a pleasant spectacle,' said Glenalmond. ' And yet, do you know, I think somehow a great one.'

' I've had a long talk with him to-night,' said Archie.

' I was supposing so,' said Glenalmond.

' And he struck me—I cannot deny that he struck me as something very big,' pursued his son. ' Yes, he is big. He never spoke about himself; only about me. I suppose I admired him. The dreadful part——'

' Suppose we did not talk about that,' interrupted Glenalmond. ' You know it very well, it cannot in any way help that you should brood upon it, and I sometimes wonder whether you and I—who are a pair of sentimentalists—are quite good judges of plain men.'

' How do you mean?' asked Archie.

' *Fair* judges, I mean,' replied Glenalmond. ' Can we be just to them? Do we not ask too much? There was a word of yours just now that impressed me a little when you asked me who we were to know all the springs of God's unfortunate creatures. You applied that, as I understood, to capital cases only. But does it—I ask myself—does it not apply all through? Is it any less difficult to judge of a good man or of a half-good man, than of the worst criminal at the bar? And may not each have relevant excuses?'

' Ah, but we do not talk of punishing the good,' cried Archie.

' No, we do not talk of it,' said Glenalmond. ' But I think we do it. Your father, for instance.'

' You think I have punished him?' cried Archie.

Lord Glenalmond bowed his head.

' I think I have,' said Archie. ' And the worst is, I think he feels it! How much, who can tell, with such a being? But I think he does.'

' And I am sure of it,' said Glenalmond.

' Has he spoken to you, then?' cried Archie.

' Oh, no,' replied the Judge.

'I tell you honestly,' said Archie. 'I want to make it up to him. I will go, I have already pledged myself to go, to Hermiston. That was to him. And now I pledge myself to you, in the sight of God, that I will close my mouth on capital punishment and all other subjects where our views may clash, for—how long shall I say? when shall I have sense enough?—ten years. Is that well?'

'It is well,' said my lord.

'As far as it goes,' said Archie. 'It is enough as regards myself, it is to lay down enough of my conceit. But as regards him, whom I have publicly insulted? What am I to do to him? How do you pay attentions to a—an Alp like that?'

'Only in one way,' replied Glenalmond. 'Only by obedience, punctual, prompt, and scrupulous.'

'And I promise that he shall have it,' answered Archie. 'I offer you my hand in pledge of it.'

'And I take your hand as a solemnity,' replied the Judge. 'God bless you, my dear, and enable you to keep your promise. God guide you in the true way, and spare your days, and preserve to you your honest heart.' At that, he kissed the young man upon the forehead in a gracious, distant, antiquated way; and instantly launched, with a marked change of voice, into another subject. 'And now, let us replenish the tankard; and I believe, if you will try my Cheddar again, you would find you had a better appetite. The Court has spoken, and the case is dismissed.'

'No, there is one thing I must say,' cried Archie. 'I must say it in justice to himself. I know—I believe faithfully, slavishly, after our talk—he will never ask me anything unjust. I am proud to feel it, that we have that much in common, I am proud to say it to you.'

The Judge, with shining eyes, raised his tankard. 'And I think perhaps that we might permit ourselves a toast,' said he. 'I should like to propose the health of a man very different from me and very much my superior—a man from whom I have often differed, who has often (in the trivial expression) rubbed me the wrong way, but whom I have never ceased to respect and, I may add, to be not a little afraid of. Shall I give you his name?'

'The Lord Justice-Clerk, Lord Hermiston,' said Archie, almost with gaiety; and the pair drank the toast deeply.

It was not precisely easy to re-establish, after these emotional passages, the natural flow of conversation. But the Judge eked out what was wanting with kind looks, produced his snuff-box (which was very rarely seen) to fill in a pause, and at last, despairing of any further social success, was upon the point of getting down a book to read a favourite passage, when there came a rather startling summons at the front door, and Carstairs ushered in my Lord Glenkindie, hot from a midnight supper. I am not aware that Glenkindie was ever a beautiful object, being short, and gross-bodied, and with an expression of sensuality comparable to a bear's. At that moment, coming in hissing from many potations, with a flushed countenance and blurred eyes, he was strikingly contrasted with the tall, pale, kingly figure of Glenalmond. A rush of confused thought came over Archie—of shame that this was one of his father's elect friends; of pride, that at the least of it Hermiston could carry his liquor; and last of all, of rage, that he would have here under his eye the man that had betrayed him. And then that, too, passed away; and he sat quiet, biding his opportunity.

The tipsy senator plunged at once into an explanation with Glenalmond. There was a point reserved yesterday, he had been able to make neither head nor tail of it, and seeing lights in the house, he had just dropped in for a glass of porter—and at this point he became aware of the third person. Archie saw the cod's mouth and the blunt lips of Glenkindie gape at him for a moment, and the recognition twinkle in his eyes.

'Who's this?' said he. 'What? is this possibly you, Don Quickshot? And how are ye? And how's your father? And what's all this we hear of you? It seems you're a most extraordinary leveller, by all tales. No king, no parliaments, and your gorge rises at the macers, worthy men! Hoot, toot! Dear, dear me! Your father's son, too! Most rideeculous!'

Archie was on his feet, flushing a little at the reappearance of his unhappy figure of speech, but perfectly self-possessed. 'My lord—and you, Lord Glenalmond, my dear friend,' he began, 'this is a happy chance for me, that I can make my confession and offer my apologies to two of you at once.'

'Ah, but I don't know about that. Confession? It'll be judeecial, my young friend,' cried the jocular Glenkindie. 'And I'm afraid to listen to ye. Think if ye were to make me a coanvert!'

'If you would allow me, my lord,' returned Archie, 'what I have to say is very serious to me; and be pleased to be humorous after I am gone!'

'Remember, I'll hear nothing against the macers!' put in the incorrigible Glenkindie.

But Archie continued as though he had not spoken. 'I have played, both yesterday and to-day, a part for which I can only offer the excuse of youth. I was so unwise as to go to an execution; it seems I made a scene at the gallows; not content with which, I spoke the same night in a college society against capital punishment. This is the extent of what I have done, and in case you hear more alleged against me, I protest my innocence. I have expressed my regret already to my father, who is so good as to pass my conduct over—in a degree, and upon the condition that I am to leave my law studies.' . . .

5

Winter on the Moors

I AT HERMISTON

THE road to Hermiston runs for a great part of the way up the valley of a stream, a favourite with anglers and with midges, full of falls and pools, and shaded by willows and natural woods of birch. Here and there, but at great distances, a byway branches off, and a gaunt farmhouse may be descried above in a fold of the hill; but the more part of the time, the road would be quite empty of passage and the hills of habitation. Hermiston parish is one of the least populous in Scotland; and, by the time you came that length, you would scarce be surprised at the inimitable smallness of the kirk, a dwarfish, ancient place seated for fifty, and standing in a green by the burnside among two-score gravestones. The manse close by, although no more than a cottage, is surrounded by the brightness of a flower-garden and the straw roofs of bees; and the whole colony, kirk and manse, garden and graveyard, finds harbourage in a grove of rowans, and is all the year round in a great silence broken only by the drone of the bees, the tinkle of the burn, and the bell on Sundays. A mile beyond the kirk the road leaves the valley by a precipitous ascent, and brings you a little after to the place of Hermiston, where it comes to an end in the back-yard before the coach-house. All beyond and about is the great field of the hills; the plover, the curlew, and the lark cry there; the wind blows as it blows in a ship's rigging, hard and cold and pure; and the hill-tops huddle one behind another like a herd of cattle into the sunset.

The house was sixty years old, unsightly, comfortable; a farm-yard and a kitchen-garden on the left, with a fruit wall where little hard green pears came to their maturity about the end of October.

The policy (as who should say the park) was of some extent, but very ill reclaimed; heather and moorfowl had crossed the boundary wall and spread and roosted within; and it would have tasked a landscape gardener to say where policy ended and unpolicied nature began. My lord had been led by the influence of Mr. Sheriff Scott into a considerable design of planting; many acres were accordingly set out with fir, and the little feathery besoms gave a false scale and lent a strange air of a toy-shop to the moors. A great, rooty sweetness of bogs was in the air, and at all seasons an infinite melancholy piping of hill birds. Standing so high and with so little shelter, it was a cold, exposed house, splashed by showers, drenched by continuous rains that made the gutters to spout, beaten upon and buffeted by all the winds of heaven; and the prospect would be often black with tempest, and often white with the snows of winter. But the house was wind and weather proof, the hearths were kept bright, and the rooms pleasant with live fires of peat; and Archie might sit of an evening and hear the squalls bugle on the moorland, and watch the fire prosper in the earthy fuel, and the smoke winding up the chimney, and drink deep of the pleasures of shelter.

Solitary as the place was, Archie did not want neighbours. Every night, if he chose, he might go down to the manse and share a 'brewst' of toddy with the minister—a hare-brained ancient gentleman, long and light and still active, though his knees were loosened with age, and his voice broke continually in childish trebles—and his lady wife, a heavy, comely dame, without a word to say for herself beyond good-even and good-day. Harum-scarum, clodpole young lairds of the neighbourhood paid him the compliment of a visit. Young Hay of Romanes rode down to call on his crop-eared pony; young Pringle of Drumanno came up on his bony gray. Hay remained on the hospitable field, and must be carried to bed; Pringle got somehow to his saddle about 3 a.m., and (as Archie stood with the lamp on the upper doorstep) lurched, uttered a senseless view-holloa, and vanished out of the small circle of illumination like a wraith. Yet a minute or two longer the clatter of his breakneck flight was audible, then it was cut off by the intervening steepness of the hill; and again, a great while after, the renewed beating of phantom horse-hoofs, far in the valley of the Hermiston, showed that the horse at least, if not his rider, was still on the homeward way.

There was a Tuesday Club at the 'Cross-keys' in Crossmichael, where the young bloods of the countryside congregated and drank deep on a percentage of the expense, so that he was left gainer who should have drunk the most. Archie had no great mind to this diversion, but he took it like a duty laid upon him, went with a decent regularity, did his manfullest with the liquor, held up his head in the local jests, and got home again and was able to put up his horse, to the admiration of Kirstie and the lass that helped her. He dined at Driffel, supped at Windielaws. He went to the new year's ball at Huntsfield and was made welcome, and thereafter rode to hounds with my Lord Muirfell, upon whose name, as that of a legitimate Lord of Parliament, in a work so full of Lords of Session, my pen should pause reverently. Yet the same fate attended him here as in Edinburgh. The habit of solitude tends to perpetuate itself, and an austerity of which he was quite unconscious, and a pride which seemed arrogance, and perhaps was chiefly shyness, discouraged and offended his new companions. Hay did not return more than twice, Pringle never at all, and there came a time when Archie even desisted from the Tuesday Club, and became in all things —what he had had the name of almost from the first—the Recluse of Hermiston. High-nosed Miss Pringle of Drumanno and high-stepping Miss Marshall of the Mains were understood to have had a difference of opinion about him the day after the ball—he was none the wiser, he could not suppose himself to be remarked by these entrancing ladies. At the ball itself my Lord Muirfell's daughter, the Lady Flora, spoke to him twice, and the second time with a touch of appeal, so that her colour rose and her voice trembled a little in his ear, like a passing grace in music. He stepped back with a heart on fire, coldly and not ungracefully excused himself, and a little after watched her dancing with young Drumanno of the empty laugh, and was harrowed at the sight, and raged to himself that this was a world in which it was given to Drumanno to please, and to himself only to stand aside and envy. He seemed excluded, as of right, from the favour of such society—seemed to extinguish mirth wherever he came, and was quick to feel the wound, and desist, and retire into solitude. If he had but understood the figure he presented, and the impression he made on these bright eyes and tender hearts; if he had but guessed that the Recluse of Hermiston, young, graceful, well spoken, but always cold, stirred the maidens of the county with the charm of Byronism when Byronism was new, it may be questioned whether his destiny might not even yet have been modified. It may be questioned, and I think it should be doubted. It was in his horoscope to be parsimonious of pain to himself, or of the chance of pain, even to the avoidance of any opportunity of pleasure; to have a Roman sense of duty, an instinctive aristocracy of manners and taste; to be the son of Adam Weir and Jean Rutherford.

II KIRSTIE

Kirstie was now over fifty, and might have sat to a sculptor. Long of limb, and still light of foot, deep-breasted, robust-loined, her golden hair not yet mingled with any trace of silver, the years had but caressed and embellished her. By the lines of a rich and vigorous maternity, she seemed destined to be the bride of heroes and the mother of their children; and behold, by the iniquity of fate, she had passed through her youth alone, and drew near to the confines of age, a childless woman. The tender ambitions that she had received at birth had been, by time and disappointment, diverted into a certain barren zeal of industry and fury of interference. She carried her thwarted ardours into housework, she washed floors with her empty heart. If she could not win the love of one with love, she must dominate all by her temper. Hasty, wordy, and wrathful, she had a drawn quarrel with most of her neighbours, and with the others not much more than armed neutrality. The grieve's wife had been 'sneisty'; the sister of the gardener who kept house for him had shown herself 'upsitten'; and she wrote to Lord Hermiston about once a year demanding the discharge of the offenders, and justifying the demand by much wealth of detail. For it must not be supposed that the quarrel rested with the wife and did not take in the husband also—or with the gardener's sister, and did not speedily include the gardener himself. As the upshot of all this petty quarrelling and intemperate speech, she was practically excluded (like a lightkeeper on his tower) from the comforts of human association; except with her own indoor drudge, who, being but a lassie and entirely at her mercy, must submit to the shifty weather of 'the mistress's' moods without complaint, and be willing to take buffets or caresses according to the temper of the hour. To Kirstie, thus situate and in the Indian summer of her heart, which was slow to submit to age, the gods sent this equivocal good thing of Archie's presence. She had known him in the cradle and paddled him when he misbehaved; and yet, as she had not so much as set eyes on him since he was eleven and had his last serious illness, the tall, slender, refined, and rather melancholy young gentleman of twenty came upon her with the shock of a new acquaintance. He was 'Young Hermiston,' 'the laird himsel' ': he had an air of distinctive superiority, a cold straight glance of his black eyes, that abashed the woman's tantrums in the beginning, and therefore the possibility of any quarrel was excluded. He was new, and therefore immediately aroused her curiosity; he was reticent, and kept it awake. And lastly he was dark and she fair, and he was male and she female, the everlasting fountains of interest.

Her feeling partook of the loyalty of a clanswoman, the hero-worship of a maiden aunt, and the idolatry due to a god. No matter what he had asked of her, ridiculous or tragic, she would have done it and joyed to do it. Her passion, for it was nothing less, entirely filled her. It was a rich physical pleasure to make his bed or light his lamp for him when he was absent, to pull off his wet boots or wait on him at dinner when he returned. A young man who should have so doted on the idea, moral and physical, of any woman, might be properly described as being in love, head and heels, and would have behaved himself accordingly. But Kirstie—though her heart leaped at his coming footsteps—though, when he patted her shoulder, her face brightened for the day—had not a hope or thought beyond the present moment and its perpetuation to the end of time. Till the end of time she would have had nothing altered, but still continue delightedly to serve her idol, and be repaid (say twice in the month) with a clap on the shoulder.

I have said her heart leaped—it is the accepted phrase. But rather, when she was alone in any chamber of the house, and heard his foot passing on the corridors, something in her bosom rose slowly until her breath was suspended, and as slowly fell again with a deep sigh, when the steps had passed and she was disappointed of her eyes' desire. This perpetual hunger and thirst of his presence kept her all day on the alert. When he went forth at morning, she would stand and follow him with admiring looks. As it grew late and drew to the time of his return, she would steal forth to a corner of the policy wall and be seen standing there sometimes by the hour together, gazing with shaded eyes, waiting the exquisite and barren pleasure of his view a mile off on the mountains. When at night she had trimmed and gathered the fire, turned down his bed, and laid out his nightgear—when there was no more to be done for the king's pleasure, but to remember him fervently in her usually very tepid prayers, and go to bed brooding upon his perfections, his future career, and what she should give him the next day for dinner—there still remained before her one more opportunity; she was still to take in the tray and say good-night. Sometimes Archie would glance up from his book with a preoccupied nod and a perfunctory salu-

tation which was in truth a dismissal; sometimes—and by degrees more often—the volume would be laid aside, he would
meet her coming with a look of relief; and the conversation would
be engaged, last out the supper, and be prolonged till the small
hours by the waning fire. It was no wonder that Archie was fond
of company after his solitary days; and Kirstie, upon her side,
exerted all the arts of her vigorous nature to ensnare his attention.
She would keep back some piece of news during dinner to be
fired off with the entrance of the supper tray, and form as it
were the *lever de rideau* of the evening's entertainment. Once he
had heard her tongue wag, she made sure of the result. From
one subject to another she moved by insidious transitions, fearing the least silence, fearing almost to give him time for an answer lest it should slip into a hint of separation. Like so many
people of her class, she was a brave narrator; her place was on
the hearthrug and she made it a rostrum, mimeing her stories
as she told them, fitting them with vital detail, spinning them
out with endless ' quo' he's ' and ' quo' she's,' her voice sinking
into a whisper over the supernatural or the horrific; until she
would suddenly spring up in affected surprise, and pointing to
the clock, ' Mercy, Mr. Archie! ' she would say, ' whatten a
time o' night is this of it! God forgive me for a daft wife! ' So it
befell, by good management, that she was not only the first to
begin these nocturnal conversations, but invariably the first to
break them off; so she managed to retire and not to be dismissed.

III A Border Family

Such an unequal intimacy has never been uncommon in Scot-
and, where the clan spirit survives; where the servant tends to
spend her life in the same service, a helpmeet at first, then a
tyrant, and at last a pensioner; where, besides, she is not necessarily destitute of the pride of birth, but is, perhaps, like Kirstie,
a connection of her master's, and at least knows the legend of
her own family, and may count kinship with some illustrious
dead. For that is the mark of the Scot of all classes: that he stands
in an attitude towards the past unthinkable to Englishmen, and
remembers and cherishes the memory of his forebears, good or
bad; and there burns alive in him a sense of identity with the
dead even to the twentieth generation. No more characteristic
instance could be found than in the family of Kirstie Elliott. They
were all, and Kirstie the first of all, ready and eager to pour
forth the particulars of their genealogy, embellished with every
detail that memory had handed down or fancy fabricated; and,

behold! from every ramification of that tree there dangled a halter. The Elliotts themselves have had a chequered history; but these Elliotts deduced, besides, from three of the most unfortunate of the border clans—the Nicksons, the Ellwalds, and the Crozers. One ancestor after another might be seen appearing a moment out of the rain and the hill mist upon his furtive business, speeding home, perhaps, with a paltry booty of lame horses and lean kine, or squealing and dealing death in some moorland feud of the ferrets and the wild cats. One after another closed his obscure adventures in mid-air, triced up to the arm of the royal gibbet or the Baron's dule-tree. For the rusty blunderbuss of Scots criminal justice, which usually hurt nobody but jurymen, became a weapon of precision for the Nicksons, the Ellwalds, and the Crozers. The exhilaration of their exploits seemed to haunt the memories of their descendants alone, and the shame to be forgotten. Pride glowed in their bosoms to publish their relationship to 'Andrew Ellwald of the Laverockstanes, called "Unchancy Dand," who was justifeed wi' seeven mair of the same name at Jeddart in the days of King James the Sax.' In all this tissue of crime and misfortune, the Elliotts of Cauldstaneslap had one boast which must appear legitimate: the males were gallows-birds, born outlaws, petty thieves, and deadly brawlers, but, according to the same tradition, the females were all chaste and faithful. The power of ancestry on the character is not limited to the inheritance of cells. If I buy ancestors by the gross from the benevolence of Lyon King of Arms, my grandson (if he is Scottish) will feel a quickening emulation of their deeds. The men of the Elliotts were proud, lawless, violent as of right, cherishing and prolonging a tradition. In like manner with the women. And the woman, essentially passionate and reckless, who crouched on the rug, in the shine of the peat fire, telling these tales, had cherished through life a wild integrity of virtue.

Her father Gilbert had been deeply pious, a savage disciplinarian in the antique style, and withal a notorious smuggler. 'I mind when I was a bairn getting mony a skelp and being shoo'd to bed like pou'try,' she would say. 'That would be when the lads and their bit kegs were on the road. We've had the riffraff of two-three counties in our kitchen, mony's the time, betwix' the twelve and the three; and their lanterns would be standing in the forecourt, ay, a score o' them at once. But there was nae ungodly talk permitted at Cauldstaneslap. My faither was a consistent man in walk and conversation; just let slip an aith, and there was the door to ye! He had that zeal for the

Lord, it was a fair wonder to hear him pray, but the family has aye had a gift that way.' This father was twice married, once to a dark woman of the old Ellwald stock, by whom he had Gilbert, presently of Cauldstaneslap; and, secondly, to the mother of Kirstie. ' He was an auld man when he married her, a fell auld man wi' a muckle voice—you could hear him rowting from the top o' the Kye-skairs,' she said; ' but for her, it appears she was a perfit wonder. It was gentle blood she had, Mr. Archie, for it was your ain. The countryside gaed gyte about her and her gowden hair. Mines is no to be mentioned wi' it, and there's few weemen has mair hair than what I have, or yet a bonnier colour. Often would I tell my dear Miss Jeannie—that was your mother, dear, she was cruel ta'en up about her hair, it was unco' tender, ye see—" Houts, Miss Jeannie," I would say, " just fling your washes and your French dentifrishes in the back o' the fire, for that's the place for them; and awa' down to a burn side, and wash yersel' in cauld hill water, and dry your bonny hair in the caller wind o' the muirs, the way that my mother aye washed hers, and that I have aye made it a practice to have washen mines —just you do what I tell ye, my dear, and ye'll give me news of it! Ye'll have hair, and routh of hair, a pigtail as thick's my arm," I said, " and the bonniest colour like the clear gowden guineas, so as the lads in kirk'll no can keep their eyes off it! " Weel, it lasted out her time, puir thing! I cuttit a lock of it upon her corp that was lying there sae cauld. I'll show it ye some of thir days if ye're good. But, as I was sayin', my mither—— '

On the death of the father there remained golden-haired Kirstie, who took service with her distant kinsfolk, the Ruther-fords, and black-a-vised Gilbert, twenty years older, who farmed the Cauldstaneslap, married, and begot four sons between 1773 and 1784, and a daughter, like a postscript, in '97, the year of Camperdown and Cape St. Vincent. It seemed it was a tradition in the family to wind up with a belated girl. In 1804, at the age of sixty, Gilbert met an end that might be called heroic. He was due home from market any time from eight at night till five in the morning, and in any condition from the quarrel-some to the speechless, for he maintained to that age the goodly customs of the Scots farmer. It was known on this occasion that he had a good bit of money to bring home; the word had gone round loosely. The laird had shown his guineas, and if anybody had but noticed it, there was an ill-looking, vagabond crew, the scum of Edinburgh, that drew out of the market long ere it was dusk and took the hill-road by Hermiston, where it was not to be believed that they had lawful business. One of the countryside, one Dickieson, they took with them to be their guide, and dear he paid for it! Of a sudden in the ford of the Broken Dykes, this vermin clan fell upon the laird, six to one, and him three parts asleep, having drunk hard. But it is ill to catch an Elliott. For a while, in the night and the black water that was deep as to his saddlegirths, he wrought with his staff like a smith at his stithy, and great was the sound of oaths and blows. With that the ambuscade was burst, and he rode for home with a pistol-ball in him, three knife wounds, the loss of his front teeth, a broken rib and bridle, and a dying horse. That was a race with death that the laird rode! In the mirk night, with his broken bridle and his head swimming, he dug his spurs to the rowels in the horse's side, and the horse, that was even worse off than himself, the poor creature! screamed out loud like a person as he went, so that the hills echoed with it, and the folks at Cauld-staneslap got to their feet about the table and looked at each other with white faces. The horse fell dead at the yard gate, the laird won the length of the house and fell there on the threshold. To the son that raised him he gave the bag of money. 'Hae,' said he. All the way up the thieves had seemed to him to be at his heels, but now the hallucination left him—he saw them again in the place of the ambuscade—and the thirst of vengeance seized on his dying mind. Raising himself and point-ing with an imperious finger into the black night from which he had come, he uttered the single command, 'Brocken Dykes,' and fainted. He had never been loved, but he had been feared in honour. At that sight, at that word, gasped out at them from a toothless and bleeding mouth, the old Elliott spirit awoke with a shout in the four sons. 'Wanting the hat,' continues my author, Kirstie, whom I but haltingly follow, for she told this tale like one inspired, 'wanting guns, for there wasna twa grains o' pouder in the house, wi' nae mair weepons than their sticks into their hands, the fower o' them took the road. Only Hob, and that was the eldest, hunkered at the doorsill where the blood had rin, fyled his hand wi' it, and haddit it up to Heeven in the way o' the auld Border aith. "Hell shall have her ain again this nicht!" he raired, and rode forth upon his errand.' It was three miles to Broken Dykes, down hill, and a sore road. Kirstie has seen men from Edinburgh dismounting there in plain day to lead their horses. But the four brothers rode it as if Auld Hornie were behind and Heaven in front. Come to the ford, and there was Dickieson. By all tales, he was not dead, but breathed and reared upon his elbow, and cried out to them for help. It was at a graceless face that he asked mercy. As soon as Hob saw, by the glint of the lantern, the eyes shining and the whiteness of the teeth in the man's face, 'Damn you!' says he; ' ye hae your teeth, hae ye?' and rode his horse to and fro upon that human remnant. Beyond that, Dandie must dismount with the lantern to be their guide; he was the youngest son, scarce twenty at the time. 'A' nicht long they gaed in the wet heath and jennipers, and whaur they gaed they neither knew nor cared, but just followed the bluid stains and the footprints o' their faither's murderers. And a' nicht Dandie had his nose to the grund like a tyke, and the ithers followed and spak' naething, neither black nor white. There was nae noise to be heard, but just the sough of the swalled burns, and Hob, the dour yin, risping his teeth as he gaed.' With the first glint of the morning they saw they were on the drove road, and at that the four stopped and had a dram to their breakfasts, for they knew that Dand must have guided them right, and the rogues could be but little ahead, hot foot for Edinburgh by the way of the Pentland Hills. By eight o' clock they had word of them—a shepherd had seen four men ' uncoly mishandled ' go by in the last hour. 'That's yin a piece,' says Clem, and swung his cudgel. 'Five o' them!' says Hob. 'God's death, but the faither was a man! And him drunk!' And then there befell them what my author termed ' a sair misbegowk,' for they were overtaken by a posse of mounted neighbours come to aid in the pursuit. Four sour faces looked on the reinforcement. 'The deil's broughten you!' said Clem, and they rode thenceforward in the rear of the party with hanging heads. Before ten they had found and secured the rogues, and by three of the afternoon, as they rode up the Vennel with their prisoners, they were aware of a concourse of people bearing in their midst something that dripped. 'For the boady of the saxt,' pursued Kirstie, 'wi' his head smashed like a hazel-nit, had been a' that nicht in the chairge o' Hermiston Water, and it dunting it on the stanes, and grunding it on the shallows, and flinging the deid thing heels-ower-hurdie at the Fa's o' Spango; and in the first o' the day Tweed had got a hold o' him and carried him off like a wind, for it was uncoly swalled, and raced wi' him, bobbing under brae-sides, and was long playing with the creature in the drumlie lynns under the castle, and at the hinder end of all cuist him up on the sterling of Crossmichael brig. Sae there they were a' thegither at last (for Dickieson had been brought in on a cart long syne), and folk could see what mainner o' man my brither had been that had held his head again' sax and saved the siller, and him drunk!' Thus died of honourable injuries and in the savour of fame Gilbert Elliott of the Cauldstaneslap; but his sons had scarce less glory out of the business. Their savage haste, the skill with which Dand had found and followed the trail, the barbarity to the wounded Dickieson (which was like an open secret in the county) and the doom which it was currently supposed they had intended for the others, struck and stirred popular imagination. Some century earlier the last of the minstrels might have fashioned the last of the ballads out of that Homeric fight and chase; but the spirit was dead, or had been reincarnated already in Mr. Sheriff Scott, and the degenerate moorsmen must be content to tell the tale in prose and to make of the ' Four Black Brothers ' a unit after the fashion of the ' Twelve Apostles ' or the ' Three Musketeers.'

Robert, Gilbert, Clement, and Andrew—in the proper Border diminutives Hob, Gib, Clem, and Dand Elliott—these ballad heroes, had much in common; in particular, their high sense of the family and the family honour; but they went diverse ways, and prospered and failed in different businesses. According to Kirstie, ' they had a' bees in their bonnets but Hob.' Hob the laird was, indeed, essentially a decent man. An elder of the Kirk, nobody had heard an oath upon his lips, save, perhaps, thrice or so at the sheep-washing, since the chase of his father's murderers. The figure he had shown on that eventful night disappeared as if swallowed by a trap. He who had ecstatically dipped his hand in the red blood, he who had ridden down Dickieson, became, from that moment on, a stiff and rather graceless model of the rustic proprieties; cannily profiting by the high war prices, and yearly stowing away a little nest-egg in the bank against calamity; approved of and sometimes consulted by the greater lairds for the massive and placid sense of what he said, when he could be induced to say anything; and particularly valued by the minister, Mr. Torrance, as a right-hand man in the parish, and a model to parents. The transfiguration had been for the moment only; some Barbarossa, some old Adam of our ancestors, sleeps in all of us till the fit circumstance shall call it into action; and for as sober as he now seemed, Hob had given once for all the measure of the devil that haunted him. He was married, and, by reason of the effulgence of that legendary night, was adored by his wife. He had a mob of little lusty, barefoot children who marched in a caravan the long miles to school, the stages of whose pilgrimage were marked by acts of spoliation and mischief, and who were qualified in the countryside as ' fair pests.' But in the house, if ' faither was in,' they were quiet as mice. In short, Hob moved through life in a great peace—the reward of any one who shall have killed his man, with any formidable and figurative circumstance, in the midst of a country gagged and swaddled with civilisation.

It was a current remark that the Elliotts were 'guid and bad, like sanguishes'; and certainly there was a curious distinction, the men of business coming alternately with the dreamers. The second brother, Gib, was a weaver by trade, had gone out early into the world to Edinburgh, and come home again with his wings singed. There was an exaltation in his nature which had led him to embrace with enthusiasm the principles of the French Revolution, and had ended by bringing him under the hawse of my Lord Hermiston in that furious onslaught of his upon the Liberals, which sent Muir and Palmer into exile and dashed the party into chaff. It was whispered that my lord, in his great scorn for the movement and prevailed upon a little by a sense of neighbourliness, had given Gib a hint. Meeting him one day in the Potterrow, my lord had stopped in front of him. 'Gib, ye eediot,' he had said, 'what's this I hear of you? Poalitics, poalitics, poalitics, weaver's poalitics, is the way of it, I hear. If ye arena a' thegither dozened with eediocy, ye'll gang your ways back to Cauldstaneslap, and ca' your loom, and ca' your loom, man!' And Gilbert had taken him at the word and returned, with an expedition almost to be called flight, to the house of his father. The clearest of his inheritance was that family gift of prayer of which Kirstie had boasted; and the baffled politician now turned his attention to religious matters—or, as others said, to heresy and schism. Every Sunday morning he was in Crossmichael, where he had gathered together, one by one, a sect of about a dozen persons, who called themselves 'God's Remnant of the True Faithful,' or, for short 'God's Remnant.' To the profane, they were known as 'Gib's Deils.' Bailie Sweedie, a noted humorist in the town, vowed that the proceedings always opened to the tune of 'The Deil Fly Away with the Exciseman,' and that the sacrament was dispensed in the form of hot whisky-toddy; both wicked hits at the evangelist, who had been suspected of smuggling in his youth, and had been overtaken (as the phrase went) on the streets of Crossmichael one Fair day. It was known that every Sunday they prayed for a blessing on the arms of Bonaparte. For this, 'God's Remnant,' as they were 'skailing' from the cottage that did duty for a temple, had been repeatedly stoned by the bairns, and Gib himself hooted by a squadron of Border volunteers in which his own brother, Dand, rode in a uniform and with a drawn sword. The 'Remnant' were believed, besides, to be 'anti-nomian in principle,' which might otherwise have been a serious charge, but the way public opinion then blew it was quite swallowed up and forgotten in the scandal about Bonaparte. For the rest, Gilbert had set up his loom in an outhouse at Cauldstaneslap, where he laboured assiduously six days of the week. His brothers, appalled by his political opinions, and willing to avoid dissension in the household, spoke but little to him; he less to them, remaining absorbed in the study of the Bible and almost constant prayer. The gaunt weaver was dry-nurse at Cauldstaneslap, and the bairns loved him dearly. Except when he was carrying an infant in his arms, he was rarely seen to smile—as, indeed, there were few smilers in that family. When his sister-in-law rallied him, and proposed that he should get a wife and bairns of his own, since he was so fond of them, 'I have no clearness of mind upon that point,' he would reply. If nobody called him in to dinner, he stayed out. Mrs. Hob, a hard, unsympathetic woman, once tried the experiment. He went without food all day, but at dusk, as the light began to fail him, he came into the house of his own accord, looking puzzled. 'I've had a great gale of prayer upon my speerit,' said he. 'I canna mind sae muckle's what I had for denner.' The creed of God's Remnant was justified in the life of its founder. 'And yet I dinna ken,' said Kirstie. 'He's maybe no more stockfish than his neeghbours! He rode wi' the rest o' them, and had a good stamach to the work, by a' that I hear! God's Remnant! The deil's clavers! There wasna muckle Christianity in the way Hob guided Johnny Dickieson, at the least of it; but Guid kens! Is he a Christian even? He might be a Mahommedan or a Deevil or a Fireworshipper, for what I ken.'

The third brother had his name on a doorplate, no less, in the city of Glasgow. 'Mr. Clement Elliott,' as long as your arm. In his case, that spirit of innovation which had shown itself timidly in the case of Hob by the admission of new manures, and which had run to waste with Gilbert in subversive politics and heretical religions, bore useful fruit in many ingenious mechanical improvements. In boyhood, from his addiction to strange devices of sticks and string, he had been counted the most eccentric of the family. But that was all by now; and he was a partner of his firm, and looked to die a bailie. He too had married, and was rearing a plentiful family in the smoke and din of Glasgow; he was wealthy, and could have bought out his brother, the cock-laird, six times over, it was whispered; and when he slipped away to Cauldstaneslap for a well-earned holiday, which he did as often as he was able, he astonished the neighbours with his broadcloth, his beaver hat, and the ample plies of his neck-cloth. Though an eminently solid man at bottom, after the pattern of Hob, he had contracted a certain Glasgow briskness and *aplomb* which set him off. All the other Elliotts were as lean as a rake, but Clement was laying on fat, and he panted sorely when he must get into his boots. Dand said, chuckling: 'Ay, Clem has the elements of a corporation.' 'A provost and corporation,' returned Clem. And his readiness was much admired.

The fourth brother, Dand, was a shepherd to his trade, and by starts, when he could bring his mind to it, excelled in the business. Nobody could train a dog like Dandie; nobody, through the peril of great storms in the winter time, could do more gallantly. But if his dexterity were exquisite, his diligence was but fitful; and served his brother for bed and board, and a trifle of pocket-money when he asked for it. He loved money well enough, knew very well how to spend it, and could make a shrewd bargain when he liked. But he preferred a vague knowledge that he was well to windward to any counted coins in the pocket; he felt himself richer so. Hob would expostulate: 'I'm an amature herd,' Dand would reply: 'I'll keep your sheep to you when I'm so minded, but I'll keep my liberty, too. Thir's no man can coandescend on what I'm worth.' Clem would expound to him the miraculous results of compound interest, and recommend investments. 'Ay, man?' Dand would say, 'and do you think, if I took Hob's siller, that I wouldna drink it or wear it on the lassies? And, anyway, my kingdom is no' of this world. Either I'm a poet or else I'm nothing.' Clem would remind him of old age. 'I'll die young, like Robbie Burns,' he would say stoutly. No question but he had a certain accomplishment in minor verse. His 'Hermiston Burn,' with its pretty refrain:—

' I love to gang thinking whaur ye gang linking, Hermiston
    burn, in the howe;'

his 'Auld, auld Elliotts, clay-cauld Elliotts, dour bauld Elliotts of auld,' and his really fascinating piece about the Praying Weaver's Stone, had gained him in the neighbourhood the reputation, still possible in Scotland, of a local bard; and, though not printed himself, he was recognised by others who were and who had become famous. Walter Scott owed to Dandie the text of the 'Raid of Wearie' in the *Minstrelsy* and made him welcome at his house, and appreciated his talents, such as they were, with all his usual generosity. The Ettrick Shepherd was his sworn crony; they would meet, drink to excess, roar out their lyrics in each other's faces, and quarrel and make it up again till bedtime. And besides these recognitions, almost to be called official, Dandie was made welcome for the sake of his gift through the farmhouses of several contiguous dales, and was thus exposed to manifold temptations which he rather sought than fled. He had figured on the stool of repentance, for once fulfilling to the letter the tradition of his hero and model. His humorous verses to Mr. Torrance on that occasion—' Kenspeckle here my lane I stand '—unfortunately too indelicate for further citation, ran through the country like a fiery cross; they were recited, quoted, paraphrased and laughed over as far away as Dumfries on the one hand and Dunbar on the other.

These four brothers were united by a close bond, the bond of that mutual admiration—or rather mutual hero-worship—which is so strong among the members of secluded families who have much ability and little culture. Even the extremes admired each other. Hob, who had as much poetry as the tongs, professed to find pleasure in Dand's verses; Clem who had no more religion than Claverhouse, nourished a heartfelt, at least an open-mouthed, admiration of Gib's prayers; and Dandie followed with relish the rise of Clem's fortunes. Indulgence followed hard on the heels of admiration. The laird, Clem, and Dand, who were Tories and patriots of the hottest quality, excused to themselves, with a certain bashfulness, the radical and revolutionary heresies of Gib. By another division of the family, the laird, Clem, and Gib, who were men exactly virtuous, swallowed the dose of Dand's irregularities as a kind of clog or drawback in the mysterious providence of God affixed to bards, and distinctly probative of poetical genius. To appreciate the simplicity of their mutual admiration, it was necessary to hear Clem, arrived upon one of his visits, and dealing in a spirit of continuous irony with the affairs and personalities of that great city of Glasgow where he lived and transacted business. The various personages, ministers of the church, municipal officers, mercantile big-wigs, whom he had occasion to introduce, were all alike denigrated, all served but as reflectors to cast back a flattering side-light on the house of Cauldstaneslap. The Provost, for whom Clem by exception entertained a measure of respect, he would liken to Hob. ' He minds me o' the laird there,' he would say. ' He has some of Hob's grand, whunstane sense, and the same way with him of steiking his mouth when he's no' very pleased.' And Hob, all unconscious, would draw down his upper lip and produce, as if for comparison, the formidable grimace referred to. The unsatisfactory incumbent of St. Enoch's Kirk was thus briefly dismissed: 'If he had but two fingers o' Gib's he would waken them up.' And Gib, honest man! would look down and secretly smile. Clem was a spy whom they had sent out into the world of men. He had come back with the good news that there was nobody to compare with the Four Black Brothers, no position that they would not adorn, no official that it would not be well they should replace, no interest of mankind, secular or spiritual, which would not immediately bloom under their supervision. The excuse of their folly is in two words: scarce the breadth of a hair divided them from the peasantry. The measure of their sense is this: that these symposia of rustic vanity were kept entirely within the family, like some secret ancestral practice. To the world their serious faces were never deformed by the suspicion of any simper of self-contentment. Yet it was known. 'They hae a guid pride o' themsel's!' was the word in the countryside.

Lastly, in a Border story, there should be added their 'to-names.' Hob was The Laird. 'Roy ne puis, prince ne daigne'; he was the laird of Couldstaneslap—say fifty acres *ipsissimus*. Clement was Mr. Elliott, as upon his door-plate, the earlier Dafty having been discarded as no longer applicable, and indeed only a reminder of misjudgment and the imbecility of the public; and the youngest, in honour of his perpetual wanderings, was known by the sobriquet of Randy Dand.

It will be understood that not all this information was communicated by the aunt, who had too much of the family failing herself to appreciate it thoroughly in others. But as time went on, Archie began to observe an omission in the family chronicle.

'Is there not a girl too?' he asked.

'Ay. Kirstie. She was named from me, or my grandmother at least—it's the same thing,' returned the aunt, and went on again about Dand, whom she secretly preferred by reason of his gallantries.

'But what is your niece like?' said Archie at the next opportunity.

'Her? As black's your hat! But I dinna suppose she would maybe be what you would ca' *ill-looked* a' thegither. Na, she's a kind of a handsome jaud—a kind o' gipsy,' said the aunt, who had two sets of scales for men and women—or perhaps it would be more fair to say that she had three, and the third and the most loaded was for girls.

'How comes it that I never see her in church?' said Archie.

' 'Deed, and I believe she's in Glesgie with Clem and his wife.

A heap good she's like to get of it! I dinna say for men folk, but where weemen folk are born, there let them bide. Glory to God, I was never far'er from here than Crossmichael.'

In the meantime it began to strike Archie as strange, that while she thus sang the praises of her kinsfolk, and manifestly relished their virtues and (I may say) their vices like a thing creditable to herself, there should appear not the least sign of cordiality between the house of Hermiston and that of Cauldstaneslap. Going to church of a Sunday, as the lady housekeeper stepped with her skirts kilted, three trucks of her white petticoat showing below, and her best India shawl upon her back (if the day were fine) in a pattern of radiant dyes, she would sometimes overtake her relatives preceding her more leisurely in the same direction. Gib of course was absent: by skriegh of day he had been gone to Crossmichael and his fellow heretics; but the rest of the family would be seen marching in open order: Hob and Dand, stiff-necked, straight-backed six-footers, with severe dark faces, and their plaids about their shoulders; the convoy of children scattering (in a state of high polish) on the wayside, and every now and again collected by the shrill summons of the mother; and the mother herself, by a suggestive circumstance which might have afforded matter of thought to a more experienced observer than Archie, wrapped in a shawl nearly identical with Kirstie's but a thought more gaudy and conspicously newer. At the sight, Kirstie grew more tall—Kirstie showed her classical profile, nose in air and nostril spread, the pure blood came in her cheek evenly in a delicate living pink.

' A braw day to ye, Mistress Elliott,' said she, and hostility and gentility were nicely mingled in her tones. ' A fine day, mem,' the laird's wife would reply with a miraculous curtsey, spreading the while her plumage—setting off, in other words, and with arts unknown to the mere man, the pattern of her India shawl. Behind her, the whole Cauldstaneslap contingent marched in closer order, and with an indescribable air of being in the presence of the foe; and while Dandie saluted his aunt with a certain familiarity as of one who was well in court, Hob marched on in awful immobility. There appeared upon the face of this attitude in the family the consequences of some dreadful feud. Presumably the two women had been principals in the original encounter, and the laird had probably been drawn into the quarrel by the ears, too late to be included in the present skin-deep reconciliation.

' Kirstie,' said Archie one day, ' what is this you have against your family? '

'I dinna complean,' said Kirstie, with a flush. 'I say naething.'

'I see you do not—not even good-day to your own nephew,' said he.

'I hae naething to be ashamed of,' said she. 'I can say the Lord's Prayer with a good grace. If Hob was ill, or in preeson or poverty, I would see to him blithely. But for curtchying and complimenting and colloguing, thank ye kindly!'

Archie had a bit of a smile: he leaned back in his chair. 'I think you and Mrs. Robert are not very good friends,' says he slyly, 'when you have your India shawls on?'

She looked upon him in silence, with a sparkling eye but an indecipherable expression; and that was all that Archie was ever destined to learn of the battle of the India shawls.

'Do none of them ever come here to see you?' he inquired.

'Mr. Archie,' said she, 'I hope that I ken my place better. It would be a queer thing, I think, if I was to clamjamfry up your faither's house—that I should say it!—wi' a dirty, black-a-vised clan, no ane o' them it was worth while to mar soap upon but just mysel'! Na, they're all damnifeed wi' the black Ellwalds. I have nae patience wi' black folk.' Then, with a sudden consciousness of the case of Archie, 'No' that it maitters for men sae muckle,' she made haste to add, 'but there's naebody can deny that it's unwomanly. Long hair is the ornament o' woman ony way; we've good warrandise for that—it's in the Bible—and wha can doubt that the Apostle had some gowden-haired lassie in his mind—Apostle and all, for what was he but just a man like yersel'?'

6

A leaf from Christina's Psalm-Book

ARCHIE was sedulous at church. Sunday after Sunday he sat down and stood up with that small company, heard the voice of Mr. Torrance leaping like an ill-played clarionet from key to key, and had an opportunity to study his moth-eaten gown and the black thread mittens that he joined together in prayer, and lifted up with a reverent solemnity in the act of benediction. Hermiston pew was a little square box, dwarfish in proportion with the kirk itself, and enclosing a table not much bigger than a footstool. There sat Archie an apparent prince, the only undeniable gentleman and the only great heritor in the parish, taking his ease in the only pew, for no other in the kirk had doors. Thence he might command an undisturbed view of that congregation of solid plaided men, strapping wives and daughters, oppressed children, and uneasy sheep-dogs. It was strange how Archie missed the look of race; except the dogs, with their refined foxy faces and inimitable curling tails, there was no one present with the least claim to gentility. The Cauld-staneslap party was scarcely an exception; Dandie, perhaps, as he amused himself making verses through the interminable burden of the service, stood out a little by the glow in his eyes and a certain superior animation of face and alertness of body; but even Dandie slouched like a rustic. The rest of the congregation, like so many sheep, oppressed him with a sense of hob-nailed routine, day following day—of physical labour in the open air, oatmeal porridge, peas bannock, the somnolent fire-side in the evening, and the night-long nasal slumbers in a box-bed. Yet he knew many of them to be shrewd and humorous, men of character, notable women, making a bustle in the world and radiating an influence from their low-browed doors. He knew besides they were like other men; below the crust of custom, rapture found a way; he had heard them beat the timbrel before Bacchus—had heard them shout and carouse over their whisky-toddy; and not the most Dutch-bottomed and severe faces among them all, not even the solemn elders themselves, but were capable of singular gambols at the voice of love. Men drawing near to an end of life's adventurous journey—maids thrilling with fear and curiosity on the threshold of entrance—women who had borne and perhaps buried children, who could remember the clinging of the small dead hands and the patter of the little feet now silent—he marvelled that among all those faces there should be no face of expectation, none that was mobile, none into which the rhythm and poetry of life had entered. ' O for a live face,' he thought; and at times he had a memory of Lady Flora; and at times he would study the living gallery before him with despair, and would see himself go on to waste his days in that joyless, pastoral place, and death come to him, and his grave be dug under the rowans, and the Spirit of the Earth laugh out in a thunder-peal at the huge fiasco.

On this particular Sunday, there was no doubt but that the spring had come at last. It was warm, with a latent shiver in the air that made the warmth only the more welcome. The shallows of the stream glittered and tinkled among bunches of primrose. Vagrant scents of the earth arrested Archie by the way with moments of ethereal intoxication. The gray, Quak-erish dale was still only awakened in places and patches from the sobriety of its wintry colouring; and he wondered at its beauty; an essential beauty of the old earth it seemed to him, not resident in particulars but breathing to him from the whole. He surprised himself by a sudden impulse to write poetry—he did so sometimes, loose, galloping octo-syllabics in the vein of Scott—and when he had taken his place on a boulder, near some fairy falls and shaded by a whip of a tree that was already radiant with new leaves, it still more surprised him that he should find nothing to write. His heart perhaps beat in time to some vast indwelling rhythm of the universe. By the time he came to a corner of the valley and could see the kirk, he had so lingered by the way that the first psalm was finishing. The nasal psalmody, full of turns and trills and graceless graces, seemed the essential voice of the kirk itself upraised in thanksgiving. ' Everything's alive,' he said; and again cries it aloud, ' Thank God, everything's alive! ' He lingered yet a while in the kirk-yard. A tuft of primroses was blooming hard by the leg of an old, black table tombstone, and he stopped to contemplate the random apologue. They stood forth on the cold earth with a trenchancy of contrast; and he was struck with a sense of incompleteness in the day, the season, and the beauty that surrounded him—the chill there was in the warmth, the gross black clods about the opening primroses, the damp earthy smell that was everywhere intermingled with the scents. The voice of the aged Torrance within rose in an ecstasy. And he wondered if Torrance also felt in his old bones the joyous influence of the spring morning; Torrance, or the shadow of what once was Torrance, that must come so soon to lie outside here in the sun and rain with all his rheumatisms, while a new minister stood in his room and thundered from his own familiar pulpit? The pity of it, and something of the chill of the grave, shook him for a moment as he made haste to enter.

He went up the aisle reverently and took his place in the pew with lowered eyes, for he feared he had already offended the kind old gentleman in the pulpit, and was sedulous to offend no further. He could not follow the prayer, not even the heads of it. Brightness of azure, clouds of fragrance, a tinkle of falling water and singing birds, rose like exhalations from some deeper, aboriginal memory, that was not his, but belonged to the flesh on his bones. His body remembered; and it seemed to him that his body was in no way gross, but ethereal and perishable like a strain of music; and he felt for it an exquisite tenderness as for a child, an innocent, full of beautiful instincts and destined to an early death. And he felt for old Torrance—of the many supplications, of the few days—a pity that was near to tears.

The prayer ended. Right over him was a tablet in the wall, the only ornament in the roughly masoned chapel—for it was no more; the tablet commemorated, I was about to say the virtues, but rather the existence of a former Rutherford of Hermiston; and Archie, under that trophy of his long descent and local greatness, leaned back in the pew and contemplated vacancy with the shadow of a smile between playful and sad, that became him strangely. Dandie's sister, sitting by the side of Clem in her new Glasgow finery, chose that moment to observe the young laird. Aware of the stir of his entrance, the little formalist had kept her eyes fastened and her face prettily composed during the prayer. It was not hypocrisy, there was no one further from a hypocrite. The girl had been taught to behave: to look up, to look down, to look unconscious, to look seriously impressed in church, and in every conjuncture to look her best. That was the game of female life, and she played it frankly. Archie was the one person in church who was of interest, who was somebody new, reputed eccentric, known to be young, and a laird, and still unseen by Christina. Small wonder that, as she stood there in her attitude of pretty decency, her mind should run upon him! If he spared a glance in her direction, he should know she was a well-behaved young lady who had been to Glasgow. In reason he must admire her clothes, and it was possible that he should think her pretty. At that her heart beat the least thing in the world; and she proceeded, by way of a corrective, to call up and dismiss a series of fancied pictures of the young man who should now, by rights, be looking at her. She settled on the plainest of them, a pink short young man with a dish face and no figure, at whose admiration she could afford to smile; but for all that, the consciousness of his gaze (which was really fixed on Torrance and his mittens) kept her in something of a flutter till the word Amen. Even then, she was far too well-bred to gratify her curiosity with any impatience. She resumed her seat languidly—this was a Glasgow touch—she composed her dress, rearranged her nosegay of primroses, looked first in front, then behind upon the other side, and at last allowed her eyes to move, without hurry, in the direction of the Hermiston pew. For a moment, they were riveted. Next she had plucked her gaze home again like a tame bird who should have meditated flight. Possibilities crowded on her; she hung over the future and grew dizzy; the image of this young man, slim, graceful, dark, with the inscrutable half-smile, attracted and repelled her like a chasm. ' I wonder, will I have met my fate? ' she thought, and her heart swelled.

Torrance was got some way into his first exposition, positing a deep layer of texts as he went along, laying the foundations of his discourse, which was to deal with a nice point in divinity, before Archie suffered his eyes to wander. They fell first of all on Clem, looking insupportably prosperous and patronising Torrance with the favour of a modified attention, as of one who was used to better things in Glasgow. Though he had never before set eyes on him, Archie had no difficulty in identifying him, and no hesitation in pronouncing him vulgar, the worst of the family. Clem was leaning forward when Archie first saw him. Presently he leaned nonchalantly back; and that deadly instrument, the maiden, was suddenly unmasked in profile. Though not quite in the front of the fashion (had anybody cared!), certain artful Glasgow mantua-makers, and her own inherent taste, had arrayed her to great advantage. Her accoutrement was, indeed, a cause of heart-burning, and almost of scandal, in that infinitesimal kirk company. Mrs. Hob had said her say at Cauldstaneslap. 'Daft-like!' she had pronounced it. 'A jaiket that'll no' meet! Whaur's the sense of a jaiket that'll no' button upon ye, if it should come to be weet? What do ye ca' thir things? Demmy brokens, d'ye say? They'll be brokens wi' a vengeance or ye can win back! Weel, I have naething to do wi' it—it's no' good taste.' Clem, whose purse had thus metamorphosed his sister, and who was not insensible to the advertisement, had come to the rescue with a 'Hoot, woman! What do you ken of good taste that has never been to the ceety?' And Hob, looking on the girl with pleased smiles, as she timidly displayed her finery in the midst of the dark kitchen, had thus ended the dispute: 'The cutty looks weel,' he had said, 'and it's no' very like rain. Wear them the day, hizzie; but it's no' a thing to make a practice o'.' In the breasts of her rivals, coming to the kirk very conscious of white underlinen, and their faces splendid with much soap, the sight of the toilet had raised a storm of varying emotion, from the mere unenvious admiration that was expressed in the long-drawn 'Eh!' to the angrier feeling that found vent in an emphatic 'Set her up!' Her frock was of straw-coloured jaconet muslin, cut low at the bosom and short at the ankle, so as to display her *demi-broquins* of Regency violet, crossing with many straps upon a yellow cobweb stocking. According to the pretty fashion in which our grandmothers did not hesitate to appear, and our great-aunts went forth armed for the pursuit and capture of our great-uncles, the dress was drawn up so as to mould the contour of both breasts, and in the nook between a cairngorm brooch maintained it. Here, too, surely in a very enviable position, trembled the nosegay of primroses. She wore on her shoulders—or rather, on her back and not her shoulders, which it scarcely passed—a French coat of sarsenet, tied in front with Margate braces, and of the same colour with her violet shoes. About her face clustered a disorder of dark ringlets, a little garland of yellow French roses surmounted her brow, and the whole was crowned by a village hat of chipped straw. Amongst all the rosy and all the weathered faces that surrounded her in church, she glowed like an open flower—girl and raiment, and the cairngorm that caught the daylight and returned it in a fiery flash, and the threads of bronze and gold that played in her hair.

Archie was attracted by the bright thing like a child. He looked at her again and yet again, and their looks crossed. The lip was lifted from her little teeth. He saw the red blood work vividly under her tawny skin. Her eye, which was great as a stag's, struck and held his gaze. He knew who she must be— Kirstie, she of the harsh diminutive, his housekeeper's niece, the sister of the rustic prophet, Gib—and he found in her the answer to his wishes.

Christina felt the shock of their encountering glances, and seemed to rise, clothed in smiles, into a region of the vague and bright. But the gratification was not more exquisite than it was brief. She looked away abruptly, and immediately began to blame herself for that abruptness. She knew what she should have done, too late—turned slowly with her nose in the air. And meantime his look was not removed, but continued to play upon her like a battery of cannon constantly aimed, and now seemed to isolate her alone with him, and now seemed to uplift her, as on a pillory, before the congregation. For Archie continued to drink her in with his eyes, even as a wayfarer comes to a well-head on a mountain, and stoops his face, and drinks with thirst unassuageable. In the cleft of her little breasts the fiery eye of the topaz and the pale florets of primrose fascinated him. He saw the breasts heave, and the flowers shake with the heaving, and marvelled what should so much discompose the girl. And Christina was conscious of his gaze—saw it, perhaps, with the dainty plaything of an ear that peeped among her ringlets; she was conscious of changing colour, conscious of her unsteady breath. Like a creature tracked, run down, surrounded, she sought in a dozen ways to give herself a countenance. She used her handkerchief—it was a really fine one—then she desisted in a panic: ' He would only think I was too warm.' She took to reading in the metrical psalms, and then remembered it was sermon-time. Last she put a 'sugar-bool' in her mouth, and the next moment repented of the step. It was such a homely-like thing! Mr. Archie would never be eating sweeties in kirk; and, with a palpable effort, she swallowed it whole, and her colour flamed high. At this signal of distress Archie awoke to a sense of his ill-behaviour. What had he been doing? He had been exquisitely rude in church to the niece of his housekeeper; he had stared like a lackey and a libertine at a beautiful and modest girl. It was possible, it was even likely, he would be presented to her after service in the kirk-yard, and then how was he to look? And there was no excuse. He had marked the tokens of her shame, of her increasing indignation, and he was such a fool that he had not understood them. Shame bowed him down, and he looked resolutely at Mr. Torrance; who little supposed, good, worthy man, as he continued to expound justification by faith, what was his true business; to play the part of derivative to a pair of children at the old game of falling in love.

Christina was greatly relieved at first. It seemed to her that she was clothed again. She looked back on what had passed. All would have been right if she had not blushed, a silly fool! There was nothing to blush at, if she *had* taken a sugar-bool. Mrs. MacTaggart, the elder's wife in St. Enoch's, took them often. And if he had looked at her, what was more natural than that a young gentleman should look at the best-dressed girl in church? And at the same time, she knew far otherwise; she knew there was nothing casual or ordinary in the look, and valued herself on its memory like a decoration. Well, it was a blessing he had found something else to look at! And presently she began to have other thoughts. It was necessary, she fancied, that she should put herself right by a repetition of the incident, better managed. If the wish was father to the thought, she did not know or she would not recognise it. It was simply as a manœuvre of propriety, as something called for to lessen the significance of what had gone before, that she should a second time meet his eyes, and this time without blushing. And at the memory of the blush, she blushed again, and became one general blush burning from head to foot. Was ever anything so indelicate, so forward, done by a girl before? And here she was, making an exhibition of herself before the congregation about nothing! She stole a glance upon her neighbours, and behold! they were steadily indifferent, and Clem had gone to sleep. And still the one idea was becoming more and more potent with her, that in common prudence she must look again before the service ended. Something of the same sort was going forward in the mind of Archie, as he struggled with the load of penitence. So it chanced that, in the flutter of the moment when the last psalm was given out, and Torrance was reading the verse, and the leaves of every psalm-book in church were rustling under busy fingers, two stealthy glances were sent out like antennæ among the pews and on the indifferent and absorbed occupants, and drew timidly nearer to the straight line between Archie and Christina. They met, they lingered together for the least fraction of time, and that was enough. A charge as of electricity passed through Christina, and behold! the leaf of her psalm-book was torn across.

Archie was outside by the gate of the graveyard, conversing with Hob and the minister and shaking hands all round with the scattering congregation, when Clem and Christina were brought up to be presented. The laird took off his hat and bowed to her with grace and respect. Christina made her Glasgow curt-sey to the laird, and went on again up the road for Hermiston and Cauldstaneslap, walking fast, breathing hurriedly with a heightened colour, and in this strange frame of mind, that when she was alone she seemed in high happiness, and when any one addressed her she resented it like a contradiction. A part of the way she had the company of some neighbour girls and a loutish young man; never had they seemed so insipid, never had she made herself so disagreeable. But these struck aside to their various destinations or were out-walked and left behind; and when she had driven off with sharp words the proffered convoy of some of her nephews and nieces, she was free to go on alone up Hermiston brae, walking on air, dwelling intoxicated among clouds of happiness. Near to the summit she heard steps behind her, a man's steps, light and very rapid. She knew the foot at once and walked the faster. 'If it's me he's wanting he can run for it,' she thought, smiling.

Archie overtook her like a man whose mind was made up.

'Miss Kirstie,' he began.

'Miss Christina, if you please, Mr. Weir,' she interrupted. 'I canna bear the contraction.'

'You forget it has a friendly sound for me. Your aunt is an old friend of mine and a very good one. I hope we shall see much of you at Hermiston?'

'My aunt and my sister-in-law doesna agree very well. Not that I have much ado with it. But still when I'm stopping in the house, if I was to be visiting my aunt, it would not look consid-erate-like.'

' I am sorry,' said Archie.

' I thank you kindly, Mr. Weir,' she said. ' I whiles think myself it's a great peety.'

' Ah, I am sure your voice would always be for peace! ' he cried.

' I wouldna be too sure of that,' she said. ' I have my days like other folk, I suppose.'

' Do you know, in our old kirk, among our good old gray dames, you make an effect like sunshine.'

' Ah, but that would be my Glasgow clothes! '

' I did not think I was so much under the influence of pretty frocks.'

She smiled with a half look at him. ' There's more than you! ' she said. ' But you see I'm only Cinderella. I'll have to put all these things by in my trunk; next Sunday I'll be as gray as the rest. They're Glasgow clothes, you see, and it would never do to make a practice of it. It would seem terrible conspicuous.'

By that they were come to the place where their ways severed. The old gray moors were all about them; in the midst a few sheep wandered; and they could see on the one hand the straggling caravan scaling the braes in front of them for Cauldstaneslap, and on the other the contingent from Hermiston bending off and beginning to disappear by detachments into the policy gate. It was in these circumstances that they turned to say farewell, and deliberately exchanged a glance as they shook hands. All passed as it should, genteelly; and in Christina's mind, as she mounted the first steep ascent for Cauldstaneslap, a gratifying sense of triumph prevailed over the recollection of minor lapses and mistakes. She had kilted her gown, as she did usually at that rugged pass; but when she spied Archie still standing and gazing after her, the skirts came down again as if by enchantment. Here was a piece of nicety for that upland parish, where the matrons marched with their coats kilted in the rain, and the lasses walked barefoot to kirk through the dust of summer, and went bravely down by the burnside, and sat on stones to make a public toilet before entering! It was perhaps an air wafted from Glasgow; or perhaps it marked a stage of that dizziness of gratified vanity, in which the instinctive act passed unperceived. He was looking after! She unloaded her bosom of a prodigious sigh that was all pleasure, and betook herself to run. When she had overtaken the stragglers of her family, she caught up the niece whom she had so recently repulsed, and kissed and slapped her, and drove her away again, and ran after her with pretty cries and laughter. Perhaps she thought the laird might still be looking! But it chanced the little scene came under the view of eyes less favourable; for she overtook Mrs. Hob marching with Clem and Dand.

' You're shürely fey,[1] lass! ' quoth Dandie.

' Think shame to yersel', miss! ' said the strident Mrs. Hob. ' Is this the gait to guide yersel' on the way hame frae kirk? You're shürely no' sponsible the day. And anyway I would mind my guid claes.'

' Hoot! ' said Christina, and went on before them, head in air, treading the rough track with the tread of a wild doe.

She was in love with herself, her destiny, the air of the hills, the benediction of the sun. All the way home, she continued under the intoxication of these sky-scraping spirits. At table she could talk freely of young Hermiston; gave her opinion of him offhand and with a loud voice, that he was a handsome young gentleman, real weil-mannered and sensible-like, but it was a pity he looked doleful. Only—the moment after—a memory of his eyes in church embarrassed her. But for this inconsiderable check, all through meal-time she had a good appetite, and she kept them laughing at table until Gib (who had returned before them from Crossmichael and his separative worship) reproved the whole of them for their levity.

Singing ' in to herself ' as she went, her mind still in the turmoil of a glad confusion, she rose and tripped upstairs to a little loft, lighted by four panes in the gable, where she slept with one of her nieces. The niece, who followed her, presuming on ' Auntie's ' high spirits, was flounced out of the apartment with small ceremony, and retired, smarting and half tearful, to bury her woes in the byre among the hay. Still humming, Christina divested herself of her finery, and put her treasures one by one in her great green trunk. The last of these was the psalm-book; it was a fine piece, the gift of Mistress Clem, in distinct old-faced type, on paper that had begun to grow foxy in the warehouse—not by service—and she was used to wrap it in a handkerchief every Sunday after its period of service was over, and bury it endwise at the head of her trunk. As she now took it in hand the book fell open where the leaf was torn, and she stood and gazed upon that evidence of her bygone discomposure. There returned again the vision of the two brown eyes staring at her, intent and bright, out of that dark corner of the kirk. The whole appearance and attitude, the smile, the suggested gesture of young Hermiston came before her in a flash at the

---

[1] Unlike yourself, strange, as persons are observed to be in the hour of approaching death or calamity.

sight of the torn page. ' I was surely fey! ' she said, echoing the words of Dandie, and at the suggested doom her high spirits deserted her. She flung herself prone upon the bed, and lay there, holding the psalmbook in her hands for hours, for the more part in a mere stupor of unconsenting pleasure and un-reasoning fear. The fear was superstitious; there came up again and again in her memory Dandie's ill-omened words, and a hundred grisly and black tales out of the immediate neighbour-hood read her a commentary on their force. The pleasure was never realised. You might say the joints of her body thought and remembered, and were gladdened, but her essential self, in the immediate theatre of consciousness, talked feverishly of some-thing else, like a nervous person at a fire. The image that she most complacently dwelt on was that of Miss Christina in her character of the Fair Lass of Cauldstaneslap, carrying all before her in the straw-coloured frock, the violet mantle, and the yellow cobweb stockings. Archie's image, on the other hand, when it presented itself, was never welcomed—far less welcomed with any ardour, and it was exposed at times to merciless criticism. In the long, vague dialogues she held in her mind, often with imaginary, often with unrealised interlocutors, Archie, if he were referred to at all, came in for savage handling. He was described as ' looking like a stirk,' ' staring like a caulf,' ' a face like a ghaist's.' ' Do you call that manners? ' she said; or, ' I soon put him in his place.' ' " *Miss Christina, if you please, Mr. Weir!* " says I, and just flyped up my skirt tails.' With gabble like this she would entertain herself long whiles together, and then her eye would perhaps fall on the torn leaf, and the eyes of Archie would appear again from the darkness of the wall, and the voluble words deserted her, and she would lie still and stupid, and think upon nothing with devotion, and be sometimes raised by a quiet sigh. Had a doctor of medicine come into that loft, he would have diagnosed a healthy, well-developed, eminently vivacious lass lying on her face in a fit of the sulks; not one who had just contracted, or was just contracting, a mortal sickness of the mind which should yet carry her towards death and despair. Had it been a doctor of psychology, he might have been pardoned for divining in the girl a passion of childish vanity, self-love *in excelsis*, and no more. It is to be understood that I have been painting chaos and describing the inarticulate. Every lineament that appears is too precise, almost every word used too strong. Take a finger-post in the mountains on a day of rolling mists; I have but copied the names that appear upon the pointers, the names of definite and famous cities far distant, and now perhaps basking in sunshine; but Christina remained all these hours, as it were, at the foot of the post itself, not moving, and enveloped in mutable and blinding wreaths of haze.

The day was growing late and the sunbeams long and level, when she sat suddenly up, and wrapped in its handkerchief and put by that psalm-book which had already played a part so decisive in the first chapter of her love-story. In the absence of the mesmerist's eye, we are told nowadays that the head of a bright nail may fill his place, if it be steadfastly regarded. So that torn page had riveted her attention on what might else have been but little, and perhaps soon forgotten; while the ominous words of Dandie—heard, not heeded, and still remembered—had lent to her thoughts, or rather to her mood, a cast of solemnity, and that idea of Fate—a pagan Fate, uncontrolled by any Christian deity, obscure, lawless, and august—moving indissuadably in the affairs of Christian men. Thus even that phenomenon of love at first sight, which is so rare and seems so simple and violent, like a disruption of life's tissue, may be decomposed into a sequence of accidents happily concurring.

She put on a gray frock and a pink kerchief, looked at herself a moment with approval in the small square of glass that served her for a toilet mirror, and went softly downstairs through the sleeping house that resounded with the sound of afternoon snoring. Just outside the door Dandie was sitting with a book in his hand, not reading, only honouring the Sabbath by a sacred vacancy of mind. She came near him and stood still.

' I'm for off up the muirs, Dandie,' she said.

There was something unusually soft in her tones that made him look up. She was pale, her eyes dark and bright; no trace remained of the levity of the morning.

' Ay, lass? Ye'll have yer ups and downs like me, I'm thinkin',' he observed.

' What for do ye say that?' she asked.

' O, for naething,' says Dand. ' Only I think ye're mair like me than the lave of them. Ye've mair of the poetic temper, tho' Guid kens little enough of the poetic taalent. It's an ill gift at the best. Look at yoursel'. At denner you were all sunshine and flowers and laughter, and now you're like the star of evening on a lake.'

She drank in this hackneyed compliment like wine, and it glowed in her veins.

' But I'm saying, Dand '—she came nearer him—' I'm for the muirs. I must have a braith of air. If Clem was to be speiring for me, try and quaiet him, will ye no'?'

' What way? ' said Dandie. ' I ken but the ae way, and that's leein'. I'll say ye had a sair heid, if ye like.'

' But I havena,' she objected.

' I daursay no,' he returned. ' I said I would say ye had; and if ye like to nay-say when ye come back, it'll no mateerially maitter, for my chara'ter's clean gane a'ready past reca'.'

' O, Dand, are ye a leear? ' she asked, lingering.

' Folks say sae,' replied the bard.

' Wha says sae? ' she pursued.

' Them that should ken the best,' he responded. ' The lassies, for ane.'

' But, Dand, you would never lee to me? ' she asked.

' I'll leave that for your pairt of it, ye girzie,' said he. ' Ye'll lee to me fast eneuch, when ye hae gotten a jo. I'm tellin' ye and it's true; when you have a jo, Miss Kirstie, it'll be for guid and ill. I ken: I was made that way mysel', but the deil was in my luck! Here, gang awa wi' ye to your muirs, and let me be; I'm in an hour of inspiraution, ye upsetting tawpie!'

But she clung to her brother's neighbourhood, she knew not why.

' Will ye no gie's a kiss, Dand? ' she asked. ' I aye likit ye fine.'

He kissed her and considered her a moment; he found something strange in her. But he was a libertine through and through, nourished equal contempt and suspicion of all womankind, and paid his way among them habitually with idle compliments.

' Gae wa' wi' ye!' said he. ' Ye're a dentie baby, and be content wi' that!'

That was Dandie's way; a kiss and a comfit to Jenny—a bawbee and my blessing to Jill—and good-night to the whole clan of ye, my dears! When anything approached the serious, it became a matter for men, he both thought and said. Women, when they did not absorb, were only children to be shoo'd away. Merely in his character of connoisseur, however, Dandie glanced carelessly after his sister as she crossed the meadow. ' The brat's no' that bad!' he thought with surprise, for though he had just been paying her compliments, he had not really looked at her. ' Hey! what's yon? ' For the gray dress was cut with short sleeves and skirts, and displayed her trim strong legs clad in pink stockings of the same shade as the kerchief she wore round her shoulders, and that shimmered as she went. This was not her way in undress; he knew her ways and the ways of the whole sex in the country-side, no one better; when they did not go barefoot, they wore stout ' rig and furrow ' woollen hose of an invisible blue mostly, when they were not black outright; and Dandie, at sight of this daintiness, put two and two together. It was a silk handkerchief, then they would be silken hose; they matched—then the whole outfit was a present of Clem's, a costly present, and not something to be worn through bog and briar, on a late afternoon of Sunday. He whistled. 'My denty May, either your heid's fair turned, or there's some on-goings!' he observed, and dismissed that subject.

She went slowly at first, but ever straighter and faster for the Cauldstaneslap, a pass among the hills to which the farm owed its name. The Slap opened like a doorway between two rounded hillocks; and through this ran the short cut to Hermiston. Immediately on the other side it went down through the Deil's Hags, a considerable marshy hollow of the hill tops, full of springs, and crouching junipers, and pools where the black peat-water slumbered. There was no view from here. A man might have sat upon the Praying Weaver's Stone a half-century, and seen none but the Cauldstaneslap children twice in the twenty-four hours on their way to the school and back again, an occasional shepherd, the irruption of a clan of sheep, or the birds who haunted about the springs, drinking and shrilly piping. So, when she had once passed the Slap, Kirstie was received into seclusion. She looked back a last time at the farm. It still lay deserted except for the figure of Dandie, who was now seen to be scribbling in his lap, the hour of expected inspiration having come to him at last. Thence she passed rapidly through the morass, and came to the farther end of it, where a sluggish burn discharges, and the path for Hermiston accompanies it on the beginning of its downward path. From this corner a wide view was opened to her of the whole stretch of braes upon the other side, still sallow and in places rusty with the winter, with the path marked boldly, here and there by the burnside a tuft of birches, and— three miles off as the crow flies—from its enclosures and young plantations, the windows of Hermiston glittering in the western sun.

Here she sat down and waited, and looked for a long time at these far-away bright panes of glass. It amused her to have so extended a view, she thought. It amused her to see the house of Hermiston—to see 'folk'; and there was an indistinguishable human unit, perhaps the gardener, visibly sauntering on the grave paths.

By the time the sun was down and all the easterly braes lay plunged in clear shadow, she was aware of another figure coming up the path at a most unequal rate of approach, now half-running, now pausing and seeming to hesitate. She watched him at first with a total suspension of thought. She held her thought as a person holds his breathing. Then she consented to recognise him. 'He'll no' be coming here, he canna be; it's no' possible.' And there began to grow upon her a subdued choking suspense. He *was* coming; his hesitations had quite ceased, his step grew firm and swift; no doubt remained; and the question loomed up before her instant: what was she to do? It was all very well to say that her brother was a laird himself; it was all very well to speak of casual intermarriages and to count cousinship, like Aunt Kirstie. The difference in their social station was trenchant; propriety, prudence, all that she had ever learned, all that she knew, bade her flee. But on the other hand the cup of life now offered to her was too enchanting. For one moment, she saw the question clearly, and definitely made her choice. She stood up and showed herself an instant in the gap relieved upon the sky line; and the next, fled trembling and sat down glowing with excitement on the Weaver's Stone. She shut her eyes, seeking, praying for composure. Her hand shook in her lap, and her mind was full of incongruous and futile speeches. What was there to make a work about? She could take care of herself, she supposed! There was no harm in seeing the laird. It was the best thing that could happen. She would mark a proper distance to him once and for all. Gradually the wheels of her nature ceased to go round so madly, and she sat in passive expectation, a quiet, solitary figure in the midst of the gray moss. I have said she was no hypocrite, but here I am at fault. She never admitted to herself that she had come up the hill to look for Archie. And perhaps after all she did not know, perhaps came as a stone falls. For the steps of love in the young, and especially in girls, are instinctive and unconscious.

In the meantime, Archie was drawing rapidly near, and he at least was consciously seeking her neighbourhood. The afternoon had turned to ashes in his mouth; the memory of the girl had kept him from reading and drawn him as with cords; and at last, as the cool of the evening began to come on, he had taken his hat and set forth, with a smothered ejaculation, by the moor path to Cauldstaneslap. He had no hope to find her; he took the off chance without expectation of result and to relieve his uneasiness. The greater was his surprise, as he surmounted the slope and came into the hollow of the Deil's Hags, to see there, like an answer to his wishes, the little womanly figure in the gray dress and the pink kerchief sitting little, and low, and lost, and acutely solitary, in these desolate surroundings and on the weather-beaten stone of the dead weaver. Those things that still smacked of winter were all rusty about her, and those things that already relished of the spring had put forth the tender and lively colours of the season. Even in the unchanging face of the death-stone changes were to be remarked; and in the channelled lettering, the moss began to renew itself in jewels of green. By an after-thought that was a stroke of art, she had turned up over her head the back of the kerchief; so that it now framed becomingly her vivacious and yet pensive face. Her feet were gathered under her on the one side, and she leaned on her bare arm, which showed out strong and round, tapered to a slim wrist, and shimmered in the fading light.

Young Hermiston was struck with a certain chill. He was reminded that he now dealt in serious matters of life and death. This was a grown woman he was approaching, endowed with her mysterious potencies and attractions, the treasury of the continued race, and he was neither better nor worse than the average of his sex and age. He had a certain delicacy which had preserved him hitherto unspotted, and which (had either of them guessed it) made him a more dangerous companion when his heart should be really stirred. His throat was dry as he came near; but the appealing sweetness of her smile stood between them like a guardian angel.

For she turned to him and smiled, though without rising. There was a shade in this cavalier greeting that neither of them perceived; neither he, who simply thought it gracious and charming as herself; nor yet she, who did not observe (quick as she was) the difference between rising to meet the laird and remaining seated to receive the expected admirer.

'Are ye stepping west, Hermiston?' said she, giving him this territorial name after the fashion of the country-side.

'I was,' said he, a little hoarsely, 'but I think I will be about the end of my stroll now. Are you like me, Miss Christina? the house would not hold me. I came here seeking air.'

He took his seat at the other end of the tombstone and studied her, wondering what was she. There was infinite import in the question alike for her and him.

'Ay,' she said. 'I couldn'a bear the roof either. It's a habit of mine to come up here about the gloaming when it's quaiet and caller.'

'It was a habit of my mother's also,' he said gravely. The recollection half startled him as he expressed it. He looked around. 'I have scarce been here since. It's peaceful,' he said, with a long breath.

'It's no' like Glasgow,' she replied. 'A weary place, yon Glasgow! But what a day have I had for my hame-coming, and what a bonny evening!'

'Indeed, it was a wonderful day,' said Archie. 'I think I will remember it years and years until I come to die. On days like this—I do not know if you feel as I do—but everything appears so brief, and fragile, and exquisite, that I am afraid to touch life. We are here for so short a time; and all the old people before us—Rutherfords of Hermiston, Elliotts of the Cauldstaneslap—that were here but a while since, riding about and keeping up a great noise in this quiet corner—making love too, and marrying—why, where are they now? It's deadly commonplace, but after all, the commonplaces are the great poetic truths.'

He was sounding her, semi-consciously, to see if she could understand him; to learn if she were only an animal the colour of flowers, or had a soul in her to keep her sweet. She, on her part, her means well in hand, watched, womanlike, for any opportunity to shine, to abound in his humour, whatever that might be. The dramatic artist, that lies dormant or only half-awake in most human beings, had in her sprung to his feet in a divine fury, and chance had served her well. She looked upon him with a subdued twilight look that became the hour of the day and the train of thought; earnestness shone through her like stars in the purple west; and from the great but controlled upheaval of her whole nature there passed into her voice, and rang in her lightest words, a thrill of emotion.

'Have you mind of Dand's song?' she answered. 'I think he'll have been trying to say what you have been thinking.'

'No, I never heard it,' he said. 'Repeat it to me, can you?'

'It's nothing wanting the tune,' said Kirstie.

'Then sing it me,' said he.

'On the Lord's Day? That would never do, Mr. Weir!'

'I am afraid I am not so strict a keeper of the Sabbath, and there is no one in this place to hear us, unless the poor old ancient under the stone.'

'No' that I'm thinking that really,' she said. 'By my way of thinking, it's just as serious as a psalm. Will I sooth it to ye, then?'

'If you please,' said he, and, drawing near to her on the tombstone, prepared to listen.

She sat up as if to sing. 'I'll only can sooth it to ye,' she explained. 'I wouldna like to sing out loud on the Sabbath. I think the birds would carry news of it to Gilbert,' and she smiled.

'It's about the Elliotts,' she continued, 'and I think there's few bonnier bits in the book-poets, though Dand has never got printed yet.'

And she began, in the low, clear tones of her half-voice, now sinking almost to a whisper, now rising to a particular note which was her best, and which Archie learned to wait for with growing emotion:——

'O they rade in the rain, in the days that are gane,
   In the rain and the wind and the lave,
They shoutit in the ha' and they routit on the hill,
   But they're a' quaitit noo in the grave.
Auld, auld Elliotts, clay-cauld Elliotts, dour, bauld
   Elliotts of auld!'

All the time she sang she looked steadfastly before her, her knees straight, her hands upon her knee, her head cast back and up. The expression was admirable throughout, for had she not learned it from the lips and under the criticism of the author? When it was done, she turned upon Archie a face softly bright, and eyes gently suffused and shining in the twilight, and his heart rose and went out to her with boundless pity and sympathy. His question was answered. She was a human being tuned to a sense of the tragedy of life; there were pathos and music and a great heart in the girl.

He arose instinctively, she also, for she saw she had gained a point, and scored the impression deeper, and she had wit enough left to flee upon a victory. They were but commonplaces that remained to be exchanged, but the low, moved voices in which they passed made them sacred in the memory. In the falling grayness of the evening he watched her figure winding through the morass, saw it turn at last and wave a hand, and then pass through the Slap; and it seemed to him as if something went along with her out of the deepest of his heart. And something surely had come, and come to dwell there. He had retained from childhood a picture, now half-obliterated by the passage of time and the multitude of fresh impressions, of his mother telling him, with the fluttered earnestness of her voice, and often with dropping tears, the tale of the 'Praying Weaver,' on the very scene of his brief tragedy and long repose. And now there was a companion piece; and he beheld, and he should behold for ever, Christina perched on the same tomb, in the gray colours of the evening, gracious, dainty, perfect as a flower, and she also singing:—

'Of old, unhappy far-off things,
And battles long ago,'

—of their common ancestors now dead, of their rude wars composed, their weapons buried with them, and of these strange changelings, their descendants, who lingered a little in their places, and would soon be gone also, and perhaps sung of by others at the gloaming hour. By one of the unconscious arts of tenderness the two women were enshrined together in his memory. Tears, in that hour of sensibility, came into his eyes indifferently at the thought of either, and the girl, from being something merely bright and shapely, was caught up into the zone of things serious as life and death and his dead mother. So that in all ways and on either side, Fate played his game artfully with this poor pair of children. The generations were prepared, the pangs were made ready, before the curtain rose on the dark drama.

In the same moment of time that she disappeared from Archie, there opened before Kirstie's eyes the cup-like hollow in which the farm lay. She saw, some five hundred feet below her, the house making itself bright with candles, and this was a broad hint to her to hurry. For they were only kindled on a Sabbath night with a view to that family worship which rounded in the incomparable tedium of the day and brought on the relaxation of supper. Already she knew that Robert must be withinsides at the head of the table, 'waling the portions'; for it was Robert in his quality of family priest and judge, not the gifted Gilbert, who officiated. She made good time accordingly down the steep ascent, and came up to the door panting as the three younger brothers, all roused at last from slumber, stood together in the cool and the dark of the evening with a fry of nephews and nieces about them, chatting and awaiting the expected signal. She stood back; she had no mind to direct attention to her late arrival or to her labouring breath.

'Kirstie, ye have shaved it this time, my lass,' said Clem. 'Whaur were ye?'

'O, just taking a dander by myself',' said Kirstie.

And the talk continued on the subject of the American war, without further reference to the truant who stood by them in the covert of the dusk, thrilling with happiness and the sense of guilt.

The signal was given, and the brothers began to go in one after another, amid the jostle and throng of Hob's children.

Only Dandie, waiting till the last, caught Kirstie by the arm.

'When did ye begin to dander in pink hosen, Mistress Elliott?' he whispered slyly.

She looked down; she was one blush. 'I maun have forgotten to change them,' said she; and went in to prayers in her turn with a troubled mind, between anxiety as to whether Dand should have observed her yellow stockings at church, and should thus detect her in a palpable falsehood, and shame that she had already made good his prophecy. She remembered the words of it, how it was to be when she had gotten a jo, and that that would be for good and evil. 'Will I have gotten my jo now?' she thought with a secret rapture.

And all through prayers, where it was her principal business to conceal the pink stockings from the eyes of the indifferent Mrs. Hob—and all through supper, as she made a feint of eating, and sat at the table radiant and constrained—and again when she had left them and come into her chamber, and was alone with her sleeping niece, and could at last lay aside the armour of society—the same words sounded within her, the same profound note of happiness, of a world all changed and renewed, of a day that had been passed in Paradise, and of a night that was to be heaven opened. All night she seemed to be conveyed smoothly upon a shallow stream of sleep and waking, and through the bowers of Beulah; all night she cherished to her heart that exquisite hope; and if, towards morning, she forgot it a while in a more profound unconsciousness, it was to catch again the rainbow thought with her first moment of awaking.

7

Enter Mephistopheles

Two days later a gig from Crossmichael deposited Frank Innes at the doors of Hermiston. Once in a way, during the past winter, Archie, in some acute phase of boredom, had written him a letter. It had contained something in the nature of an invitation, or a reference to an invitation—precisely what, neither of them now remembered. When Innes had received it, there had been nothing further from his mind than to bury himself in the moors with Archie; but not even the most acute political heads are guided through the steps of life with unerring directness. That would require a gift of prophecy which has been denied to man. For instance, who could have imagined that, not a month after he had received the letter, and turned it into mockery, and put off answering it, and in the end lost it, misfortunes of a gloomy cast should begin to thicken over Frank's career? His case may be briefly stated. His father, a small Morayshire laird with a large family, became recalcitrant and cut off the supplies; he had fitted himself out with the beginnings of quite a good law library, which, upon some sudden losses on the turf, he had been obliged to sell before they were paid for; and his bookseller, hearing some rumour of the event, took out a warrant for his arrest. Innes had early word of it, and was able to take precautions. In this immediate welter of his affairs, with an unpleasant charge hanging over him, he had judged it the part of prudence to be off instantly, had written a fervid letter to his father at Inverauld, and put himself in the coach for Cross-michael. Any port in a storm! He was manfully turning his back on the Parliament House and its gay babble, on porter and oysters, the racecourse and the ring; and manfully prepared, until these clouds should have blown by, to share a living grave with Archie Weir at Hermiston.

To do him justice, he was no less surprised to be going than Archie was to see him come; and he carried off his wonder with an infinitely better grace.

'Well, here I am!' said he, as he alighted. 'Pylades has come to Orestes at last. By the way, did you get my answer? No? How very provoking! Well, here I am to answer for myself and that's better still.'

'I am very glad to see you, of course,' said Archie. 'I make you heartily welcome, of course. But you surely have not come to stay, with the Courts still sitting; is that not most unwise?'

'Damn the Courts!' says Frank. 'What are the Courts to friendship and a little fishing?'

And so it was agreed that he was to stay, with no term to the visit but the term which he had privily set to it himself—the day, namely, when his father should have come down with the dust, and he should be able pacify the bookseller. On such vague conditions there began for these two young men (who were not even friends) a life of great familiarity and, as the days grew on, less and less intimacy. They were together at mealtimes, together o' nights when the hour had come for whisky-toddy; but it might have been noticed (had there been any one to pay heed) that they were rarely so much together by day. Archie had Hermiston to attend to, multifarious activities in the hills, in which he did not require, and had even refused, Frank's escort. He would be off sometimes in the morning and leave only a note on the breakfast-table to announce the fact; and sometimes, with no notice at all, he would not return for dinner until the hour was long past. Innes groaned under these desertions; it required all his philosophy to sit down to a solitary breakfast with composure, and all his unaffected good-nature to be able to greet Archie with friendliness on the more rare occasions when he came home late for dinner.

'I wonder what on earth he finds to do, Mrs. Elliott?' said he one morning, after he had just read the hasty billet and sat down to table.

'I suppose it will be business, sir,' replied the housekeeper dryly, measuring his distance off to him by an indicated curtsey.

'But I can't imagine what business!' he reiterated.

'I suppose it will be *his* business,' retorted the austere Kirstie.

He turned to her with that happy brightness that made the charm of his disposition, and broke into a peal of healthy and natural laughter.

'Well played, Mrs. Elliott!' he cried, and the housekeeper's face relaxed into the shadow of an iron smile. 'Well played indeed!' said he. 'But you must not be making a stranger of me like that. Why, Archie and I were at the High School together, and we've been to College together, and we were going to the Bar together, when—you know! Dear me, dear me! what a pity that was! A life spoiled, a fine young fellow as good as buried here in the wilderness with rustics; and all for what? A frolic, silly, if you like, but no more. God, how good your scones are, Mrs. Elliott!'

'They're no' mines, it was the lassie made them,' said Kirstie; 'and, saving your presence, there's little sense in taking the Lord's name in vain about idle vivers that you fill your kyte wi'.'

'I daresay you're perfectly right, ma'am,' quoth the imperturbable Frank. 'But, as I was saying, this is a pitiable business, this about poor Archie; and you and I might do worse than put our heads together, like a couple of sensible people, and bring it to an end. Let me tell you, ma'am, that Archie is really quite a promising young man, and in my opinion he would do well at the Bar. As for his father, no one can deny his ability, and I don't fancy any one would care to deny that he has the deil's own temper——'

'If you'll excuse me, Mr. Innes, I think the lass is crying on me,' said Kirstie, and flounced from the room.

'The damned, cross-grained old broomstick!' ejaculated Innes.

In the meantime, Kirstie had escaped into the kitchen, and before her vassal gave vent to her feelings.

'Here, ettercap! Ye'll have to wait on yon Innes! I canna
haud myself in. "Puir Erchie"! I'd "puir Erchie" him, if I
had my way! And Hermiston with the deil's ain temper! God,
let him take Hermiston's scones out of his mouth first. There's
no' a hair on ayther o' the Weirs that hasna mair spunk and
dirdum to it than what he has in his hale dwaibly body!
Settin' up his snash to me! Let him gang to the black toon
where he's mebbe wantit—birling in a curricle—wi' pimatum
on his heid—making a mess o' himsel' wi' nesty hizzies—a fair
disgrace!' It was impossible to hear without admiration Kirstie's
graduated disgust, as she brought forth, one after another, these
somewhat baseless charges. Then she remembered her immediate purpose, and turned again on her fascinated auditor. 'Do
ye no' hear me, tawpie? Do ye no' hear what I'm tellin' ye?
Will I have to shoo ye in to him? If I come to attend to ye, mistress!' And the maid fled the kitchen, which had become practically dangerous, to attend on Innes's wants in the front parlour.

Tantaene irae? Has the reader perceived the reason? Since
Frank's coming there were no more hours of gossip over the
supper tray! All his blandishments were in vain; he had started handicapped on the race for Mrs. Elliott's favour.

But it was a strange thing how misfortune dogged him in his
efforts to be genial. I must guard the reader against accepting
Kirstie's epithets as evidence; she was more concerned for their
vigour than for their accuracy. Dwaibly, for instance; nothing
could be more calumnious. Frank was the very picture of good
looks, good-humour, and manly youth. He had bright eyes with
a sparkle and a dance to them, curly hair, a charming smile,
brilliant teeth, an admirable carriage of the head, the look of a
gentleman, the address of one accustomed to please at first sight
and to improve the impression. And with all these advantages,
he failed with every one about Hermiston; with the silent shepherd, with the obsequious grieve, with the groom who was also
the ploughman, with the gardener and the gardener's sister—
pious, down-hearted woman with a shawl over her ears—he
failed equally and flatly. They did not like him, and they showed
it. The little maid, indeed, was an exception; she admired him
devoutly, probably dreamed of him in her private hours; but
she was accustomed to play the part of silent auditor to Kirstie's
tirades and silent recipient of Kirstie's buffets, and she had
learned not only to be a very capable girl of her years, but a very
secret and prudent one besides. Frank was thus conscious that
he had one ally and sympathiser in the midst of that general
union of disfavour that surrounded, watched, and waited on

him in the house of Hermiston; but he had little comfort or society from that alliance, and the demure little maid (twelve on her last birthday) preserved her own counsel, and tripped on his service, brisk, dumbly responsive, but inexorably unconversational. For the others, they were beyond hope and beyond endurance. Never had a young Apollo been cast among such rustic barbarians. But perhaps the cause of his ill-success lay in one trait which was habitual and unconscious with him, yet diagnostic of the man. It was his practice to approach any one person at the expense of some one else. He offered you an alliance against the some one else; he flattered you by slighting him; you were drawn into a small intrigue against him before you knew how. Wonderful are the virtues of this process generally; but Frank's mistake was in the choice of the some one else. He was not politic in that; he listened to the voice of irritation. Archie had offended him at first by what he had felt to be rather a dry reception; had offended him since by his frequent absences. He was besides the one figure continually present in Frank's eye; and it was to his immediate dependants that Frank could offer the snare of his sympathy. Now the truth is that the Weirs, father and son, were surrounded by a posse of strenuous loyalists. Of my lord they were vastly proud. It was a distinction in itself to be one of the vassals of the 'Hanging Judge,' and his gross, formidable joviality was far from unpopular in the neighbourhood of his home. For Archie they had, one and all, a sensitive affection and respect which recoiled from a word of belittlement.

Nor was Frank more successful when he went farther afield. To the Four Black Brothers, for instance, he was antipathetic in the highest degree. Hob thought him too light, Gib too profane. Clem, who saw him but for a day or two before he went to Glasgow, wanted to know what the fule's business was, and whether he meant to stay here all session time! 'Yon's a drone,' he pronounced. As for Dand, it will be enough to describe their first meeting, when Frank had been whipping a river and the rustic celebrity chanced to come along the path.

'I'm told you are quite a poet,' Frank had said.

'Wha tell 't ye that, mannie?' had been the unconciliating answer.

'O, everybody,' says Frank.

'God! Here's fame!' said the sardonic poet, and he had passed on his way.

Come to think of it, we have here perhaps a truer explanation of Frank's failures. Had he met Mr. Sheriff Scott he could have turned a neater compliment, because Mr. Scott would have been a friend worth making. Dand, on the other hand, he did not value sixpence, and he showed it even while he tried to flatter. Condescension is an excellent thing, but it is strange how one-sided the pleasure of it is! He who goes fishing among the Scots peasantry with condescension for a bait will have an empty basket by evening.

In proof of this theory Frank made a great success of it at the Crossmichael Club, to which Archie took him immediately on his arrival; his own last appearance on that scene of gaiety. Frank was made welcome there at once, continued to go regularly, and had attended a meeting (as the members ever after loved to tell) on the evening before his death. Young Hay and young Pringle appeared again. There was another supper at Windielaws, another dinner at Driffel; and it resulted in Frank being taken to the bosom of the county people as unreservedly as he had been repudiated by the country folk. He occupied Hermiston after the manner of an invader in a conquered capital. He was perpetually issuing from it, as from a base, to toddy parties, fishing parties, and dinner parties, to which Archie was not invited, or to which Archie would not go. It was now that the name of The Recluse became general for the young man. Some say that Innes invented it; Innes, at least, spread it abroad.

'How's all with your Recluse to-day?' people would ask.

'O, reclusing away!' Innes would declare, with his bright air of saying something witty; and immediately interrupt the general laughter which he had provoked much more by his air than his words, 'Mind you, it's all very well laughing, but I'm not very well pleased. Poor Archie is a good fellow, an excellent fellow, a fellow I always liked. I think it small of him to take his little disgrace so hard and shut himself up. " Grant that it is a ridiculous story, painfully ridiculous," I keep telling him. " Be a man! Live it down, man!" But not he. Of course it's just solitude, and shame, and all that. But I confess I'm beginning to fear the result. It would be all the pities in the world if a really promising fellow like Weir was to end ill. I'm seriously tempted to write to Lord Hermiston, and put it plainly to him.'

'I would if I were you,' some of his auditors would say, shaking the head, sitting bewildered and confused at this new view of the matter, so deftly indicated by a single word. 'A capital idea!' they would add, and wonder at the *aplomb* and position of this young man, who talked as a matter of course of writing to Hermiston and correcting him upon his private affairs.

And Frank would proceed, sweetly confidential: ' I'll give you an idea, now. He's actually sore about the way that I'm received and he's left out in the county—actually jealous and sore. I've rallied him and I've reasoned with him, told him that every one was most kindly inclined towards him, told him even that *I* was received merely because I was his guest. But it's no use. He will neither accept the invitations he gets, nor stop brooding about the ones where he's left out. What I'm afraid of is that the wound's ulcerating. He had always one of those dark, secret, angry natures—a little underhand and plenty of bile—you know the sort. He must have inherited it from the Weirs, whom I suspect to have been a worthy family of weavers somewhere; what's the cant phrase!—sedentary occupation. It's precisely the kind of character to go wrong in a false position like what his father's made for him, or he's making for himself, whichever you like to call it. And for my part, I think it a disgrace,' Frank would say generously.

Presently the sorrow and anxiety of this disinterested friend took shape. He began in private, in conversations of two, to talk vaguely of bad habits and low habits. ' I must say I'm a-fraid he's going wrong altogether,' he would say. ' I'll tell you plainly, and between ourselves, I scarcely like to stay there any longer; only, man, I'm positively afraid to leave him alone. You'll see, I shall be blamed for it later on. I'm staying at a great sacrifice. I'm hindering my chances at the Bar, and I can't blind my eyes to it. And what I'm afraid of is that I'm going to get kicked for it all round before all's done. You see, nobody believes in friendship nowadays.'

' Well, Innes,' his interlocutor would reply, ' it's very good of you, I must say that. If there's any blame going you'll always be sure of *my* good word, for one thing.'

' Well,' Frank would continue, ' candidly, I don't say it's pleasant. He has a very rough way with him; his father's son, you know. I don't say he's rude—of course, I couldn't be expected to stand that—but he steers very near the wind. No, it's not pleasant; but I tell ye, man, in conscience I don't think it would be fair to leave him. Mind you, I don't say there's anything actually wrong. What I say is that I don't like the looks of it, man!' and he would press the arm of his momentary confidant.

In the early stages I am persuaded there was no malice. He talked but for the pleasure of airing himself. He was essentially glib, as becomes the young advocate, and essentially careless of the truth, which is the mark of the young ass; and so he talked at random. There was no particular bias, but that one which is indigenous and universal, to flatter himself and to please and interest the present friend. And by thus milling air out of his mouth, he had presently built up a presentation of Archie which was known and talked of in all corners of the county. Wherever there was a residential house and a walled garden, wherever there was a dwarfish castle and a park, wherever a quadruple cottage by the ruins of a peel-tower showed an old family going down, and wherever a handsome villa with a carriage approach and a shrubbery marked the coming up of a new one—probably on the wheels of machinery—Archie began to be regarded in the light of a dark, perhaps a vicious mystery, and the future developments of his career to be looked for with uneasiness and confidential whispering. He had done something disgraceful, my dear. What, was not precisely known, and that good kind young man, Mr. Innes, did his best to make light of it. But there it was. And Mr. Innes was very anxious about him now; he was really uneasy, my dear; he was positively wrecking his own prospects because he dared not leave him alone. How wholly we all lie at the mercy of a single prater, not needfully with any malign purpose! And if a man but talks of himself in the right spirit, refers to his virtuous actions by the way, and never applies to them the name of virtue, how easily his evidence is accepted in the court of public opinion!

All this while, however, there was a more poisonous ferment at work between the two lads, which came late indeed to the surface, but had modified and magnified their dissensions from the first. To an idle, shallow, easy-going customer like Frank, the smell of a mystery was attractive. It gave his mind something to play with, like a new toy to a child; and it took him on the weak side, for like many young men coming to the Bar, and before they have been tried and found wanting, he flattered himself he was a fellow of unusual quickness and penetration. They knew nothing of Sherlock Holmes in these days, but there was a good deal said of Talleyrand. And if you could have caught Frank off his guard, he would have confessed with a smirk, that, if he resembled any one, it was the Marquis de Talleyrand-Périgord. It was on the occasion of Archie's first absence that this interest took root. It was vastly deepened when Kirstie resented his curiosity at breakfast, and that same afternoon there occurred another scene which clinched the business. He was fishing Swingleburn, Archie accompanying him, when the latter looked at his watch.

'Well, good-bye,' said he. 'I have something to do. See you at dinner.'

'Don't be in such a hurry,' cries Frank. 'Hold on till I get my rod up. I'll go with you; I'm sick of flogging this ditch.'

And he began to reel up his line.

Archie stood speechless. He took a long while to recover his wits under this direct attack; but by the time he was ready with his answer, and the angle was almost packed up, he had become completely Weir, and the hanging face gloomed on his young shoulders. He spoke with a laboured composure, a laboured kindness even; but a child could see that his mind was made up.

' I beg your pardon, Innes; I don't want to be disagreeable, but let us understand one another from the beginning. When I want your company, I'll let you know.'

' Oh!' cries Frank, ' you don't want my company, don't you?'

' Apparently not just now,' replied Archie. ' I even indicated to you when I did, if you'll remember—and that was at dinner. If we two fellows are to live together pleasantly—and I see no reason why we should not—it can only be by respecting each other's privacy. If we begin intruding—— '

' Oh, come! I'll take this at no man's hands. Is this the way you treat a guest and an old friend?' cried Innes.

' Just go home and think over what I said by yourself,' continued Archie, ' whether it's reasonable, or whether it's really offensive or not; and let's meet at dinner as though nothing had happened. I'll put it this way, if you like—that I know my own character, that I'm looking forward (with great pleasure, I assure you) to a long visit from you, and that I'm taking precautions at the first. I see the thing that we—that I, if you like— might fall out upon, and I step in and *obsto principiis*. I wager you five pounds you'll end by seeing that I mean friendliness, and I assure you, Francie, I do,' he added, relenting.

Bursting with anger, but incapable of speech, Innes shouldered his rod, made a gesture of farewell, and strode off down the burnside. Archie watched him go without moving. He was sorry, but quite unashamed. He hated to be inhospitable, but in one thing he was his father's son. He had a strong sense that his house was his own and no man else's; and to lie at a guest's mercy was what he refused. He hated to seem harsh. But that was Frank's look-out. If Frank had been commonly discreet, he would have been decently courteous. And there was another consideration. The secret he was protecting was not his own merely; it was hers; it belonged to that inexpressible she who was fast taking possession of his soul, and whom he would soon have defended at the cost of burning cities. By the time he had watched Frank as far as the Swingleburnfoot, appearing and disappearing in the tarnished heather, still stalking at a fierce gait but already dwindled in the distance into less than the smallness of Lilliput, he could afford to smile at the occurrence. Either Frank would go, and that would be a relief—or he would continue to stay, and his host must continue to endure him. And Archie was now free—by devious paths, behind hillocks and in the hollow of burns—to make for the trysting-place where Kirstie, cried about by the curlew and the plover, waited and burned for his coming by the Covenanter's stone.

Innes went off down-hill in a passion of resentment, easy to be understood, but which yielded progressively to the needs of his situation. He cursed Archie for a cold-hearted, unfriendly, rude dog; and himself still more passionately for a fool in having come to Hermiston when he might have sought refuge in almost any other house in Scotland, but the step once taken was practically irretrievable. He had no more ready money to go anywhere else; he would have to borrow from Archie the next club-night; and ill as he thought of his host's manners, he was sure of his practical generosity. Frank's resemblance to Talleyrand strikes me as imaginary; but at least not Talleyrand himself could have more obediently taken his lesson from the facts. He met Archie at dinner without resentment, almost with cordiality. You must take your friends as you find them, he would have said. Archie couldn't help being his father's son, or his grandfather's, the hypothetical weaver's grandson. The son of a hunks, he was still a hunks at heart, incapable of true generosity and consideration; but he had other qualities with which Frank could divert himself in the meanwhile, and to enjoy which it was necessary that Frank should keep his temper.

So excellently was it controlled that he awoke next morning with his head full of a different, though a cognate subject. What was Archie's little game? Why did he shun Frank's company? What was he keeping secret? Was he keeping tryst with somebody, and was it a woman? It would be a good joke and a fair revenge to discover. To that task he set himself with a great deal of patience, which might have surprised his friends, for he had been always credited not with patience so much as brilliancy; and little by little, from one point to another, he at last succeeded in piecing out the situation. First he remarked that, although Archie set out in all the directions of the compass, he always, came home again from some point between the south and west. From the study of a map, and in consideration of the great expanse of untenanted moorland running in that direction towards the sources of the Clyde, he laid his finger on Cauldstaneslap and two other neighbouring farms, Kingsmuirs and Polintarf.

But it was difficult to advance farther. With his rod for a pretext, he vainly visited each of them in turn; nothing was to be seen suspicious about this trinity of moorland settlements. He would have tried to follow Archie, had it been the least possible, but the nature of the land precluded the idea. He did the next best, ensconced himself in a quiet corner, and pursued his movements with a telescope. It was equally in vain, and he soon wearied of his futile vigilance, left the telescope at home, and had almost given the matter up in despair, when, on the twenty-seventh day of his visit, he was suddenly confronted with the person whom he sought. The first Sunday Kirstie had managed to stay away from kirk on some pretext of indisposition, which was more truly modesty; the pleasure of beholding Archie seeming too sacred, too vivid for that public place. On the two following, Frank had himself been absent on some of his excursions among the neighbouring families. It was not until the fourth, accordingly, that Frank had occasion to set eyes on the enchantress. With the first look, all hesitation was over. She came with the Cauldstaneslap party; then she lived at Cauldstaneslap. Here was Archie's secret, here was the woman, and more than that—though I have need here of every manageable attenuation of language—with the first look, he had already entered himself as rival. It was a good deal in pique, it was a little in revenge, it was much in genuine admiration: the devil may decide the proportions; I cannot, and it is very likely that Frank could not.

'Mighty attractive milkmaid,' he observed, on the way home.

'Who?' said Archie.

'O, the girl you're looking at—aren't you? Forward there on the road. She came attended by the rustic bard; presumably, therefore, belongs to his exalted family. The single objection! for the Four Black Brothers are awkward customers. If anything were to go wrong, Gib would gibber, and Clem would prove inclement; and Dand fly in danders, and Hob blow up in gobbets. It would be a Helliott of a business!'

'Very humorous, I am sure,' said Archie.

'Well, I am trying to be so,' said Frank. 'It's none too easy in this place, and with your solemn society, my dear fellow. But confess that the milkmaid has found favour in your eyes or resign all claim to be a man of taste.'

'It is no matter,' returned Archie.

But the other continued to look at him, steadily and quizzically, and his colour slowly rose and deepened under the glance, until not impudence itself could have denied that he was blushing. And at this Archie lost some of his control. He changed his stick from one hand to the other, and—' O, for God's sake, don't be an ass!' he cried.

'Ass? That's the retort delicate without doubt,' says Frank. ' Beware of the homespun brothers, dear. If they come into the dance, you'll see who's an ass. Think now, if they only applied (say) a quarter as much talent as I have applied to the question of what Mr. Archie does with his evening hours, and why he is so unaffectedly nasty when the subject's touched on—— '

' You are touching on it now,' interrupted Archie, with a wince.

' Thank you. That was all I wanted, an articulate confession,' said Frank.

' I beg to remind you—— ' began Archie.

But he was interrupted in turn. ' My dear fellow, don't. It's quite needless. The subject's dead and buried.'

And Frank began to talk hastily on other matters, an art in which he was an adept, for it was his gift to be fluent on anything or nothing. But although Archie had the grace or the timidity to suffer him to rattle on, he was by no means done with the subject. When he came home to dinner, he was greeted with a sly demand, how things were looking ' Cauldstaneslap ways.' Frank took his first glass of port out after dinner to the toast of Kirstie, and later in the evening he returned to the charge again.

' I say, Weir, you'll excuse me for returning again to this affair. I've been thinking it over, and I wish to beg you very seriously to be more careful. It's not a safe business. Not safe, my boy,' said he.

' What? ' said Archie.

' Well, it's your own fault if I must put a name on the thing; but really, as a friend, I cannot stand by and see you rushing head down into these dangers. My dear boy,' said he, holding up a warming cigar, ' consider what is to be the end of it? '

' The end of what? —Archie, helpless with irritation, persisted in this dangerous and ungracious guard.

' Well, the end of the milkmaid; or, to speak more by the card, the end of Miss Christina Elliott of the Cauldstaneslap? '

' I assure you,' Archie broke out, ' this is all a figment of your imagination. There is nothing to be said against that young lady; you have no right to introduce her name into the conversation.'

' I'll make a note of it,' said Frank. ' She shall henceforth be nameless, nameless, nameless, Gregarach! I make a note besides of your valuable testimony to her character. I only want to look at this thing as a man of the world. Admitted she's an angel—but, my good fellow, is she a lady?'

This was torture to Archie. 'I beg your pardon,' he said, struggling to be composed, ' but because you have wormed yourself into my confidence——'

'Oh, come!' cried Frank. 'Your confidence? It was rosy but unconsenting. Your confidence, indeed! Now, look! This is what I must say, Weir, for it concerns your safety and good character, and therefore my honour as your friend. You say I wormed myself into your confidence. Wormed is good. But what have I done? I have put two and two together, just as the parish will be doing to-morrow, and the whole of Tweeddale in two weeks, and the Black Brothers—well, I won't put a date on that; it will be a dark and stormy morning. Your secret, in other words, is poor Poll's. And I want to ask of you as a friend whether you like the prospect? There are two horns to your dilemma, and I must say for myself I should look mighty ruefully on either. Do you see yourself explaining to the Four Black Brothers? or do you see yourself presenting the milkmaid to papa as the future lady of Hermiston? Do you? I tell you plainly, I don't.'

Archie rose. ' I will hear no more of this,' he said in a trembling voice.

But Frank again held up his cigar. 'Tell me one thing first. Tell me if this is not a friend's part that I am playing?'

' I believe you think it so,' replied Archie. ' I can go as far as that. I can do so much justice to your motives. But I will hear no more of it. I am going to bed.'

'That's right, Weir,' said Frank, heartily. 'Go to bed and think over it; and I say, man, don't forget your prayers! I don't often do the moral—don't go in for that sort of thing—but when I do there's one thing sure, that I mean it.'

So Archie marched off to bed, and Frank sat alone by the table for another hour or so, smiling to himself richly. There was nothing vindictive in his nature; but, if revenge came in his way, it might as well be good, and the thought of Archie's pillow reflections that night was indescribably sweet to him. He felt a pleasant sense of power. He looked down on Archie as on a very little boy whose strings he pulled—as on a horse whom he had backed and bridled by sheer power of intelligence, and whom he might ride to glory or the grave at pleasure. Which was it to be? He lingered long, relishing the details of schemes that he was too idle to pursue. Poor cork upon a torrent, he tasted that night the sweets of omnipotence, and brooded like a deity over the strands of that intrigue which was to shatter him before the summer waned.

8

A nocturnal visit

KIRSTIE had many causes of distress. More and more as we grow old—and yet more and more as we grow old and are women, frozen by the fear of age—we come to rely on the voice as the single outlet of the soul. Only thus, in the curtailment of our means, can we relieve the straitened cry of the passion within us; only thus, in the bitter and sensitive shyness of advancing years, can we maintain relations with those vivacious figures of the young that still show before us and tend daily to become no more than the moving wallpaper of life. Talk is the last link, the last relation. But with the end of the conversation, when the voice stops and the bright face of the listener is turned away, solitude falls again on the bruised heart. Kirstie had lost her 'cannie hour at e'en'; she could no more wander with Archie, a ghost, if you will, but a happy ghost, in fields Elysian. And to her it was as if the whole world had fallen silent; to him, but an unremarkable change of amusements. And she raged to know it. The effervescency of her passionate and irritable nature rose within her at times to bursting point.

This is the price paid by age for unseasonable ardours of feeling. It must have been so for Kirstie at any time when the occasion chanced; but it so fell out that she was deprived of this delight in the hour when she had most need of it, when she had most to say, most to ask, and when she trembled to recognise her sovereignty not merely in abeyance but annulled. For, with the clairvoyance of a genuine love, she had pierced the mystery that had so long embarrassed Frank. She was conscious, even before it was carried out, even on that Sunday night when it began, of an invasion of her rights; and a voice told her the invader's name. Since then, by arts, by accident, by small things observed, and by the general drift of Archie's humour, she had passed beyond all possibility of doubt. With a sense of justice that Lord Hermiston might have envied, she had that day in church considered and admitted the attractions of the younger Kirstie; and with the profound humanity and sentimentality of her nature, she had recognised the coming of fate. Not thus would she have chosen. She had seen, in imagination, Archie wedded to some tall, powerful, and rosy heroine of the golden locks, made in her own image, for whom she would have strewed the bride-bed with delight; and now she could have wept to see the ambition falsified. But the gods had pronounced, and her doom was otherwise.

She lay tossing in bed that night, besieged with feverish thoughts. There were dangerous matters pending, a battle was toward, over the fate of which she hung in jealousy, sympathy, fear, and alternate loyalty and disloyalty to either side. Now she was reincarnated in her niece, and now in Archie. Now she saw, through the girl's eyes, the youth on his knees to her, heard his persuasive instances with a deadly weakness, and received his over-mastering caresses. Anon, with a revulsion, her temper raged to see such utmost favour of fortune and love squandered on a brat of a girl, one of her own house, using her own name—a deadly ingredient—and that ' didna ken her ain mind an' was as black's your hat.' Now she trembled lest her deity should plead in vain, loving the idea of success for him like a triumph of nature; anon, with returning loyalty to her own family and sex, she trembled for Kirstie and the credit of the Elliotts. And again she had a vision of herself, the day over for her old-world tales and local gossip, bidding farewell to her last link with life and brightness and love; and behind and beyond, she saw but the blank butt-end where she must crawl to die. Had she then come to the lees? she, so great, so beautiful, with a heart as fresh as a girl's and strong as womanhood? It could not be, and yet it was so; and for a moment her bed was horrible to her as the sides of the grave. And she looked forward over a waste of hours, and saw herself go on to rage, and tremble, and be softened, and rage again, until the day came and the labours of the day must be renewed.

Suddenly she heard feet on the stairs—his feet, and soon after the sound of a window-sash flung open. She sat up with her heart beating. He had gone to his room alone, and he had not gone to bed. She might again have one of her night cracks; and at the entrancing prospect, a change came over her mind; with the approach of this hope of pleasure, all the baser metal became immediately obliterated from her thoughts. She rose, all woman, and all the best of woman, tender, pitiful, hating the wrong, loyal to her own sex—and all the weakest of that dear miscellany, nourishing, cherishing next her soft heart, voicelessly flattering, hopes that she would have died sooner than have acknowledged. She tore off her night-cap, and her hair fell about her shoulders in profusion. Undying coquetry awoke.

By the faint light of her nocturnal rush, she stood before the looking-glass, carried her shapely arms above her head, and gathered up the treasures of her tresses. She was never backward to admire herself; that kind of modesty was a stranger to her nature; and she paused, struck with a pleased wonder at the sight. 'Ye daft auld wife!' she said, answering a thought that was not; and she blushed with the innocent consciousness of a child. Hastily she did up the massive and shining coils, hastily donned a wrapper, and with the rush-light in her hand, stole into the hall. Below stairs she heard the clock ticking the deliberate seconds, and Frank jingling with the decanters in the dining-room. Aversion rose in her, bitter and momentary. 'Nesty, tippling puggy!' she thought; and the next moment she had knocked guardedly at Archie's door and was bidden enter.

Archie had been looking out into the ancient blackness, pierced here and there with a rayless star; taking the sweet air of the moors and the night into his bosom deeply; seeking, perhaps finding, peace after the manner of the unhappy. He turned round as she came in, and showed her a pale face against the window-frame.

'Is that you, Kirstie?' he asked. 'Come in!'

'It's unco' late, my dear,' said Kirstie, affecting unwillingness.

'No, no,' he answered, 'not at all. Come in, if you want a crack. I am not sleepy, God knows!'

She advanced, took a chair by the toilet-table and the candle, and set the rush-light at her foot. Something—it might be in the comparative disorder of her dress, it might be the emotion that now welled in her bosom—had touched her with a wand of transformation, and she seemed young with the youth of goddesses.

'Mr. Erchie,' she began, 'what's this that's come to ye?'

'I am not aware of anything that has come,' said Archie, and blushed and repented bitterly that he had let her in.

'Oh, my dear, that'll no dae!' said Kirstie. 'It's ill to blind the eyes of love. Oh, Mr. Erchie, tak' a thocht ere it's ower late. Ye shouldna be impatient o' the braws o' life, they'll a' come in their saison, like the sun and the rain. Ye're young yet; ye've money cantie years afore ye. See and dinna wreck yersel' at the outset like sae mony ithers! Hae patience—they told me aye that was the owercome o' life—hae patience, there's a braw day coming yet. Gude kens it never cam' to me; and here I am wi' nayther man nor bairn to ca' my ain, wearyin' a' folks wi' my ill tongue, and you just the first, Mr. Erchie!'

'I have a difficulty in knowing what you mean,' said Archie.

'Weel, and I'll tell ye,' she said. 'It's just this, that I'm fear-ed. I'm feared for ye, my dear. Remember, your faither is a hard man, reapin' where he hasna sowed and gaitherin' where he hasna strawed. It's easy speakin', but mind! Ye'll have to look in the gurly face o'm, where it's ill to look, and vain to look for mercy. Ye mind me o' a bonny ship pitten oot into the black and gowsty seas—ye're a' safe still, sittin' quait and crackin' wi' Kirstie in your lown chalmer; but whaur will ye be the morn, and in whatten horror o' the fearsome tempest, cryin' on the hils to cover ye?'

'Why, Kirstie, you're very enigmatical to-night—and very eloquent,' Archie put in.

'And, my dear Mr. Erchie,' she continued, with a change of voice, 'ye mauna think that I canna sympathise wi' ye. Ye mauna think that I havena been young mysel'. Lang syne, when I was a bit lassie, no' twenty yet——' She paused and sighed. 'Clean and caller, wi' a fit like the hinney bee,' she continued. 'I was aye big and buirdly, ye maun understand; a bonny figure o' a woman, though I say it that suldna—built to rear bairns—braw bairns they suld hae been, and grand I would hae likit it! But I was young, dear, wi' the bonny glint o' youth in my e'en, and little I dreamed I'd ever be tellin' ye this, an auld, lanely, rudas wife! Weel, Mr. Erchie, there was a lad cam' courtin' me, as was but naetural. Mony had come before, and I would nane o' them. But this yin had a tongue to wile the birds frae the lift and the bees frae the foxglove bells. Deary me, but it's lang syne. Folk have dee'd sinsyne and been buried, and are forgotten, and bairns been born and got merrit and got bairns o' their ain. Sinsyne woods have been plantit, and have grawn up and are bonny trees, and the joes sit in their shadow, and sinsyne auld estates have changed hands, and there have been wars and rumours of wars on the face of the earth. And here I'm still—like an auld droopit craw—lookin' on and craik-in'. But, Mr. Erchie, do ye no' think that I have mind o' it a' still? I was dwallin' then in my faither's house; and it's a curious thing that we were whiles trysted in the Deil's Hags. And do ye no' think that I have mind of the bonny simmer days, the lang miles o' the bluid-red heather, the cryin' o' the whaups, and the lad and the lassie that was trysted? Do ye no' think that I mind how the hilly sweetness ran about my hairt? Ay, Mr. Erchie, I ken the way o' it—fine do I ken the way—how the grace o' God takes them like Paul of Tarsus, when they think it least, and drives the pair o' them into a land which is like a dream, and the world and the folks in't are nae mair than clouds to the puir lassie, and Heeven nae mair than windle-straes, if she can but pleesure him! Until Tam dee'd—that was my story,' she broke off to say, ' he dee'd, and I wasna at the buryin'. But while he was here, I could take care o' mysel'. And can yon puir lassie?'

Kirstie, her eyes shining with unshed tears, stretched out her hand towards him appealingly; the bright and the dull gold of her hair flashed and smouldered in the coils behind her comely head, like the rays of an eternal youth; the pure colour had risen in her face; and Archie was abashed alike by her beauty and her story. He came towards her slowly from the window, took up her hand in his and kissed it.

' Kirstie,' he said hoarsely, ' you have misjudged me sorely. I have always thought of her, I wouldna harm her for the universe, my woman! '

' Eh, lad, and that's easy sayin',' cried Kirstie, ' but it's nae sae easy doin'! Man, do ye no' comprehend that it's God's wull we should be blendit and glamoured, and have nae command over our ain members at a time like that? My bairn,' she cried, still holding his hand, ' think o' the puir lass! have pity upon her, Erchie! and O, be wise for twa! Think o' the risk she rins! I have seen ye, and what's to prevent ithers? I saw ye once in the Hags, in my ain howf, and I was wae to see ye there—in pairt for the omen, for I think there's a weird on the place—and in pairt for puir nakit envy and bitterness o' hairt. It's strange ye should forgather there tae! God! but yon puir, thrawn, auld Covenanter's seen a heap o' human natur since he lookit his last on the musket-barrels, if he never saw nane afore,' she added, with a kind of wonder in her eyes.

' I swear by my honour I have done her no wrong,' said Archie. ' I swear by my honour and the redemption of my soul that there shall none be done her. I have heard of this before. I have been foolish, Kirstie, not unkind, and, above all, not base.'

' There's my bairn! ' said Kirstie, rising. ' I'll can trust ye noo, I'll can gang to my bed wi' an easy hairt.' And then she saw in a flash how barren had been her triumph. Archie had promised to spare the girl, and he would keep it; but who had promised to spare Archie? What was to be the end of it? Over a maze of difficulties she glanced, and saw, at the end of every passage, the flinty countenance of Hermiston. And a kind of horror fell upon her at what she had done. She wore a tragic mask. ' Erchie, the Lord peety you, dear, and peety me! I have buildit on this foundation,'—laying her hand heavily on his shoulder—'and buildit hie, and pit my hairt in the buildin' of it. If the hale hypothec were to fa', I think, laddie, I would dee! Excuse a daft wife that loves ye, and that kenned your mither. And for His name's sake keep yersel' frae inordinate desires; haud your hairt in baith your hands, carry it canny and laigh; dinna send it up like a bairn's kite into the collieshangie o' the wunds! Mind, Maister Erchie dear, that this life's a disappointment, and a mouthfu' o' mools is the appointed end.'

'Ay, but Kirstie, my woman, you're asking me ower much at last,' said Archie, profoundly moved, and lapsing into the broad Scots. 'Ye're asking what nae man can grant ye, what only the Lord of heaven can grant ye if He see fit. Ay! And can even He? I can promise ye what I shall do, and you can depend on that. But how I shall feel—my woman, that is long past thinking of!'

They were both standing by now opposite each other. The face of Archie wore the wretched semblance of a smile; hers was convulsed for a moment.

'Promise me ae thing,' she cried, in a sharp voice. 'Promise me ye'll never do naething without telling me.'

'No, Kirstie, I canna promise ye that,' he replied. 'I have promised enough, God kens!'

'May the blessing of God lift and rest upon ye, dear!' she said.

'God bless ye, my old friend,' said he.

9

At the Weaver's stone

IT was late in the afternoon when Archie drew near by the hill path to the Praying Weaver's Stone. The Hags were in shadow. But still, through the gate of the Slap, the sun shot a last arrow, which sped far and straight across the surface of the moss, here and there touching and shining on a tussock, and lighted at length on the gravestone and the small figure awaiting him there. The emptiness and solitude of the great moors seemed to be concentrated there, and Kirstie pointed out by that finger of sunshine for the only inhabitant. His first sight of her was thus excruciatingly sad, like a glimpse of a world from which all light, comfort, and society were on the point of vanishing. And the next moment, when she had turned her face to him and the quick smile had enlightened it, the whole face of nature smiled upon him in her smile of welcome. Archie's slow pace was quickened; his legs hasted to her though his heart was hanging back. The girl, upon her side, drew herself together slowly and stood up, expectant; she was all languor, her face was gone white; her arms ached for him, her soul was on tip-toes. But he deceived her, pausing a few steps away, not less white than herself, and holding up his hand with a gesture of denial.

'No, Christina, not to-day,' he said. 'To-day I have to talk to you seriously. Sit ye down, please, there where you were. Please!' he repeated.

The revulsion of feeling in Christina's heart was violent. To have longed and waited these weary hours for him, rehearsing her endearments—to have seen him at last come—to have been ready there, breathless, wholly passive, his to do what he would with—and suddenly to have found herself confronted with a gray-faced, harsh schoolmaster—it was too rude a shock. She sat down on the stone, from which she had arisen, part with the instinct of obedience, part as though she had been thrust there. What was this? Why was she rejected? Had she ceased to please? She stood here offering her wares, and he would none of them! And yet they were all his! His to take and keep; not his to refuse, though! In her quick petulant nature, a moment ago on fire with hope, thwarted love and wounded vanity wrought. The schoolmaster that there is in all men, to the de-spair of all girls and most women, was now completely in pos-session of Archie. He had passed a night of sermons; a day of reflection; he had come wound up to do his duty; and the set mouth, which in him only betrayed the effort of his will, to her seemed the expression of an averted heart. It was the same with his constrained voice and embarrassed utterance; and if so—if it was all over—the pang of the thought took away from her the power of thinking.

He stood before her some way off. 'Kirstie, there's been too much of this. We've seen too much of each other.' She looked up quickly and her eyes contracted. 'There's no good ever comes of these secret meetings. They're not frank, not honest truly, and I ought to have seen it. People have begun to talk; and it's not right of me. Do you see?'

'I see somebody will have been talking to ye,' she said sullenly.

'They have, more than one of them,' replied Archie.

'And whae were they?' she cried. 'And what kind o' love do ye ca' that, that's ready to gang round like a whirligig at folk talking? Do ye think they havena talked to me?'

'Have they indeed?' said Archie, with a quick breath. 'That is what I feared. Who were they? Who has dared——'

Archie was on the point of losing his temper.

As a matter of fact, not any one had talked to Christina on the matter; and she strenuously repeated her own first question in a panic of self-defence.

'Ah, well! what does it matter?' he said. 'They were good folk that wished well to us, and the great affair is that there are people talking. My dear girl, we have to be wise. We must not wreck our lives at the outset. They may be long and happy yet, and we must see to it, Kirstie, like God's rational creatures and not like fool children. There is one thing we must see to before all. You're worth waiting for, Kirstie! worth waiting for a generation; it would be enough reward.'—And here he remembered the schoolmaster again, and very unwisely took to following wisdom. 'The first thing that we must see to, is that there shall be no scandal about, for my father's sake. That would ruin all; do ye no' see that?'

Kirstie was a little pleased, there had been some show of warmth of sentiment in what Archie had said last. But the dull irritation still persisted in her bosom; with the aboriginal instinct, having suffered herself, she wished to make Archie suffer.

And besides, there had come out the word she had always feared to hear from his lips, the name of his father. It is not to be supposed that, during so many days with a love avowed between them, some reference had not been made to their conjoint future. It had in fact been often touched upon, and from the first had been the sore point. Kirstie had wilfully closed the eye of thought; she would not argue even with herself; gallant, desperate little heart, she had accepted the command of that supreme attraction like the call of fate and marched blindfold on her doom. But Archie, with his masculine sense of responsibility, must reason; he must dwell on some future good, when the present good was all in all to Kirstie; he must talk—and talk lamely, as necessity drove him—of what was to be. Again and again he had touched on marriage; again and again been driven back into indistinctness by a memory of Lord Hermiston. And Kirstie had been swift to understand and quick to choke down and smother the understanding; swift to leap up in flame at a mention of that hope, which spoke volumes to her vanity and her love, that she might one day be Mrs. Weir of Hermiston; swift, also, to recognise in his stumbling or throttled utterance the death-knell of these expectations, and constant, poor girl!

in her large-minded madness, to go on and to reck nothing of the future. But these unfinished references, these blinks in which his heart spoke, and his memory and reason rose up to silence it before the words were well uttered, gave her unqualifiable agony. She was raised up and dashed down again bleeding. The recurrence of the subject forced her, for however short a time, to open her eyes on what she did not wish to see; and it had invariably ended in another disappointment. So now again, at the mere wind of its coming, at the mere mention of his father's name—who might seem indeed to have accompanied them in their moorland courtship, an awful figure in a wig with an ironical and bitter smile, present to guilty consciousness—she fled from it head down.

'Ye havena told me yet,' she said, 'who was it spoke?'

'Your aunt for one,' said Archie.

'Auntie Kirstie?' she cried. 'And what do I care for my Auntie Kirstie?'

'She cares a great deal for her niece,' replied Archie, in kind reproof.

'Troth, and it's the first I've heard of it,' retorted the girl.

'The question here is not who it is, but what they say, what they have noticed,' pursued the lucid schoolmaster. 'That is what we have to think of in self-defence!'

'Auntie Kirstie, indeed! A bitter, thrawn auld maid that's fomented trouble in the country before I was born, and will be doing it still, I daur say, when I'm deid! It's in her nature; it's as natural for her as it's for a sheep to eat.'

'Pardon me, Kirstie, she was not the only one,' interposed Archie. 'I had two warnings, two sermons, last night, both most kind and considerate. Had you been there, I promise you you would have grat, my dear! And they opened my eyes. I saw we were going a wrong way.'

'Who was the other one?' Kirstie demanded.

By this time Archie was in the condition of a hunted beast. He had come, braced and resolute; he was to trace out a line of conduct for the pair of them in a few cold, convincing sentences; he had now been there some time, and he was still staggering round the outworks and undergoing what he felt to be a savage cross-examination.

'Mr. Frank!' she cried. 'What nex', I would like to ken?'

'He spoke most kindly and truly.'

'What like did he say?'

'I am not going to tell you; you have nothing to do with that,' cried Archie, startled to find he had admitted so much.

'Oh, I have naething to do with it!' she repeated, springing to her feet. 'A'body at Hermiston's free to pass their opinions upon me, but I have naething to do wi' it! Was this at prayers like? Did ye ca' the grieve into the consultation? Little wonder if a'body's talking, when you make a'body ye're confidants! But as you say, Mr. Weir—most kindly, most considerately, most truly, I'm sure—I have naething to do with it. And I think I'll better be going. I'll be wishing you good-evening, Mr. Weir.' And she made him a stately curtsey, shaking as she did so from head to foot, with the barren ecstasy of temper.

Poor Archie stood dumbfounded. She had moved some steps away from him before he recovered the gift of articulate speech.

'Kirstie!' he cried. 'Oh, Kirstie woman!'

There was in his voice a ring of appeal, a clang of mere astonishment that showed the schoolmaster was vanquished.

She turned round on him. 'What do ye Kirstie me for?' she retorted. 'What have ye to do wi' me? Gang to your ain freends and deave them!'

He could only repeat the appealing 'Kirstie!'

'Kirstie, indeed!' cried the girl, her eyes blazing in her white face. 'My name is Miss Christina Elliott, I would have ye to ken, and I daur ye to ca' me out of it. If I canna get love, I'll have respect, Mr. Weir. I'm come of decent people, and I'll have respect. What have I done that ye should lightly me? What have I done? What have I done? Oh, what have I done?' and her voice rose upon the third repetition. 'I thocht —I thocht—I thocht I was sae happy!' and the first sob broke from her like the paroxysm of some mortal sickness.

Archie ran to her. He took the poor child in his arms, and she nestled to his breast as to a mother's, and clasped him in hands that were strong like vices. He felt her whole body shaken by the throes of distress, and had pity upon her beyond speech. Pity, and at the same time a bewildered fear of this explosive engine in his arms, whose works he did not understand, and yet had been tampering with. There arose from before him the curtains of boyhood, and he saw for the first time the ambiguous face of woman as she is. In vain he looked back over the interview; he saw not where he had offended. It seemed unprovoked, a wilful convulsion of brute nature....

GLOSSARY

ae, *one.*

antinomian, *one of a sect which holds that under the Gospel dispensation the moral law is not obligatory.*

Auld Hornie, *the Devil.*

ballant, *ballad.*

bauchles, *brogues, old shoes.*

bauld, *bold.*

bees in their bonnet, *eccentricities.*

birling, *whirling.*

black-a-vised, *dark-complexioned.*

bonnet-laird, *small landed proprietor, yeoman.*

bool, *ball,* technically, *marble;* here, *sugar-plum.*

brae, *rising ground.*

brig, *bridge.*

buff, play buff on, *to make a fool of, to deceive.*

burn, *stream.*

butt end, *end of a cottage.*

byre, *cow-house.*

ca', *drive.*

caller, *fresh.*

canna, *cannot.*

canny, *careful, shrewd.*

cantie, *cheerful.*

carline, *an old woman.*

chalmer, *chamber.*

claes, *clothes.*

clamjamfry, *crowd.*

clavers, *idle talk.*

cock-laird, *a yeoman.*

collieshangie, *turmoil.*

crack, *to converse.*

cuddy, *donkey.*

cuist, *cast.*

cutty, *jade;* also used playfully = *brat.*

daft, *mad, frolicsome.*

dander, *to saunter.*

danders, *cinders.*

daurna, *dare not.*

deave, *to deafen.*

demmy brokens, *demi-broquins.*

denty, *dainty.*

dirdum, *vigour.*

disjaskit, *worn-out, disreputable-looking.*

doer, *law agent.*

dour, *hard.*

drumlie, *dark.*

dule-tree, *the tree of lamentation, the hanging tree;* dule *is also Scots for boundary, and* it *may mean the boundary tree, the tree on which the baron hung interlopers.*

dunting, *knocking.*

dwaibly, *infirm, rickety.*

earand, *errand.*

ettercap, *vixen.*

fechting, *fighting.*

feck, *quantity, portion.*

feckless, *feeble, powerless.*

fell, *strong and fiery.*

fey, *unlike yourself, strange, as persons are observed to be in the hour of approaching death or disaster.*

fit, *foot.*

flit, *to depart.*

flyped, *turned up, turned inside out.*

forbye, *in addition to.*

forgather, *to fall in with.*

fower, *four.*

fule, *fool.*

füshionless, *pithless, weak.*

fyle, *to soil, to defile.*

fylement, *obloquy, defilement.*

gaed, *went.*

gang, *to go.*

gey an', *very.*

gigot, *leg of mutton.*

girzie, *lit., diminutive of Grizel; here, a playful nickname.*

glaur, *mud.*

glint, *glance, sparkle.*

gloaming, *twilight.*

glower, *to scowl.*

gobbets, *small lumps.*

gowden, *golden.*

gowsty, *gusty.*

grat, *wept.*

grieve, *land-steward.*

guddle, *to catch fish with the hands by groping under the stones or banks.*

guid, *good.*

gumption, *common-sense, judgment.*

gurley, *stormy, surly.*

gyte, *beside itself.*

haddit, *held.*

hae, *have, take.*

hale, *whole.*

heels-ower-hurdie, *heels over head.*

hinney, *honey.*

hirstle, *to bustle.*

hizzie, *wench.*

howe, *hollow.*

howf, *haunt.*

hunkered, *crouched.*

hypothec, *lit., a term in Scots law meaning the security given by a tenant to a landlord, as furniture, produce, etc.; by metonymy and colloquially, 'the whole structure,' 'the whole affair.'*

idleset, *idleness.*

infeftment, *a term in Scots law originally synonymous with investiture.*

jaud, *jade.*

jeely-piece, *a slice of bread and jelly.*

jennipers, *juniper.*

jo, *sweetheart.*

justifeed, *executed, made the victim of justice.*

jyle, *jail.*

kebbuck, *cheese.*

ken, *to know.*

kenspeckle, *conspicuous.*

kilted, *tucked up.*

kyte, *belly.*

laigh, *low.*

laird, *landed proprietor.*

lane, *alone.*

lave, *rest, remainder.*

linking, *tripping.*

lown, *lonely, still.*

lynn, *cataract.*

Lyon King of Arms, *the chief of the Court of Heraldry in Scotland.*

macers, *officers of the supreme court* [cf. *Guy Mannering,* last chapter].

maun, *must.*

menseful, *of good manners.*

mirk, *dark.*

misbegowk, *deception, disappointment.*

mools, *mould, earth.*

muckle, *much, great, big.*

my lane, *by myself.*

nowt, *black cattle.*

palmering, *walking infirmly.*

panel, *in Scots law, the accused person in a criminal action, the prisoner.*

peel, *a fortified watch-tower.*

plew-stilts, *plough-handles.*

policy, *ornamental grounds of a country mansion.*

puddock, *frog.*

quean, *wench.*

rair, *to roar.*

riffraff, *rabble.*

risping, *grating.*

rowt, *to roar, to rant.*
rowth, *abundance.*
rudas, *haggard (old woman).*
runt, *an old cow past breeding;* opprobriously, *an old woman.*

sab, *sob.*
sanguishes, *sandwiches.*
sasine, in Scots law, *the act of giving legal possession of feudal property,* or, colloquially, *the deed by which that possession is proved.*
sclamber, *to scramble.*
sculduddery, *impropriety, grossness.*
session, *the Court of Session, the supreme court of Scotland.*
shauchling, *shuffling.*
shoo, *to chase gently.*
siller, *money.*
sinsyne, *since then.*
skailing, *dispersing.*
skelp, *slap.*
skirling, *screaming.*
skreigh-o'-day, *daybreak.*
snash, *abuse.*
sneisty, *supercilious.*
sooth, *to hum.*
sough, *sound, murmur.*
Spec., *The Speculative Society,* a debating society connected with Edinburgh University.
speir, *to ask.*
speldering, *sprawling.*

splairge, *to splash.*
spunk, *spirit, fire.*
steik, *to shut.*
stirk, *a young bullock.*
stockfish, *hard, savourless.*
sugar-bool, *sugar-plum.*
syne, *since.*

tawpie, *a slow, foolish slut.*
telling you, *a good thing for you.*
thir, *these.*
thrawn, *cross-grained.*
toon, *town.*
two-names, *local sobriquets in addition to patronymic.*
tyke, *dog.*

unchancy, *unlucky.*
unco, *strange, extraordinary, very.*
upsitten, *impertinent.*

vivers, *victuals.*

wae, *sad, unhappy.*
waling, *choosing.*
warrandise, *warranty.*
waur, *worse.*
weird, *destiny.*
whammle, *to upset.*
whaup, *curlew.*
windlestrae, *crested dog's-tail grass.*
wund, *wind.*

yin, *one.*

OTHER FRAGMENTS

The Great North Road
The Young Chevalier
Heathercat

CONTENTS

THE GREAT NORTH ROAD

CONTENTS

Nance at the 'Green Dragon'

NANCE HOLDAWAY was on her knees before the fire, blowing the green wood that voluminously smoked upon the dogs, and only now and then shot forth a smothered flame; her knees already ached and her eyes smarted, for she had been some while at this ungrateful task, but her mind was gone far away to meet the coming stranger. Now she met him in the wood, now at the castle gate, now in the kitchen by candle-light; each fresh presentment eclipsed the one before; a form so elegant, manners so sedate, a countenance so brave and comely, a voice so winning and resolute—sure such a man was never seen! The thick-coming fancies poured and brightened in her head like the smoke and flames upon the hearth.

Presently the heavy foot of her Uncle Jonathan was heard upon the stair, and as he entered the room she bent the closer to her work. He glanced at the green fagots with a sneer, and looked askance at the bed and the white sheets, at the strip of carpet laid, like an island, on the great expanse of the stone floor, and at the broken glazing of the casement clumsily repaired with paper.

'Leave that fire a-be,' he cried. 'What, have I toiled all my life to turn innkeeper at the hind end? Leave it a-be, I say.'

'La, uncle, it doesn't burn a bit; it only smokes,' said Nance, looking up from her position.

'You are come of decent people on both sides,' returned the old man. 'Who are you to blow the coals for any Robin-run-agate? Get up, get on your hood, make yourself useful, and be off to the "Green Dragon."'

'I thought you was to go yourself,' Nance faltered.

'So did I,' quoth Jonathan; 'but it appears I was mistook.'

The very excess of her eagerness alarmed her, and she began to hang back. 'I think I would rather not, dear uncle,' she said. 'Night is at hand, and I think, dear, I would rather not.'

'Now you look here,' replied Jonathan; 'I have my lord's orders, have I not? Little he gives me, but it's all my livelihood. And do you fancy if I disobey my lord, I'm likely to turn round for a lass like you? No; I've that hell-fire of pain in my old knee, I wouldn't walk a mile, not for King George upon his bended knees.' And he walked to the window and looked down the steep scarp to where the river foamed in the bottom of the dell.

Nance stayed for no more bidding. In her own room, by the glimmer of the twilight, she washed her hands and pulled on her Sunday mittens; adjusted her black hood, and tied a dozen times its cherry ribbons; and in less than ten minutes, with a fluttering heart and excellently bright eyes, she passed forth under the arch and over the bridge, into the thickening shadows of the groves. A well-marked wheel-track conducted her. The wood, which upon both sides of the river dell was a mere scrambling thicket of hazel, hawthorn, and holly, boasted on the level of more considerable timber. Beeches came to a good growth, with here and there an oak; and the track now passed under a high arcade of branches, and now ran under the open sky in glades. As the girl proceeded these glades became more frequent, the trees began again to decline in size, and the wood to degenerate into furzy coverts. Last of all there was a fringe of elders; and beyond that the track came forth upon an open, rolling moorland, dotted with wind-bowed and scanty bushes, and all golden-brown with the winter, like a grouse. Right over against the girl the last red embers of the sunset burned under horizontal clouds; the night fell clear and still and frosty, and the track in low and marshy passages began to crackle underfoot with ice.

Some half a mile beyond the borders of the wood the lights of the ' Green Dragon ' hove in sight, and running close beside them, very faint in the dying dusk, the pale ribbon of the Great North Road. It was the back of the post-house that was presented to Nance Holdaway; and as she continued to draw near and the night to fall more completely, she became aware of an unusual brightness and bustle.

A post-chaise stood in the yard, its lamps already lighted: light shone hospitably in the windows and from the open door; moving lights and shadows testified to the activity of servants bearing lanterns. The clank of pails, the stamping of hoofs on the firm causeway, the jingle of harness, and, last of all, the energetic hissing of a groom, began to fall upon her ear. By the stir you would have thought the mail was at the door, but it was still too early in the night. The down mail was not due at the ' Green Dragon ' for hard upon an hour; the up mail from Scotland not before two in the black morning.

Nance entered the yard somewhat dazzled. Sam, the tall hostler, was polishing the curb-chain with sand; the lantern at his feet letting up spouts of candle-light through the holes with which its conical roof was peppered.

'Hey, miss,' said he, jocularly, 'you won't look at me any more, now you have gentry at the castle.'

Her cheeks burned with anger.

'That's my lord's chay,' the man continued, nodding at the chaise; 'Lord Windermoor's. Came all in a fluster—dinner, bowl of punch, and put the horses to. For all the world like a runaway match, my dear—bar the bride. He brought Mr. Archer in the chay with him.'

'Is that Holdaway?' cried the landlord from the lighted entry, where he stood shading his eyes.

'Only me, sir,' answered Nance.

'O, you Miss Nance,' he said. 'Well, come in quick, my pretty. My lord is waiting for your uncle.'

And he ushered Nance into a room cased with yellow wainscot and lighted by tall candles, where two gentlemen sat at a table finishing a bowl of punch. One of these was stout, elderly, and irascible, with a face like a full moon, well dyed with liquor, thick tremulous lips, a short purple hand, in which he brandished a long pipe, and an abrupt and gobbling utterance. This was my Lord Windermoor. In his companion Nance beheld a younger man, tall, quiet, grave, demurely dressed, and wearing his own hair. Her glance but lighted on him, and she flushed, for in that second she made sure that she had twice betrayed herself—betrayed by the involuntary flash of her black eyes her secret impatience to behold this new companion, and, what was far worse, betrayed her disappointment in the realisation of her dreams. He, meanwhile, as if unconscious, continued to regard her with unmoved decorum.

'O, a man of wood,' thought Nance.

'What—what?' said his lordship. 'Who is this?'

'If you please, my lord, I am Holdaway's niece,' replied Nance, with a curtsey.

'Should have been here himself,' observed his lordship. 'Well, you tell Holdaway that I'm aground; not a stiver—not a stiver. I'm running for the beagles—going abroad, tell Holdaway. And he need look for no more wages: glad of 'em myself, if I could get 'em. He can live in the castle if he likes, or go to the devil. O, and here is Mr. Archer; and I recommend him to take him in—a friend of mine—and Mr. Archer will pay, as I wrote. And I regard that in the light of a precious good thing for Holdaway, let me tell you, and a set-off against the wages.'

'But O, my lord!' cried Nance, 'we live upon the wages, and what are we to do without?'

'What am I to do?—what am I to do?' replied Lord Winder-

moor, with some exasperation. ' I have no wages. And there is
Mr. Archer. And if Holdaway doesn't like it, he can go to the
devil, and you with him!—and you with him! '

' And yet, my lord,' said Mr. Archer, ' these good people will
have as keen a sense of loss as you or I; keener, perhaps, since
they have done nothing to deserve it.'

' Deserve it? ' cried the peer. ' What? What? If a rascally
highwayman comes up to me with a confounded pistol, do you
say that I've deserved it? How often am I to tell you, sir, that
I was cheated—that I was cheated? '

' You are happy in the belief,' returned Mr. Archer gravely.

' Archer, you would be the death of me! ' exclaimed his lordship. ' You know you're drunk; you know it, sir; and yet you
can't get up a spark of animation.'

' I have drunk fair, my lord,' replied the younger man; ' but
I own I am conscious of no exhilaration.'

' If you had as black a look-out as me, sir,' cried the peer,
' you would be very glad of a little innocent exhilaration, let me
tell you. I am glad of it—glad of it, and I only wish I was
drunker. For let me tell you it's a cruel hard thing upon a man
of my time of life and my position, to be brought down to beggary
because the world is full of thieves and rascals—thieves and
rascals. What? For all I know, you may be a thief and a rascal
yourself; and I would fight you for a pinch of snuff—a pinch
of snuff,' exclaimed his lordship.

Here Mr. Archer turned to Nance Holdaway with a pleasant
smile, so full of sweetness, kindness, and composure that, at one
bound, her dreams returned to her.

' My good Miss Holdaway,' said he, ' if you are willing to
show me the road, I am eager to be gone. As for his lordship
and myself, compose yourself; there is no fear; this is his lordship's way.'

' What? What? ' cried his lordship. ' My way? Ish no such
a thing, my way.'

' Come, my lord,' cried Archer; ' you and I very thoroughly
understand each other; and let me suggest, it is time that both
of us were gone. The mail will soon be due. Here, then, my
lord, I take my leave of you, with the most earnest assurance of
my gratitude for the past, and a sincere offer of any services I
may be able to render in the future.'

' Archer,' exclaimed Lord Windermoor, ' I love you like a son.
Le' 's have another bowl.'

' My lord, for both our sakes, you will excuse me,' replied

Mr. Archer. 'We both require caution; we must both, for some while at least, avoid the chance of a pursuit.'

'Archer,' quoth his lordship, 'this is a rank ingratishood. What? I'm to go firing away in the dark in the cold po'-chaise, and not so much as a game of écarté possible, unless I stop and play with the postillion—the postillion; and the whole country swarming with thieves and rascals and highwaymen.'

'I beg your lordship's pardon,' put in the landlord, who now appeared in the doorway to announce the chaise, 'but this part of the North Road is known for safety. There has not been a robbery, to call a robbery, this five years' time. Farther south, of course, it's nearer London, and another story,' he added.

'Well, then, if that's so,' concluded my lord, 'le' 's have t' other bowl and a pack of cards.'

'My lord, you forget,' said Archer, 'I might still gain, but it is hardly possible for me to lose.'

'Think I'm a sharper?' inquired the peer. 'Gen'leman's parole's all I ask.'

But Mr. Archer was proof against these blandishments, and said farewell gravely enough to Lord Windermoor, shaking his hand and at the same time bowing very low. 'You will never know,' said he, 'the service you have done me.' And with that, and before my lord had finally taken up his meaning, he had slipped about the table, touched Nance lightly but imperiously on the arm, and left the room. In face of the outbreak of his lordship's lamentations, she made haste to follow the truant.

2

In which Mr. Archer is installed

THE chaise had been driven around to the front door; the courtyard lay all deserted, and only lit by a lantern set upon a window-sill. Through this Nance rapidly led the way, and began to ascend the swellings of the moor with a heart that somewhat fluttered in her bosom. She was not afraid, but in the course of these last passages with Lord Windermoor Mr. Archer had ascended to that pedestal on which her fancy waited to install him. The reality, she felt, excelled her dreams, and this cold night walk was the first romantic incident in her experience.

It was the rule in those days to see gentlemen unsteady after dinner, yet Nance was both surprised and amused when her companion, who had spoken so soberly, began to stumble and waver by her side with the most airy divagations. Sometimes he would get so close to her that she must edge away; and at others lurch clear out of the track and plough among deep heather. His courtesy and gravity meanwhile remained unaltered. He asked her how far they had to go; whether the way lay all upon the moorland, and when he learned they had to pass a wood expressed his pleasure. ' For,' said he, ' I am passionately fond of trees. Trees and fair lawns, if you consider of it rightly, are the ornaments of nature, as palaces and fine approaches—— ' And here he stumbled into a patch of slough and nearly fell. The girl had hard work not to laugh, but at heart she was lost in admiration for one who talked so elegantly.

They had got to about a quarter of a mile from the ' Green Dragon,' and were near the summit of the rise, when a sudden rush of wheels arrested them. Turning and looking back, they saw the post-house, now much declined in brightness; and speeding away northward the two tremulous bright dots of my Lord Windermoor's chaise-lamps. Mr. Archer followed these yellow and unsteady stars until they dwindled into points and disappeared.

' There goes my only friend,' he said. ' Death has cut off those that loved me, and change of fortune estranged my flatterers; and but for you, poor bankrupt, my life is as lonely as this moor.'

The tone of his voice affected both of them. They stood there on the side of the moor, and became thrillingly conscious of the void waste of the night, without a feature for the eye, and except for the fainting whisper of the carriage-wheels without a murmur for the ear. And instantly, like a mockery, there broke out, very far way, but clear and jolly, the note of the mail-guard's horn. ' Over the hills,' was his air. It rose to the two watchers on the moor with the most cheerful sentiment of human company and travel, and at the same time in and around the ' Green Dragon ' it woke up a great bustle of lights running to and fro and clattering hoofs. Presently after, out of the darkness to southward, the mail drew near with a growing rumble. Its lamps were very large and bright, and threw their radiance forward in overlapping cones; the four cantering horses swarmed and steamed; the body of the coach followed like a great shadow; and this lit picture slid with a sort of ineffectual swiftness over the black field of night, and was eclipsed by the buildings of the ' Green Dragon.'

Mr. Archer turned abruptly and resumed his former walk; only that he was now more steady, kept better alongside his young conductor, and had fallen into a silence broken by sighs.

Nance waxed very pitiful over his fate, contrasting an imaginary past of courts and great society, and perhaps the King himself, with the tumbledown ruin in a wood to which she was now conducting him.

' You must try, sir, to keep your spirits up,' said she. ' To be sure, this is a great change for one like you; but who knows the future? '

Mr. Archer turned towards her in the darkness, and she could clearly perceive that he smiled upon her very kindly. ' There spoke a sweet nature,' said he, ' and I must thank you for these words. But I would not have you fancy that I regret the past for any happiness found in it, or that I fear the simplicity and hardship of the country. I am a man that has been much tossed about in life; now up, now down; and do you think that I shall not be able to support what you support—you who are kind, and therefore know how to feel pain; who are beautiful, and therefore hope; who are young, and therefore (or am I the more mistaken?) discontented? '

' Nay, sir, not that, at least,' said Nance; ' not discontented. If I were to be discontented how should I look those that have real sorrows in the face? I have faults enough, but not that fault; and I have my merits too, for I have a good opinion of myself. But for beauty, I am not so simple but that I can tell a banter from a compliment.'

' Nay, nay,' said Mr. Archer, ' I had half forgotten; grief is selfish, and I was thinking of myself and not of you, or I had never blurted out so bold a piece of praise. 'Tis the best proof of my sincerity. But come, now, I would lay a wager you are no coward? '

' Indeed, sir, I am not more afraid than another,' said Nance. ' None of my blood are given to fear.'

' And you are honest? ' he returned.

' I will answer for that,' said she.

' Well, then, to be brave, to be honest, to be kind, and to be contented, since you say you are so—is not that to fill up a great part of virtue? '

' I fear you are but a flatterer,' said Nance, but she did not say it clearly, for what with bewilderment and satisfaction, her heart was quite oppressed.

There could be no harm, certainly, in these grave compliments; but yet they charmed and frightened her, and to find favour, for reasons however obscure, in the eyes of this elegant, serious, and most unfortunate young gentleman, was a giddy elevation, was almost an apotheosis, for a country maid.

But she was to be no more exercised; for Mr. Archer, disclaiming any thought of flattery, turned to other subjects, and held her all through the wood in conversation, addressing her with an air of perfect sincerity, and listening to her answers with every mark of interest. Had open flattery continued, Nance would have soon found refuge in good sense; but the more subtle lure she could not suspect, much less avoid. It was the first time she had ever taken part in a conversation illuminated by any ideas. All was then true that she had heard and dreamed of gentlemen; they were a race apart, like deities knowing good and evil. And then there burst upon her soul a divine thought, hope's glorious sunrise: since she could understand, since it seemed that she too, even she, could interest this sorrowful Apollo, might she not learn? Or was she not learning? Would not her soul awake and put forth wings? Was she not, in fact, an enchanted princess, waiting but a touch to become royal? She saw herself transformed, radiantly attired, but in the most exquisite taste; her face grown longer and more refined; her tint etherealised; and she heard herself with delighted wonder talking like a book.

Meanwhile they had arrived at where the track comes out above the river dell, and saw in front of them the castle, faintly shadowed on the night, covering with its broken battlements a bold projection of the bank, and showing at the extreme end where were the habitable tower and wing, some crevices of candle-light. Hence she called loudly upon her uncle, and he was seen to issue, lantern in hand, from the tower door, and, where the ruins did not intervene, to pick his way over the swarded courtyard, avoiding treacherous cellars and winding among blocks of fallen masonry. The arch of the great gate was still entire, flanked by two tottering bastions, and it was here that Jonathan met them, standing at the edge of the bridge, bent somewhat forward, and blinking at them through the glow of his own lantern. Mr. Archer greeted him with civility; but the old man was in no humour of compliance. He guided the new-comer across the courtyard, looking sharply and quickly in his face, and grumbling all the time about the cold, and the discomfort and dilapidation of the castle.

He was sure he hoped that Mr. Archer would like it; but in truth he could not think what brought him there. Doubtless he had a good reason—this with a look of cunning scrutiny—but, indeed, the place was quite unfit for any person of repute; he himself was eaten up with the rheumatics. It was the most rheumaticky place in England, and, some fine day, the whole habitable part (to call it habitable) would fetch away bodily and go down the slope into the river. He had seen the cracks widening; there was a plaguy issue in the bank below; he thought a spring was mining it; it might be to-morrow, it might be next day; but they were all sure of a come-down sooner or later. 'And that is a poor death,' said he, 'for any one, let alone a gentleman, to have a whole old ruin dumped upon his belly. Have a care to your left there: these cellar vaults have all broke down, and the grass and the hemlock hide 'em. Well, sir, here is welcome to you, such as it is, and wishing you well away.'

And with that Jonathan ushered his guest through the tower door, and down three steps on the left hand into the kitchen or common room of the castle. It was a huge, low room, as large as a meadow, occupying the whole width of the habitable wing, with six barred windows looking on the court, and two into the river valley. A dresser, a table, and a few chairs stood dotted here and there upon the uneven flags. Under the great chimney a good fire burned in an iron firebasket; a high old settle, rudely carved with figures and Gothic lettering, flanked it on either side; there were a hinge table and a stone bench in the chimney corner, and above the arch hung guns, axes, lanterns, and great sheaves of rusty keys.

Jonathan looked about him, holding up the lantern, and shrugged his shoulders with a pitying grimace. 'Here it is,' he said. 'See the damp on the floor, look at the moss; where there's moss you may be sure that it's rheumaticky. Try and get near that fire for to warm yourself; it'll blow the coat off your back. And with a young gentleman with a face like yours, as pale as a tallow candle, I'd be afeared of a churchyard cough and a galloping decline,' said Jonathan, naming the maladies with gloomy gusto, 'or the cold might strike and turn your blood,' he added.

Mr. Archer fairly laughed. 'My good Mr. Holdaway,' said he, 'I was born with that same tallow-candle face, and the only fear that you inspire me with is the fear that I intrude unwelcomely upon your private hours. But I tkink I can promise you that I am very little troublesome, and I am inclined to hope that the terms which I can offer may still pay you the derangement.'

'Yes, the terms,' said Jonathan, 'I was thinking of that. As you say, they are very small,' and he shook his head.

'Unhappily, I can afford no more,' said Mr. Archer. 'But this we have arranged already,' he added with a certain stiffness;

'and as I am aware that Miss Holdaway has matter to communicate, I will, if you permit, retire at once. To-night I must bivouac; to-morrow my trunk is to follow from the "Dragon." So, if you will show me to my room I shall wish you a good slumber and a better awakening.'

Jonathan silently gave the lantern to Nance, and she, turning and curtseying in the doorway, proceeded to conduct their guest up the broad winding staircase of the tower. He followed with a very brooding face.

'Alas!' cried Nance, as she entered the room, 'your fire is black out,' and setting down the lantern, she clapped upon her knees before the chimney and began to rearrange the charred and still smouldering remains. Mr. Archer looked about the gaunt apartment with a sort of shudder. The great height, the bare stone, the shattered windows, the aspect of the uncurtained bed, with one of its four fluted columns broken short, all struck a chill upon his fancy. From this dismal survey his eyes turned to Nance crouching before the fire, the candle in one hand and artfully puffing at the embers; the flames as they broke forth played upon the soft outline of her cheek—she was alive and young, colored with the bright hues of life, and a woman. He looked upon her, softening; and then set down and continued to admire the picture.

'There, sir,' said she, getting upon her feet, 'your fire is doing bravely now. Good night.' He rose and held out his hand. 'Come,' said he, 'you are my only friend in these parts, and you must shake hands.'

She brushed her hand upon her skirt, and offered it, blushing.

'God bless you, my dear,' said he.

And then, when he was alone, he opened one of the windows, and stared down into the dark valley. A gentle wimpling of the river among stones ascended to his ear; the trees upon the other bank stood very black against the sky; farther away an owl was hooting. It was dreary and cold, and as he turned back to the hearth and the fine glow of fire, 'Heavens!' said he to himself, 'what an unfortunate destiny is mine!'

He went to bed, but sleep only visited his pillow in uneasy snatches. Outbreaks of loud speech came up the staircase; he heard the old stones of the castle crack in the frosty night with sharp reverberations, and the bed complained under his tossings. Lastly, far on into the morning, he awakened from a doze to hear, very far off, in the extreme and breathless quiet, a wailing flourish on the horn. The down mail was drawing near to the 'Green Dragon.' He sat up in bed; the sound was tragical by distance, and the modulation appealed to his ear like human speech. It seemed to call upon him with a dreary insistence—to call him far away, to address him personally, and to have a meaning that he failed to seize. It was thus, at least, in this nodding castle, in a cold, miry woodland, and so far from men and society, that the traffic on the Great North Road spoke to him in the intervals of slumber.

3
Jonathan Holdaway

NANCE descended the stair, pausing at every step. She was in no hurry to confront her uncle with bad news, and she must dwell a little longer on the rich note of Mr. Archer's voice, the charm of his kind words, and the beauty of his manner and person. But, once at the stair-foot, she threw aside the spell and recovered her sensible and workaday self.

Jonathan was seated in the middle of the settle, a mug of ale beside him, in the attitude of one prepared for trouble; but he did not speak, and suffered her to fetch her supper and eat of it, with a very excellent appetite, in silence. When she had done, she, too, drew a tankard of home-brewed, and came and planted herself in front of him upon the settle.

' Well? ' said Jonathan.

' My Lord has run away,' said Nance.

' What? ' cried the old man.

' Abroad,' she continued. ' Run away from creditors. He said he had not a stiver, but he was drunk enough. He said you might live on in the castle, and Mr. Archer would pay you; but you was to look for no more wages, since he would be glad of them himself.'

Jonathan's face contracted; the flush of a black, bilious anger mounted to the roots of his hair; he gave in an inarticulate cry, leapt upon his feet, and began rapidly pacing the stone floor. At first he kept his hands behind his back in a tight knot; then he began to gesticulate as he turned.

' This man—this lord,' he shouted, ' who is he? He was born with a gold spoon in his mouth, and I with a dirty straw. He rolled in his coach when he was a baby. I have dug and toiled and laboured since I was that high—that high.' And he shouted again. ' I'm bent and broke, and full of pains. D'ye think I don't know the taste of sweat? Many's the gallon I've drunk of it—ay, in the midwinter, toiling like a slave. All through, what has my life been? Bend, bend, bend my old creaking back till it would ache like breaking; wade about in the foul mire, never a dry stitch; empty belly, sore hands, hat off to my Lord Redface; kicks and ha'pence; and now, here, at the hind end, when I'm worn to my poor bones, a kick and done with it.' He walked a little while in silence and then, extending his hand, 'Now, you Nance Holdaway,' said he, 'you come of my blood, and you're a good girl. When that man was a boy I used to carry his gun for him. I carried the gun all day on my two feet, and many a stitch I had, and chewed a bullet for. He rode upon a horse with feathers in his hat, but it was him that had the shots and took the game home. Did I complain? Not I. I knew my station. What did I ask, but just the chance to live and die honest? Nance Holdaway, don't let them deny it to me —don't let them do it. I've been poor as Job, and honest as the day, but now, my girl, you mark these words of mine, I'm getting tired of it.'

'I wouldn't say such words, at least,' said Nance.

'You wouldn't?' said the old man grimly. 'Well, and did I when I was your age? Wait till your back's broke, and your hands tremble, and your eyes fail, and you're weary of the battle, and ask no more but to lie down in your bed and give the ghost up like an honest man; and then let there up and come some insolent, ungodly fellow—ah! if I had him in these hands! "Where's my money that you gambled?" I should say. "Where's my money that you drank and diced?" "Thief!" is what I would say; "thief!"' he roared, '"thief!"'

'Mr. Archer will hear you, if you don't take care,' said Nance; 'and I would be ashamed, for one, that he should hear a brave, old, honest hard-working man like Jonathan Holdaway talk nonsense like a boy.'

'D'ye think I mind for Mr. Archer?' he cried shrilly, with a clack of laughter; and then he came close up to her, stooped down with his two palms upon his knees, and looked her in the eyes, with a strange hard expression, something like a smile. 'Do I mind for God, my girl?' he said; 'that's what it's come to be now, do I mind for God?'

'Uncle Jonathan,' she said, getting up and taking him by the arm; 'you sit down again, where you were sitting. There, sit still; I'll have no more of this; you'll do yourself a mischief. Come, take a drink of this good ale, and I'll warm a tankard for you. La, we'll pull through, you'll see. I'm young, as you say, and it's my turn to carry the bundle; and don't you worry your bile, or we'll have sickness, too, as well as sorrow.'

'D'ye think that I'd forgotten you?' said Jonathan, with something like a groan; and thereupon his teeth clicked to, and he sat silent with the tankard in his hand and staring straight before him.

'Why,' says Nance, setting on the ale to mull, 'men are always children, they say, however old; and if ever I heard a thing like this, to set to and make yourself sick, just when the money's failing! Keep a good heart up; you haven't kept a good heart these seventy years, nigh hand, to break down about a pound or two. Here's this Mr. Archer come to lodge, that you disliked so much. Well, now you see it was a clear providence. Come, let's think upon our mercies. And here is the ale mulling lovely; smell of it; I'll take a drop myself, it smells so sweet. And, Uncle Jonathan, you let me say one word. You've lost more than money before now; you lost my aunt, and bore it like a man. Bear this.'

His face once more contracted; his fist doubled and shot forth into the air, and trembled. 'Let them look out!' he shouted. 'Here, I warn all men; I've done with this foul kennel of knaves. Let them look out.'

'Hush, hush! for pity's sake,' cried Nance.

And then all of a sudden he dropped his face into his hands, and broke out with a great hiccoughing dry sob that was horrible to hear. 'O,' he cried, 'my God, if my son hadn't left me, if my Dick was here!' and the sobs shook him; Nance sitting still and watching him, with distress. 'O, if he were here to help his father!' he went on again. 'If I had a son like other fathers, he would save me now, when all is breaking down; O, he would save me! Ay, but where is he? Raking taverns, a thief perhaps. My curse be on him!' he added, rising again into wrath.

'Hush!' cried Nance, springing to her feet: 'your boy, your dead wife's boy—Aunt Susan's baby, that she loved—would you curse him? O, God forbid!'

The energy of her address surprised him from his mood. He looked upon her, tearless and confused. 'Let me go to my bed,' he said at last, and he rose and, shaking as with ague, but quite silent, lighted his candle, and left the kitchen.

Poor Nance! the pleasant current of her dreams was all diverted. She beheld a golden city, where she aspired to dwell; she had spoken with a deity, and had told herself that she might rise to be his equal; and now the earthly ligaments that bound her down had been straitened. She was like a tree looking skyward, her roots were in the ground. It seemed to her a thing so coarse, so rustic, to be thus concerned about a loss in money; when Mr. Archer, fallen from the sky-level of counts and nobles, faced his changed destiny with so immovable a courage. To weary of honesty; that, at least, no one could do, but even to name it was already a disgrace; and she beheld in fancy her uncle, and the young lad, all laced and feathered, hand upon hip, bestriding his small horse. The opposition seemed to perpetuate itself from generation to generation; one side still doomed to the clumsy and the servile, the other born to beauty.

She thought of the golden zones in which gentlemen were bred, and figured with so excellent a grace; zones in which wisdom and smooth words, white linen and slim hands, were the mark of the desired inhabitants; where low temptations were unknown, and honesty no virtue, but a thing as natural as breathing.

4

Mingling threads

IT was nearly seven before Mr. Archer left his apartment. On the landing he found another door beside his own, opening on a roofless corridor, and presently he was walking on the top of the ruins. On one hand he could look down a good depth into the green courtyard; on the other his eye roved along the downward course of the river, the wet woods all smoking, the shadows long and blue, the mists golden and rosy in the sun, here and there the water flashing across an obstacle. His heart expanded and softened to a grateful melancholy, and with his eye fixed upon the distance, and no thought of present danger, he continued to stroll along the elevated and treacherous promenade.

A terror-stricken cry rose to him from the courtyard. He looked down, and saw in a glimpse Nance standing below with hands clasped in horror and his own foot trembling on the margin of a gulf. He recoiled and leant against a pillar, quaking from head to foot, and covering his face with his hands; and Nance had time to run round by the stair and rejoin him where he stood before he had changed a line of his position.

'Ah!' he cried, and clutched her wrist; 'don't leave me. The place rocks; I have no head for altitudes.'

'Sit down against that pillar,' said Nance. 'Don't you be afraid; I won't leave you; and don't look up or down: look straight at me. How white you are!'

'The gulf,' he said, and closed his eyes again and shuddered.

'Why,' said Nance, 'what a poor climber you must be! That was where my cousin Dick used to get out of the castle after Uncle Jonathan had shut the gate. I've been down there myself with him helping me. I wouldn't try with you,' she said, and laughed merrily.

The sound of her laughter was sincere and musical, and perhaps its beauty barbed the offence to Mr. Archer. The blood came into his face with a quick jet, and then left it paler than before. 'It is a physical weakness,' he said harshly, 'and very droll, no doubt, but one that I can conquer on necessity. See, I am still shaking. Well, I advance to the battlements and look down. Show me your cousin's path.'

'He would go sure-foot along that little ledge,' said Nance, pointing as she spoke; 'then out through the breach and down by yonder buttress. It is easier coming back, of course, because you see where you are going. From the bruttress-foot a sheep-walk goes along the scarp—see, you can follow it from here in the dry grass. And now, sir,' she added, with a touch of womanly pity, 'I would come away from here if I were you, for indeed you are not fit.'

Sure enough, Mr. Archer's pallor and agitation had continued to increase; his cheeks were deathly, his clenched fingers trembled pitifully. 'The weakness is physical,' he sighed, and had nearly fallen. Nance led him from the spot, and he was no sooner back in the tower stair, than he fell heavily against the wall and put his arm across his eyes. A cup of brandy had to be brought him before he could descend to breakfast; and the perfection of Nance's dream was for the first time troubled.

Jonathan was waiting for them at table, with yellow, blood-shot eyes and a peculiar dusky complexion. He hardly waited till they found their seats, before, raising one hand, and stooping with his mouth above his plate, he put up a prayer for a blessing on the food and a spirit of gratitude in the eaters, and thereupon, and without more civility, fell to. But it was notable that he was no less speedily satisfied than he had been greedy to begin. He pushed his plate away and drummed upon the table.

'These are silly prayers,' said he, 'that they teach us. Eat and be thankful, that's no such wonder. Speak to me of starving —there's the touch. You're a man, they tell me, Mr. Archer, that has met with some reverses?'

'I have met with many,' replied Mr. Archer.

'Ha!' said Jonathan, 'none reckons but the last. Now, see; I tried to make this girl here understand me.'

'Uncle,' said Nance, 'what should Mr. Archer care for your

concerns? He hath troubles of his own, and came to be at peace, I think.'

'I tried to make her understand me,' repeated Jonathan, doggedly; 'and now I'll try you. Do you think this world is fair?'

'Fair and false!' quoth Mr. Archer.

The old man laughed immoderately. 'Good,' said he; 'very good. But what I mean is this: do you know what it is to get up early and go to bed late, and never take so much as a holiday but four; and one of these your own marriage day, and the other three the funerals of folk you loved, and all that, to have a quiet old age in shelter, and bread for your old belly, and a bed to lay your crazy bones upon, with a clear conscience?'

'Sir,' said Mr. Archer, with an inclination of his head, 'you portray a very brave existence.'

'Well,' continued Jonathan, 'and in the end thieves deceive you, thieves rob and rook you, thieves turn you out in your old age and send you begging. What have you got for all your honesty? A fine return! You that might have stole scores of pounds, there you are out in the rain with your rheumatics!'

Mr. Archer had forgotten to eat; with his hand upon his chin he was studying the old man's countenance. 'And you conclude?' he asked.

'Conclude!' cried Jonathan. 'I conclude I'll be upsides with them.'

'Ay,' said the other, 'we are all tempted to revenge.'

'You have lost money?' asked Jonathan.

'A great estate,' said Archer, quietly.

'See now!' says Jonathan, 'and where is it?'

'Nay, I sometimes think that every one has had his share of it but me,' was the reply. 'All England hath paid his taxes with my patrimony; I was a sheep that left my wool on every brier.'

'And you sit down under that?' cried the old man. 'Come now, Mr. Archer, you and me belong to different stations; and I know mine—no man better—but since we have both been rooked, and are both sore with it, why, here's my hand with a very good heart, and I ask for yours, and no offence, I hope.'

'There is surely no offence, my friend,' returned Mr. Archer, as they shook hands across the table; 'for, believe me, my sympathies are quite acquired to you. This life is an arena where we fight with beasts; and, indeed,' he added, sighing, 'I sometimes marvel why we go down to it unarmed.'

In the meanwhile, a creaking of ungreased axles had been

heard descending through the wood; and presently after the door opened, and the tall hostler entered the kitchen carrying one end of Mr. Archer's trunks. The other was carried by an aged beggar man of that district, known and welcome for some twenty miles about under the name of 'Old Cumberland.' Each was soon perched upon a settle, with a cup of ale; and the hostler, who valued himself upon his affability, began to entertain the company, still with half an eye on Nance, to whom in gallant terms he expressly dedicated every sip of ale. First he told of the trouble they had to get his Lordship started in the chaise; and how he had dropped a rouleau of gold on the threshold, and the passage and doorstep had been strewn with guinea-pieces. At this old Jonathan looked at Mr. Archer. Next the visitor turned to news of a more thrilling character; how the down mail had been stopped again near Grantham by three men on horseback—a white and two bays; how they had handkerchiefs on their faces; how Tom the guard's blunderbuss missed fire, but he swore he had winged one of them with a pistol; and how they had got clean away with seventy pounds in money, some valuable papers, and a watch or two.

'Brave, brave!' cried Jonathan, in ecstasy. 'Seventy pounds! O, it's brave!'

'Well, I don't see the great bravery,' observed the hostler, misapprehending him. 'Three men, and you may call that three to one. I'll call it brave when some one stops the mail single-handed; that's a risk.'

'And why should they hesitate?' inquired Mr. Archer. 'The poor souls who are fallen to such a way of life, pray, what have they to lose? If they get the money, well; but if a ball should put them from their troubles, why, so better.'

'Well, sir,' said the hostler, 'I believe you'll find they won't agree with you. They count on a good fling, you see; or who would risk it?—And here's my best respects to you, Miss Nance.'

'And I forgot the part of cowardice,' resumed Mr. Archer. 'All men fear.'

'O, surely not!' cried Nance.

'All men,' reiterated Mr. Archer.

'Ay, that's a true word,' observed Old Cumberland, 'and a thief, anyway, for it's a coward's trade.'

'But these fellows, now,' said Jonathan, with a curious, appealing manner—'these fellows with their seventy pounds! Perhaps, Mr. Archer, they were no true thieves after all, but just people who had been robbed and tried to get their own again. What was that you said, about all England and the taxes?

One takes, another gives; why, that's almost fair. If I've been rooked and robbed, and the coat taken off my back, I call it most fair to take another's.'

'Ask Old Cumberland,' observed the hostler, 'you ask Old Cumberland, Miss Nance!' and he bestowed a wink upon his favoured fair one.

'Why that?' asked Jonathan.

'He had his coat taken, ay, and his shirt too,' returned the hostler.

'Is that so?' cried Jonathan, eagerly. 'Was you robbed too?'

'That was I,' replied Cumberland, 'with a warrant! I was a well-to-do man when I was young.'

'Ay! See that!' says Jonathan. 'And you don't long for a revenge?'

'Eh! Not me!' answered the beggar. 'It's too long ago. But if you'll give me another mug of your good ale, my pretty lady, I won't say no to that.'

'And shalt have! And shalt have!' cried Jonathan; 'or brandy even, if you like it better.'

And as Cumberland did like it better, and the hostler chimed in, the party pledged each other in a dram of brandy before separating.

As for Nance, she slipped forth into the ruins, partly to avoid the hostler's gallantries, partly to lament over the defects of Mr. Archer. Plainly, he was no hero. She pitied him; she began to feel a protecting interest mingle with and almost supersede her admiration, and was at the same time disappointed and yet drawn to him. She was, indeed, conscious of such unshaken fortitude in her own heart, that she was almost tempted by an occasion to be bold for two. She saw herself, in a brave attitude, shielding her imperfect hero from the world; and she saw, like a piece of Heaven, his gratitude for her protection.

5

Life in the Castle

FROM that day forth the life of these three persons in the ruins ran very smoothly. Mr. Archer now sat by the fire with a book, and now passed whole days abroad, returning late, dead weary. His manner was a mask; but it was half transparent; through the even tenor of his gravity and courtesy profound revolutions of feeling were betrayed, seasons of numb despair, of restlessness, of aching temper. For days he would say nothing beyond his usual courtesies and solemn compliments; and then, all of a sudden, some fine evening beside the kitchen fire, he would fall into a vein of elegant gossip, tell of strange and interesting events, the secrets of families, brave deeds of war, the miraculous discovery of crime, the visitations of the dead. Nance and her uncle would sit till the small hours with eyes wide open: Jonathan applauding the unexpected incidents with many a slap of his big hand: Nance, perhaps, more pleased with the narrator's eloquence and wise reflections. And then, again, days would follow of abstraction, of listless humming, of frequent apologies and long hours of silence. Once only, and then after a week of unrelieved melancholy, he went over to the ' Green Dragon,' spent the afternoon with the landlord and a bowl of punch, and returned as on the first night, devious in step, but courteous and unperturbed of speech.

If he seemed more natural and more at his ease, it was when he found Nance alone; and laying by some of his reserve, talked before her rather than to her of his destiny, character, and hopes. To Nance these interviews were but a doubtful privilege. At times he would seem to take a pleasure in her presence, to consult her gravely, to hear and discuss her counsels; at times even, but these were rare and brief, he would talk of herself, praise the qualities that she possessed, touch indulgently on her defects, and lend her books to read and even examine her upon her reading; but far more often he would fall into a half-unconsciousness, put her a question and then answer it himself, drop into the veiled tone of voice of one soliloquising, and leave her at last as though he had forgotten her existence. It was odd, too, that in all this random converse not a fact of his past life, and scarce a name, should ever cross his lips. A profound reserve kept watch upon his most unguarded moments. He spoke continually of himself, indeed, but still in enigmas; the veiled prophet of egoism.

The base of Nance's feeling for Mr. Archer was admiration as for a superior being; and with this, his treatment, consciously or not, accorded happily. When he forgot her, she took the blame upon herself. His formal politeness was so exquisite that this essential brutality stood excused. His compliments, besides, were always grave and rational; he would offer reason for his praise, convict her of merit, and thus disarm suspicion. Nay, and the very hours when he forgot and remembered her alternately could by the ardent fallacies of youth be read in the light of an attention. She might be far from his confidence; but still she was nearer it than any one. He might ignore her presence, but yet he sought it.

Moreover, she, upon her side, was conscious of one point of superiority. Beside this rather dismal, rather effeminate man, who recoiled from a worm, who grew giddy on the castle wall, who bore so helplessly the weight of his misfortunes, she felt herself a head and shoulders taller in cheerful and sterling courage. She could walk, head in air, along the most precarious rafter; her hand feared neither the grossness nor the harshness of life's web, but was thrust cheerfully, if need were, into the brier bush, and could take hold of any crawling horror. Ruin was mining the walls of her cottage, as already it had mined and subverted Mr. Archer's palace. Well, she faced it with a bright countenance and a busy hand. She had got some washing, some rough seamstress work from the 'Green Dragon,' and from another neighbour ten miles across the moor. At this she cheerfully laboured, and from that height she could afford to pity the useless talents and poor attitude of Mr. Archer. It did not change her admiration, but it made it bearable. He was above her in all ways; but she was above him in one. She kept it to herself, and hugged it. When, like all young creatures, she made long stories to justify, to nourish, and to forecast the course of her affection, it was this private superiority that made all rosy, that cut the knot, and that, at last, in some great situation, fetched to her knees the dazzling but imperfect hero. With this pretty exercise she beguiled the hours of labour, and consoled herself for Mr. Archer's bearing. Pity was her weapon and her weakness. To accept the loved one's faults, although it has an air of freedom, is to kiss the chain, and this pity it was which, lying nearer to her heart, lent the one element of true emotion to a fanciful and merely brain-sick love.

Thus it fell out one day that she had gone to the 'Green Dragon' and brought back thence a letter to Mr. Archer. He, upon seeing it, winced like a man under the knife: pain, shame, sorrow, and the most trenchant edge of mortification cut into his heart and wrung the steady composure of his face.

'Dear heart! have you bad news?' she cried.

But he only replied by a gesture and fled to his room, and when, later on, she ventured to refer to it, he stopped her on the threshold, as if with words prepared beforehand. 'There are some pains,' said he, 'too acute for consolation, or I would bring them to my kind consoler. Let the memory of that letter, if you please, be buried.' And then as she continued to gaze at him, being, in spite of herself, pained by his elaborate phrase, doubtfully sincere in word and matter: ' Let it be enough,' he added haughtily, ' that if this matter wring my heart, it doth not touch my conscience. I am a man, I would have you to know, who suffers undeservedly.'

He had never spoken so directly: never with so convincing an emotion; and her heart thrilled for him. She could have taken his pains and died for them with joy.

Meanwhile she was left without support. Jonathan now swore by his lodger, and lived for him. He was a fine talker. He knew the finest sight of stories; he was a man and a gentleman, take him for all in all, and a perfect credit to Old England. Such were the old man's declared sentiments, and sure enough he clung to Mr. Archer's side, hung upon his utterance when he spoke, and watched him with unwearying interest when he was silent. And yet his feeling was not clear; in the partial wreck of his mind, which was leaning to decay, some afterthought was strongly present. As he gazed in Mr. Archer's face a sudden brightness would kindle in his rheumy eyes, his eyebrows would lift as with a sudden thought, his mouth would open as though to speak, and close again in silence. Once or twice he even called Mr. Archer mysteriously forth into the dark courtyard, took him by the button, and laid a demonstrative finger on his chest; but there his ideas or his courage failed him; he would shufflingly excuse himself and return to his position by the fire without a word of explanation. ' The good man was growing old,' said Mr. Archer, with a suspicion of a shrug. But the good man had his idea, and even when he was alone the name of Mr. Archer fell from his lips continually in the course of mumbled and gesticulative conversation.

6

The bad half-crown

HOWEVER early Nance arose, and she was no sluggard, the old man, who had begun to outlive the earthly habit of slumber, would usually have been up long before, the fire would be burning brightly, and she would see him wandering among the ruins, lantern in hand, and talking assiduously to himself. One day, however, after he had returned late from the market town, she found that she had stolen a march upon that indefatigable early riser. The kitchen was all blackness. She crossed the castleyard to the wood-cellar, her steps printing the thick hoar-frost. A scathing breeze blew out of the north-east and slowly carried a regiment of black and tattered clouds over the face of heaven, which was already kindled with the wild light of morning, but where she walked, in shelter of the ruins, the flame of her candle burned steady. The extreme cold smote upon her conscience. She could not bear to think this bitter business fell usually to the lot of one so old as Jonathan, and made desperate resolutions to be earlier in the future.

The fire was a good blaze before he entered, limping dismally into the kitchen. ' Nance,' said he, ' I be all knotted up with the rheumatics; will you rub me a bit ? ' She came and rubbed him where and how he bade her. ' This is a cruel thing that old age should be rheumaticky,' said he. ' When I was young I stood my turn of the teethache like a man ! for why ? because it couldn't last for ever; but these rheumatics come to live and die with you. Your aunt was took before the time came; never had an ache to mention. Now I lie all night in my single bed and the blood never warms in me; this knee of mine it seems like lighted up with the rheumatics; it seems as though you could see to sew by it; and all the strings of my old body ache, as if devils was pulling 'em. Thank you kindly; that's someways easier now, but an old man, my dear, has little to look for; it's pain, pain, pain to the end of the business, and I'll never be rightly warm again till I get under the sod,' he said, and looked down at her with a face so aged and weary that she had nearly wept.

' I lay awake all night,' he continued; ' I do so mostly, and a long walk kills me. Eh, deary me, to think that life should run to such a puddle ! And I remember long syne when I was strong, and the blood all hot and good about me, and I loved to run, too—deary me, to run ! Well, that's all by. You'd better pray to be took early, Nance, and not live on till you get to be like me, and are robbed in your gray old age, your cold, shivering, dark old age, that's like a winter's morning; ' and he bitterly shuddered, spreading his hands before the fire.

' Come now,' said Nance, ' the more you say the less you'll like it, Uncle Jonathan; but if I were you I would be proud for to have lived all your days honest and beloved, and come near the end with your good name; isn't that a fine thing to be proud of? Mr. Archer was telling me in some strange land they used to run races each with a lighted candle, and the art was to keep the candle burning. Well, now, I thought that was like life: a man's good conscience is the flame he gets to carry, and if he comes to the winning-post with that still burning, why, take it how you will, the man's a hero—even if he was low-born like you and me.'

' Did Mr. Archer tell you that? ' asked Jonathan.

' No, dear,' said she, ' that's my own thought about it. He told me of the race. But see, now,' she continued, putting on the porridge, ' you say old age is a hard season, but so is youth. You're half out of the battle, I would say; you loved my aunt and got her, and buried her, and some of these days soon you'll go to meet her; and take her my love and tell her I tried to take good care of you; for so I do, Uncle Jonathan.'

Jonathan struck with his fist upon the settle. D'ye think I want to die, ye vixen! ' he shouted. ' I want to live ten hundred years.'

This was a mystery beyond Nance's penetration, and she stared in wonder as she made the porridge.

' I want to live,' he continued, ' I want to live and to grow rich. I want to drive my carriage and to dice in hells and see the ring, I do. Is this a life that I lived? I want to be a rake, d'ye understand? I want to know what things are like. I don't want to die like a blind kitten, and me seventy-six.'

' O fie! ' said Nance.

The old man thrust out his jaw at her, with the grimace of an irreverent schoolboy. Upon that aged face it seemed a blasphemy. Then he took out of his bosom a long leather purse, and emptying its contents on the settle, began to count and recount the pieces, ringing and examining each, and suddenly he leapt like a young man. 'What! ' he screamed. ' Bad? O Lord! I'm robbed again! ' And falling on his knees before the settle he began to pour forth the most dreadful curses on the head of his deceiver. His eyes were shut, for to him this vile solemnity was prayer. He held up the bad half-crown in his right hand, as though he were displaying it to Heaven; and what increased the horror of the scene, the curses he invoked were those whose efficacy he had tasted—old age and poverty, rheumatism and an ungrateful son. Nance listened appalled; than she sprang forward and dragged down his arm and laid her hand upon his mouth.

' Whist! ' she cried. ' Whist ye, for God's sake! O my man, whist ye! If Heaven were to hear; if poor Aunt Susan were to hear! Think, she may be listening.' And with the histrionism of strong emotion she pointed to a corner of the kitchen.

His eyes followed her finger. He looked there for a little, thinking, blinking; then he got stiffly to his feet and resumed his place upon the settle, the bad piece still in his hand. So he sat for some time, looking upon the half-crown, and now wondering to himself on the injustice and partiality of the law, now computing again and again the nature of his loss. So he was still sitting when Mr. Archer entered the kitchen. At this a light came into his face, and after some seconds of rumination he despatched Nance upon an errand.

'Mr. Archer,' said he, as soon as they were alone together, 'would you give me a guinea-piece for silver?'

'Why, sir, I believe I can,' said Mr. Archer.

And the exchange was just effected when Nance re-entered the apartment. The blood shot into her face. 'What's to do here?' she asked rudely.

'Nothing, my deary,' said old Jonathan, with a touch of whine.

'What's to do?' she said again.

'Your uncle was but changing me a piece of gold,' returned Mr. Archer.

'Let me see what he hath given you, Mr. Archer,' replied the girl. 'I had a bad piece, and I fear it is mixed up among the good.'

'Well, well,' replied Mr. Archer, smiling, 'I must take the merchant's risk of it. The money is now mixed.'

'I know my piece,' quoth Nance. 'Come, let me see your silver, Mr. Archer. If I have to get it by a theft I'll see that money,' she cried.

'Nay, child, if you put as much passion to be honest as the world to steal, I must give way, though I betray myself,' said Mr. Archer. 'There it is as I received it.'

Nance quickly found the bad half-crown. 'Give him another,' she said, looking Jonathan in the face; and when that had been done, she walked over to the chimney and flung the guilty piece into the reddest of the fire. Its base constituents began immediately to run; even as she watched it the disc crumpled, and the lineaments of the King became confused. Jonathan, who had followed close behind, beheld these changes from over her shoulder, and his face darkened sorely.

'Now,' said she, 'come back to table, and to-day it is I that shall say grace, as I used to do in the old times, day about with Dick;' and covering her eyes with one hand, 'O Lord,' said she, with deep emotion, 'make us thankful; and, O Lord, deliver us from evil! For the love of the poor souls that watch for us in Heaven, O deliver us from evil!'

THE year moved on to March; and March, though it blew bitter keen from the North Sea, yet blinked kindly between whiles on the river dell. The mire dried up in the closest covert; life ran in the bare branches, and the air of the afternoon would be suddenly sweet with the fragrance of new grass.

Above and below the castle the river crooked like the letter " S." The lower loop was to the left, and embraced the high and steep projection which was crowned by the ruins; the upper loop enclosed a lawny promontory fringed by thorn and willow. It was easy to reach it from the castle side, for the river ran in this part very quietly among innumerable boulders and over dam-like walls of rock. The place was all enclosed, the wind a stranger, the turf smooth and solid; so it was chosen by Nance to be her bleaching-green.

One day she brought a bucketful of linen, and had but begun to wring and lay them out when Mr. Archer stepped from the thicket on the far side, drew very deliberately near, and sat down in silence on the grass. Nance looked up to greet him with a smile, but finding her smile was not returned, she fell into embarrassment and stuck the more busily to her employment. Man or woman, the whole world looks well at any work to which they are accustomed; but the girl was ashamed of what she did. She was ashamed, besides, of the sun-bonnet that so well became her, and ashamed of her bare arms, which were her greatest beauty.

' Nausicaä,' said Mr. Archer, at last, ' I find you like Nausicaä.'

' And who was she? ' asked Nance, and laughed in spite of herself, an empty and embarrassed laugh, that sounded in Mr. Archer's ears, indeed, like music, but to her own like the last grossness of rusticity.

' She was a princess of the Grecian islands,' he replied. ' A king, being shipwrecked, found her washing by the shore. Certainly I, too, was shipwrecked,' he continued, plucking at the grass. ' There was never a more desperate castaway—to fall from polite life, fortune, a shrine of honour, a grateful conscience, duties willingly taken up and faithfully discharged; and to fall to this—idleness, poverty, inutility, remorse.' He seemed to have forgotten her presence but here he remembered her again. ' Nance,' said he, ' would you have a man sit down and suffer or rise up and strive? '

'Nay,' she said. 'I would always rather see him doing.'

'Ha!' said Mr. Archer, 'but yet you speak from an imperfect knowledge. Conceive a man damned to a choice of only evil—misconduct upon either side, not a fault behind him, and yet naught before him but this choice of sins. How would you say then?'

'I would say that he was much deceived, Mr. Archer,' returned Nance. 'I would say there was a third choice, and that the right one.'

'I tell you,' said Mr. Archer, 'the man I have in view hath two ways open, and no more. One to wait, like a poor mewling baby, till Fate save or ruin him; the other to take his troubles in his hand, and to perish or be saved at once. It is no point of morals; both are wrong. Either way this step-child of Providence must fall; which shall he choose, by doing, or not doing?'

'Fall, then, is what I would say,' replied Nance. 'Fall where you will, but do it! For O, Mr. Archer,' she continued, stooping to her work, 'you that are good and kind and so wise, it doth sometimes go against my heart to see you live on here like a sheep in a turnipfield! If you were braver——' and here she paused, conscience-smitten.

'Do I, indeed, lack courage?' inquired Mr. Archer of himself. 'Courage, the footstool of the virtues, upon which they stand? Courage, that a poor private carrying a musket has to spare of; that does not fail a weasel or a rat; that is a brutish faculty? I to fail there, I wonder? But what is courage, then? The constancy to endure oneself or to see others suffer? The itch of ill-advised actvity—mere shuttle-wittedness—or to be still and patient? To inquire of the significance of words is to rob ourselves of what we seem to know, and yet, of all things, certainly to stand still is the least heroic. Nance,' he said, 'did you ever hear of *Hamlet*?'

'Never,' said Nance.

''Tis an old play,' returned Mr. Archer, 'and frequently enacted. This while I have been talking Hamlet. You must know this Hamlet was a Prince among the Danes,' and he told her the play in a very good style, here and there quoting a verse or two with solemn emphasis.

'It is strange,' said Nance; 'he was then a very poor creature?'

'That was what he could not tell,' said Mr. Archer. 'Look at me; am I as poor a creature?'

She looked, and what she saw was the familiar thought of all her hours; the tall figure very plainly habited in black, the spotless ruffles, the slim hands; the long, well-shapen, serious, shaven face, the wide and somewhat thin-lipped mouth, the dark eyes that were so full of depth and change and colour. He was gazing at her with his brows a little knit, his chin upon one hand and that elbow resting on his knee.

'Ye look a man!' she cried, 'ay, and should be a great one! The more shame to you to lie here idle like a dog before the fire.'

'My fair Holdaway,' quoth Mr. Archer, 'you are much set on action. I cannot dig, to beg I am ashamed,' he continued, looking at her with a half-absent fixity: ''Tis a strange thing, certainly, that in my years of fortune I should never taste happiness, and now when I am broke, enjoy so much of it, for was I ever happier than to-day? Was the grass softer, the stream pleasanter in sound, the air milder, the heart more at peace? Why should I not sink? To dig—why, after all, it should be easy To take a mate, too? Love is of all grades since Jupiter; love fails to none; and children—— ' but here he passed his hand suddenly over his eyes. 'O fool and coward, fool and coward!' he said bitterly; 'can you forget your fetters? You did not know that I was fettered, Nance!' he asked again, addressing her. But Nance was somewhat sore. 'I know you keep talking,' she said, and, turning half away from him, began to wring out a sheet across her shoulder. 'I wonder you are not wearied of your voice. When the hands lie abed the tongue takes a walk.'

Mr. Archer laughed unpleasantly, rose and moved to the water's edge. In this part the body of the river poured across a little narrow fell, ran some ten feet very smoothly over a bed of pebbles, then getting wind, as it were, of another shelf of rock which barred the channel, began, by imperceptible degrees, to separate towards either shore in dancing currents, and to leave the middle clear and stagnant. The set towards either side was nearly equal; about one half of the whole water plunged on the side of the castle, through a narrow gullet; about one half ran lipping past the margin of the green and slipped across a babbling rapid.

'Here,' said Mr. Archer, after he had looked for some time at the fine and shifting demarcation of these currents, 'come here and see me try my fortune.'

'I am not like a man,' said Nance; 'I have no time to waste.'

'Come here,' he said again. 'I ask you seriously, Nance. We are not always childish when we seem so.'

She drew a little nearer.

'Now,' said he, 'you see these two channels—choose one.'

'I'll choose the nearest, to save time,' said Nance.

'Well, that shall be for action,' returned Mr. Archer. 'And

since I wish to have the odds against me, not only the other channel but yon stagnant water in the midst shall be for lying still. You see this?' he continued, pulling up a withered rush, ' I break it in three. I shall put each separately at the top of the upper fall, and according as they go by your way or by the other I shall guide my life.'

' This is very silly,' said Nance, with a movement of her shoulders.

' I do not think it so,' said Mr. Archer.

' And then,' she resumed, ' if you are to try your fortune, why not evenly?'

' Nay,' returned Mr. Archer, with a smile, ' no man can put complete reliance in blind Fate; he must still cog the dice.'

By this time he had got upon the rock beside the upper fall, and, bidding her look out, dropped a piece of rush into the middle of the intake. The rusty fragment was sucked at once over the fall, came up again far on the right hand, leaned ever more and more in the same direction, and disappeared under the hanging grasses on the castle side.

' One,' said Mr. Archer, ' one for standing still.'

But the next launch had a different fate, and after hanging for a while about the edge of the stagnant water, steadily approached the bleaching-green and danced down the rapid under Nance's eyes.

' One for me,' she cried with some exultation; and then she observed that Mr. Archer had grown pale, and was kneeling on the rock, with his hand raised like a person petrified. ' Why,' said she, ' you do not mind it, do you?'

' Does a man not mind a throw of dice by which a fortune hangs?' said Mr. Archer, rather hoarsely. ' And this is more than fortune. Nance, if you have any kindness for my fate, put up a prayer before I launch the next one.'

' A prayer,' she cried, ' about a game like this? I would not be so heathen.'

' Well,' said he, ' then without,' and he closed his eyes and dropped the piece of rush. This time there was no doubt. It went for the rapid as straight as any arrow.

' Action, then!' said Mr. Archer, getting to his feet; ' and then God forgive us,' he added, almost to himself.

' God forgive us, indeed,' cried Nance, ' for wasting the good daylight! But come, Mr. Archer, if I see you look so serious I shall begin to think you was in earnest.'

' Nay,' he said, turning upon her suddenly, with a full smile; ' but is not this good advice? I have consulted God and demigod; the nymph of the river, and what I far more admire and trust, my blue-eyed Minerva. Both have said the same. My own heart was telling it already. Action, then, be mine; and into the deep sea with all this paralysing casuistry. I am happy to-day for the first time.'

8

The Mail-Guard

SOMEWHERE about two in the morning a squall had burst upon the castle, a clap of screaming wind that made the towers rock, and a copious drift of rain that streamed from the windows. The wind soon blew itself out, but the day broke cloudy and dripping, and when the little party assembled at breakfast, their humours appeared to have changed with the change of weather. Nance had been brooding on the scene at the river-side, applying it in various way to her particular aspirations, and the result, which was hardly to her mind, had taken the colour out of her cheeks. Mr. Archer, too, was somewhat absent; his thoughts were of a mingled strain; and even upon his usually impassive countenance there were betrayed successive depths of depression and starts of exultation, which the girl translated in terms of her own hopes and fears. But Jonathan was the most altered: he was strangely silent, hardly passing a word, and watched Mr. Archer with an eager and furtive eye. It seemed as if the idea that had so long hovered before him had now taken a more solid shape, and while it still attracted, somewhat alarmed his imagination.

At this rate, conversation languished into a silence which was only broken by the gentle and ghostly noises of the rain on the stone roof and about all that field of ruins; and they were all relieved when the note of a man whistling and the sound of approaching footsteps in the grassy court announced a visitor. It was the hostler from the ' Green Dragon ' bringing a letter for Mr. Archer. Nance saw her hero's face contract and then relax again at the sight of it; and she thought that she knew why, for the sprawling, gross black characters of the address were easily distinguishable from the fine writing on the former letter that had so much disturbed him. He opened it and began to read; while the hostler sat down to table with a pot of ale and proceeded to make himself agreeable after his fashion.

' Fine doings down our way, Miss Nance,' said he. ' I haven't been abed this blessed night.'

Nance expressed a polite interest, but her eye was on Mr. Archer, who was reading his letter with a face of such extreme indifference that she was tempted to suspect him of assumption.

'Yes,' continued the hostler, 'not been the like of it this fifteen years: the North Mail stopped at the three stones.'

Jonathan's cup was at his lip, but at this moment he choked with a great splutter; and Mr. Archer, as if startled by the noise, made so sudden a movement that one corner of the sheet tore off and stayed between his finger and thumb. It was some little time before the old man was sufficiently recovered to beg the hostler to go on, and he still kept coughing and crying and rubbing his eyes. Mr. Archer, on his side, laid the letter down, and putting his hands in his pocket, listened gravely to the tale.

'Yes,' resumed Sam, 'the North Mail, was stopped by a single horseman; dash my wig, but I admire him! There were four insides and two out, and poor Tom Oglethorpe, the guard. Tom showed himself a man; let fly his blunderbuss at him; had him covered too, and could swear to that; but the Captain never let on, up with a pistol and fetched poor Tom a bullet through the body. Tom, he squelched upon the seat, all over blood. Up comes the Captain to the window. "Oblige me," says he, "with what you have." Would you believe it? not a man says cheep! —not them! "Thy hands over thy head." Four watches, rings, snuff-boxes, seven-and-forty pounds overhead in gold. One Dicksee, a grazier, tries it on: gives him a guinea. "Beg your pardon," says the Captain, "I think too highly of you to take it at your hand. I will not take less than ten from such a gentleman." This Dicksee had his money in his stocking, but there was the pistol at his eye. Down he goes, offs with his stocking, and there was thirty golden guineas. "Now," says the Captain, "you've tried it on with me, but I scorns the advantage. Ten, I said," he says, "and ten I take." So, dash my buttons, I call that man a man!' cried Sam, in cordial admiration.

'Well, and then?' says Mr. Archer.

'Then,' resumed Sam, 'that old fat fagot Engleton, him as held the ribbons and drew up like a lamb when he was told to, picks up his cattle, and drives off again. Down they came to the "Dragon," all singing like as if they was scalded, and poor Tom saying nothing. You would 'a' thought they had all lost the King's crown to hear them. Down gets this Dicksee. "Postmaster," he says, taking him by the arm, "this is a most abominable thing," he says. Down gets a Major Clayton, and gets the old man by the other arm. "We've been robbed," he cries, "robbed!" Down gets the others, and all round the old man telling their story, and what they had lost, and how they was all as good as ruined; till at last old Engleton says, says he, " How about Oglethorpe? " says he. " Ay," says the others, " how about the guard? " Well, with that we bousted him down, as white as a rag and all blooded like a sop. I thought he was dead. Well, he ain't dead; but he's dying, I fancy.'

' Did you say four watches? ' said Jonathan.

' Four, I think. I wish it had been forty,' cried Sam. ' Such a party of soused herrings I never did see—not a man among them bar poor Tom. But us that are the servants on the road have all the risk and none of the profit.'

' And this brave fellow,' asked Mr. Archer, very quietly, ' this Oglethorpe—how is he now? '

' Well, sir, with my respects, I take it he has a hole bang through him,' said Sam. ' The doctor hasn't been yet. He'd 'a' been bright and early if it had been a passenger. But, doctor or no, I'll make a good guess that Tom won't see to-morrow. He'll die on a Sunday, will poor Tom; and they do say that's fortunate.'

' Did Tom see him that did it? ' asked Jonathan.

' Well, he saw him,' replied Sam, ' but not to swear by. Said he was a very tall man, and very big, and had a 'andkerchief about his face, and a very quick shot, and sat his horse like a thorough gentleman, as he is.'

' A gentleman! ' cried Nance. ' The dirty knave! '

' Well, I calls a man like that a gentleman,' returned the hostler; ' that's what I mean by a gentleman.'

' You don't know much of them, then,' said Nance. ' A gentleman would scorn to stoop to such a thing. I call my uncle a better gentleman than any thief.'

' And you would be right,' said Mr. Archer.

' How many snuff-boxes did he get? ' asked Jonathan.

' O, dang me if I know,' said Sam; ' I didn't take an inventory.'

' I will go back with you, if you please,' said Mr. Archer. ' I should like to see poor Oglethorpe. He has behaved well.'

' At your service, sir,' said Sam, jumping to his feet. ' I dare to say a gentleman like you would not forget a poor fellow like Tom—no, nor a plain man like me, sir, that went without his sleep to nurse him. And excuse me, sir,' added Sam, ' you won't forget about the letter, neither? '

' Surely not,' said Mr. Archer.

Oglethorpe lay in a low bed, one of several in a long garret of the inn. The rain soaked in places through the roof and fell in minute drops; there was but one small window; the beds were occupied by servants, the air of the garret was both close and chilly. Mr. Archer's heart sank at the threshold to see a man lying perhaps mortally hurt in so poor a sick-room, and as he drew near the low bed he took his hat off. The guard was a big, blowsy, innocent-looking soul with a thick lip and a broad nose, comically turned up; his cheeks were crimson, and when Mr. Archer laid a finger on his brow he found him burning with fever.

'I fear you suffer much,' he said, with a catch in his voice, as he sat down on the bedside.

'I suppose I do, sir,' returned Oglethorpe; 'it is main sore.'

'I am used to wounds and wounded men,' returned the visitor. 'I have been in the wars and nursed brave fellows before now; and, if you will suffer me, I propose to stay beside you till the doctor comes.'

'It is very good of you, sir, I am sure,' said Oglethorpe. 'The trouble is they won't none of them let me drink.'

'If you will not tell the doctor,' said Mr. Archer, 'I will give you some water. They say it is bad for a green wound, but in the Low Countries we all drank water when we found the chance, and I could never perceive we were the worse for it.'

'Been wounded yourself, sir, perhaps?' called Oglethorpe.

'Twice,' said Mr. Archer, 'and was as proud of these hurts as any lady of her bracelets. 'Tis a fine thing to smart for one's duty; even in the pangs of it there is contentment.'

'Ah, well!' replied the guard, 'if you've been shot yourself, that explains. But as for contentment, why, sir, you see, it smarts, as you say. And then, I have a good wife, you see, and a bit of a brat—a little thing, so high.'

'Don't move,' said Mr. Archer.

'No, sir, I will not, and thank you kindly,' said Oglethorpe. 'At York they are. A very good lass is my wife—far too good for me. And the little rascal—well, I don't know how to say, but he sort of comes round you. If I were to go, sir, it would be hard on my poor girl—main hard on her!'

'Ay, you must feel bitter hardly to the rogue that laid you here,' said Mr. Archer.

'Why, no, sir, more against Engleton and the passengers,' replied the guard. 'He played his hand, if you come to look at it; and I wish he had shot worse, or me better. And yet I'll go to my grave but what I covered him,' he cried. 'It looks like witchcraft. I'll go to my grave but what he was drove full of slugs like a pepper-box.'

'Quietly,' said Mr. Archer, 'you must not excite yourself. These deceptions are very usual in war; the eye, in a moment of alert, is hardly to be trusted, and when the smoke blows away you see the man you fired at, taking aim, it may be at yourself. You should observe, too, that you were in the dark night, and somewhat dazzled by the lamps, and that the sudden stopping of the mail had jolted you. In such circumstances a man may miss, ay, even with a blunderbuss, and no blame attach to his marksmanship.' . . .

THE YOUNG CHEVALIER

CONTENTS

PROLOGUE

The Wine-Seller's Wife

THERE was a wine-seller's shop, as you went down to the river in the city of the Anti-popes. There a man was served with good wine of the country and plain country fare; and the place being clean and quiet, with a prospect on the river, certain gentlemen who dwelt in that city in attendance on a great personage made it a practice (when they had any silver in their purses) to come and eat there and be private.

They called the wine-seller Paradou. He was built more like a bullock than a man, huge in bone and brawn, high in colour, and with a hand like a baby for size. Marie-Madeleine was the name of his wife; she was of Marseilles, a city of entrancing women, nor was any fairer than herself. She was tall, being almost of a height with Paradou; full-girdled, point-device in every form, with an exquisite delicacy in the face; her nose and nostrils a delight to look at from the fineness of the sculpture, her eyes inclined a hair's-breadth inward, her colour between dark and fair, and laid on even like a flower's. A faint rose dwelt in it, as though she had been found unawares bathing, and had blushed from head to foot. She was of a grave countenance, rarely smiling; yet it seemed to be written upon every part of her that she rejoiced in life. Her husband loved the heels of her feet and the knuckles of her fingers; he loved her like a glutton and a brute; his love hung about her like an atmosphere; one that came by chance into the wine-shop was aware of that passion; and it might be said that by the strength of it the woman had been drugged or spell-bound. She knew not if she loved or loathed him; he was always in her eyes like something monstrous—monstrous in his love, monstrous in his person, horrific but imposing in his violence; and her sentiment swung back and forward from desire to sickness. But the mean, where it dwelt chiefly, was an apathetic fascination, partly of horror; as of Europa in mid-ocean with her bull.

On the 10th November, 1749, there sat two of the foreign gentlemen in the wine-seller's shop. They were both handsome men of a good presence, richly dressed. The first was swarthy and long and lean, with an alert, black look, and a mole upon his cheek. The other was more fair. He seemed very easy and sedate, and a little melancholy for so young a man, but his smile was charming. In his gray eyes there was much abstraction, as of one recalling fondly that which was past and lost. Yet there was strength and swiftness in his limbs; and his mouth set straight across his face, the under lip a thought upon side, like that of a man accustomed to resolve. These two talked together in a rude outlandish speech that no frequenter of that wine-shop understood. The swarthy man answered to the name of *Ballantrae*; he of the dreamy eyes was sometimes called *Balmile*, and sometimes *my Lord*, or *my Lord Gladsmuir*; but when the title was given him, seemed to put it by as if in jesting, not without bitterness.

The mistral blew in the city. The first day of that wind, they say in the countries where its voice is heard, it blows away all the dust, the second all the stones, and the third it blows back others from the mountains. It was now come to the third day; outside the pebbles flew like hail, and the face of the river was puckered, and the very building-stones in the walls of houses seemed to be curdled, with the savage cold and fury of that continuous blast. It could be heard to hoot in all the chimneys of the city; it swept about the wine-shop, filling the room with eddies; the chill and gritty touch of it passed between the nearest clothes and the bare flesh; and the two gentlemen at the far table kept their mantles loose about their shoulders. The roughness of these outer hulls, for they were plain travellers' cloaks that had seen service, set the greater mark of richness on what showed below of their laced clothes; for the one was in scarlet and the other in violet and white, like men come from a scene of ceremony; as indeed they were.

It chanced that these fine clothes were not without their influence on the scene which followed, and which makes the prologue of our tale. For a long time Balmile was in the habit to come to the wine-shop and eat a meal or drink a measure of wine; sometimes with a comrade; more often alone, when he would sit and dream and drum upon the table, and the thoughts would show in the man's face in little glooms and lightenings, like the sun and the clouds upon a water. For a long time Marie-Madeleine had observed him apart. His sadness, the beauty of his smile when by any chance he remembered her existence and addressed her, the changes of his mind signalled forth by an abstruse play of feature, the mere fact that he was foreign and a thing detached from the local and the accustomed, insensibly attracted and affected her. Kindness was ready in her mind; it but lacked the touch of an occasion to effervesce and crystallise. Now, Balmile had come hitherto in a very poor plain habit;

and this day of the mistral, when his mantle was just open, and she saw beneath it the glancing of the violet and the velvet and the silver, and the clustering fineness of the lace, it seemed to set the man in a new light, with which he shone resplendent to her fancy.

The high inhuman note of the wind, the violence and continuity of its outpouring, and the fierce touch of it upon man's whole periphery, accelerated the functions of the mind. It set thoughts whirling, as it whirled the trees of the forest; it stirred them up in flights, as it stirred up the dust in chambers. As brief as sparks, the fancies glittered and succeeded each other in the mind of Marie-Madeleine; and the grave man with the smile, and the bright clothes under the plain mantle, haunted her with incongruous explanations. She considered him, the unknown, the speaker of an unknown tongue, the hero (as she placed him) of an unknown romance, the dweller upon unknown memories. She recalled him sitting there alone, so immersed, so stupefied; yet she was sure he was not stupid. She recalled one day when he had remained a long time motionless, with parted lips, like one in the act of starting up, his eyes fixed on vacancy. Any one else must have looked foolish; but not he. She tried to conceive what manner of memory had thus entranced him; she forged for him a past; she showed him to herself in every light of heroism and greatness and misfortune; she brooded with petulant intensity on all she knew and guessed of him. Yet, though she was already gone so deep, she was still unashamed, still unalarmed; her thoughts were still disinterested; she had still to reach the stage at which—beside the image of that other whom we love to contemplate and to adorn—we place the image of ourself and behold them together with delight.

She stood within the counter, her hands clasped behind her back, her shoulders pressed against the wall, her feet braced out. Her face was bright with the wind and her own thoughts; as a fire in a similar day of tempest glows and brightens on a hearth, so she seemed to glow, standing there, and to breathe out energy. It was the first time Ballantrae had visited that wine-seller's, the first time he had seen the wife; and his eyes were true to her.

' I perceive your reason for carrying me to this very draughty tavern,' he said at last.

' I believe it is propinquity,' returned Balmile.

' You play dark,' said Ballantrae, ' but have a care! Be more frank with me, or I will cut you out. I go through no form of qualifying my threat, which would be commonplace and not conscientious. There is only one point in these campaigns: that is the degree of admiration offered by the man; and to our hostess I am in a posture to make victorious love.'

' If you think you have the time, or the game worth the candle,' replied the other, with a shrug.

' One would suppose you were never at the pains to observe her,' said Ballantrae.

' I am not very observant,' said Balmile. ' She seems comely.'

' You very dear and dull dog!' cried Ballantrae; ' chastity is the most besotting of the virtues. Why, she has a look in her face beyond singing! I believe, if you were to push me hard, I might trace it home to a trifle of a squint. What matters? The height of beauty is in the touch that's wrong, that's the modulation in a tune. 'Tis the devil we all love; I owe many a conquest to my mole'—he touched it as he spoke with a smile, and his eyes glittered; ' we are all hunchbacks, and beauty is only that kind of deformity that I happen to admire. But come! Because you are chaste, for which I am sure I pay you my respects, that is no reason why you should be blind. Look at her, look at the delicious nose of her, look at her cheek, look at her ear, look at her hand and wrist—look at the whole baggage from heels to crown, and tell me if she wouldn't melt on a man's tongue.'

As Ballantrae spoke, half jesting, half enthusiastic, Balmile was constrained to do as he was bidden. He looked at the woman, admired her excellences, and was at the same time ashamed for himself and his companion. So it befell that when Marie-Madeleine raised her eyes, she met those of the subject of her contemplations fixed directly on herself with a look that is unmistakable, the look of a person measuring and valuing another—and, to clench the false impression, that his glance was instantly and guiltily withdrawn. The blood beat back upon her heart and leaped again; her obscure thoughts flashed clear before her; she flew in fancy straight to his arms like a wanton, and fled again on the instant like a nymph. And at that moment there chanced an interruption, which not only spared her embarrassment, but set the last consecration on her now articulate love.

Into the wine-shop there came a French gentleman, arrayed in the last refinement of the fashion, though a little tumbled by his passage in the wind. It was to be judged he had come from the same formal gathering at which the others had preceded him; and perhaps that he had gone there in the hope to meet with them, for he came up to Ballantrae with unceremonious eagerness.

' At last, here you are! ' he cried in French. ' I thought I was to miss you altogether.'

The Scotsmen rose, and Ballantrae, after the first greetings, laid his hand on his companion's shoulder.

' My Lord,' said he, ' allow me to present to you one of my best friends and one of our best soldiers, the Lord Viscount Gladsmuir.'

The two bowed with the elaborate elegance of the period.

' *Monseigneur*,' said Balmile, ' *je n'ai pas la prétention de m'affubler d'un titre que la mauvaise fortune de mon roi ne me permet pas de porter comme il sied. Je m'appelle, pour vous servir, Blair de Balmile tout court.*' (' My Lord, I have not the effrontery to cumber myself with a title which the ill fortunes of my king will not suffer me to bear the way it should be. I call myself, at your service, plain Blair of Balmile.')

' *Monsieur le Vicomte ou Monsieur Bler' de Balmaíl*,' replied the new-comer, ' *le nom n'y fait rien, et l'on connaît vos beaux faits.*' (' The name matters nothing; your gallant actions are known.')

A few more ceremonies, and these three, sitting down together to the table, called for wine. It was the happiness of Marie-Madeleine to wait unobserved upon the prince of her desires. She poured the wine, he drank of it; and that link between them seemed, to her for the moment, close as a caress. Though they lowered their tones, she surprised great names passing in their conversation, names of kings, the names of de Gesvre and Belle-Isle; and the man who dealt in these high matters, and she who was now coupled with him in her own thoughts, seemed to swim in mid-air in a transfiguration. Love is a crude core, but it has singular and far-reaching fringes; in that passionate attraction for the stranger that now swayed and mastered her, his harsh incomprehensible language and these names of grandees in his talk, were each an element.

The Frenchman stayed not long, but it was plain he left behind him matter of much interest to his companions; they spoke together earnestly, their heads down, the woman of the wine-shop totally forgotten; and they were still so occupied when Paradou returned.

This man's love was unsleeping. The even bluster of the mistral, with which he had been combating some hours, had not suspended, though it had embittered, that predominant passion. His first look was for his wife, a look of hope and suspicion, menace and humility and love, that made the over-blooming brute appear for the moment almost beautiful. She returned his glance, at first as though she knew him not, then with a swiftly waxing coldness of intent; and at last, without changing their direction, she had closed her eyes.

There passed across her mind during that period much that Paradou could not have understood had it been told to him in words: chiefly the sense of an enlightening contrast betwixt the man who talked of kings and the man who kept a wine-shop, betwixt the love she yearned for and that to which she had been long exposed like a victim bound upon the altar. There swelled upon her, swifter than the Rhone, a tide of abhorrence and disgust. She had succumbed to the monster, humbling herself below animals; and now she loved a hero, aspiring to the semi-divine. It was in the pang of that humiliating thought that she had closed her eyes.

Paradou—quick, as beasts are quick, to translate silence—felt the insult through his blood; his inarticulate soul bellowed within him for revenge. He glanced about the shop. He saw the two indifferent gentlemen deep in talk, and passed them over: his fancy flying not so high. There was but one other present, a country lout who stood swallowing his wine, equally unobserved by all and unobserving; to him he dealt a glance of murderous suspicion and turned direct upon his wife. The wine-shop had lain hitherto, a space of shelter, the scene of a few ceremonial passages and some whispered conversation, in the howling river of the wind; the clock had not yet ticked a score of times since Paradou's appearance; and now, as he suddenly gave tongue, it seemed as though the mistral had entered at his heels.

'What ails you, woman?' he cried, smiting on the counter.

'Nothing ails me,' she replied. It was strange; but she spoke and stood at that moment like a lady of degree, drawn upward by her aspirations.

'You speak to me, by God, as though you scorned me!' cried the husband.

The man's passion was always formidable; she had often looked on upon its violence with a thrill—it had been one ingredient in her fascination; and she was now surprised to behold him, as from afar off, gesticulating but impotent. His fury might be dangerous like a torrent or a gust of wind, but it was inhuman; it might be feared or braved, it should never be respected. And with that there came in her a sudden glow of courage and that readiness to die which attends so closely upon all strong passions.

'I do scorn you,' she said.

'What is that?' he cried.

'I scorn you,' she repeated, smiling.

'You love another man!' said he.

'With all my soul,' was her reply.

The wine-seller roared aloud so that the house rang and shook with it.

'Is this the——?' he cried, using a foul word, common in the South; and he seized the young countryman and dashed him to the ground. There he lay for the least interval of time insensible; then fled from the house, the most terrified person in the county. The heavy measure had escaped from his hands, splashing the wine high upon the wall. Paradou caught it. 'And you?' he roared to his wife, giving her the same name in feminine, and he aimed at her the deadly missile. She expected it, motionless, with radiant eyes.

But before it sped, Paradou was met by another adversary, and the unconscious rivals stood confronted. It was hard to say at that moment which appeared the more formidable. In Paradou, the whole muddy and truculent depths of the half-man were stirred to frenzy; the lust of destruction raged in him; there was not a feature in his face but it talked murder. Balmile had dropped his cloak; he shone out at once in his finery, and stood to his full stature; girt in mind and body, all his resources, all his temper, perfectly in command; in his face the light of battle. Neither spoke; there was no blow nor threat of one; it was war reduced to its last element, the spiritual; and the huge wine-seller slowly lowered his weapon. Balmile was a noble, he a commoner; Balmile exulted in an honourable cause. Paradou already perhaps began to be ashamed of his violence. Of a sudden, at least, the tortured brute turned and fled from the shop, in the footsteps of his former victim, to whose continued flight his reappearance added wings.

So soon as Balmile appeared between her husband and herself, Marie-Madeleine transferred to him her eyes. It might be her last moment, and she fed upon that face; reading there inimitable courage and illimitable valour to protect. And when the momentary peril was gone by, and the champion turned a little awkwardly towards her whom he had rescued, it was to meet, and quail before, a gaze of admiration more distinct than words. He bowed, he stammered, his words failed him; he who had crossed the floor a moment ago, like a young god, to smite, returned like one discomfited: got somehow to his place by the table, muffled himself again in his discarded cloak, and for a last touch of the ridiculous, seeking for anything to restore his countenance, drank of the wine before him, deep as a porter after a heavy lift. It was little wonder if Ballantrae, reading the scene with malevolent eyes, laughed out loud and brief, and drank with raised glass, ‘ To the champion of the Fair.’

Marie-Madeleine stood in her old place within the counter; she disdained the mocking laughter; it fell on her ears, but it did not reach her spirit. For her, the world of living persons was all resumed again into one pair, as in the days of Eden; there was but the one end in life, the one hope before her, the one thing needful, the one thing possible—to be his.

I

The Prince

THAT same night there was in the city of Avignon a young man in distress of mind. Now he sat, now walked in a high apartment, full of draughts and shadows. A single candle made the darkness visible; and the light scarce sufficed to show upon the wall, where they had been recently and rudely nailed, a few miniatures and a copper medal of the young man's head. The same was being sold that year in London to admiring thousands. The original was fair; he had beautiful brown eyes, a beautiful bright open face; a little feminine, a little hard, a little weak; still full of the light of youth, but already beginning to be vulgarised; a sordid bloom come upon it, the lines coarsened with a touch of puffiness. He was dressed as, for a gala, in peach-colour and silver; his breast sparkled with stars and was bright with ribbons; for he had held a levee in the afternoon and received a distinguished personage incognito. Now he sat with a bowed head, now walked precipitately to and fro, now went and gazed from the uncurtained window, where the wind was still blowing, and the lights winked in the darkness.

The bells of Avignon rose into song as he was gazing; and the high notes and the deep tossed and drowned, boomed suddenly near or were suddenly swallowed up, in the current of the mistral. Tears sprang in the pale blue eyes; the expression of his face was changed to that of a more active misery; it seemed as if the voices of the bells reached, and touched and pained him, in a waste of vacancy where even pain was welcome. Outside in the night they continued to sound on, swelling and fainting; and the listener heard in his memory, as it were, their harmonies, joy-bells clashing in a northern city, and the acclamations of a multitude, the cries of battle, the gross voices of cannon, the stridor of an animated life. And then all died away, and he stood face to face with himself in the waste of vacancy, and a horror upon his mind, and a faintness on his brain, such as seizes men upon the brink of cliffs.

On the table, by the side of the candle, stood a tray of glasses, a bottle, and a silver bell. He went thither swiftly, then his hand lowered first above the bell, then settled on the bottle. Slowly he filled a glass, slowly drank it out; and, as a tide of animal warmth recomforted the recesses of his nature, stood there smiling at himself. He remembered he was young; the funeral curtains rose, and he saw his life shine and broaden and flow out majestically, like a river sunward. The smile still on his lips, he lit a second candle, and a third; a fire stood ready built in a chimney, he lit that also; and the fir-cones and the gnarled olive billets were swift to break in flame and to crackle on the hearth, and the room brightened and enlarged about him like his hopes. To and fro, to and fro, he went, his hands lightly clasped, his breath deeply and pleasurably taken. Victory walked with him; he marched to crowns and empires among shouting followers; glory was his dress. And presently again the shadows closed upon the solitary. Under the gilt of flame and candle-light, the stone walls of the apartment showed down bare and cold; behind the depicted triumph loomed up the actual failure: defeat, the long distress of the flight, exile, despair, broken followers, mourning faces, empty pockets, friends estranged. The memory of his father rose in his mind: he, too, estranged and defied; despair sharpened into wrath. There was one who had led armies in the field, who had staked his life upon the family enterprise, a man of action and experience, of the open air, the camp, the court, the council-room; and he was to accept direction from an old, pompous gentleman in a home in Italy, and buzzed about by priests? A pretty king, if he had not a martial son to lean upon! A king at all?

'There was a weaver (of all people) joined me at St. Ninians; he was more of a man than my papa!' he thought. 'I saw him lie doubled in his blood and a grenadier below him—and he died for my papa! All died for him, or risked the dying, and I lay for him all those months in the rain and skulked in heather like a fox; and now he writes me his advice! calls me Carluccio— me, the man of the house, the only king in that king's race!' He ground his teeth. 'The only king in Europe! Who else? Who has done and suffered except me? who has lain and run and hidden with his faithful subjects, like a second Bruce? Not my accursed cousin, Louis of France, at least, the lewd effeminate traitor!' And filling the glass to the brim, he drank a king's damnation. Ah, if he had the power of Louis, what a king were here!

The minutes followed each other into the past, and still he persevered in this debilitating cycle of emotions, still fed the fire of his excitement with driblets of Rhine wine; a boy at odds with life, a boy with a spark of the heroic, which he was now burning out and drowning down in futile reverie and solitary excess.

From two rooms beyond, the sudden sound of a raised voice attracted him.

'By . . .

HEATHERCAT

CONTENTS

PART ONE—THE KILLING-TIME

THE KILLING-TIME

I

Traquairs of Montroymont

THE period of this tale is in the heat of the *killing-time*; the scene laid for the most part in solitary hills and morasses, haunted only by the so-called Mountain Wanderers, the dragoons that came in chase of them, the women that wept on their dead bodies, and the wild birds of the moorland that have cried there since the beginning. It is a land of many rain-clouds; a land of much mute history, written there in prehistoric symbols. Strange green raths are to be seen commonly in the country, above all by the kirkyards; barrows of the dead, standing stones; beside these, the faint, durable footprints and handmarks of the Roman; and an antiquity older perhaps than any, and still living and active—a complete Celtic nomenclature and a scarce-mingled Celtic population. These rugged and gray hills were once included in the boundaries of the Caledonian Forest. Merlin sat here below his apple-tree and lamented Gwendolen; here spoke with Kentigern; here fell into his enchanted trance. And the legend of his slumber seems to body forth the story of that Celtic race, deprived for so many centuries of their authentic speech, surviving with their ancestral inheritance of melancholy perversity and patient, unfortunate courage.

The Traquairs of Montroymont (*Mons Romanus*, as the erudite expound it) had long held their seat about the head waters of the Dule and in the black parts of the moorland parish of Balweary. For two hundred years they had enjoyed in these upland quarters a certain decency (almost to be named distinction) of repute; and the annals of their house, or what is remembered of them, were obscure and bloody. Ninian Traquair was 'cruallie slochtered' by the Crozers at the kirk-door of Balweary, anno 1482. Francis killed Simon Ruthven of Drumshoreland, anno 1540; bought letters of slayers at the widow and heir, and, by a barbarous form of compounding, married (without tocher) Simon's daughter Grizzel, which is the way the Traquairs and Ruthvens came first to an intermarriage. About the last Traquair and Ruthven marriage, it is the business of this book, among many other things, to tell.

The Traquairs were always strong for the Covenant; for the King also, but the Covenant first; and it began to be ill days for Montroymont when the Bishops came in and the dragoons at the heels of them. Ninian (then laird) was an anxious husband of himself and the property, as the times required, and it may be said of him that he lost both. He was heavily suspected of the Pentland Hills rebellion. When it came the length of Bothwell Brig, he stood his trial before the Secret Council, and was convicted of talking to some insurgents by the wayside, the subject of the conversation not very clearly appearing, and of the reset and maintenance of one Gale, a gardener-man, who was seen before Bothwell with a musket, and afterwards, for a continuance of months, delved the garden at Montroymont. Matters went very ill with Ninian at the Council; some of the lords were clear for treason; and even the boot was talked of. But he was spared that torture; and at last, having pretty good friendship among great men, he came off with a fine of seven thousand marks, that caused the estate to groan. In this case, as in so many others, it was the wife that made the trouble. She was a great keeper of conventicles; would ride ten miles to one, and when she was fined, rejoiced greatly to suffer for the Kirk; but it was rather her husband that suffered. She had their only son, Francis, baptised privately by the hands of Mr. Kidd; there was that much the more to pay for! She could neither be driven nor wiled into the parish kirk; as for taking the sacrament at the hands of any Episcopalian curate, and tenfold more at those of Curate Haddo, there was nothing further from her purposes; and Montroymont had to put his hand in his pocket month by month and year by year. Once, indeed, the little lady was cast in prison, and the laird, worthy, heavy, uninterested man, had to ride up and take her place; from which he was not discharged under nine months and a sharp fine. It scarce seemed she had any gratitude to him; she came out of jail herself, and plunged immediately deeper in conventicles, resetting recusants, and all her old, expensive folly, only with greater vigour and openness, because Montroymont was safe in the Tolbooth and she had no witness to consider. When he was liberated and came back, with his fingers singed, in December, 1680, and late in the black night, my lady was from home. He came into the house at his alighting, with a riding-rod yet in his hand; and, on the servant-maid telling him, caught her by the scruff of the neck, beat her violently, flung her down in the passageway, and went upstairs to his bed fasting and without a light. It was three in the morning when my lady returned from that conventicle, and, hearing of the assault (because the maid had sat up for her, weeping), went to their common chamber with a lantern in hand and stamping with her shoes so as to wake the dead; it was supposed, by those that heard her, from a design to have it out with the goodman at once. The house-servants gathered on the stair, because it was a main interest with them to know which of these two was the better horse; and for the space of two hours they were heard to go at the matter, hammer and tongs. Montroymont alleged he was at the end of his possibilities; it was no longer within his power to pay the annual rents, she had served him basely by keeping conventicles while he lay in prison for her sake; his friends were weary, and there was nothing else before him but the entire loss of the family lands, and to begin life again by the wayside as a common beggar. She took him up very sharp and high, called upon him, if he were a Christian? and which he most considered, the loss of a few dirty, miry glebes, or of his soul? Presently he was heard to weep, and my lady's voice to go on continually like a running burn, only the words indistinguishable; whereupon it was supposed a victory for her ladyship, and the domestics took themselves to bed. The next day Traquair appeared like a man who had gone under the harrows; and his lady wife thenceforward continued in her old course without the least deflection.

Thenceforward Ninian went on his way without complaint, and suffered his wife to go on hers without remonstrance. He still minded his estate, of which, it might be said, he took daily a fresh farewell, and counted it already lost; looking ruefully on the acres and the graves of his fathers, on the moorlands where the wild-fowl consorted, the low, gurgling pool of the trout, and the high, windy place of the calling curlews—things that were yet his for the day and would be another's to-morrow; coming back again, and sitting ciphering till the dusk at his approaching ruin, which no device of arithmetic could postpone beyond a year or two. He was essentially the simple ancient man, the farmer and landholder; he would have been content to watch the seasons come and go, and his cattle increase, until the limit of age; he would have been content at any time to die, if he could have left the estates undiminished to an heir male of his ancestors, that duty standing first in his instinctive calendar. And now he saw everywhere the image of the new proprietor come to meet him, and go sowing and reaping, or fowling for his pleasure on the red moors, or eating the very gooseberries in the Place garden; and saw always, on the other hand, the figure of Francis go forth, a beggar, into the broad world.

It was in vain the poor gentleman sought to moderate; took every test and took advantage of every indulgence; went and drank with the dragoons in Balweary; attended the communion and came regularly to the church to Curate Haddo, with his son beside him. The mad, raging, Presbyterian zealot of a wife at home made all of no avail; and indeed the house must have fallen years before if it had not been for the secret indulgence of the curate, who had a great sympathy with the laird, and winked hard at the doings in Montroymont. This curate was a man very ill reputed in the countryside, and indeed in all Scotland. ' Infamous Haddo ' is Shield's expression. But Patrick Walker is more copious. ' Curate Hall Haddo,' says he, *sub voce* Peden, ' or *Hell* Haddo as he was more justly to be called, a pokeful of old condemned errors and the filthy vile lusts of the flesh, a published whoremonger, a common gross drunkard, continually and godlessly scraping and skirling on a fiddle, continually breathing flames against the remnant of Israel. But the Lord put an end to his piping, and all these offences were composed into one bloody grave.' No doubt this was written to excuse his slaughter; and I have never heard it claimed for Walker that he was either a just witness or an indulgent judge. At least, in a merely human character, Haddo comes off not wholly amiss in the matter of these Traquairs: not that he showed any graces of the Christian, but had a sort of Pagan decency, which might almost tempt one to be concerned about his sudden, violent, and unprepared fate.

2

Francie

FRANCIE was eleven years old, shy, secret, and rather childish of his age, though not backward in schooling, which had been pushed on far by a private governor, one M'Brair, a forfeited minister harboured in that capacity at Montroymont. The boy, already much employed in secret by his mother, was the most apt hand conceivable to run upon a message, to carry food to lurking fugitives, or to stand sentry on the sky-line above a conventicle. It seemed no place on the moorlands was so naked but what he would find cover there; and as he knew every hag, boulder, and heatherbush in a circuit of seven miles about Montroymont, there was scarce any spot but what he could leave or approach it unseen. This dexterity had won him a reputation in that part of the country; and among the many children employed in these dangerous affairs, he passed under the by-name of Heathercat.

How much his father knew of this employment might be doubted. He took more forethought for the boy's future, seeing he was like to be left so poorly, and would sometimes assist at his lessons, sighing heavily, yawning deep, and now and again patting Francie on the shoulder if he seemed to be doing ill, by way of a private, kind encouragement. But a great part of the day was passed in aimless wanderings with his eyes sealed, or in his cabinet sitting bemused over the particulars of the coming bankruptcy; and the boy would be absent a dozen times for once that his father would observe it.

On the 2nd of July, 1682, the boy had an errand from his mother, which must be kept private from all, the father included in the first of them. Crossing the braes, he hears the clatter of a horse's shoes, and claps down incontinent in a hag by the way-side. And presently he spied his father come riding from one direction, and Curate Haddo walking from another; and Mon-troymont leaning down from the saddle, and Haddo getting on his toes (for he was a little, ruddy, bald-pated man, more like a dwarf), they greeted kindly, and came to a halt within two fathoms of the child.

'Montroymont,' the curate said, 'the de'il's in 't but I'll have to denunciate your leddy again.'

'De'il's in 't indeed!' says the laird.

'Man! can ye no induce her to come to the kirk?' pursues Haddo; 'or to a communion at the least of it. For the conven-ticles, let be! and the same for yon solemn fule, M'Brair: I can blink at them. But she's got to come to the kirk, Montroy-mont.'

'Dinna speak of it,' says the laird. 'I can do nothing with her.'

'Couldn't ye try the stick to her? It works wonders whiles,' suggested Haddo. 'No? I'm wae to hear it. And I suppose ye ken where you're going?'

'Fine!' said Montroymont. 'Fine do I ken where: Bank-rup'cy and the Bass Rock!'

'Praise to my bones that I never married!' cried the curate. 'Well, it's a grievous thing to me to see an auld house dung down that was here before Flodden Field. But naebody can say it was with my wish.'

'No more they can, Haddo!' says the laird. 'A good friend ye've been to me, first and last. I can give you that character with a clear conscience.'

Whereupon they separated, and Montroymont rode briskly down into the Dule Valley. But of the curate Francie was not to be quit so easily. He went on with his little, brisk steps to the corner of a dyke, and stopped and whistled and waved upon a lassie that was herding cattle there. This Janet M'Clour was a big lass, being taller than the curate; and what made her look the more so, she was kilted very high. It seemed for a while she would not come, and Francie heard her calling Haddo a 'daft auld fule,' and saw her running and dodging him among the whins and hags till he was fairly blown. But at the last he gets a bottle from his plaid-neuk and holds it up to her; whereupon she came at once into a composition, and the pair sat, drinking of the bottle, and daffing and laughing together, on a mound of heather. The boy had scarce heard of these vanities, or he might have been minded of a nymph and satyr, if anybody could have taken long-leggit Janet for a nymph. But they seemed to be huge friends, he thought; and was the more surprised, when the curate had taken his leave, to see the lassie fling stones after him with screeches of laughter, and Haddo turn about and caper, and shake his staff at her, and laugh louder than herself. A wonderful merry pair, they seemed; and when Francie crawled out of the hag, he had a great deal to consider in his mind. It was possible they were all fallen in error about Mr. Haddo, he reflected—having seen him so tender with Montroymont, and so kind and playful with the lass Janet; and he had a temptation to go out of his road and question her herself upon the matter. But he had a strong spirit of duty on him; and plodded on instead over the braes till he came near the House of Cairngorm. There, in a hollow place by the burn-side that was shaded by some birks, he was aware of a barefoot boy, perhaps a matter of three years older than himself. The two approached with the precautions of a pair of strange dogs, looking at each other queerly.

'It's ill weather on the hill,' said the stranger, giving the watchword.

'For a season,' said Francie, 'but the Lord will appear.'

'Richt,' said the barefoot boy. 'Wha're ye frae?'

'The Leddy Montroymont,' says Francie.

'Ha'e then!' says the stranger, and handed him a folded paper, and they stood and looked at each other again. 'It's unco' het,' said the boy.

'Dooms het,' says Francie.

'What do they ca' ye?' says the other.

'Francie,' says he. 'I'm young Montroymont. They ca' me Heathercat.'

'I'm Jock Crozer,' said the boy. And there was another pause, while each rolled a stone under his foot.

'Cast your jaiket and I'll fecht ye for a bawbee,' cried the elder boy, with sudden violence, and dramatically throwing back his jacket.

'Na, I have nae time the now,' said Francie, with a sharp thrill of alarm, because Crozer was much the heavier boy.

'Ye're feared. Heathercat indeed!' said Crozer, for among this infantile army of spies and messeggers the fame of Crozer had gone forth and was resented by his rivals. And with that they separated.

On his way home Francie was a good deal occupied with the recollection of this untoward incident. The challenge had been fairly offered and basely refused: the tale would be carried all over the country, and the lustre of the name of Heathercat be dimmed. But the scene between Curate Haddo and Janet M'Clour had also given him much to think of; and he was still puzzling over the case of the curate, and why such ill words were said of him, and why, if he were so merry-spirited, he should yet preach so dry, when, coming over a knowe, whom should he see but Janet, sitting with her back to him, minding her cattle! He was always a great child for secret, stealthy ways, having been employed by his mother on errands when the same was necessary; and he came behind the lass without her hearing.

'Jennet,' says he.

'Keep me!' cries Janet, springing up. 'O, it's you, Maister Francie! Save us, what a fricht ye gied me!'

'Ay, it's me,' said Francie. 'I've been thinking, Jennet; I saw you and the curate a while back——'

'Brat!' cried Janet, and coloured up crimson; and the one moment made as if she would have stricken him with a ragged stick she had to chase her bestial with, and the next was begging and praying that he would mention it to none. It was 'nae-body's business, whatever,' she said; 'it would just start a clash in the country'; and there would be nothing left for her but to drown herself in Dule Water.

'Why?' says Francie.

The girl looked at him and grew scarlet again.

'And it isna that, anyway,' continued Francie. 'It was just that he seemed so good to ye—like our Father in Heaven, I thought; and I thought that mebbe, perhaps, we had all been wrong about him from the first. But I'll have to tell Mr. M'Brair, I'm under a kind of a bargain to him to tell him all.'

' Tell it to the divil of ye like for me!' cried the lass. ' I've naething to be ashamed of. Tell M'Brair to mind his ain affairs,' she cried again; ' they'll be hot eneuch for him, if Haddie likes!' And so strode off, shoving her beasts before her, and ever and again looking back and crying angry words to the boy, where he stood mystified.

By the time he had got home his mind was made up that he would say nothing to his mother. My Lady Montroymont was in the keeping-room, reading a godly book; she was a wonderful frail little wife to make so much noise in the world and be able to steer about that patient sheep her husband; her eyes were like sloes, the fingers of her hands were like tobacco-pipe shanks, her mouth shut tight like a trap; and even when she was the most serious, and still more when she was angry, there hung about her face the terrifying semblance of a smile.

' Have ye gotten the billet, Francie?' said she; and when he had handed it over, and she had read and burned it, ' Did you see anybody?' she asked.

' I saw the laird,' said Francie.

' He didna see you, though?' asked his mother.

' De'il a fear,' from Francie.

' Francie!' she cried. ' What's that I hear? an aith? The Lord forgive me, have I broughten forth a brand for the burning, a fagot for hell-fire?'

' I'm very sorry, ma'am,' said Francie. ' I humbly beg the Lord's pardon, and yours, for my wickedness.'

' H'm,' grunted the lady. ' Did ye see nobody else?'

' No, ma'am,' said Francie, with the face of an angel, ' except Jock Crozer, that gied me the billet.'

' Jock Crozer!' cried the lady. ' I'll Crozer them! Crozers indeed! What next? Are we to repose the lives of a suffering remnant in Crozers? The whole clan of them wants hanging, and if I had my way of it, they wouldna want it long. Are you aware, sir, that these Crozers killed your forebear at the kirk-door?'

' You see, he was bigger 'n me,' said Francie.

' Jock Crozer,' continued the lady. ' That'll be Clement's son, the biggest thief and reiver in the countryside. To trust a note to him! But I'll give the benefit of my opinions to Lady Whitecross when we two forgather. Let her look to herself! I have no patience with half-hearted carlines, that complies on the Lord's day morning with the kirk, and comes taigling the

same night to the conventicle. The one or the other! is what I
saw: Hell or Heaven—Haddie's abominations or the pure word
of God dreeping from the lips of Mr. Arnot.

> ' " Like honey from the honeycomb
>   That dreepeth, sweeter far." '

My lady was now fairly launched, and that upon two congenial subjects: the deficiencies of the Lady Whitecross, and the
turpitudes of the whole Crozer race—which, indeed, had never
been conspicuous for respectability. She pursued the pair of
them for twenty minutes on the clock with wonderful animation
and detail, something of the pulpit manner, and the spirit of
one possessed. ' O hellish compliance! ' she exclaimed. ' I
would not suffer a complier to break bread with Christian folk.
Of all the sins of this day there is not one so God-defying, so
Christ-humiliating, as damnable compliance '; the boy standing
before her meanwhile, and brokenly pursuing other thoughts,
mainly of Haddo and Janet, and Jock Crozer stripping off his
jacket. And yet, with all his distraction, it might be argued that
he heard too much; his father and himself being ' compliers '
—that is to say, attending the church of the parish as the law
required.

Presently, the lady's passion beginning to decline or her flux
of ill words to be exhausted, she dismissed her audience. Francie bowed low, left the room, closed the door behind him; and
then turned him about in the passageway, and with a low voice,
but a prodigious deal of sentiment, repeated the name of the
evil one twenty times over, to the end of which, for the greater
efficacy, he tacked on ' damnable ' and ' hellish.' *Fas est ab hoste
doceri*—disrespect is made more pungent by quotation; and
there is no doubt but he felt relieved, and went upstairs into his
tutor's chamber with a quiet mind. M'Brair sat by the cheek of
the peat-fire and shivered, for he had a quartan ague and this
was his day. The great nightcap and plaid, the dark unshaven
cheeks of the man, and the white, thin hands, that held the plaid
about his chittering body, made a sorrowful picture. But Francie knew and loved him; came straight in, nestled close to the
refugee, and told his story. M'Brair had been at the College
with Haddo; the Presbytery had licensed both on the same day;
and at this tale, told with so much innocency by the boy, the
heart of the tutor was commoved.

' Woe upon him! Woe upon that man! ' he cried, ' O the
unfaithful shepherd! O the hireling and apostate minister! Make

my matters hot for me? quo' she! the shameless limmer! And true it is that he could repose me in that nasty, stinking hole, the Canongate Tolbooth, from which your mother drew me out—the Lord reward her for it!—or to that cold, unbieldy, marine place of the Bass Rock, which, with my delicate kist, would be fair ruin to me. But I will be valiant in my Master's service. I have a duty here: a duty to my God, to myself, and to Haddo: in His strength, I will perform it.'

Then he straightly discharged Francie to repeat the tale, and bade him in the future to avert his very eyes from the doings of the curate. 'You must go to his place of idolatry; look upon him there!' says he, 'but nowhere else. Avert your eyes, close your ears, pass him by like a three days' corp'. He is like that damnable monster Basiliscus, which defiles—yea, poisons!—by the sight.' All which was hardly claratory to the boy's mind.

Presently Montroymont came home, and called up the stairs to Francie. Traquair was a good shot and swordsman; and it was his pleasure to walk with his son over the braes of the moor-fowl, or to teach him arms in the back court, when they made a mighty comely pair, the child being so lean and light and active, and the laird himself a man of a manly, pretty stature, his hair (the periwig being laid aside) showing already white with many anxieties, and his face of an even, flaccid red. But this day Francie's heart was not in the fencing.

'Sir,' says he, suddenly lowering his point, 'will ye tell me a thing if I was to ask it?'

'Ask away,' says the father.

'Well, it's this,' said Francie: 'Why do you and me comply if it's so wicked?'

'Ay, ye have the cant of it, too!' cries Montroymont. 'But I'll tell ye for all that. It's to try and see if we can keep the rigging on this house, Francie. If she had her way, we would be beggar-folk and hold our hands out by the wayside. When ye hear her—when ye hear folk,' he corrected himself briskly, 'call me a coward, and one that betrayed the Lord, and I kenna what else, just mind it was to keep a bed to ye to sleep in and a bite for ye to eat.—On guard!' he cried, and the lesson proceeded again till they were called to supper.

'There's another thing yet,' said Francie, stopping his father. 'There's another thing that I am not sure I am very caring for. She—she sends me errands.'

'Obey her, then, as is your bounden duty,' said Traquair.

'Ay, but wait till I tell ye,' says the boy. 'If I was to see you I was to hide.'

Montroymont sighed. 'Well, and that's good of her, too,' said he. 'The less that I ken of thir doings the better for me; and the best thing you can do is just to obey her, and see and be a good son to her, the same as ye are to me, Francie.'

At the tenderness of this expression the heart of Francie swelled within his bosom, and his remorse was poured out. 'Faither!' he cried, 'I said, " de'il " to-day; many's the time I said it, and " *damnable* " too, and " *hellitsh*." I ken they're all right; they're beeblical. But I didna say them beeblically; I said them for sweir-words—that's the truth of it.'

'Hout, ye silly bairn!' said the father; 'dinna do it nae mair, and come in by to your supper.' And he took the boy, and drew him close to him a moment, as they went through the door, with something very fond and secret, like a caress between a pair of lovers.

The next day M'Brair was abroad in the afternoon, and had a long advising with Janet on the braes where she herded cattle. What passed was never wholly known; but the lass wept bitterly, and fell on her knees to him among the whins. The same night, as soon as it was dark, he took the road again for Balweary. In the Kirkton, where the dragoons quartered, he saw many lights, and heard the noise of a ranting song and people laughing grossly, which was highly offensive to his mind. He gave it the wider berth, keeping among the fields; and came down at last by the water-side, where the manse stands solitary between the river and the road. He tapped at the back door, and the old woman called upon him to come in, and guided him through the house to the study, as they still called it, though there was little enough study there in Haddo's days, and more song-books than theology.

'Here's yin to speak wi' ye, Mr. Haddie!' cries the old wife.

And M'Brair, opening the door and entering, found the little, round, red man seated in one chair and his feet upon another. A clear fire and a tallow dip lighted him barely. He was taking tobacco in a pipe, and smiling to himself; and a brandy-bottle and glass, and his fiddle and bow, were beside him on the table.

'Hech, Patey M'Brair, is this you?' said he, a trifle tipsily. 'Step in by, man, and have a drop brandy: for the stomach's sake! Even the de'il can quote Scripture—eh, Patey?'

'I will neither eat nor drink with you,' replied M'Brair. 'I am come upon my Master's errand: woe be upon me if I should anyways mince the same. Hall Haddo, I summon you to quit this kirk which you encumber.'

'Muckle obleeged!' says Haddo winking.

'You and me have been to kirk and market together,' pursued M'Brair: 'we have had blessed seasons in the kirk, we have sat in the same teaching-rooms and read in the same book; and I know you still retain for me some carnal kindness. It would be my shame if I denied it; I live here at your mercy and by your favour, and glory to acknowledge it. You have pity on my wretched body, which is but grass, and must soon be trodden under; but O, Haddo! how much greater is the yearning with which I yearn after and pity your immortal soul! Come now, let us reason together! I drop all points of controversy, weighty though these be; I take your defaced and damnified kirk on your own terms; and I ask you, Are you a worthy minister? The communion season approaches; how can you pronounce thir solemn words, "The elders will now bring forrit the elements," and not quail? A parishioner may be summoned to-night; you may have to rise from your miserable orgies; and I ask you, Haddo, what does your conscience tell you? Are you fit? Are you fit to smooth the pillow of a parting Christian? And if the summons should be for yourself, how then?'

Haddo was startled out of all composure and the better part of his temper. 'What's this of it?' he cried. 'I'm no waur than my neebours. I never set up to be speeritual; I never did. I'm a plain, canty creature; godliness is cheerfulness, says I; give me my fiddle and a dram, and I wouldna hairm a flee.'

'And I repeat my question,' said M'Brair: 'Are you fit—fit for this great charge? fit to carry and save souls?'

'Fit? Blethers! As fit's yoursel',' cried Haddo.

'Are you so great a self-deceiver?' said M'Brair. 'Wretched man, trampler upon God's covenants, crucifier of your Lord afresh! I will ding you to the earth with one word: How about the young woman, Janet M'Clour?'

'Well, what about her? what do I ken?' cries Haddo. 'M'Brair, ye daft auld wife, I tell ye as true's truth, I never meddled her. It was just daffing, I tell ye: daffing, and nae mair: a piece of fun, like! I'm no' denying but what I'm fond of fun, sma' blame to me! But for onything sarious—hout, man, it might come to a deposeetion! I'll sweir it to ye. Where's a Bible, till you hear me sweir?'

'There is nae Bible in your study,' said M'Brair severely.

And Haddo, after a few distracted turns, was constrained to accept the fact.

'Weel, and suppose there isna?' he cried, stamping. 'What mair can ye say of us, but just that I'm fond of my joke, and so's she? I declare to God, by what I ken, she might be the Virgin

Mary—if she would just keep clear of the dragoons. But me! na, de'il haet o' me!'

'She is penitent at least,' said M'Brair.

'Do you mean to actually up and tell me to my face that she accused me?' cried the curate.

'I canna just say that,' replied M'Brair. 'But I rebuked her in the name of God, and she repented before me on her bended knees.'

'Weel, I daursay she's been ower far wi' the dragoons,' said Haddo. 'I never denied that. I ken naething by it.'

'Man, you but show your nakedness the more plainly,' said M'Brair. 'Poor, blind, besotted creature—and I see you stoitering on the brink of dissolution: your light out, and your hours numbered. Awake, man!' he shouted with a formidable voice, 'awake, or it be ower late.'

'Be damned if I stand this!' exclaimed Haddo, casting his tobacco-pipe violently on the table, where it was smashed in pieces. 'Out of my house with ye, or I'll call for the dragoons.'

'The speerit of the Lord is upon me,' said M'Brair, with solemn ecstasy. 'I sist you to compear before the Great White Throne, and I warn you the summons shall be bloody and sudden.'

And at this, with more agility than could have been expected, he got clear of the room and slammed the door behind him in the face of the pursuing curate. The next Lord's day the curate was ill, and the kirk closed, but, for all his ill words, Mr. M'Brair abode unmolested in the house of Montroymont.

3

The hill-end of Drumlowe

THIS was a bit of a steep broken hill that overlooked upon the west a moorish valley, full of ink-black pools. These presently drained into a burn that made off, with little noise and no celerity of pace, about the corner of the hill. On the far side the ground swelled into a bare heath, black with junipers, and spotted with the presence of the standing stones for which the place was famous. They were many in that part, shapeless, white with lichen—you would have said with age; and had made their abode there for untold centuries, since first the heathens shouted for their installation. The ancients had hallowed them to some ill religion, and their neighbourhood had long been avoided by the prudent before the fall of day; but of late, on the upspringing of new requirements, these lonely stones on the moor had again become a place of assembly. A watchful picket on the Hill-end commanded all the northern and eastern approaches; and such was the disposition of the ground, that by certain cunningly posted sentries the west also could be made secure against surprise: there was no place in the country where a conventicle could meet with more quiet of mind or a more certain retreat open, in the case of interference from the dragoons. The minister spoke from a knowe close to the edge of the Ring, and poured out the words God gave him on the very threshold of the devils of yore. When they pitched a tent (which was often in wet weather, upon a communion occasion) it was rigged over the huge isolated pillar that had the name of Anes-Errand, none knew why. And the congregation sat partly clustered on the slope below, and partly among the idolatrous monoliths and on the turfy soil of the Ring itself. In truth the situation was well qualified to give a zest to Christian doctrines, had there been any wanted. But these congregations assembled under conditions at once so formidable and romantic as made a zealot of the most cold. They were the last of the faithful; God, who had averted His face from all other countries of the world, still leaned from Heaven to observe, with swelling sympathy, the doings of His moorland remnant; Christ was by them with His eternal wounds, with dropping tears; the Holy Ghost (never perfectly realised nor firmly adopted by Protestant imaginations) was dimly supposed to be in the heart of each and on the lips of the minister. And over against them was the army of the hierarchies, from the men Charles and James Stuart, on to King Lewie and the Emperor; and the scarlet Pope, and the muckle black devil himself, peering out the red mouth of hell in an ecstasy of hate and hope. ' One pull more! ' he seemed to cry; ' one pull more, and it's done. There's only Clydesdale and the Stewartry, and the three Bailieries of Ayr, left for God.' And with such an angust assistance of powers and principalities looking on at the last conflict of good and evil, it was scarce possible to spare a thought to those old, infirm, debile *ab agendo* devils whose holy place they were now violating.

There might have been three hundred to four hundred present. At least there were three hundred horses tethered for the most part in the Ring; though some of the hearers on the outskirts of the crowd stood with their bridles in their hand, ready to mount at the first signal. The circle of faces was strangely characteristic; long, serious, strongly marked, the tackle standing out in the lean brown cheeks, the mouth set and the eyes shining with a fierce enthusiasm; the shepherd, the labouring man, and the rarer laird, stood there in their broad blue bonnets or laced hats, and presenting an essential identity of type. From time to time a long-drawn groan of adhesion rose in this audience, and was propagated like a wave to the outskirts, and died away among the keepers of the horses. It had a name; it was called 'a holy groan.'

A squall came up; a great volley of flying mist went out before it and whelmed the scene; the wind stormed with a sudden fierceness that carried away the minister's voice and twitched his tails and made him stagger, and turned the congregation for a moment into a mere pother of blowing plaid-ends and prancing horses; and the rain followed and was dashed straight into their faces. Men and women panted aloud in the shock of that violent shower-bath; the teeth were bared along all the line in an involuntary grimace; plaids, mantles, and riding-coats were proved vain, and the worshippers felt the water stream on their naked flesh. The minister, reinforcing his great and shrill voice, continued to contend against and triumph over the rising of the squall and the dashing of the rain.

' In that day ye may go thirty mile and not hear a crawing cock,' he said; ' and fifty mile and not get a light to your pipe; and an hundred mile and not see a smoking house. For there'll be naething in all Scotland but deid men's banes and blackness, and the living anger of the Lord. O, where to find a bield—O sirs, where to find a bield from the wind of the Lord's anger? Do ye call *this* a wind? Bethankit! Sirs, this is but a temporary dispensation; this is but a puff of wind, this is but a spit of rain and by with it. Already there's a blue bow in the west, and the sun will take the crown of the causeway again, and your things'll be dried upon ye, and your flesh will be warm upon your bones. But O, sirs, sirs! for the day of the Lord's anger!'

His rhetoric was set forth with an ear-piercing elocution, and a voice that sometimes crashed like cannon. Such as it was, it was the gift of all hill preachers, to a singular degree of likeness or identity. Their images scarce ranged beyond the red horizon of the moor and the rainy hill-top, the shepherd and his sheep, a fowling-piece, a spade, a pipe, a dunghill, a crowing cock, the shining and the withdrawal of the sun. An occasional pathos of simple humanity, and frequent patches of big biblical words, relieved the homely tissue. It was a poetry apart; bleak, austere, but genuine, and redolent of the soil.

A little before the coming of the squall there was a different scene enacting at the outposts. For the most part the sentinels were faithful to their important duty; the Hill-end of Drumlowe was known to be a safe meeting-place; and the out-pickets on this particular day had been somewhat lax from the beginning, and grew laxer during the inordinate length of the discourse. Francie lay there in his appointed hiding-hole, looking abroad between two whin-bushes. His view was across the course of the burn, then over a piece of plain moorland, to a gap between two hills; nothing moved but grouse, and some cattle who slowly traversed his field of view, heading northward: he heard the psalms, and sang words of his own to the savage and melancholy music; for he had his own design in hand, and terror and cowardice prevailed in his bosom alternately, like the hot and the cold fit of an ague. Courage was uppermost during the singing, which he accompanied all its length with this impromptu strain:

> ' And I will ding Jock Crozer down
> No later than the day.'

Presently the voice of the preacher came to him in wafts, at the wind's will, as by the opening and shutting of a door; wild spasms of screaming, as of some undiscerned gigantic hill-bird stirred with inordinate passion, succeeded to intervals of silence; and Francie heard them with a critical ear. ' Ay,' he thought at last, ' he'll do; he has the bit in his mou' fairly.'

He had observed that his friend or rather his enemy, Jock Crozer, had been established at a very critical part of the line of outposts; namely, where the burn issues by an abrupt gorge from the semicircle of high moors. If anything was calculated to nerve him to battle it was this. The post was important; next to the Hill-end itself, it might be called the key to the position; and it was where the cover was bad, and in which it was most natural to place a child. It should have been Heathercat's; why had it been given to Crozer? An exquisite fear of what should be the answer passed through his marrow every time he faced the question. Was it possible that Crozer could have boasted? that there were rumours abroad to his—Heathercat's —discredit? that his honour was publicly sullied? All the world went dark about him at the thought; he sank without a struggle into the midnight pool of despair; and every time he so sank, he brought back with him—not drowned heroism indeed, but half-drowned courage by the locks. His heart beat very slowly as he deserted his station, and began to crawl towards that of

Crozer. Something pulled him back, and it was not the sense of duty, but a remembrance of Crozer's build and hateful readiness of fist. Duty, as he conceived it, pointed him forward on the rueful path that he was travelling. Duty bade him redeem his name if he were able, at the risk of broken bones; and his bones and every tooth in his head ached by anticipation. An awful subsidiary fear whispered him that if he were hurt, he should disgrace himself by weeping. He consoled himself, boy-like, with the consideration that he was not yet committed; he could easily steal over unseen to Crozer's post, and he had a continuous private idea that he would very probably steal back again. His course took him so near the minister that he could hear some of his words: ' What news, minister, of Claver'se? He's going round like a roaring, rampaging lion . . .'

BIBLIOGRAPHY

NOVELS AND SHORT STORIES:

    1882   The Story of a Lie
              New Arabian Nights (2 vols.)
    1883   Treasure Island
    1885   Prince Otto
              More Arabian Nights
    1886   The Strange Case of Dr. Jekyll and Mr. Hyde
              Kidnapped
    1887   The Merry Men, and Other Tales
    1888   The Black Arrow
    1889   The Misadventures of John Nicholson
              The Master of Ballantrae
              The Wrong Box
    1892   The Wrecker
    1893   Island Night's Entertainments
              Catriona
    1894   The Ebb-Tide

POSTHUMOUSLY PUBLISHED:

    1895   The Body-Snatcher
    1896   Weir of Hermiston
    1897   St. Ives (Finished by Sir A. T. Quiller-Couch)
    1916   The Waif Woman
    1921   When the Devil Was Well
    1923   Ticonderoga

POEMS AND PLAYS:

    1880   Deacon Brodie ⎫
    1884   Beau Austin   ⎬ Written in conjunction with
              Admiral Guinea ⎨ W. E. Henley and privately
    1885   Macaire   ⎭ printed
    1885   A Child's Garden of Verses
    1887   Underwoods
              Ticonderoga (privately printed)
    1890   Ballads

POSTHUMOUSLY PUBLISHED:

1896 Songs of Travel and Other Verses
1898 Three Short Poems
1899 R. L. S. Teuila
1913 Complete Edition of Poems and Ballads (New York Edition)
1914 The Hanging Judge
1916 An Ode of Horace (privately printed)
      Poems Hitherto Unpublished (Boston Bibliophile Soc.)
1918 New Poems and Variant Readings (Boston Bibliophile Soc.)

NUMEROUS ESSAYS AND OTHER MISCELLANEOUS WRITINGS INCLUDING:

1878 An Inland Voyage
1879 Travels with a Donkey in the Cevennes
1892 A Footnote to History.
1893 War in Samoa (privately printed)

Also the *Vailima Letters* and other published collections of his correspondences.

COLLECTED EDITIONS OF HIS WORKS:

Edinburgh Edition   1894-98 (28 vols.)
Vailima Edition   1922-23 (26 vols.)
Tusitala Edition   1923-24 (35 vols.)

FOLLOWING CONTAIN INFORMATION ON HIS LIFE AND WORKS:

Partial Portraits (1888) and *Notes on Novelists* (1914) by Henry James
Robert Louis Stevenson by Sir W. Raleigh (1895)
Robert Louis Stevenson by L. C. Cornford (1899)
Life of Robert Louis Stevenson by Graham Balfour (1901)
With Stevenson in Samoa by H. J. Moore (1911)
Memories of Vailima by I. Strong and Lloyd Osbourne (1911)
On the Trail of Stevenson by H. Clayton
R. L. S. A Critical Study by F. Swinnerton (1914)
Life of Robert Louis Stevenson by R. O. Masson (1923)
An Intimate Portrait of Robert Louis Stevenson by Lord Osbourne (New York, 1924)

Presbyterian Pirate by Doris N. Dalglish (1937)

Home from the Sea by Richard A. Berman (1939)

Selected Writings of Robert Louis Stevenson Ed. by Saxe Commins (1947)

Novels and Stories by Robert Louis Stevenson by V. S. Pritchett (1947)

Robert Louis Stevenson by Lettice Cooper (1947)

Our Mountain Hermitage (Silverado and Robert Louis Stevenson) by Anne Roller Issler (1950)

Stevenson and Edinburgh (A Centenary Study) by Moray Mac Laren (1951)

The Strange Case of Robert Louis Stevenson by Malcolm Elwin (1951)

Robert Louis Stevenson: Collected Poems (Editor) Janet Adam Smith (1951)

Voyage to Windward: The Life of Robert Louis Stevenson by G. C. Furness (1951)

Tusitala of the South Seas: The story of Robert Louis Stevenson's life in the South Pacific by Joseph W. Ellison (1953)

R. L. S.: Stevenson's Letters to Charles Baxter. Edited by DeLancey Ferguson and Marshall Waingrow (1956)

Our Samoan Adventure by Fanny and Robert Louis Stevenson (1956)

Portrait of a Rebel, by Richard Aldington (1957)